# Asparagus
## *and other stories*

Nicholas Worskett

*for my brother and my sister,*
*and for Uma Turan and Nigel Fairs*

## Acknowledgements

I have many people to thank for many things, but, in relation very specifically to this collection, I would like to thank Linda Baker, Dominic Berry, Aisha Bridgman, Matthew Brotherton, Glynis Casson, Sara Cooper, Heli Croft, Nicholas Davidson, Sya Elwes, Nigel Fairs, Margot Krebs Neale, Richard Lamplough, Graham Lipscomb, Jonathan Miller, Rupert Neelands, Antony Pickthall, William Rouse, Mark Shepherd and Freya Stacpoole; and, especially, Nick Bernstein

2

# Contents

# These Things Happen

The worst thing about the news of my terminal illness was how well other people took it. People like my sister, for example. I phoned her the moment I got home from the hospital.

"It's me," I said.

"'Me'?"

"Your brother."

"Oh hello Andrew."

"No, Imogen, the other one. Adam."

"Adam. Of course. To what do I owe this pleasure?"

"I'm afraid I have some rather bad news."

"You didn't get the promotion."

"Forget the promotion. It's nothing to do with the promotion. I've just been to see the doctor. You remember that appointment I told you about? at Kingston Hospital? with Dr Mulligan? the oncologist? … Imogen? are you there?"

"Yes, yes, I'm here," she said, in that provisional way which meant she'd stopped listening but that I should carry on speaking anyway. I heard domestic activity in the background, the day-long squabble which seemed to constitute family life, a condition I had narrowly avoided. Five years before I had made the mistake of asking Jennifer Slater to marry me and she had looked at me witheringly and said "You *are* joking, I presume," before running off (appropriately enough) with her personal trainer Doug with the biceps, and then, presumably, doing a few press-ups with him on his kitchen table.

"You don't remember about the appointment at Kingston Hospital?" I said.

"Which one are you again?"

"Adam. *Adam.*"

"Sorry, Adam, it's been such a madhouse here these last few days what with the sproglets going back to school and then trying to plan this skiing trip to Switzerland …"

"Well, I'm afraid it's not good news, Imogen. In fact, it's pretty well the worst news imaginable. He … Dr Mulligan … he says …" I took a breath of the universe's dark matter. "Imogen, he says I've probably got … eight weeks … a *maximum* of eight weeks …" There was an extended pause. I imagined her standing in the middle of her bright kitchen in Sunningdale in a state of catatonic shock. "Imogen?" I said, gently. I knew it was going to be tough for those closest to me. "Are you okay?"

"Sorry, Adam, Lucy was trampling mud into the hall and I'm trying to get their tea ready. You were saying something about mulligatawny soup?"

"*Dr* Mulligan. The specialist. At Kingston Hospital. Imogen, he told me I've got eight weeks."

"Eight weeks? To do what?"

"*Live* Imogen. Eight weeks to *live*."

"That's a bummer. So that's, what? About two months? At the *most*. Where are we now?" I imagined her studying the calendar by the sink with its pictures of thatched cottages and kittens. "It's September. Or is it November? I can't believe I don't even know what month it is: I told you it's been like a madhouse here. And how are things otherwise?"

"'Otherwise'? *What* 'otherwise'? I no longer have any 'otherwise'."

"I've just thought. If it's eight weeks you'll miss Christmas." She laughed, convincingly. "One less present to worry about, I suppose," she said.

"Imogen, forgive me, but I'm not really in the mood for levity right now. In fact, I'm on something of a downer. It's almost impossible to describe … it's as if I'm falling through space … into this … black, bottomless pit … I just don't know how I'm going to …"

"Oh hang on, Andrew. Someone's at the door. Can I call you back?"

"Yes. Call me back. And it's Adam. *Adam*. Don't …"

The line went dead, and purred.

Would death be like that? a cutting-off? a hanging-up? or would it be like being put on hold, forever, but without the Vivaldi?

How different a room looks when you know you're going to die: ornaments take on a special quality of nothingness. I had never known that a vase could be so sullen, a candlestick so wantonly incommunicative.

Of course, we all know we're going to die, eventually, as much as we know anything. But I'm talking about having an *itinerary*: that was the difference in my case. For most of our lives we have only a notional sense of our inevitable demise; we conceive of it as something that will vaguely happen at some nebulous point in the future, like getting served at the Post Office. Unless we're in total denial or are of a religious disposition, this imprecision comes as our only defence. I no longer had it. Dr Mulligan had said "eight weeks" and I suspected his sense of timing was as perfect as his bespoke Jermyn Street suit (I guessed he did a lot of private work). On the bus home I'd had the time to do the fearful arithmetic, the summing up. Eight times seven is fifty-six. Fifty-six days. *In the best case scenario.* Fifty-six multiplied by twenty four … one-thousand-three-hundred-and-forty-four hours remaining of my visit to this weird spinning planet in this weird spinning universe. I sat with my head, now also spinning and weird, in my hands, waiting for Imogen to call back, trying to imagine one-thousand-three-hundred-and-forty-four hours – or, rather, one-thousand-three-hundred-and-forty-three-hours now, since I had left the hospital an hour before – and what I should do with this particular one, the first of my meagre remaining allowance. Should I listen to the lunchtime news? pour myself a brandy? introduce myself to a prostitute? do a bungee jump? engage in charitable work? consult a faith healer? read the Bible? or the Koran, to keep my options open? or perhaps chase up that nice man from the Jehovah's Witnesses who seemed so interested in my hallway? or should I just hurl myself under a bus and get the whole rotten deal over with?

Twenty minutes passed in a cloud of anxiety and confusion which suddenly evaporated in a moment of small, but piquant, irritation. Imogen hadn't called back, or else she had called Andrew by mistake. I checked my watch. Twenty precious minutes, wasted. *Gone*.

So I phoned her.

"Imogen?"

"Hello Adam."

"It's Adam, for God's sake!"

"I *said* Adam."

"Did you? So you did. Sorry. You were meant to call me back."

"Oh, sorry!" She actually sang this. "I forgot."

"You *forgot*?"

"Mr Fisher from down the road knocked on the door. You know, the man with the sideburns? Tabitha's gone missing again and he wanted me to check the shed."

"Who's Tabitha? His wife?"

"His cat. So we just went to the shed."

"Oh right. The shed."

"And then I started making lunch and I completely forgot. Anyway. Where were we? *How are you*?"

"*How am I*? I *told* you."

"Oh, of course. Sorry. You *said*. Poor booby, it must be *awful*. Anyway. What else has been going on in your life? How's work? What's the latest on the promotion?"

"*Work*? *The promotion*? Imogen, work's over for me now."

"Oh my God. Because of the cuts?"

"What do you mean 'the cuts'?"

"The council cuts? They've made you redundant?"

I work in local government. But that was now, frankly, irrelevant, like everything. "Because I'm *dying*!" I cried out.

"Okay," she said. "Don't get your knickers in a twist. These things happen. It's not *that* big a deal."

I must confess, at this point, that a flash of anger went through me.

"What did you just say?" I said, my voice tightening.

"I said it's not *that* big a deal."

"It's not 'that big a deal'? I cannot believe you just said that. Imogen, death *is* quite a big deal, actually. For *me*, at least. For you it may be just another part of your crowded schedule, I appreciate that. But for me – call me over-sensitive – it's going to lead to some pretty serious changes around here, I can tell you. You know, over the years, I've sort of got used to having me around. I've grown rather fond of … buses and Rice Krispies and hedgehogs and street corners … *stuff*."

"Yes, okay, it is *quite* a big deal if you think of it like that, but it's not such a big deal if you think how it happens to everyone, in the end. It's not *uncommon*. And after you've died you'll be no different from how you were before you were born and you weren't afraid of that, were you?"

"In those halcyon days before I was born I didn't have any expectations. My conception came completely out of the blue. Besides, the past isn't exactly at the top of my agenda right now. I can live with the past, that's all good: it's the *future* that gives me grave cause for concern."

"But you won't even be there to *know* you're not there, will you? so what is there to be afraid of?"

"That! What you just said! *Exactly* what you just said!"

Her sigh rumbled against the mouthpiece, like distant thunder. "We just have to live with it, Adam," she said, and I could tell from her straining voice that she was engaged in some minor physical chore at the sink, like peeling an avocado. "We live, we die. End of story."

"You say that but is it the end of the story? I wonder. I mean, what about all this God stuff everyone keeps going on about?"

"What God stuff?"

"Well, about an afterlife and so on."

"Oh that's all made up."

"Shit. *Is* it?"

I would have preferred it if she'd been a little more circumspect on the matter of an afterlife, a little more agnostic and tactful; if she'd kept a few options open, even if only out of politeness. I suppose that her bracing pragmatism, her instinct for normalising everything, should have been comforting insofar as it precluded panic. Cats, sheds, fish fingers, skiing trips, promotion, death: they were all the same to Imogen, all part of the same 'rich tapestry'.

Later that afternoon I tried calling my parents but their line was constantly engaged. Finally, I got through.

"Oh hello Andrew," Dad said. "I'm afraid your mother's popped out."

"It's Adam."

"What?"

"This is Adam. You called me Andrew."

"Sorry. Adam. Let me get my glasses."

"What do you need your glasses for?"

"I don't know. Perhaps I mean my hearing aid. As I said, your mother's not here."

"That's fine, Dad. I'm more than happy to talk to you in her absence. Has Imogen spoken to you?"

"Just now, funnily enough. We had a good long chat about everything."

"Well, at least you know. Oh, it's pretty bad, Dad."

"What is?"

"Well, about *me*."

"About you? I don't think she mentioned anything about you."

"She didn't tell you?"

"Tell me what? I do wish you'd stop being so mysterious."

"My news."

"No. What news? Don't tell me. You got the promotion! Congratulations!"

"No, Dad, it's nothing to do with the bloody promotion."

"Well what then?"

"I have eight weeks to live."

"No, she didn't mention that, or if she did I must have missed it. My hearing's not what it used to be. Do you think she's all right? She didn't seem quite herself somehow, entirely preoccupied with the children going back to school and then she started going on about some missing cat or something and then this ridiculous idea about some skiing holiday in Switzerland. Did she mention that to you? How she thinks I can afford …"

"Dad. Dad. Did you hear what I just said?"

"About what?"

"About having eight weeks to live."

"Yes, of course I did. I'm not deaf." Stifling a yawn, he added, "It's very sad, isn't it? But, oh well, you know what they say."

"Who? What? What do who say?"

"I forget. Something like, it's not how *long* you live, it's … I forget now … Life begins at forty? No, that's not it."

"Well, thanks for being so philosophical, Dad."

"Tell me, how old are you now?"

"I'm forty-seven."

"Are you *really*? You know, I was just reading that in Medieval times the average life expectancy was thirty-five years. And in certain parts of sub-Saharan Africa I believe it still is."

"Yes, Dad, but this isn't Medieval times and I live in Thames Ditton."

"So, in a way, you've done pretty well, I'd say. Of course your Uncle Kenneth was only forty-two when he fell off the perch. Funny old business. A 'pulmonary embolism'." He said 'pulmonary embolism' as if it was an achievement of enormous distinction.

"*Dad*. Most people can expect to live well into their seventies or eighties in the 21st century and in an advanced western civilisation."

"Yes, you've sort of fallen between two stools, haven't you?" he said. I was surprised to hear him laugh. "Too old to be tragically young and yet too young to be in the 'good innings' category. Oh well. These things happen."

"Yes, so everyone keeps saying," I said. "I'm sorry for letting the side down and for being such a disappointment. I'll try to be a little more considerate next time I die so I'm not a cause of," my voice rose wildly here, "*general embarrassment.*"

"Erm, listen, do you mind if we don't chat now? 'Cash in the Attic' is just starting."

"'Cash in the Attic'."

"Yes. I've become quite addicted to it. It's this antiques programme where they …"

"Yes, Dad, I know what 'Cash in the Attic' is. You go and watch your programme. Tell Mum I phoned, won't you?"

"Of course. I know she'd love to hear all your news. I'll give you a call later in the week. Oh! There's the music starting! Got to go! 'Bye Andrew!"

I found myself staring at the telephone purring in my hand. Then I found myself staring at the wall. I sensed that I was going to be doing a lot of staring at walls over the next few days, weeks and … well, weeks.


I gave up on my family and decided to call Jeremy Phipps instead. Jeremy is my oldest friend: we were at school together, although we went our different ways afterwards and he became a famous professional baritone. 'Gramophone' had enthused of him, 'this young and charismatic singer seems destined for immortality', which gave him quite a lot to live up to. Despite this, we have kept in touch. I told him that I needed to see him urgently and that I had some 'news', choosing a deliberately neutral term but hoping that its very neutrality might forewarn him of my catastrophe. We arranged to meet in our usual pub, 'The Windmill' on Clapham Common, near where we'd once shared a flat together, and where he still lived. He was half an hour late. I was half an hour early, despite the fact that I had come by train all the way from Thames Ditton which had, unusually, involved a change at Surbiton. But I figured that if we drank a lot – as seemed likely, in the circumstances – I didn't want to be stuck with the car.

When he had bought himself a pint, without offering to get me one, he elaborately removed his trademark thespian overcoat with its big flapping lapels – the same overcoat he'd worn in the heroic swaggering picture of him in 'Gramophone' – and sat down.

"Hey," he said, like an American, and left it at that.

Feeling that perhaps he should have instigated our conversation with a breathless enquiry about my 'news', I was forced into asking, in the same American vernacular, "How's it going?" I might have added 'buddy', but I didn't.

"Fine," he said. "I've just come straight from Abbey Road."

I felt he expected a follow-up question and so I dutifully provided one. "What were you doing at Abbey Road?" I said.

"Recording some lesser-known Sibelius repertoire for baritone and orchestra with the London Phil."

"As one does," I said, wearily.

"For the new album."

'Album', I thought. Jeremy was one of those classical musicians who appropriated the vocabulary of popular music, thereby irritating classical musicians and patronising popular ones: for him, a concert was a 'gig', an aria a 'number' and a violin a 'fiddle'.

"Did you know," I said, wanting to gently introduce the idea of mortality into our conversation, "that Sibelius died in *1957*?"

"Yes," he said.

"If you'd have asked me, I'd have said he died in *1857*."

"Well that's the thing: I wouldn't have asked you, would I? The fact that you think Sibelius might have died in *1857* shows how little you understand Sibelius."

A little taken-aback by his irritability, I made an even-handed 'fair enough' expression, and then waited. And waited some more. Jeremy sat, sipping his beer, looking more absent than distracted.

Finally, I said, "Well don't you want to hear my news?"

"What news?"

"The news I told you about and which is the reason we have convened at this ale house."

"Go on then."

"I'm dying."

He did then, at least, raise his eyebrows a little, but quickly returned them. "Well, we're all *dying*," he pointed out.

"I don't mean it like that, Jeremy, I don't mean it like a … philosophical point, or even a generalisation. I mean, for once, I can be very specific. I've got eight weeks."

"That's a bit annoying," he said, glancing at the clock on the wall behind the bar. "Eight weeks."

There was a ruminative pause during which he made no further enquiries. One thing that surprised me was that he, like everyone else, seemed not remotely interested in the nature of my illness, the size or position or disposition of the tumour. Neither did he seem remotely curious about the cruel stages through which hope had progressively been denied me, the stages of my fall, the ending of my story, since he didn't seem inclined to ask: the thinking myself well; the thinking myself moderately well, but perhaps just a little under the weather; the thinking myself unwell, but curable; the thinking myself ill; the thinking myself very ill indeed, but in remission, with the luxury of a long, managed, seemingly interminable, decline …

The thinking myself Saved.

Now there were no rungs left at the foot of the dreadful ladder, and I was at the bottom of the pit.

After a while, Jeremy, who kept glancing at the clock, said, distractedly, "You should go on holiday."

"Holiday?"

"Yes. A holiday. To fill in the time. Take a few days off work.

Speak to your HR department. By the way, any news on the promotion?"

"No."

"I'm sure they'd understand. Then bugger off to Spain or Italy or the North Pole or something. I'd join you but I'm booked up to the hilt right now, and not just with the Sibelius project. Why don't you go away with Julie?"

"Julie?"

"Yes."

"Who's 'Julie'?"

"Er, your *girlfriend*?"

"*Jennifer*," I said. "Not Julie. *Jennifer*. Jeremy, Jennifer and I split up five years ago and I haven't seen her since, not since she ran away with her personal trainer, Doug, remember? with the biceps?"

He looked puzzled. "I'm sure it was Julie," he said, distantly.

"No," I said, with clipped patience. "I'm reasonably confident – having gone out with her for five years, and lived with her for four – that her name was Jennifer."

I noticed that another unexpected petulance had settled upon us, whereas I had been counting on an all-encompassing warmth. I had even thought we might hold each other in a bear-hug, and weep, like in a buddy movie, and he'd say things like 'you're the best mate this young and charismatic singer could have'. Instead, Jeremy Phipps glanced at the clock again and there was another uneasy, even gloomy, silence.

"Listen, Adam," he said. "I really have to go. I've got a rehearsal for Fauré's Requiem. We're doing it at the RFH. It's corny, I know, the Fauré, but people seem to like it and they know the *Agnus Dei* from the Lurpak ad. You should come along."

"When is the concert?"

"Ah. Good point. In four weeks." He stood up, drained his pint and pulled on his overcoat. "If you've got eight weeks then you should still be around for it. I'll tell you what what we'll do. I'll get the ticket for you anyway and if you die before the concert I can either give it to someone else or get a refund. It seems stupid to waste it."

"I wouldn't countenance it," I said.

Standing by the table with his great big floppy lapels, he gave me one last look: a significant one, I felt, in that it lingered a little, and seemed, in some way, to process me anew. I returned it expectantly and felt my pulse quicken with expectation. He seemed to be gathering himself for some final declaration, something he *had* to say but found too difficult. I knew how men – men in particular – often had difficulty expressing their emotions.

"Go on," I pressed him.

"We're doing it with the English Chamber Orchestra," he said.

The next day I saw Dr Mulligan again and asked him what options, if any, were left open to me. He shook his head with a suitably perplexed expression and then mentioned the famous 'clinic' in Zürich. I was passed a lavishly-illustrated brochure which might have been for a Country Club, a last resort. There were pictures of a conservatory with basket chairs and low coffee tables; a garden refulgent with rhododendrons where an elderly couple meandered; and there was a white room where alluring young women wearing glasses (indicating they were clinicians) placed their hands on the arms of quaint old men who, smiling gently, relaxed into narcotic stupefaction and, presumably, oblivion. These images, however sanitised they might have been, held a certain appeal for me. But I immediately sensed Dr Mulligan's ambivalence about the place and he snatched the brochure back, saying he thought it over-priced for what it offered and that it was usually booked up for months, if not years, which made it of little use to me. Then, registering my irked expression, he seemed to have another idea. He reached furtively into a compartment in his desk from which he removed a leaflet and passed it to me. It looked like something a window cleaner might shove through your letterbox.

"You could always try this place instead," he said, confidentially. "It offers a very similar service, but – how shall I put it? – without the frills."

The leaflet was for a clinic called 'Krankenhaus des Todes' and it was also in Zürich. There was no question about it: Zürich was clearly the place to be, or *not* to be.

"Thank you," I said.

"If you do decide to book it," he said, "tell them Dr Mulligan sent you. Dr Mulligan."

And he winked at me.


I had always thought, perhaps naively, that a clinic was a place where they made you better, not dead. Now, I understood that making you dead could be a way of making you better. But I knew that it was important for me to end my own life under my own terms rather than have them imposed upon me by the heedless rota of biology. Our bodies make their own decisions: they are, after all, only machines for living in and, like all machines, are subject to obsolescence, breaking down and seizing up.

I made a booking online, to the 'no frills' place Dr Mulligan had recommended, then flew out to Zürich a few days prior to my appointment, to give me time to think things over.

Zürich, I must say, came as a pleasant surprise. I had imagined it as a place dedicated to banking with the appropriately banal corporate architecture. While it had its share of that, I found, at its tight core, something straight out of a Medieval woodcut or a fairy tale and I badly needed fairy tales.

My hotel was a five-star establishment on the *Stadthausquai*. I had decided to go out in style with what limited money I had left over, the bottom line, the grand total, of my existence. Each evening a pianist and a violinist played in the lobby among the ferns, engendering a feeling of well-being at cocktail hour. One night, I met some American financiers and we went out on the town. I told them nothing about myself, or, at least, nothing that was true: I even gave them a false name. (I told them I was called Andrew.) We ended up in a strip bar and I remember thinking, as I watched the spot-lit writhing of the semi-naked women, the leering ministrations of men, how strange this would all seem after a thousand years, a million, an eternity, of disembodied non-existence! how impossible to describe! to account for!

When I returned to my hotel room, drunk and exhausted, I lay on my bed and stared at the ceiling with a completely new and profound – I might almost say stabilised – despair. I thought I could get used to this and that I might find a way to get through it, even on my own. It was as if, layer by layer, assumption by assumption, I was shedding the tenets of my existence. I was beginning to understand that it might not be necessary for me to exist at all.

On my final evening, I stood on the balcony of my room with something from the minibar and looked out across the river – the lit spires, the mirrored boats, the golden melting of the water, the whole forsaken beauty of the world – and realised that I had, indeed, come to a decision. After this brief intermission in Zürich, I understood that my life had at last begun to make sense and that I was therefore in a position to relinquish it.

The bells of the *Grossmünster* rang out. Did they ring for me?

I checked out the next morning. Even phrases like 'checked out' seemed to have taken on a deeper resonance. I took a taxi to the clinic. The driver eyed me in the mirror after I had given the address.

"Just visiting?" he said.

"Yes," I said. "Just visiting."

That phrase, too, resonated. It struck me then, as I watched the streets of Zürich passing in the sure knowledge that I would never see them again, that the only claim we could ever make of the world – if we could make any claims on it at all – was that we had always been, from the very outset, 'just visiting'.

The clinic was situated in the outskirts of the city on a trading estate of warehouses and low red-brick seventies office buildings. It was raining. No, let me rephrase that: it was drizzling. If anywhere was Godless, it was here, in this place, and in this drizzle. But the place seemed deathless, too, as if it would be impossible to do anything so Gothic and frivolous as die in an environment of such bland and secular modernity. What I had not been expecting, however, was the stack of coffins beside the building and more crammed into lorries which were parked on the tarmac in front. As I walked between them I heard someone bang on the side of one and shout "Bereit zu gehen!" to the driver. The lorry coughed into life.

The receptionist cheerfully took my details in the sunny reception. A radio was playing in the background: not music, but a traffic report, in busy German. It was nice to think that people were just driving around out there.

"English?" she said, perkily. I thought I would miss her, and all the indiscretion of her vitality, more than anyone else alive.

"Yes," I said and, as she busied herself with her terminal, I added, conversationally, "Do you get many English?"

"Oh, many, many English come here for our procedures," she said, as if picking up on some charming national idiosyncrasy. "We accept all major credit cards."

She took my payment, gave me my paperwork and showed me through into a waiting room. There were twelve people sitting around the walls on plastic chairs. All of them were reading lifestyle magazines. I had to stand, since there were no chairs free. The only sound in the room was the stupendously grave and tactless ticking of a clock on the wall. Now, it was even more than ever a countdown.

A buzzer sounded harshly.

"Herr von Ribbentrop?" came an amplified German voice. "Herr von Ribbentrop? Tür B. Von Ribbentrop. Tür B."

Von Ribbentrop went, and I replaced him in his still-warm chair. The man beside me offered a futile smile.

"Afternoon," he said, immediately understanding from my appearance that I was English. He was too.

I nodded. There hardly seemed much point in initiating a conversation at this late stage.

"What you in for?" he persisted.

I wasn't sure what the correct term was. "The house special?" I said. "What about you?"

"The same," he said. "A 'termination'."

Thankfully, that was to be the limit of our conversation. The next moment, the amplified voice said, in an English that was startling for its clarity and directness, "Mr Wilson. Door A. Mr Wilson. Door A. Go at once to Door A."

He stood. "That's me," he said. "I'm Wilson. Or I used to be."

Oddly, we shook hands. Why do we do that? I read somewhere that it was originally to show we were not carrying weapons, that we meant no harm.

"Well," I said. "Goodbye, Wilson."

"Cheerio," he said. "See you in the hereafter!"

"Absolutely," I said, and even sounded like I meant it.

I decided to call Imogen one last time. I took out my mobile and pressed the numbers, including the code. It rang, and rang, and went to voicemail. I heard the automated voice: "The person you have called is unavailable. Please try again later." Having no 'later', I didn't. Then I thought of phoning Mum and Dad and began dialling their number but the man next to me, pointing at a sign on the wall which I hadn't noticed up until then – a picture of a mobile phone with a red line drawn diagonally across it – commanded, with a Teutonic fury that was terrible for its restraint, "*Schalten Sie das Telefon*."

Ten minutes later my name was called, followed by an order to proceed to Door C. As I stood, a janitor in overalls entered the waiting room with a vacuum cleaner. Whistling, he began picking up the wastepaper bins and emptying them into his sack.

I went to Door C, knocked and entered a consulting room. A trolley was being wheeled out through some industrial rubber doors, the sort you might find at the back of a supermarket, and I noted two feet poking out, at an odd angle, from beneath a sheet, or shroud. A man was sitting at a desk. He looked like a completely normal man. It struck me then that this foreign stranger, this doctor, would be the last human being I would ever see; this consulting room, which smelt faintly of methylated spirit, the last place I would ever inhabit.

"I won't keep you a moment," he said. "Do take a seat." He was shuffling papers on the desk in front of him, like a newsreader. I noticed that the top sheet had a passport photograph of my head pinned to it. At last, he put the papers down and said, "Well, everything seems to be in order, Mr Lubbock."

"Lucas," I said.

"Was hast du gesagt? I mean, what did you say?"

"I'm Lucas. Adam Lucas."

"I am sorry. Herr Lucas, of course. I'm getting myself all muddled-up here. It's been a long day. Thirty-five appointments. *That* was Lubbock."

He tipped his head after the departed trolley, but then turned back to me, and I noticed how he couldn't look me in the eye. Instead, he appeared to be looking at a place half way up my forehead. The effect was disconcerting: I felt I needed to touch the place he was looking at, to conceal it, or wipe away a stain. He signalled for me to pass my own paperwork, which I did. Breezily, he went through it, whistling to himself, or, more exactly, exhaling tunefully, providing a clicked rhythm on his palate.

"How's your blood pressure?" he asked.

"Fine," I said. "Normal."

"I don't know why we have to ask that, but we do."

"Do you want to take my blood pressure?"

"No, I'm sure it will be fine," he said. "So, you're sure about this?"

"About what?"

"Well, about the procedure."

"Yes, I'm sure," I said, "at least …"

"Okay." He stamped the last of the sheets, stapled them and flung them into his thickly-stacked Out Tray from where my miniature punctured head stared up at the polystyrene tiles. "We'll get on with it, shall we?"

He showed me to a bench covered in rubber which bore the faint indentations of a human being. It reminded me of the Turin Shroud.

"Here?" I said.

"Yes," he said. "Just there."

I sat down. The bench was still warm from the previous incumbent, the man on the trolley.

The doctor glanced at his watch. "You don't mind the television?" he said. "I want to catch the news. About the war."

I shrugged. "Feel free," I said.

Attached to the wall was a television, blank-faced as an Easter Island god, staring to the horizon. He pressed the remote control. Men were fighting. Gun-toting soldiers, shambolic as mercenaries, gave V-signs to the camera from the backs of bouncing trucks. Across the desert, black smoke was stilled by distance into leaning funnels; the dunes were scattered with burning tanks; women conducted their wailing. Foreign grief was so articulate, so imploring.

"Bloody Arabs," he said. "We should nuke the lot of them."

I found myself despising him, although I knew it was best to keep on his good side. I didn't want him botching this up. Then his phone rang. He looked distractedly at the number.

"I have to take this," he said, turning down the television.

"Please do," I said.

He said into the phone, "Ja." His eyes moved from side to side as he listened. Then he said, "Ich werde als sechs zu Hause sein. Es muss etwas zu essen im Kühlschrank sein." He put the phone down, and scowled. "My wife," he said. "Are you married?"

"No."

Beside him on the desk was a jug and a tumbler. The jug contained a pink liquid. He poured the pink liquid into the tumbler, then held it up to the light, to check the level. He came over with it.

"Just relax," he said. He passed me the tumbler. "Here," he said. "Drink this." Some old phrase came back to me then, some dim memory of something that had been said before, by other people, in other places: an old hope. "Drink it quickly," he added. "In one. Straight down. Imagine it's a shot of vodka."

I drank it in one. It tasted of strawberries but with a sour edge. Then I sat back.

"Does it take long?" I said.

"I should have given you a leaflet," he said. "We have too many leaflets." He glanced at his watch. He looked tired, I thought, as if he needed a holiday. "Two to three minutes, usually," he said. "It depends on several factors. How much food you have in your stomach, for instance."

"That affects it, does it?"

"Not much," he said. He turned to watch the television. "I'll just turn it up a little," he said. "You don't mind? The war, you know."

"That's fine," I told him.

"There are some English magazines there. Shouldn't be long now." I picked one up from the table. It was a magazine of puzzles. He glanced at me and said, "There are some 'quick crosswords' at the back. Do you want a pen?"

"Don't worry, it's fine."

I flicked through the magazine. Some of the crosswords had a few clues filled in. On others, a pen had trailed a line, forlornly, down the page. None of the crosswords had been completed.

The doctor had turned up the television but I was aware that the world was already fading for me. I heard some German narration and the feeble inverted horn of a foreign ambulance, machine-gun fire, the thunder of ordnance, the toll of spent shells, the warbling of communal grief. Oh, it would be good to get away from all that, at least.

Then I heard something at once puzzling and yet familiar which seemed, for a moment, to tug me back into the world, even as I fell into darkness: the drone and thump of the vacuum cleaner coming from the next room.

## Green Birds

We may as well begin with my diary entry for Saturday 9th December.

'Took M. to London and to Regent Street to see the lights. Bought the new dress for her party. Home at 7pm.'

That particular entry is remarkable not so much for what it does say as for what it doesn't, for an event took place on that visit to London with my daughter Margaret which was to transform my life utterly, and yet, for reasons which remain a mystery to me, I chose not to record it in my diary, even obliquely.

There were, of course, many things I chose not to record: no diary can ever be fully comprehensive, after all. I did not mention, for instance, how Margaret and I had popped into the V&A to see the Raphael cartoons (she was mightily bored, particularly when she realised they were not the sort of cartoons I may have, inadvertently, led her to expect), gazed at the preposterous wedding-cake interior of The Brompton Oratory (still bored), seen Peter Pan playing his panpipes in Kensington Gardens (neutral) and then sat in the café by the Serpentine where we had tea and chocolate cake and watched flamingos tiptoe on their reflections (totally *un*-bored). On our way to Regent Street, as the dusk began to gather, we stopped outside Fortnum & Mason in Piccadilly to watch the famous clock in action. Sure enough, at 3pm precisely, the bells began to whirr and jangle, giving the impression of some enormously complicated inner mechanism, and the doors of the two decorative booths opened and out came the foppish figures of Messrs Fortnum and Mason, in 18th-century dress complete with powdered wigs and tailcoats. They bowed to each other, then went back the way they'd come, and the little doors closed after them. It was almost as if you'd imagined the whole thing. Margaret filmed it on her phone and then put it on

Facebook. I imagine that my daughter believes that, if it's not on Facebook, you might just as well have imagined the whole thing anyway.

This action of the clock, however, was not the transformative event that I have alluded to. After all, it rings and goes through the same performance every day, on the hour, for the delight of office-workers and tourists alike. No. What caught my attention on that otherwise ordinary day was something quite different. As Margaret and I stood on the pavement opposite the illustrious department store, and just as the bell started ringing – almost as if its appearance had been summoned by it in just the same way as it had summoned the figures of Messrs Fortnum and Mason – an enormous lolloping *green bird* emerged from the entrance and took its place in the ceaseless flow of pedestrians. My first impression was of its magnificent absurdity, if those two qualities can co-exist in one being. It was considerably taller than a human being and its feathers, which were a luminous shade of green, were shaggy and thick. Its head resembled that of a duck, except the beak was rather less pronounced and red or orange in colour. The eyes were black, beady and strangely alert but cross-eyed, with long eyelashes. It had a protuberant belly, giving the creature a ludicrous bottom-heavy pear- or bell-shape which contributed to the lumbering quality of its gait: it seemed to rest its entire weight on first one foot, then the other. Its shoe-less feet were webbed.

The sight of the creature was so astonishing to me that my first instinct was to laugh, but something made me hold me back, something not unlike fear. Then, as its bobbing avian head was subsumed into the mass of bobbing human ones, I tugged at Margaret's shoulder and, diverting her attention from the clock, said, in a hoarse whisper, "Did you *see* that?"

Of course I hadn't appreciated that she was in the process of filming and she mouthed her injunction, with that stroppy authority that a fifteen-year-old can summon towards a geriatric father, "Quiet!"

Only afterwards, as we pressed through the crowds of Piccadilly towards Regent Street, did I say to her, with a pretence of casualness, "Did you see that bird, Margaret? that strange green bird? coming out of the store, just as the bells rang?"

"Yes," she said with a tone of such apparent obviousness that I was at once crestfallen, and reminded of how much my daughter was growing up. She'd put me in my place.

And so reason and logic took over in the busy boardroom of my head. A meeting of logicians was hastily convened. There were flow charts and graphs, coffee and biscuits and an over-head projector. Plausible explanations jostled. Clearly the bird was part of a marketing campaign, although for what product I could hardly imagine. I had some vague memories of a bird called 'Buzby' being used in the advertisements for the privatisation of British Telecom in the 1970s. There seemed to be no rationale behind the choice of a bird for *that* particular campaign but I remembered that it had been enormously successful so why should they not try something similar again? And then I remembered that there was some new musical which had recently opened in the West End and that the cast were dressed in all manner of outlandish animal and bird costumes, a veritable menagerie or vivarium of a stage show. It may or may not have been performed on roller-skates. And then – the rationales piling up, just as they tumbled down – of course it was *Christmas*, a season that encouraged all sorts of eccentricities of behaviour and belief, not least of all that Jesus Christ was born to a virgin in a manger!

While I satisfied myself that any of these very plausible explanations would suffice to account for my unsettling vision, there remained with me throughout that day – as we gazed at the angel-wing lights in Regent Street and, afterwards, caught the tube to Victoria, and the train to Rochester – a feeling that a subtle but resonant disturbance had taken place in the very fabric of reality, or, at least, *my* reality; yes, that something was not quite right. Perhaps at its root, ironically, was precisely my very vivid apprehension of the bird's *reality*, how it had seemed entirely naturalistic and nothing like a person in a bird costume, still less a puppet in the manner of Rod Hull's psychopathic 'Emu', or yet some form of highly realistic automaton or animatronic which you find these days even in supposedly serious museums of natural history.

And the other aspect of its existence – and, perhaps, in some ways, the most remarkable, puzzling and unsettling to me – was that absolutely no one, including my fifteen-year-old daughter, had taken a blind bit of notice.

Had it been, then, a *hallucination*?

As my diary records, we were home by 7pm. On some invented pretext I went at once to my study, logged onto my computer and went straight to Margaret's Facebook page. Sure enough, there was her post of the clock at Fortnum & Mason. After I had found time to be moderately hurt at her accompanying comment ('In London with boring old Dad but saw this great clock', which, I noted, adding to my pain, several of her friends had 'liked', and even one of their parents), I watched the clip which lasted all of twenty seconds. Margaret had timed it perfectly so that she caught the very beginning of the chimes. And there it was, poking into the bottom of the frame, just as I remembered: the green bird coming out of the store and turning right to join the ordinary people on the pavement; at which point Margaret, understandably, zoomed in on the two figures emerging from the clock's mechanism and so we missed the creature's stately progress down Piccadilly. Just at the end of the clip you could hear me saying, in the background, so that it is barely detectable, "Did you *see* that?" and then the film shook as I tugged at her shoulder.

I must have watched that clip twenty or thirty times.

Afterwards, I went downstairs and came upon a scene that immediately ousted all of my former preoccupations: my wife, Jane, was clasping her hands together while Margaret – looking almost like a young woman – curtsied towards her in her new party dress. I barely recognised her, my own daughter.

After dinner that evening, when Margaret had gone to bed, Jane and I huddled up on the sofa to watch a film. I have no memory of the film whatsoever. My mind was elsewhere.

After we had not spoken for several minutes, she said my name.

"Robin," she said. Except she didn't say it like that. She said, in a long rising appealing interrogative, as if she were about to ask some far-fetched favour of me, "*Roooobin*?"

"Yes, light of my life?" I said, belying my slight foreboding.

"Thank you for taking Margaret to London today and for buying that beautiful dress for her," she said. "She adores it."

I acknowledged this with a sort of grunt. Then I waited a while before I said, "And?" When she didn't reply, I said, "*And*?"

"You know she's going to this party next Friday, don't you?"

"Of course. That's what the dress is for."

"She wants to go ... with a boy."

I let this sink in. Then I said, "You mean, like a boyfriend?"

"Sort of."

"Jane," I said. "She's fifteen. Isn't she a bit young to be going to parties with boyfriends? I didn't have my first girlfriend until I was twenty-two."

"Yes, your cousin Beth, when you were at the seminary. You told me all about it."

"We only held hands," I confessed.

"They grow up so fast these days. You saw her today, how she looks and, more importantly, behaves. She's a proper young woman now. And we have to trust her not to ..."

"Not to?"

"... do anything ... stupid."

"Ugh, the thought of it."

"Don't be like that, Robin. At some point you're going to have to let her go. You have to try to remember what it's like being that age. You were young once. Apparently."

"Steady." I leant forward and put a new log on the fire, where the embers gave a warm roar. "Who is this 'boyfriend' then?" I said. "Tell me about him."

"He's called Kevin."

"Kevin? Really? That's not a good start."

"Think of it as … Norse … or Viking … and he *sounds* lovely, not at all like a Kevin."

"I've no idea what a 'Kevin' sounds like. So you've not actually met him?"

"No. But Margaret's told me all about him."

"She never mentioned him to me. Why did she tell you and not me?"

"His father's an architect."

"Oh, well, that's all right then."

"And I said we would have no objection to her going to the party with him."

"That was the Royal 'we' was it?"

"Don't be horrid."

"It would be nice to feel I played some part, however small, in our daughter's upbringing."

"That's not fair."

It wasn't fair, and I knew it. So I nuzzled her for a bit, by way of mitigation.

"I'm sure it'll be fine," I whispered directly into her ear. My wife had excellent ears.

"Good," she said.

"I'm happy if you're happy."

"That's funny," she said. "So am I!"


At 11pm Jane went up to read. I stayed down to have another nightcap and watch the headlines. There were demonstrations in Paris and they were showing newsreel footage of them from earlier in the evening. Because all of the placards were in French, and my French is rusty – much rustier than my Latin, Hebrew and Aramaic – I had little idea what they were demonstrating about. I assumed, in line with our tiresome *zeitgeist*, that they would be either pro-Muslim or, more likely, anti-Muslim. What is wrong with people? Then I saw that the word 'Immigration' featured prominently on a number of placards; helpfully, the word was the same in French as it was in English. So therefore, I assumed, the demonstration was either pro- or anti-immigration. Judging by the demeanour, and general approach, of the demonstrators, and their many tattoos, it seemed more probable that it was the latter.

Then, I saw it. I put my drink down and stared. Very slowly, I slid from the sofa and began crawling, panther-like, across the floor towards the television until my face was virtually pressed to the screen.

There – now only semi-formed in a crowd of vibrating pixels – was exactly the same green bird I'd seen in Piccadilly, only now it was marching down the Champs Elysées with a placard jutting from beneath its wing which read, 'ARRETER IMMEDIATEMENT TOUTE IMMIGRATION!'

I pulled back from the screen, shocked, and the bird re-formed into the whole podgy magnificent feathered thing. Without doubt it was the same one that I had seen in London. But how could that be? The television's footage had been filmed, according to the digits in the corner, at 6.30pm that evening. I did a swift calculation. I had seen the bird in London at *exactly* 3pm. I knew that from the chiming of the clock as it had exited Fortnum & Mason. If the bird had been in Piccadilly at 3pm, it could conceivably have made it to St Pancras by, say, 3.15pm and then, assuming it had caught a train immediately, could have been at Paris Gard du Nord for 5.45pm, which would have given it ample time to get to the Champs Elysées by Métro, and to the demonstration, for 6.30pm. But then I thought: wasn't Paris an hour ahead of London? Presumably, the time given on the video footage would have been local time – 6.30pm in Paris would be 5.30pm in London – meaning my bird would have lost an hour to get there, which would have rendered the journey practically impossible.

But all that considered – I took a swig of scotch – what the hell was the green bird doing there anyway? in Paris? demonstrating against immigration?

The next day I spent the morning clearing out the garage, something I had been meaning to do for months. Jane and I had talked about converting it into a sort of games or activity room. Despite my advanced age, I still hankered for a train set.

So much stuff! How had we managed to accumulate three watering cans? I stacked up some boxes full of old bank statements, horrified to find beneath one a swarm of spiders which, as they were revealed, scattered away. Then I turned my attention to the shelves.

"Who are you talking to, Daddy?"

I almost fell off the ladder. "Margaret!" I cried. "Don't do that!"

"Who were you talking to?"

"I wasn't talking to anyone so far as I know."

In fact I had been ruminating over a formulation that had come to me in my troubled sleep the previous night, like an annunciation, although one delivered less on the wings of an angel than on those of a tatty old crow: 'Just because God doesn't exist doesn't mean he does exist.' Had I actually said it *out loud*?

Margaret said, craftily, "Were you saying a prayer?"

"I'm afraid I wasn't, sweetheart," I said. "God and I aren't talking right now. We've had a strop."

"What about?"

She was ready to hear these grown-up things, I felt. "Chiefly on whether he's a figment of my imagination or not," I said.

Descending the ladder, I saw that Margaret, now frowning at me in the light of my revelation, was wearing her woolly jumper with sheep gambolling on it, and I realised then how much it was the new dress that had transformed her, the day before, into the young woman I knew she would soon become. But, for now, she was my dear child again and I felt an overwhelming protectiveness towards her; or, at least, this precious and transient manifestation of her. And the way she called me 'Daddy': it broke my heart, or mended it, I could hardly tell which.

"I made you some coffee," she said, and handed me my Pluto mug which I'd had since I was a child myself. I saw immediately what she had done: she had put ground coffee in, meant for the filter machine, instead of instant, and then added milk and water. I wasn't going to say anything so I took a sip and realised that she had used salt instead of sugar. Was my own daughter trying to poison me?

"Thank you, sweetheart," I said, placing the mug on a shelf. "That's very thoughtful of you."

"Are we really going to the park this afternoon, like you promised?"

"Of course, if I promised. Come and have a look at this." I took her over to where the boxes were. "Ready?" I said.

I lifted one of the boxes, like a magician's reveal. Spiders swarmed from beneath it in every direction. Margaret grabbed my arm but didn't screech, as I'd half expected her to.

"Suddenly they realise there's a whole new world out there," I said.

Margaret didn't look convinced. She dawdled for a while, before she said, with what I detected as a hint of censure, "Where will the spiders go now that their home's been destroyed?"

"I'm sure they'll find somewhere else to live," I said, "somewhere better than under a dark old box."

I wondered whether to extend this idea, for her benefit, into a parable relating to adolescence, the onset of puberty and all the dangerous changes these things wrought; or perhaps into a parable on the Church of England and its urgent need for renewal. But her still-imploring face, her tug at my sleeve, her small white laced-up pumps, made it impossible for me to speak plainly, and so I placed my hand on her tousled head instead, like a benediction.

In my line of business it is very rare for me to have a Sunday off, particularly in the lead up to Christmas, and so, that afternoon, there was a sense of occasion as Jane, Margaret and I headed for the park. Although there was a wintry chill in the air, the sun beamed and, walking between Jane and Margaret, holding hands with both of them, I had one of those rare and seemingly causeless surges of wellbeing when all the parts of life – green bird or no green bird – seem, if only for a moment, to fall into place and make sense. Sometimes, in winter, the fall of sunlight across your face recalls a summer more lovely than has ever been, or will. I looked up into the enamelled Botticelli blue of the sky, the sort of sky where *putti* hang out, and found it so intensely blue that it seemed touched with something golden; and, against it, I saw a bird, an ordinary sort of bird – perhaps a sparrow, small and brown, but high and free and wheeling – dipping on its invisible trapeze, trailing its ribbon of song.

We sat outside the café and had a pot of tea and some carrot cake. Across the lawn, happy dogs leapt in pursuit of stick and ball and ducks squabbled in the boating lake. Often parishioners would come by and feel it their duty to make polite conversation, usually pertaining to the weather: we were well-known in Rochester and I was fair game for such idle pleasantries as "Lovely out!" and "It's like Spring is here already!"

The green bird sat at the next table. Awkwardly, it picked up the menu with its wings and I watched, with fascination, as its beady eyes swivelled from left to right as it read. Everyone paid it no attention whatsoever.

"Don't *stare*, Dad," said Margaret, under her breath.

"I'm s-s-sorry," I stammered, and looked away, although I surreptitiously continued my surveillance of the being.

After a while, the waitress approached it and took an order for "cake" (at least that's what it sounded like). This confirmed the evidence of both Margaret's Facebook film and the newsreel footage from Paris: this thing was *not* a hallucination. It was real. The waitress had clearly interacted with it. But then a further troubling notion hit me: what if this was all part of the hallucination too? The waitress, the café, the park, the Paris mob? the bustling Piccadilly pavement? my daughter? my wife? my faith itself? all part of an enormous substructure of deception and artifice? At that moment it seemed to me as if there were no clear demarcation between where hallucination began and reality ended, or, for that matter, between where hallucination ended and reality began.

I said to Jane and Margaret, very carefully, "Well, perhaps we'd better be making a move. When the waitress brings that green bird its order will you ask for the bill?"

Neither of them showed the slightest sign of perturbation at the vision seated at the next table; they merely acquiesced to my reasonable suggestion. And I thought: there is a large green bird out there and no one, *no one*, is taking a blind bit of notice.

At home, I took my newspaper into the conservatory and pretended to read it. If I could only *pretend* that everything was normal then perhaps I could go some way to convincing myself that it was.

A story caught my eye. The headline read: 'Distinguished Lecturer to visit Moscow.' I read on.

'Dr Paul Anderson, from the London School of Hygiene and Tropical Medicine, has been invited to deliver the annual Sergei and Yulia Skripal Memorial Lecture at the prestigious Vladimir Putin Medical School in Moscow. This is the first time that such an honour has been conferred by the institution upon a foreign academic.'

Beneath the story was a picture of Dr Paul Anderson. The distinguished academic was wearing a gown and descending a flight of stone steps. Under his left wing was tucked a diploma and balanced on his beak were a pair of horn-rimmed spectacles.

I thought: they are legion. They *must* be. Here, in addition to the sighting in the café, was further evidence, before my very eyes. Up until then, I had, perhaps naively, believed that there existed only one of these green birds and that it was in some way connected with me, perhaps following me, perhaps trying to tell me something, deliver a warning, a portent or a prophecy. It had even crossed my mind, believe it or not, that it might have been a manifestation of the Holy Spirit itself, although, in Christian iconography, the Holy Spirit more usually takes the form of a dove. Now, with the appearance of Dr Paul Anderson, I realised that I was completely mistaken and that these creatures were insidiously infiltrating the whole of our society, at every level, and that they had absolutely nothing to do with me and no interest in me whatsoever.

The next morning I walked to the Cathedral as usual. I feel that I should point out here that I am the Bishop of Rochester. This fact often comes as a complete surprise to me too. Sometimes I will wake up in the morning and think, "Well, bugger me, if I'm not the Bishop of Rochester!"

It is only a short walk – five minutes at the most – and I took my usual route. During this walk I witnessed a green bird standing in the tinsel-crowded bay window of a house on St Margaret's Street, apparently dusting; a green bird driving a minicab on Boley Hill; a green bird among a group of carol singers in College Yard; and a green bird wearing a red scarf dismounting a bicycle outside the castle. It was clearly a student.

Instead of heading straight to my office in the Cathedral, I went to the Lady Chapel which contains the splendidly elaborate monument to Bishop Godfrey Somerset. I had it to myself that morning and prayed for a while there. The church teaches us that if you repeat things over and over again, and at the same times each day, eventually they become true. It doesn't mean that, through repetition, they become to *seem* true; it means that, through repetition, they literally become so. This is how prayer works, although it has never worked for me. Despite this, I bowed my head and muttered the following prayer to my elusive paymaster: "Dear God, thank you for your manifold blessings and for all the richness of your creation, both of which go without saying, and I'm sorry if I may have seemed a little aloof recently, but I wonder whether at some point in the next few days you could find it in your power to enlighten me as to why the world is increasingly populated by large green birds? In the Name of the Father, the Son, and the Holy Bird. *Ghost*, I mean. *Ghost.* Amen." I crossed myself. Then I hurried off to a ten o'clock meeting in the Chapter House with the Deacon about funding urgent repairs to the tower's weathervane. We had it on good authority – that of a steeplejack – that the golden cockerel which topped it was in danger of falling off. From that height, if it fell, it could quite easily kill someone.

Why do weathervanes on churches so often sport a cockerel? Forgive my digression, but it's an interesting story. Well, it's fairly interesting. In the sixth century, Pope Gregory decreed that the cockerel was the most suitable emblem of Christianity since it was also the emblem of Saint Peter, a reference to Luke 22:34 in which Jesus predicts that Peter will deny him three times 'before the cock crows.' As a result of this, the cock became a common feature of weathervanes on church spires, and in the 9th-century Pope Nicholas actually stipulated that the figure should be placed on *all* church steeples. It is ironic, then, that a cock – a symbol of doubt – should adorn so many of our religious buildings. And telling, too, that even here, in the sanctuary of this great Cathedral, I was watched over by yet another large flightless bird.


I will not provide an exhaustive tally of the many sightings I had that week. But it would be true to say that by Friday I had become accustomed to the green birds and became accordingly less surprised by their appearance, in whatever form or function they presented themselves to me, and had begun to think of them as being an intrinsic part of my flock. It dawned on me that they must always have existed but that I had simply never noticed them before, however improbable that notion seemed. But I will just mention, however, the ordination of the new Bishop of Salisbury which featured on the television news on Wednesday evening. The sight of His Most Reverend Excellency processing to the roar of the great organ down that magnificent nave in all his pomp and regalia, mitre perched atop his beaked head, crosier tucked under a wing, big webbed feet slapping on the ancient floor, was not something I shall forget in a hurry, although Jane and Margaret watched the proceedings with completely straight faces throughout and did not seem to consider that extraordinary procession worthy of even a passing comment, except for Margaret who, at the end of the bulletin, asked, "Will he be more important than the Bishop of Rochester?"

I was not able to provide her with a definitive answer.


On Friday I came home to find a great deal of excitement in the house. Upstairs, Margaret was getting ready for her party and Jane – with, I felt, a nostalgic re-enactment of her own youth – was helping her. Loud pop music was playing from Margaret's bedroom: she was a huge fan of 'One Direction', despite my attempts to win her over to the polyphonic glories of William Byrd to which she seemed almost completely insusceptible. I imagined them both jumping up and down on the bed.

I was sitting in the drawing room when, at exactly 7pm – this punctuality was a good sign, I felt – I heard the doorbell chiming (that's a sort of ecclesiastical joke on my part – the doorbell sounds remarkably like the chimes at Rochester). As I had been fore-warned, Kevin had turned up to collect Margaret. Of course I had mixed feelings still about the whole thing; I still felt, genuinely, that Margaret was too young to be going to parties with boys. But perhaps I was just imposing upon her some of the prejudices which had come as a consequence of my own late development, and my age. As Jane had said, they grow up so quickly these days, and perhaps this was something I simply had to attune myself to. However, I sat there for a while longer, wanting to delay the inevitable, for I had now begun to see my daughter's departure for the party as the beginning not only of her departure from childhood, but her departure from me, her doting father.

When the bell chimed a second time, I shouted, "Is someone going to get that?"

Margaret and Jane came tumbling down the stairs and went into the hall. I heard the door open and Jane's warm greeting, "Kevin, it's so lovely to meet you at last!"

I stood, and, taking a breath, went into the hall. You know what happens next. There was Kevin, in his extravagant green plumage. I strode up to him and, unshaken by even the faintest alarm, shook his wing warmly. He seemed inordinately nervous and kept hopping from one webbed foot to the other, making loud slapping sounds on the parquet. There was a strong smell of birdseed and he had a piece of cuttlebone sticking out from the side of his beak.

"It's very good to meet you, Kevin," I said, perhaps a little blandly.

His beak opened and he produced a remarkably piercing screech: "*Kaaark*! *Kaaark*!" At which point about a dozen droppings, the size of golf balls, fell from his nether regions and thumped dully onto the floor. My wife continued to smile seraphically, and I, taking her hint, chose to ignore them too.

I felt I had to say it, even if I framed it as a joke. Looking at him over my spectacles – a look of stern admonition I have cultivated for some of my more insufferable parishioners – I said, "I do hope, young man, that you are going to take good care of our little girl."

"*Daaaad*!" cried Margaret, in a voice I was getting used to, and one which, I suspected, I was going to be hearing a lot more of in the future, before I ceased to hear it at all.

"*Kaaark*! *Kaaark*!" screeched Kevin, clearly in a state of great excitement.

Later, I was sitting in the drawing room with Jane. We'd had dinner – it had been very pleasant with just the two of us and I even lit a candle – and now we were having a nightcap. Byrd was on the CD player, the fire was crackling away, the grandfather clock was ticking portentously and our Christmas tree could not have been more pagan. Despite all this, I was very restless.

"If you look at that clock one more time …" said Jane.

"I'm not looking at the clock."

"Margaret said she'd be home by ten-thirty at the latest."

"I know, I know."

"So give her the benefit of the doubt."

"I will. I will give her the benefit of the doubt."

"And, while you're doing it, give me a kiss, Bish."

I kissed her, perhaps a little peremptorily. "I do worry," I said.

She plucked at my lip with her finger. "I know you do, you silly old Episcopal sausage," she said. Then, in a more wary tone of voice, she said, "Did you like him?"

"Kevin, you mean? Very much."

"Was he what you were expecting?"

"Well …"

"Tell me."

"He seemed very … nice. Sort of … *normal*. Oh my God, the droppings."

"I did them."

"Bless you," I said, which, coming from a Bishop, always had a ring to it. I drained the last of my scotch. "Do you know what? I think I'll turn in."

"Turn in? Robin, it's nine o'clock."

"I know," I said, "but it's been a busy week and I shall only sit here and worry about Margaret when I might as well lie in bed and worry about Margaret. You stay and finish your drink and wait for her to come back." I stood, and kissed her on the cheek. "And, Jane?" I said.

"Yes, my darling?"

"Tell Margaret that I love her very much, won't you?"

"She knows that, Robin."

"Still. Tell her for me."

She nodded, and smiled. "Okay."

One more surprise awaited me. I took my glass into the kitchen, tipped half an inch of scotch into it, and started up the stairs. Half way up, on the landing, a window gave a view over the neighbouring gardens to the tower of the Cathedral, glowing in orange floodlight which made it seem to float, ethereal against the darkness. I would usually pause here to observe my domain and wonder at the happy lot I had drawn in life.

And it was then, just as I heard the bells of the Cathedral ring the hour, that I saw them silhouetted and transfigured against the pale-faced moon: a perfect V-formation of twelve gold-green birds.

My God, I thought: they can *fly*!

# Cala Romantica

Mr Hurd's brother-in-law, Frank, was dealing out his Polaroids. Most of them were of Frank in the nude.

Mrs Hurd said, "Where's Carol?"

Carol was Frank's wife.

"Taking the pictures, where do you think?" said Frank. He was always short with her. "This is me on the beach."

"Goodness me," said Mrs Hurd.

"And this is me in front of the hotel," he said. There he was, flexing his bronzed muscles in his jutting skin-tight speedos.

"It looks very *big*," said Mr Hurd.

"You're not wrong there," said Frank, for whom 'big' was always a compliment. "Six bars and four restaurants, two Olympic-sized swimming pools and a little one for the kids shaped like Mickey Mouse."

With his croupier's *élan* he slapped another picture down.

"What's this?" said Mrs Hurd, staring with alarm at what appeared to be a blurred close-up of some piece of human anatomy.

"That's Carol's nose," said Frank. He took a sideways sip of tea: they didn't keep lager in the house. "She took it by accident when she was loading the film."

"It's nice to see *one* of Carol," said Mrs Hurd, a little primly, but she'd made her point. "Even her nose."

The Polaroids remained laid out in rows like an abandoned game of Patience.

"Is that it?" said Mr Hurd. "No pictures of the children then?"

Frank and Carol had five strapping kids.

Mrs Hurd interrupted with an air of closure which just avoided brusqueness. "Well, thank you, Frank, for showing them to us," she said. She was always polite with him but, after the dreadful incident at the Chilcotts' party, she'd never trusted him, and never would again. But they didn't talk about that.

Mr Hurd knew what was coming next: Frank was going to suggest that *they* went to Cala Romantica.

"I don't know," he said, anticipating him.

"Tony," said Frank. "It's a *no-brainer*."

He often used phrases like this – 'no-brainer', 'no-hoper', 'non-starter' – phrases which Mr Hurd was vaguely aware of, in the same way that he was vaguely aware of the existence of 'portable phones' and 'emails'.

"But it's very expensive, isn't it?" he said.

"Three hundred and fifty quid a week, all in," said Frank.

"For both of us?"

"Don't be a plonker, Tony: this is the *Med* we're talking about now, not Skeggy. *Each*. But that includes your flight, coach transfer from the airport and full English breakfast. Not lunch or dinner or drinks but drinks are cheap as chips out there: a pint for a quid. Imagine that! You can get shit-faced on a tenner!"

Mrs Hurd, tight-lipped, began clearing the tea things. Frank's way of speaking reminded her that he came from a different background. What poor Carol had to endure at his hands didn't bear thinking about. But as she went through into the kitchen the picture of him on the beach lying face down in his G-string came back to her, his body livid as a barbecued steak, his buttocks white as two hard-boiled eggs, and so much hair crawling over the man's back!


They changed their minds: they'd go. So they booked a week in the resort of Cala Romantica on Majorca's sunny north-east coast. Two weeks had seemed an indulgence, and a risk; a week seemed safer, in case they hated it.

In the Travel Agents, Mr Hurd watched the young woman with the long caramel neck and the hair bun feed the information into her computer. Behind her on the wall was a poster. 'España', it said, the word thrillingly italicised, like a matador's flourish. Beneath it was a stock image of a yellow sun, some blue water and a green palm tree which could have been anywhere, even the 'Water Waves Fun Centre' in Blackburn. 'Sun, Sea and Sangria' it added at the bottom, by way of clarification. Mr Hurd puzzled over it, vaguely aware that the third 'S' was usually 'Sex'. Or was it 'Sand'?

The young woman handed them the tickets which were still warm and fragrant from the machine.

"All done for you," she said. "One week in the Hotel Playa Flamenco Nights in Cala Romantica, a double with sea view."

"Thank you, *Laura*," said Mr Hurd, expansively. He knew her name from the badge pinned to her chest.

Mrs Hurd stiffened beside him: something in her revolted against her husband when he was too familiar with attractive young women.

"We've never been abroad before," she admitted, to put him in context.

"How exciting it will be for you!" said Laura. Then she added, confidentially, "You know, Majorca's *completely* different from what people think."

Because they had no idea what people thought about Majorca, the notion that it was completely different from what people thought about it wasn't very helpful. But Mr Hurd didn't mind: in the twenty minutes that they had been sitting in the Travel Agents he had fallen very deeply in love with Laura. That was all it took these days.

And just two weeks later – cue the strum of a flamenco guitar and the rattle of castanets – they were in an impossibly hot coach with tinted windows and dark orange air vents the colour of headaches, racing across an arid landscape of scorched maize and scattered rock, alleviated occasionally by the shock of crimson azaleas. Mr Hurd watched 'abroad' pass by and wondered what all the fuss was about. It was *different*, certainly, but the array of new sense-impressions only left him bewildered. Vast advertisement hoardings in the shape of bulls or bottles of rum were set like easels on the hills and shabby white unvisited towns passed in a flurry of dust with their shuttered shop fronts, huddles of old men sitting around playing cards, dogs not bothering to look up. Everyone on the coach was still singing what they'd started on the plane: "We're off to sunny sunny Spain! Eviva España!"

Mr Hurd pretended to sing along but Mrs Hurd remained silent, her head pressed against the window. She hadn't spoken, let alone sung, since they'd boarded the flight at Manchester, except once, to reprimand her husband for winking at a stewardess. In fact, she'd hardly spoken since the holiday had been booked. Mr Hurd was aware, peripherally, that she would rather have gone to Skegness, as usual. Even after forty-five years of marriage he still didn't know how to deal with these sullen incommunicative moods of hers, so he settled into a reciprocal strop, trying to enjoy the liberation from enforced small-talk but, instead, all the time worrying about her and feeling guilty and wanting them to be back to normal again and knowing that somehow *they had to talk about things*.

They needed a break after the last year which would not go down as the best of their married lives. For a start there'd been the shock of Carol's illness, but at least she seemed to be responding to the chemotherapy. Then there was that horrible business about Frank at the Chilcotts' party which they'd never *really* got to the bottom of and which Mrs Hurd didn't want to talk about, but it just wouldn't seem to go away. Frank had been very drunk and done something stupid to Mrs Hurd which he shouldn't have done, and that was all there was to it. But it still riled Mr Hurd that his brother-in-law had never apologised or even admitted any wrongdoing. He had decided that this was typical of Frank's cavalier attitude towards life: it only confirmed his original opinions of the man, as it had, in its more immediate way, his wife's. And then there'd been Monty dying. Mrs Hurd had taken it particularly badly: she'd loved that dog. They both had. It hadn't seemed right, putting him to sleep like that, when he could still wag his tail and watch you with that counting pant, that eyebrow-cocked entreaty.

44

And beneath these alluvial layers of their care was the single fact which had dominated their lives together but about which they had never spoken, either to each other or to anyone else: forty years before, their first, their only, child, Lottie – for whom they had prepared a room with pink walls, a cot, dolls, a mobile, even a name ('Lottie' was short for Charlotte, but they knew she'd always be Lottie) – had been stillborn. The tiny lifeless body had been hastily taken from them and disposed of without even the dignity of a proper burial. Their grief broke them, and they didn't think to ask about her body.

Then came more bad news. They were told that they could never have children. They could never replace Lottie, even if they had wanted to.

The coach pulled up outside the big white building and sneezed conclusively. The sudden silence instigated a flurry of activity. Mr and Mrs Hurd followed everyone onto the baking tarmac where some men were unloading the suitcases, hurling them into an untidy row. They followed another man into a marble hall which was cold as a fridge. As they waited in line, Mr Hurd looked up to the ceiling where a phalanx of slowly revolving fans redistributed the flies. Occasionally, seasoned holidaymakers, rippling and semi-naked, with that settled-in chatty unhurried air of the acclimatized, passed through, carrying their plastic inflatables, heading for the beach with a mastication of flip-flops.

They were allotted a room by a man at the desk with a moustache and then another man, also with a moustache, picked up their suitcase, glanced at the docket they'd been given, and hurried off. They presumed they were meant to follow him. They rode in a lift to the fifth floor, then proceeded along a corridor lined with identical white numbered doors. The sheer scale of it was all quite new to Mr and Mrs Hurd. There was a pleasant cool smell of freshly-baked bread and a hint of polish. Mr Hurd caught a glimpse, through a half-open door, of someone else's room, revealing an opened suitcase on a bed with its mess of belongings scattered about it, clothes, guidebooks, a camera: the disarray of someone else's private unpacked life.

After a while the man stopped, took out a set of keys and opened a door. He gestured for them to enter and humped the suitcase in after them.

"All right to leave here?" he said, putting the suitcase by the bed.

"Very good there indeed," said Mr Hurd, in the slow patois and unnatural arrangement of words he thought a foreigner might understand.

"Here you have bathroom, television, doors onto balcony, light switch, air condition, and," with a fetching, white-toothed smile, "I hope you very happy stay with us."

"Thank you," said Mr Hurd.

Placing their keys on the desk, the man concluded, "Buenos dias," and was gone.

Mr Hurd felt a thrill go through him at their sudden autonomy, their custodianship of these new and exotic surroundings.

"Do you think we should have given him a tip?" whispered Mrs Hurd, as if the man was on the other side of the door with his ear pressed against it.

"Oh, I don't know," said Mr Hurd, implying he didn't much care either – they were *abroad,* anything would go – and he put his arms around his wife, her familiar stocky body which once he'd craved but for which, now, he felt a safer less urgent desire. She didn't protest and he knew he was forgiven. "Listen," he said, touching noses. "We're here to enjoy ourselves. Understand? We're here to put everything behind us: Monty, Carol's illness ... Frank ... and ... well, everything that's happened ..."

He felt her flinch at the mention of Frank's name which he had carefully put towards the end of his inventory of their misfortunes; or had she understood what he had meant by 'everything that's happened'? He could not bring himself to say 'Lottie' but he hoped she knew what he meant. For a while they held each other in the dark room.

Then she said, her voice still muted, "There's a very funny smell in here."

Mr Hurd had noticed it too but hadn't been going to say anything. "Let's open the curtains and get some air in here," he said, detaching himself.

But there weren't any curtains, just some shutters with a tricky metal catch. When he had figured it out, he opened them with a theatrical flourish and stepped out into the oven of the day and onto a small balcony, its floor pink and marbled like nougat, the hiss and chatter of crickets almost deafening. He admired the view; or, at least, he took it in, already preparing his positive angle. Instead of the vista of wide blue sea and nodding palms which the shutters had somehow implied, there was a skeleton of metal girders, some encased in concrete. At its base was a pool of stagnant water, rainbowed with petrol, and, sitting in it, a yellow excavator. There were some filthy gaping concrete mixers with grey porridge around their mouths. He heard the pounding clatter of a drill.

"There's a lot of building work going on!" he called encouragingly into the room. "Obviously a very popular resort! Come and take a look! Enid? Are you there?"

Behind him, he heard the zips on the case swiftly going. She'd come out in her own time: it was best to leave her. He drummed his fingers on the hot balcony rail, and listened. Beyond the sound of the drill, there was a remote thump of music, the ululation of laughter, the hum of bar-chat: somewhere out there, people were having fun. The sun beat squarely onto his face, forcing him to squint as his eyes tracked the further view across the building sites, the pink serrated roofs of villa developments, a couple of taller hotels with their names in letters, Hollywood-style, on top, a water tank flashing like its own sun, until they settled on a wedge of shaking oxyacetylene blue, twinkling silently like stadium photography … and with a thrill he realised it was, could only be, the *sea*! The Mediterranean! Cradle of civilization! Playground of the rich!

He went back into the dark room which now pulsed with a palimpsest of sunlight.

Mrs Hurd had gone.

"Enid?" he said. "Are you there?"

Then he noticed the bathroom door was closed and that there was a line of light beneath it. She would be freshening up after the journey.

He sat on the bed beside the suitcase with its unfastened straps. The plastic toiletries bag, decorated with a lattice of pink hearts, was half open and Mr Hurd noticed, with only vague curiosity, a carton of Dulcolax protruding from it. Why was his wife taking *laxatives*? he wondered.

She was being a long time.

Then he looked at the wall. There was a print, in the modern style, of a palm-fringed bay, the paradise he had dreamt of, and been sold, but which in reality seemed to have eluded him.

He continued sitting there for a while, deflated, until he became aware of the toilet flushing for the third or fourth time, followed by the cistern's tired resumption of breath.

"Enid?" he called out with happy mischief in his voice. "Are you all right in there? You've been an awfully long time."

The answer came in the form of another dry clanking and what sounded like a grunt. He stood and went to the bathroom door and playfully tapped on it, with a knuckle.

"Enid?" he said.

"Don't come in!" she shouted, and he heard the lock go.

This sounded like another tantrum. He stood for a while in the middle of the room and found the whole thing a little comical. Then he heard the door unlock and Mrs Hurd came out, looking flushed. She closed the door, resolutely, behind her.

"Enid?" he said again, with more insistent concern. "Is everything all right? I was worried about you."

She was breathing with extreme self-control. Then she did something she very rarely did and which filled him with dread: she said his name.

"*Tony*," she said.

"Enid? What is it? You're … *shaking*."

"It's this foreign … *toilet*."

"Do you want me to take a look?"

"No I do not. Why don't you go down and have a drink in that bar by reception? I'll unpack and join you in half an hour."

It didn't get much better than this: he was being commanded to do precisely the very thing he wanted to do.

"If you're sure," he said, wondering over this strange unaccounted-for 'half an hour' – perhaps she wanted to do the unpacking herself, he knew how particular she was – but he was guiltily pleased at its prospect.

As he tripped along the corridor he called "Buenos dias!" to two young women in bikinis and sombreros and in the lift he chatted to a brown barefooted English boy who showed him the coloured transfers on his arms which he told him he got free with Chupa Chups lollies which they sold on the beach.

Jaunty guitar music was playing in the bar which he recognised from the holiday programmes. He asked for a beer and the young barman said, as if affronted, "*Una cerveza*?" and Mr Hurd had to comically repeat the Spanish word to him two or three times until he was satisfied with his pronunciation, and then he was passed a big frosty amber goblet of *San Miguel* – not a pint glass, but he wasn't about to complain – which it was explained he could pay for *later* – he wasn't about to complain about that either – and he took it to the only unoccupied table which sat in a blazing parallelogram of sunlight. He sipped. The beer was fizzy and lip-numbingly cold; not what he was used to at The Swan, but nice all the same, and perfect for the climate.

Ten minutes later, he went for another.

"*Una* …" he began.

"… *cerveza*!" cried the barman, on cue, and gave him one. Mr Hurd knew they were going to become great friends in the week ahead. He introduced himself. The barman was called Mateo and it was clear that this was how Mr Hurd should refer to him from now on.

When he was half way through his second *San Miguel*, he spotted Mrs Hurd coming towards him, looking grim. Wordlessly, she sat down. He calculated: she would think this was his first drink.

"Would you like … *una cerveza*?" he said.

"No thank you."

"You don't even know what it is."

"I'll have a cup of English tea."

"Don't have a cup of English tea. You're on holiday! In Spain! What about … a glass of sherry? That's Spanish, you know. Sherry."

"It's four o'clock."

"Don't have tea, dear."

"I'll have a small glass of white wine then, if it makes you happy. Not too dry. I do wish there was a table in the shade."

At the bar, Mateo poured the wine and then, before Mr Hurd could stop him, added some ice. Mr Hurd imagined it was normal in Spain to put ice in wine. On the way back to their table he picked up some leaflets.

"There's lots of excursions we can go on," he said when he had sat down, determined not to be colonised by her lack of enthusiasm. He fanned out the leaflets. "Look. A flamenco night."

"We don't want to be gallivanting all over the place."

He watched as she mechanically removed the ice from her wine and placed it in the ashtray.

"Or what about this?" he said. "'The Caves of Drach'!"

"No thank you very much."

"They do sound a bit ghoulish, don't they? Well what about a boat trip to … 'Port d' Alcúdia'? Lovely harbour. Look at all the restaurants by the water and the yachts. Look at the yachts, Enid."

"*No*, Tony."

"You're right," he said, putting the leaflets aside. "We've come here to relax."

"I do wish there was a table in the shade," she said again. She seemed very restless.

"So you keep saying," said Mr Hurd. "As you can see, there isn't one, but if one becomes available we'll move straight to it. Here. I'll fan you with a leaflet."

"Excuse me."

She stood up.

"*Now* where are you going?"

"I've got to go upstairs for something."

"You just came down!"

But she was gone and Mr Hurd settled back into his guilty relief and the growing and very real possibility of a third *San Miguel*.

A fly landed on the beermat and busily rubbed its hands together, as if plotting something. Mr Hurd laughed to think of its nationality: a Spanish fly! He was a bit tipsy on the beer. This fact, and the foreignness, was making him restless to explore. He often had dreams in which the world's impossible richness and potential was beckoning to him and seemed, all at once, within reach. Sometimes, in these dreams, he would fly far from Blackburn and its terraces and chimneys, across a dazzling and impossibly detailed landscape, somewhere he'd never ventured, but bright and real as stained glass. Then he'd wake with a start, to find himself in their bedroom, with Mrs Hurd snoring beside him, the rain scuttling down the windowpane.

Ten minutes later he saw Mrs Hurd approaching like a one-woman diaspora, her shoes clipping on the marble. He partially stood, out of some half-forgotten chivalry. She sat down tersely.

"Tony," she said, in the same manner.

"What is it, dear?"

"The foreign toilet," she said, in an undertone. "I don't *like* it. It's disgusting, and unhygienic."

Mr Hurd found his wife's preoccupation with plumbing comical.

"When in Rome!" he said. "We have to get used to their funny ways."

"Well, I'm not sure I *can* get used to 'their funny ways', or that I want to."

Mateo placed a hand-written bill on the table in front of them.

"Three beers and one white wine," he said, his jokey demeanour now jettisoned. "One thousand two hundred pesetas."

"*Three* beers?" said Mrs Hurd.

"Goodness me," said Mr Hurd. He reached into his jacket. "It does sound a lot, doesn't it?"

"*Three* beers, Tony?"

"I mean it sounds a lot in pesetas. But we must remember the exchange rate and not worry too much. Divide everything by a hundred Frank said …" He felt the empty interior of his pocket. "Oh dear. My wallet. I think it's still in the suitcase. I'll have to go up and fetch it."

Mateo said, in his newly acquired textbook English, "You can always put it on your room bill, if you'd prefer."

"Yes, let's do that," said Mrs Hurd, although she had no idea what the man was talking about.

Mr Hurd decided to put his foot down. "No thank you, Mateo," he said, "we don't want to start building up debt. And, besides, we'll need money if we're going to eat out tonight."

"Surely we can eat in the hotel?" said Mrs Hurd.

"But I felt like a little local colour this evening," said Mr Hurd, glancing at Mateo who was scratching his head and looking out of the window where a pretty young woman on a moped was semaphoring at him. Mr Hurd wondered whether she was his girlfriend. It seemed more than likely because now she had blown him a kiss.

"I think I've had quite enough local colour for one day," said Mrs Hurd.

"I'll pop up and get my wallet," said Mr Hurd.

"I'll go," said Mrs Hurd.

"Don't be *silly*," said Mr Hurd, surprised by how firm he sounded. "You've already been up twice. I can't think what all the fuss is about. You sit tight and finish your drink. Here. Fan yourself with these."

Back in the room he located his wallet. His wife, he noticed, had closed the doors onto the balcony and there was that smell of drains again. He wondered whether he should speak to someone about it. As he was leaving, he noticed the light under the bathroom door. For the twin reasons of his own parsimony – he couldn't bear a light left on, even if it wasn't his own – and the fact that he had drunk three *San Miguels* and needed to have a pee anyway, he went into the bathroom. The lid on the seat was closed. He lifted it.

"Holy *crap*," he said – a phrase he'd once heard Frank use but had never found a personal use for, until now.

The sight that met his eyes was not a pleasant one. Lying from the top to the furthest recess of the illogically angled bowl was a shining tapering monster of a turd, by *far* the largest he had ever seen. It was the size, the shape and the colour of an aubergine. Swiftly – as a horrified reflex action – he pushed the flusher on top of the cistern.

When the froth had cleared it was still there, exactly as before, only more shiny.

He stared at it for some time as the cistern began refilling.

After several more abortive flushes – perhaps ten – which produced no signs of movement, he left the room and made his way distractedly down the stairs. He had decided not to take the lift as he needed time to gather his thoughts, although not so much time that Mrs Hurd would wonder what had happened to him and perhaps even guess what he had seen. As he descended each landing his dilemma seemed only to grow in its complexity and awfulness. Was it really possible that his own wife could have produced such a thing? Obviously, *clearly*, there was going to be a problem with moving it: the toilet's own mechanism was evidently powerless in the face of such an adversary. But he felt the dilemma more acutely in its psychological than in its physical dimension. Of course, he had been 'intimate' with Mrs Hurd in the past but he suspected that this latest development might force him into a kind and degree of intimacy he didn't want: that is, a *verbal* one. For, while he could quite happily make love to his wife – although, admittedly, with rather less frequency than he used to – he would have found it impossible to describe that same act in language, either in the technical language of biology or – heaven forbid – the cruder vernacular. And now there was this.

On the third landing down he had to settle himself against the wall as he found himself, to his surprise, suddenly and uncontrollably laughing, but with a violent inner perturbation which from the outside must have looked like some form of seizure: that preposterous great *sausage*! – he could barely think of it! – it made him wonder if he'd ever really *known* his wife at *all*?

Suddenly, she was standing in front of him.

"Tony?" she said, noticing his tribulation.

"*Enid*!" he cried, with a superfluity of joy and surprise, as if they hadn't seen each other for years and had just happened to meet by chance on this Spanish staircase.

"Whatever are you doing?" she said. "I heard you laughing from two floors down."

"Just a sort of … private joke," he said, "as I was coming downstairs. What about you?"

"I was popping up for something," she said, wary of him now, suspecting all his motives.

"Well," said Mr Hurd. "I shall … see you downstairs."

They parted like strangers, after an inconclusive hiatus, unable to find the correct form of words to mark their parting since they would be seeing each other again so soon.

He went quickly to the bar, keen for another drink to steady his nerves, and it was as he stood at the bar, delving into every pocket he possessed – and even a few he didn't – that three realisations dawned on him simultaneously and to disastrous effect: first, he realised he didn't have his wallet with him. Second, he recalled, with devastating clarity, what had been, at the time, an act of numb absent-mindedness as he had leant forward to peer more closely at the indelectable stool: he had placed his wallet on top of the cistern. And the third realisation tumbled horribly into his consciousness: in all likelihood, his wife was, at that very moment, looking from the wallet to the turd and back again, putting two and two together.

Momentarily unable to reason and filled with a sense that he must *do* something urgently – *anything* – he crossed the bar and started bounding up the stairs. But on the second landing, he saw the lift pass slowly downwards – it was one of those lifts that has tall rectangular frosted glass windows in its doors – and he saw through the windows the distinctive, if blurred, form of Mrs Hurd.

He turned and ran down the stairs.

When, a few seconds later, Mrs Hurd found him, he was sitting at their usual table with an entirely casual outward appearance and a lackadaisical smile; but when, wordlessly, she handed him the wallet, she noticed that he was heaving inwardly, gasping for air, and that his forehead was shining with perspiration.

The next few hours were negotiated between them with the dazed surrender to protocol and careful attention to detail of the final stages of an execution by lethal injection. There was no escape, no chance of a timely call from the Governor's office: it was just a question of somehow getting through it.

They took a walk around the grounds of the hotel – all wiry grass, pine cones and chattering lawn sprinklers sewing rainbows in the air – and then Mr Hurd had another *San Miguel* and Mrs Hurd another white wine at one of the many bars, and then they had dinner in one of the many restaurants: this one was Spanish themed. Mr Hurd had Spanish chicken; Mrs Hurd had Spanish beef. They left most of it. Mr

Hurd ordered sangria – a drink Frank had told him about, and which he remembered from the poster in the Travel Agents above the head of the lovely Laura – and it arrived in a sort of glass watering can. The idea, apparently, was to pour it into your mouth from a great height: Mr Hurd remembered seeing Judith Chalmers doing it on 'Wish You Were Here?'

All around, chains of fairy lights marked the trees and there were pools of illumination amid the vegetation. Mr Hurd had never seen plants lit like that and he liked the luxurious effect. The pool, now closed to swimmers, glowed a deep blue, its fretted surface like the shiver of human skin. The water magnified and melted the tiles beneath. Elsewhere, the music from the bars was becoming ever more insistent and eloquent. But nothing could drown out the chatter of the crickets which seemed to get louder and louder, more all-consuming, the more you listened to it.

Mr Hurd said, once the waiter had taken their plates away, "We'll go for a swim in the pool tomorrow, if you like. I might even have a little dip before breakfast."

"You'll need one to clear your head after all that … whatever that stuff is called."

"Sangria," said Mr Hurd, who was becoming quite an expert on the local beverages.

"Whatever it is."

"It's mostly fruit juice." Then, draining his glass, he said, "I'll just go and see what time the pool opens in the morning."

"Now?" said Mrs Hurd.

She was right. As an excuse, it wasn't wholly convincing but it was the best he could manage. The sangria had made him resolved and pioneering and he had a job to do. It wasn't going to be a particularly pleasant job but in his present state of mind he knew he was equal to it. He'd planned it over dinner, which partly accounted for his lack of appetite. A toothbrush was what he needed, or perhaps the handle of a toilet brush: anything to give it a good, firm prod, or exercise a little leverage.

In her husband's absence, Mrs Hurd sat, looking at the happy people all around her, some dancing, some kissing, some just sitting dreamily, holding hands. It was a warm evening with a breeze that carried the scent of jasmine and pine which reminded her of toilet freshener. While she was not happy, she was, at least, aware of the *possibility* of happiness in a place such as this, where the whole world was, essentially, built for pleasure and repose, at a cost. But one thing dominated her thoughts. It was intolerable, the burden of it; the waiting for the truth to be made explicit between them. That was the worst thing, worse than the thing itself: the *not talking about the thing.*

Suddenly, a feeling of resolve overcame her, engendered by a desire to share, at last, in the carefree happiness that was being exhibited all around her. But before that could happen she knew she had an onerous duty to perform. She rose purposefully from her chair, walked briskly into the hotel, across the hall, up the stairs (too impatient to wait for the lift) and into the room, not even noticing that the door was already open. Without hesitation at the thought of her repellent adversary, she flung open the door of the bathroom.

At first she did not recognise the man crouching over the toilet bowl. All she registered, with a terrible swoon, was that a strange man was there, poking exploratively with the handle of a toothbrush.

When she recognised him there was nothing for her to do but to burst into tears. Mr Hurd leapt up, carefully placing the toothbrush on the sink, and held her in his arms, rocking her gently back and forth.

"Hey, hey, no crying now, no crying now," he kept repeating, "we'll sort something out. We'll sort something."

And he clasped her to himself.


On the terrace the dancing had begun. Mr and Mrs Hurd sat side by side, tapping their feet in time to the orchestra. In reality, the orchestra was a man on an electric organ but he managed to make it sound like an orchestra. Mr Hurd had invested in another watering can of sangria and was relieved when Mrs Hurd didn't object or even seem to notice. Occasionally, she dabbed her eyes with a handkerchief. In solidarity, Mr Hurd squeezed her hand.

The incident in the bathroom had brought them face to face with something quite new. Mr Hurd could not help thinking, on this warm, sensual evening – with the music and the stars, the great pale moon floating low among the pines – that for the first time in perhaps twenty years he felt *affectionate* towards his wife. He would always love her, of course; that was written into the agreement of their marriage and neither of them were in the habit of breaking their promises. But *loving* someone wasn't the same as *liking* them. And sitting there Mr Hurd realised, rather to his surprise, that he also *liked* Mrs Hurd.

The music suddenly became up-tempo – it was 'By the Rivers of Babylon' – and a conga line formed spontaneously around the pool. Mr Hurd drained his sangria in one, stood up, and turned to his wife.

"Care to dance, Mrs Hurd?" he said, extending his arm towards her.

It was like a scene in a film. The music in the background even had that ghostly aura of music in films, carefully placed to one side and muffled, so you could catch the dialogue.

"You go," she said.

So he went. He didn't ask her again or seek her permission. He went. And every time he came jigging past her, his hands planted on the hard rhythmic hips of the young woman in front of him, he saw she was clapping her hands and her mouth was moving to the words he was surprised she even knew: 'By the Rivers of Babylon … there we sat down … yea, we wept … when we remembered Zion …'

Later, precautions were taken. The general feeling was that the problem could better be dealt with in the morning, in the clear light of day. And that's exactly how it seemed from this vantage point: the next morning, all would be right again under a Spanish sun, and their holiday could begin in earnest. In fact, the whole thing seemed rather silly. As they had aided each other up the stairs, pausing on each landing to count it out and giggle – *ssshhhing* each other, in case they woke the other guests – they decided that yes, really, the whole thing was very funny.

In the room, the smell had gathered and thickened. Mr Hurd opened the doors onto the balcony and stood there for a moment, gasping at the sweet night air. He heard the boom of music issuing from the bars that were still open; the manic persistence of conversation. And it was past eleven o'clock! Then he took another deep breath and entered the bathroom. He grabbed several reams of toilet paper and placed them, like a shroud, over the offending article, which had turned darker in colour, he thought.

They went to bed. Mrs Hurd seemed to fall asleep immediately. It had been a long and difficult day. It was almost impossible to believe that they had been in Blackburn that morning. Mr Hurd lay still, staring up at the ceiling, occasionally giggling to himself. It was very funny. He wondered if there was *anyone* he could tell this to? Frank, possibly. But then *he'd* go and tell everyone, he was such a blabbermouth, and Mrs Hurd would be mortified if such a story got out since she, in a sense, was the butt of it. He giggled again. *Butt*! And the thought occurred to him that, probably, it would be gone in the morning anyway. It would make its own way down under the sheer force of gravity. The universe was benevolent. With that comforting thought – and the promise of a few lengths in the pool – he fell at once into a deep sleep.

Mrs Hurd was lying on her side, away from him. Although she was breathing regularly, as if she was asleep, her eyes remained wide open. Against the thump of music coming from outside, the distant laughter, she had rigidly fixed her attention on the dark shape of the empty suitcase sitting by the table, divested of all their belongings.

Mr Hurd slept long and soundly and dreamt repeatedly of flushed-clean toilet bowls. But he woke with an immediate sense of anxiety and a lousy headache. He sat up. His wife's side of the bed was empty. From outside he heard the rattle of the builder's drill.

"Enid?" he said.

He was aware of the sound of a cistern filling. The bathroom light was on. He climbed out of bed and threw open the shutters. The brightness ached in his eyes, arousing a deeper, more profound, ache in the back of his neck. On the balcony, some flies were spinning around something dead.

He went to the bathroom. Enid was sitting on the closed toilet seat with her head in her hands.

"It hasn't moved!" she cried, and went distractedly to the sink where she clutched her face in the lit mirror.

"Let's have a look," said Mr Hurd.

With foreboding, he lifted the lid and peered in. There it lay, bound and mummified in its discoloured swaddling, exuding a rich peaty animal smell. "Oh, I think it has moved slightly!" he said, brightly. "I think it's a little further down than it was."

He pushed the flusher. For a moment the bowl became a force 10 gale, then, quite suddenly, accompanied by the now-familiar cistern's resumption of breath, it stopped. The water shone, becalmed, tilting. There was a dripping sound. The bandaged patient remained.

"It'll never go!" cried Mrs Hurd, and, for once, Mr Hurd thought she might be right. They were going to have to try something else.

"Why don't I speak to someone?" he said.

"*Speak* to someone? Who?"

"Well, someone from the hotel? from maintenance? I'm sure it can't be the first time it's happened. It's the way the bowl is angled: it's a design flaw. They probably have some sort of specialist equipment."

"'Specialist equipment'?"

"Yes. Tongs of some sort."

"*Tongs*?" cried Mrs Hurd. "No, no, *no*."

"But, dear …"

"Imagine what they'd *think*!"

"We need a Plan B then," said Mr Hurd. "Let's think. Perhaps if I get a big stick from the grounds? Perhaps I can give him a good prod with that?"

"Oh don't, Tony!" cried Mrs Hurd. "Don't, for pity's sake, start calling it 'him'!"

"One good firm prod with a big stick," said Mr Hurd. "That'll do the trick."

After their showers they descended for a breakfast of coffee, bread rolls, butter and peach jam. Everything tasted odd, even the butter. No one seemed, particularly, to be staring at them. They had no appetite. Then they went to the hall.

"Why don't you go up and wait for me in the room?" said Mr Hurd.

"No," she said. "I don't want to be alone with … that … *thing*."

"I understand," said Mr Hurd. "Wait here. I won't be long."

He walked across the bar and stepped out onto a narrow track that ran beside the hotel. On the other side of it was a fence made of flax; bursting through it was a voluminous umbrella-like plant with thrusting red stamens. He turned left and started walking, towards the bay. The white earth ached in his eyes and threw the gathering morning heat into his face: the breeze, tangy with sea-water, was like a hairdryer turned onto full-heat. He passed a rattling extractor fan and a badly-parked Seat *Toledo* with no wheels, noticing its funny number plate with too many small square numbers and a little coloured flag. Then he came to a shop whose crowded entrance was shaded by an awning. Set out before it was a trestle table upon which were crates of onions, potatoes and dusty tomatoes. Hanging in the shade were various inflated plastic animals, a small fat dinghy with the head of the Loch Ness Monster and some more sensible rubber rings and arm bands. There was a cabinet of orange sun screen and orange sunglasses and a warm *Walls* freezer of ice cream. Behind a counter there were rows of postcards showing identical beaches, aquamarine coves and one of spookily-lit stalactites. Another had a pair of female buttocks on it, covered in sand. Standing half in the sun was a revolving display of newspapers, already wilting at the edges: *Le Monde, Die Zeit, La Repubblica, The Daily Mail.* A short distance further on was a tree with bark the colour of mackerel. Mr Hurd stooped to pick up a stick from beneath it, about two feet in length. Then, concealing it down his trouser leg, he returned, in a hobbling gait, to the hotel, and he and Mrs Hurd took the lift up to their floor.

It was as they turned into their corridor that Mrs Hurd let out a cry and started running.

"No! No! No!" she cried.

Mr Hurd saw immediately the cause of her alarm. A maid with a trolley was in the process of letting herself into their room. They had forgotten to put out the 'Do Not Disturb' sign.

The maid, unsure of her offence, pulled back from the door and held her hands up. Mrs Hurd grasped her arm.

"No!" she cried. "You not go into our room? Do you understand? You NOT go into our room!"

"Not today thank you!" called out Mr Hurd, in a jocular voice as he hurried up behind his wife. He had removed the stick from his trousers to enable him to run faster and now found that he was waving it in the air.

The maid, glancing nervously at it, forced a desperate conciliatory smile.

"I understand," she said, but clearly she didn't because she tried to unlock the door again.

Then, in a voice which Mr Hurd, even after forty-five years of marriage, had never heard before, Mrs Hurd screamed, "Get away! Get away! Get away!" and made a grab for her.

The maid ran off.

Gasping, Mrs Hurd unlocked the door and went in. Mr Hurd followed and closed the door after them, and locked it. Mrs Hurd went into bathroom. Mr Hurd heard two or three flushes. A minute or two later Mrs Hurd came out. She stood in the middle of the room, facing away from him towards the shutter's light. Her body was heaving.

"I don't want anyone … *anyone*," she said, "coming in here!"

"No one's going to," said Mr Hurd. "I've locked the door. Now calm down. Calm down. You're going to have a fit if you carry on like this!"

There was a moment of calm. They sat in silence for what seemed like several minutes as Mr Hurd fingered the knobbly stick in his grasp.

Then there was a knock at the door, swift and businesslike.

"She's back!" cried Mrs Hurd, in a stage whisper. "The little *minx*!"

Mr Hurd called out, in a bright high voice trembling on the edge of normality, "Who is it?"

"Señor Benedicto Alvarez," came the stern reply.

"Who?" whispered Mrs Hurd.

"'Señor Benedicto Alvarez'," whispered Mr Hurd.

"Who is Señor Benedicto Alvarez?"

"I've no idea."

"Well *ask*."

Mr Hurd cleared his throat and called out, "I'm sorry, but who are you? We're having a … fiesta?"

"My name is Señor Benedicto Alvarez," said Señor Benedicto Alvarez. "I am the Manager of the Hotel."

"Oh. My. *God*," said Mrs Hurd.

"Keep calm," said Mr Hurd. "I'll deal with this."

He crossed the room, unlocked the door and stepped out into the corridor, closing the door after him, standing with his back pressed against it. Señor Benedicto Alvarez was tall, dark, and wearing a black suit. He looked like an undertaker.

"Mr Hurd?" he said.

"Yes," said Mr Hurd, with a shudder of fear, wondering how he knew his name. He had always nurtured a deep-seated fear of authority, of being found out, of being *exposed*.

"I have had a complaint from one of the maids," said Señor Benedicto Alvarez. He was going to get straight to the point. "She said she was assaulted by your wife."

"Oh no, no," said Mr Hurd. "There's been a misunderstanding."

"And she said that you attacked her," he said, "with a stick."

Mr Hurd found that he had to think on his feet. "Oh, no," he said. "A complete misunderstanding, Mr Alva …"

"… rez."

"Alvarez. There was no stick."

Señor Benedicto Alvarez's dark eyes had fallen to the stick that Mr Hurd had forgotten he was still holding.

"You are holding a stick," he said.

"Ah," said Mr Hurd, as if in sudden enlightenment, "*this* stick! I have a gammy leg, you see? so I walk on a stick. To take the weight off it."

He demonstrated, a little hobble to the left, then to the right.

Unmoved, Señor Benedicto Alvarez said, "The maid said that you would not let her service your room."

"Now, for that," said Mr Hurd, "there is a very straightforward explanation."

"I am waiting to hear it."

Mr Hurd leant in towards Señor Benedicto Alvarez. "May I call you Señor?" he said.

"Señor means Mister in Spanish."

"Ah," said Mr Hurd. "Mr Alvarez. *Señor* Alvarez. My wife has a problem. A sort of … psychological problem."

"Go on," said Señor Benedicto Alvarez, and one manicured eyebrow lifted with curiosity.

"You see – Mr Alvarez – my wife is … how can I put this? … she's fanatical about cleaning. It's like a sort of … a sort of *disorder* with her, and she always insists – I mean, *insists* – on doing her own, even when we're in a guest house. Or a hotel, of course. Between you and me, it can be quite embarrassing at times. I think it must go back to some … childhood trauma."

"It is certainly unusual," said Señor Benedicto Alvarez. "I have never heard of a similar case."

"I'm sorry if the maid misinterpreted her," said Mr Hurd.

Señor Benedicto Alvarez looked as if he remained to be convinced. But then he probably looked like that all the time.

"Very well," he said. "On this occasion, I will overlook it. In future, any disputes should be settled amicably, through Management, and preferably without threatening behaviour. I would suggest that a better, more civilised, method would be to put the 'Do Not Disturb' sign out. And one more thing, Mr Hurd."

"Yes?"

"It's a *siesta*, not a *fiesta*."

Mr Hurd felt a moment of pique at the Manager's superior attitude and faultless English which seemed only heightened by the Spanish accent in which he delivered it: what had happened to the customer always being right? But he only nodded, forever in abeyance, and waited until the Manager had gone before going back into the room. Mrs Hurd was lying on the bed, staring at the ceiling.

"He's gone," he said.

She didn't reply.

"Now," said Mr Hurd, "I'll go and get this sorted out, for once and for all."

He went into the bathroom. The smell was now choking. Feeling a wave of nausea rush over him, he grabbed the towel and wrapped it around his face. Then he knelt at the bowl and, slowly, began poking at it, with the stick.


"Well?"

Mrs Hurd was sitting up on the bed. She turned the bedside lamp on. Mr Hurd stood in the bright doorway, defeated. He threw the towel aside.

"No good," he said.

"But surely," said Mrs Hurd, "with a stick that size?"

Mr Hurd noticed, with a movement of pity, how small she looked, hunched up on the bed, her face dishevelled and tear-stained. He sat beside her and put an arm over her shoulder.

"All I've succeeded in doing is to break a few pieces off, no more," he explained. He continued, as if he was an astronomer describing a newly-discovered planet, "It seems to have a hard outer crust. Underneath I imagine it's actually quite …"

"Stop it! Stop it! Stop it!" cried Mrs Hurd. "I can't *bear* it!"

"There now! There now!"

He began earnestly caressing his wife's back and his eyes strayed across the room to the bedside table, the unread guidebook – what excitement, what promise, that had held for him! – the lamp with its flex, the …

"That's it!" he said.

"What's it?"

"The flex!"

"We'll hang ourselves?"

"No! Wire! That's what we need! Wire!"

"*Wire*?"

"Yes. Don't you see? I can hook it round the end, then pull it up. It'll cut through no problem, like a wire through cheese!"

"But then what? It'll still be there!"

"Well, if it won't flush down we'll have to find a way of getting it out of the building. But let's cross that bridge when we come to it."

"Oh Tony, I hope you're right."

Mr Hurd stood up, heroically, and gave her a peck on the cheek.

"Sit tight," he said, and left the room.

It took him half an hour to find what he was looking for: a short length of copper wire from the edge of one of the many building sites. As he came back to the hotel he noticed a group of people standing around by a coach evidently about to leave on an excursion, perhaps to the ominous 'Caves of Drach'. He noticed that each of them was carrying a plastic box which presumably contained their packed lunches. This gave him an idea. One of the day trippers had placed her box on the wall beside her as she did something with her camera. Mr Hurd walked past and expertly picked up the plastic box, concealing it under his shirt. Then he went to the shop and bought a child's spade.

Back in the room, he explained the plan to Mrs Hurd. Then he wrapped the towel around his face and gave her an astronaut-like wave.

He went in.

Five minutes later the wire had done the trick. The turd bobbed in the water: it was what they called a 'floater'. On the side of the bowl was a dark stain but some bleach and a scrubbing brush would soon see to that.

He pressed the flusher.

At first he thought it had gone, but then he watched as its black tip appeared, and a moment later it was bobbing again.

"Plan B," said Mr Hurd.

He took the plastic box and removed the lid. Inside was an apple, a chicken breast, some coleslaw and a chocolate bar. He removed them and placed them on the edge of the bath. Then he took the spade …

"Got him!" he cried, holding the box forward with its amorphous dark shape inside.

"Is it done?" said Mrs Hurd, looking up from the edge of the bed.

"Yes," said Mr Hurd. "It's done. I had to cut the little beggar in two to get him in the box, but he's – *it's* – in there, safe and sound."

"Now what?" said Mrs Hurd.

"Now to put the next part of our plan into action. We dispose of it tonight, under cover of darkness." He sat beside her on the bed and placed an arm around her, gathering her close. "Listen," he said quietly, but with new conviction, and he even kissed her, just above her ear. "Think of that *thing* in the box as being all of our troubles and tribulations over the last few years … everything bad that's happened to us … which we are now going to put behind us … dispose of. Bury away, out of sight. Yes?" She didn't say anything. "Yes?" he said again, encouragingly, nudging her with his shoulder. She nodded briskly. "There," he said, and gave her a squeeze. "Now, we begin our holiday! The rest of our life! What about a spot of lunch down by the pool? I feel a nice cold *San Miguel* coming on! and then we must go to the beach! We haven't even been to the beach yet! We've come all this way and we haven't even had a paddle!"

It was late and darkness had fallen across Cala Romantica. Anyone sitting on one of the rear balconies of the Hotel Playa Flamenco Nights, perhaps taking a nightcap, might have observed two figures emerge from it. A closer observer might have noticed that one of them was holding a small box.

The elopers set off precariously along the main road, heading away from the lights of the resort. After twenty minutes or so they were in low hilly country. They turned to admire the view, the bay with its trembling arc of lights mirrored fuzzily in the sea, the remotest suggestion of late-night revelry. Then, like illicit lovers, they left the road and passed between the low khaki trees of an olive grove with its notation of olives.

After a while, Mr Hurd stopped.

"Here," he said, with solemnity. "This is the place."

Mrs Hurd stood to one side, keeping a watch. Mr Hurd took out the child's spade and began digging at the dry earth, still warm from the day. Then he took the box and placed it, gently, in the small hole. He replaced the soil over it and pressed it down with his foot.

"Job done," he said. "Or should I say *big job* done?"

Mrs Hurd pursed her lips but Mr Hurd thought he detected a trace of a smile there. Perhaps this meant that things could be different now, between them.

There were some goats in the next field. One or two of them idly crossed over to see what was going on in their little grove. Their bells clanked. They watched Mr and Mrs Hurd dancing in a circle, with linked arms, dancing first this way, then that.

"We're off off off to sunny Spain!" Mr Hurd was singing.

"Eviva España!" came Mrs Hurd's reply.

Exhausted they collapsed to the ground; surprised each other by kissing. Then they kissed more deeply.

"Well, well, well," said Mr Hurd, snuggling her.

"You know what?" she said. "I feel forty years younger."

"That's funny!" said Mr Hurd. "I was about to say exactly the same thing!"

They sat for a long while among the olive trees, the chirruping crickets. The goats wandered off with their dull mournful bells.

Mr Hurd suddenly felt the need to speak. He often felt the need to speak, but he never acted upon it. He wanted to tell his wife how much he loved her, how he had loved her all his life, ever since they had first met, how she was the most important person in the world to him. He put his arms about her.

"Mrs Hurd?" he said, nuzzling her nose with his.

"Yes, Mr Hurd?"

He opened his mouth to speak, but nothing, immediately, came out. How did you say what he wanted, so ardently, to say? in what form of words?

"Yes, Mr Hurd?" she said again.

Mr Hurd spoke, but they were not the words he wanted to say.

"I think," he said, with mock gravity, "we've learnt one very important lesson from all this."

"Oh yes?" said Mrs Hurd. "And what's that?"

"No more laxatives for *you*, young lady!"

He laughed with a new abandon. They could talk about anything now, he could tell her everything, ask her everything.

But he felt his wife turn to stone in his arms.

"Enid?" he said, the laughter still in his voice.

"What do you mean?" she said, coldly. "What did you mean by

that?"

"I'm sorry," he said, warmly, pulling her closer. "I couldn't help but notice those laxatives in the bag. I was only trying to be funny. No, my darling, my little love, what I wanted to say was ..."

He stopped speaking. She was silent. He saw the expression on her face.

"Enid?" he said, and felt a terrible chill go through him.

She pulled away from him.

"Enid, dear," he said. "Don't be like that! It was only a little joke!"

She rose up.

"Enid?" he said, still not quite relinquishing the laughter; thinking she might be play-acting, as she sometimes did. But when she turned to him he saw that she was not play-acting at all.

Through gritted teeth, she said, "You thought ... you thought ... *I* did that ... that *thing*?"

He felt again his old fear of her, a fear that went through him like his fear of all people, of their judgement. And at the same moment he saw his terrible error.

"No," he said, deciding that lying was the only course of action available to him, if he wanted to save his marriage. "Of course not! *Enid*!"

"You thought I did that thing! You thought it was *all* my fault, all along? That I was to blame for it?"

"No! I was *joking*! No one was to blame! No one!"

"It was already there!" she cried. "When we arrived! It was there all along! It was always there!"

"My love, my love, I know, I know ..."

She turned and walked away, then started half-running, away through the trees, down the hill.

"Enid!" he called. "*Enid*!"

"I'm going back to the hotel!" he heard her cry. "I don't want to see you! You disgust me!"

"Enid, I know ..."

"You disgust me!"

He put his head into his hands. Then, he stood. He felt a violent angry force go through him, like a bolt of electricity: he felt this was the grand heroic moment of his whole life.

"Enid!" he commanded. "You come back here!" She was lost in the darkness, a dark shape that he would barely have recognised. "Enid? Do you hear me? You come back here at once!"

He started to follow her but stopped. He felt weightless. And then the words came, the wild wayward words, hurled after her, into the dark.

"Everyone knows all about you! Everyone! Everyone knows about you and Frank! Do you hear me? Enid? Everyone knows it was *you* who tried to kiss *him* at the Chilcotts'! Do you hear me? Everyone knows! Even Carol knows! And you're ridiculous! a laughing stock! a laughing stock! Do you hear me? As if *he'd* ever look at someone like you! Enid? Do you hear me? As if he'd ever look at someone like you! You're a bloody … a bloody *laughing stock*!"

There. It was done. He'd told his greatest fear, at last. But as he began stumbling down the slope through the trees he was calling her name again, only now his voice was broken and choking with anguish and grief and love for her.

And then he stopped, and listened, and he heard, coming from far away, a sound he hadn't heard for forty years: his wife, quietly weeping.

71

# Transamerica Pyramid

*Transamerica Pyramid ... The elegant, 48-storey office tower (1972) gracing San Francisco's Financial District skyline is a recognised symbol of the city ... The 853ft pyramid was designed to absorb earthquake shocks by swaying with the motion of the earth.*
Michelin Guide to California

On the morning of 17th October 1989 San Francisco was shaken by an earthquake that registered 7.1 on the Richter scale. People found themselves buried in the rubble of their homes or trapped by the collapse of the Oakland Bay Bridge and the Cypress Street Viaduct. The violent tremor interrupted broadcasts of the World Series game at Candlestick Park. Hundreds of buildings were destroyed, both by the quake itself and in the ensuing fires, and many paid the ultimate price.

In Britain, we woke to the news on radio and television. How could we ever forget that aerial footage of the world in collapse, transmitted against the fretful chop of helicopter blades?

These things did not affect me. They happen, after all, then life returns to an only marginally-altered normality. The baseball game was re-played, the viaduct and the bridge rebuilt, the dead dug-up and re-buried.

Then, just a few months later, came *another* quake, even more powerful, even more devastating, than the first. By then earthquakes were old news. They'd been done. You'd seen one, you'd seen them all. They happened to other people. Interest from the media, I remember, was pretty well non-existent in Britain and even in the San Francisco Herald it merited only a half-column inch on an inside page beneath the small-ads. 'Second quake devastates city,' read the inconspicuous headline, 'Thousands believed dead.' This was followed by a story about a missing cat. On the television news, the story came near the bulletin's end, as an adjunct to the more serious business of political tantrum and celebrity gossip. News anchor Bob

Schieffer, adjusting his wad of papers, concluded lightly, and with the faintest air of exasperation, "And, finally, San Francisco was today devastated by yet another earthquake, can you believe? It registered a mighty 7.9 on the Richter scale and so it was even bigger than the last one. We are expecting a high casualty figure." Then he added, with a mischievous twinkle in his eye, "Did the Earth move for *you*? And now, sport …"

That day, I was watching the news in the Emergency Room of the San Francisco General. I just happened to be in the city to give a lecture and, for those few seismic seconds, I was its epicentre. My universe turned on its dark side, the world fell to ruin around me, and I thought I would die. I received basic medical care and counselling for trauma but I had other things on my mind at the time, not least of all a divorce.

Slowly, over the ensuing days and months, I became conscious that it wasn't just the news anchor who exhibited a cavalier and irresponsible attitude to what had happened then: it was as if the whole populace were completely indifferent, and wantonly so. People were meant to care about the victims of disasters, weren't they? Then I became aware of the outright deniers, the conspiracy theorists, the general population; people who claimed that there had been no second quake at all. If they were right, what, then, was the cause of my scars? my fever? my fear?

Recuperating, I watched people carrying on with their lives as if nothing had happened. I saw the ferries plying the bay, laying their lines of white spume, the planes coming into SFO, the cable cars clanking up Taylor Street and the traffic heavy on the Golden Gate. I made the decision to stay in the city and to dedicate myself to publicising its neglected catastrophe. Over the next few months, as I began to wither away, I became a veteran campaigner and was considered by some, in this city of cranks, the crank *ne plus ultra*. Tour guides pointed me out. I wore my hair about my shoulders and grew a long untidy beard. I got some tattoos. With placards I marched in City Square declaring to anyone who would listen, "Remember the dead of the second quake! Remember the dead of the second quake!" My wife got what she wanted and my parents and children disowned me. I slept rough in a parking lot on Hyde Street.

Funnily enough – and what is funnier than an earthquake? – it was earthquakes which had originally brought me to San Francisco with such near-lethal timing. I'm a seismologist; I *study* the damn things. In February 1990 I was attending a conference of seismologists at the California Academy of Sciences. If you're going to talk earthquakes where better than in a city built on top of the San Andreas fault?

The second quake – what I have come to think of as *my* quake – struck on the morning of 16th February. No one knows why – not even those of us who make our living studying and predicting them – but quakes tend to be early risers. They favour the morning. It guarantees them a high body count.

I was shaving in the hotel mirror. In its reflection, beyond the stubbly planet of my horrified face, I could see my prostitute lying on the bed in the room behind me. There was water in the glass by the sink. Its surface remained flat and undisturbed. A towel was hanging on the rail. It did not move.

"What in God's name was that?" I said.

My prostitute looked up from a magazine and said, "I didn't hear anything."

"Put some clothes on," I said.

"Sure. Whatever."

The photograph of my wife and children on the bedside table remained exactly where it was.

"Come on," I said, "let's get out of here before the whole place comes down."

"Sure. Whatever. You owe me."

"I'll give you the money later. We have to get out now."

The light remained switched on and the bare bulb hung absolutely still from the centre of the ceiling. My briefcase, which contained the notes for my forthcoming lecture, was open on the bed.

My prostitute, unmoving, took out a piece of paper and read out loud, "'… Earthquakes vary in size from those that are so weak they cannot be detected to those violent enough to propel objects and people into the air and wreak havoc and destruction across entire cities … ' What are you? An earthquake guy?"

"A seismologist, yes."

"That's kinda interesting."

"Can this wait? Leave your belongings. We have to get out of here."

"Sure."

In the bathroom the mirror hadn't shattered. My toothbrush and my razor were exactly where I had left them. The wardrobe remained just where it was. None of the coat-hangers was rattling. I put on my jacket.

"I'm not waiting any longer," I said.

My prostitute was dressed at last. We left the room and followed the emergency exit signs. In the corridor a janitor was mopping the floor. He stood aside to let us pass and wished us a good morning. He was completely calm. We emerged into the street.

"You want to get a drink?" said my prostitute, squinting in the wintry sunlight.

"I can't," I said.

"Why not?"

"Because I'm an alcoholic."

"I'd have thought, if anything, that would make you *want* to get a drink."

"You just don't get it, do you? Any of it?"

I turned to look at the surrounding scene of devastation. I hardly need describe it. But what I remember most vividly at that moment is the sound of police sirens, wailing, whooping, weeping. A police car stopped nearby, its blue light spinning, Pentecostal. A police officer got out and approached us with his tool-belt, his charm bracelet, of guns, tasers and pepper sprays.

He said to me, "You got yourself a cut there, mister."

I touched my chin. There was a trace of blood on my fingers.

"Officer," I said. "What's happened here?"

"Nothing," he said. "Move along now. There's nothing to see. Everything's normal."

"*Normal*?" I said.

"Yeah," he said, turning to survey the street. He took his cap off and scratched his bald policeman's head. "I can't figure it out," he said. "It's actually kinda creepy."

There was ruin all about us. The street was covered in trash. Some people were passing by on the sidewalk. Two had stopped to chat outside a liquor store. One of the houses had a window open. Another house had a picket fence in front of it. The edge of the road was painted with a yellow line. There was a tree and a lamp post and a call box. There was a fire hydrant and a bookstore. The bars were open. There were some cars. And, beyond, above the serried rooftops, the Transamerica Pyramid stood out like a colossal 'A' against a lachrymose winter sky, and it was then that I remembered how pyramids, among the ancient Egyptians, marked the desert with the final resting places of their dead.

# The Case for Obscurity

In the seventies summers were like Ladybird books. My memory of them is in primary colours: skies, lawns, seasides, toy boats, ice cream vans.

This may be my memory of Ladybird books.

You can easily get confused. I always believed that there was a particular ice cream van which used to stop outside our house and play the Magic Roundabout music. It was an unusual shape for an ice cream van, rectangular, like a hearse, but liveried in blue and red stripes with a green awning protruding over the serving hatch. Then, one day, in a second-hand bookshop, I came across a Ladybird book called *We Have Fun* and there it was: an identical ice cream van with happy children queuing in the sunshine for their cornets.

I was not among them.

In 1976 it stopped raining. Week after week, the unchallenged sun baked the earth. There was a hosepipe ban and the grass died. I was fourteen and in love. Being in love seemed to be connected in some way with the drought.

I was in love with Chloë Singleton. She was in the sixth form which meant that she was three years older than me and that's a lot of years when you're fourteen. Her name had an accent on the 'e' which only added to her exoticism. I later found out that this accent, in this application, was not an *umlaut* but a *diaeresis*, the Greek word for 'division' or 'separate'. Chloë Singleton had honeyed hair and eggshell-blue eyes and she wore brightly-coloured jewellery and bangles and beads, and fingerless gloves. I once got up close enough to her to see the psoriasis on her hands, like gold-leaf, and to witness her anxious fingers which were forever twisting the hair at her temple into golden braids, braids with which a fourteen-year-old schoolboy could quite easily hang himself. When she moved, her accessories clunked and rang like rigging on a yacht. She did not know that I existed, nor did she care. As a result, I was very unhappy all the time.

I'd sit in the woods thinking about her impossible possibility, then walk home slowly through the dusk which was always filled with bright fragments of startled birdsong. I wanted to find a cave and hibernate, or, ideally, never wake up, but, instead, I went home for tea and TV. My parents, who, under the cover of parental concern, vigilantly tracked my every move, like the Stasi, tried to make friends with me but I didn't want to be friends with them or with anyone else for that matter, or see anyone or say anything or do anything and that included, in no particular order, shovelling manure in the back garden, O-levels and picking up socks. All I wanted was to think of Chloë Singleton or to go into the woods or to watch TV … or to watch my tropical fish, which was a bit like watching TV. I had an aquarium, a glassy self-contained world of ferns and gravel and quartz-like red and blue *neon tetra*. The constant thrum of its aerator, spewing its column of bubbles, provided the white noise of my childhood.

One day, I was lying on my bed when I noticed a sock on the carpet. I wondered whether I should pick it up. Where was its twin, its sole-mate? The darned thing lay there, mocking me. I was going to have to pick it up. But *Spem in Alium* was on the stereo – that bit where the forty parts begin to rise and swirl towards the end in delirious polyphony – so I abandoned the whole crazy sock plan.

Personally, I blame the school. Greencoat's had got on perfectly well without girls for 400 years. Its statutes specifically decreed that it was for poor *boys*. Then, suddenly, out of the blue, the school had decided to admit twelve girls into the sixth form, as a vanguard, an experiment. They turned out to be the first of many and the beginning of the school's progression to becoming fully co-educational. Couldn't they see that they were asking for trouble, when we were all at such a difficult age, so prone to hormonal disturbance and roving eyes and hearts? They arrived, one day, this advance posse of willowy gum-chewing Marlboro-smoking girls, perfectly happy, it seemed, in their autonomy and expert heartlessness: the creamy progeny of the

English middle classes, leaning against a wall, smoking, not giving a damn if you lived or died.

There was to be, one Saturday, a school fête. A fête worse than death. From the windows of the laboratory block we watched it being assembled on the playing fields like a Medieval military encampment complete with striped tents, flags and coloured bunting. A loud-speaker on a pole, its electric voice riven by scrapes of thunder, declared: "*Testing Testing Testing.*"

It was the eternal voice of adults.

Saturday arrived, like every Saturday, in those days of perpetual summer: long, bright and crowned by *The Pink Panther Show* and *Doctor Who*, then mud-slinging and trespass in dusky gardens. The fête was in full swing by the time we arrived in the green Cortina. I managed to lose my family at once: if Chloë Singleton should happen to be there I didn't want her seeing what I shared a gene pool with. Some people were throwing wet sponges at Mr Redman in the stocks. The loud-speaker crackled, "Try your luck at the Lucky Dip!" There was a real Dalek. A sad donkey, bereft of the seaside, was giving rides. On a stage, the rival school bands 'Plantagenet' (prog. rock) and 'Destroy Eastbourne' (punk) were tuning up, which was pretty pointless. There were tea urns in tents whose shade smelt of warm rubber; cakes and cups were lined-up on trestle tables. I bought a raffle ticket.

Towards the end of the afternoon the results of the raffle were announced by the sky-voice. I won fourth prize. It was a book: just my luck. Winning a book was like winning a dental appointment. When I went to collect it there was a splatter of applause, as if luck, even bad luck, was an achievement. The man tried to take the raffle ticket from me but I insisted on keeping it. It was much more important than the lousy prize: it was the *idea* of a prize, it was talismanic. I had a magical superstitious frame of mind in those days, nourished by the hope and despair of unrequited love which endlessly seeks out clues and hidden meanings, and perhaps even this fourth prize meant my fortunes were changing at last.

The resumed applause, flat and ironic in the open air, receded as I withdrew with my book and slunk across the parched playing field pock-marked with last-season's football studs, but still with its galaxy of daisies, all the time scanning the crowds for Chloë Singleton. She was not there.

I sat under a tree, out of the sun. Only then did it occur to me to see what book I had won. I opened it. It was called *An English Poesy*. Even the title made me want to puke, and that was before I'd read any of the actual poems. It had been published in 1954 in a limited edition of a thousand copies, each signed and numbered by the author in a hand of laboured, nearly psychotic, neatness: 'Arthur Somerset'. My copy was numbered '14'. This number seemed to possess no significance whatsoever.

I started to read. *An English Poesy* was a collection of very bad poems. Even at fourteen, I knew that any half-decent self-respecting poem didn't *rhyme*; that was one of its principal requirements. I also knew that, to qualify as good *modern* poetry, it had to say simple things in a way that was impossible to understand; that is, unless you happened to know about other stuff like the myths of Ancient Greece or the Upanishads. But these poems by Arthur Somerset seemed pretty straightforward to me with their descriptions of fields and trees and rivers and sunsets, like A. E. Housman who I was doing for O-level. There were even a few 'lads' in there too, doing wholesome laddish things like swimming naked in ponds or climbing trees, but none of them were about to drown themselves or hang themselves. There weren't too many 'lasses' to keep them company, I noticed, which, perhaps, explained their lack of suicidal impulses. On the back cover was some 'blurb', the printed judgement of one 'C. Grayling' (whoever he was): 'A hundred years from now,' he wrote, 'when the likes of T. S. Eliot and Ezra Pound are consigned to the dustbin of literary history, people will still be reading, and cherishing, the beautiful *poesy* of Arthur Somerset.' That word 'cherishing' made me want to throw up almost as much as 'poesy' did, and consigning Eliot and Pound to 'the dustbin of literary history' seemed too spiteful an assessment for the back of a collection of anodyne verse. I flicked through the hand-made leaves, already wondering if the bookshop in town would offer me anything for it, until my eye alighted upon a particular poem. It was a sonnet and was remarkable not so much for its brevity (most of the poems were several pages long) but for the fact that it bore a dedication.

The dedication read, "For C****."

Chloë, I thought: this poem is for *Chloë*. It began:

*These clouds are where you are and shine*
*No less in your remoter sky ...*

I knew all about this. The day before I had been standing in a field, praying for a bolt of judicious summer lightning, when I had seen an effulgent *cumulus nimbus* rearing over the town and it had struck me, with intense poetic force, that this same distinctive cloud, this isle of sky, would be visible to Chloë Singleton and visible *at exactly the same moment that I was looking at it.* But this triangulation, this synchronicity, gave me no cause for optimism; on the contrary, it seemed crucial to my dejection. It only made me realise that Chloë Singleton was in a different place, and far away, and therefore out of bounds, and that this cloud would mean nothing to her.

By the end of the day, I had learnt that poem by heart. I marked its place in the book with the raffle ticket.

A few days later I came home from school to find my father reading the book. I was outraged.

"Can I have that please?" I said.

"Is it yours?" he said. "You left it on the kitchen table this morning."

"Can I have it please?"

"Where did you find it?"

"I didn't find it. I won it at the school fête in the raffle. Can I have it back, please, Dad?"

"Dreadful poems."

"Can I have it back?"

"I knew Arthur Somerset," he said.

"Can I … you what?"

"I knew Arthur Somerset. He taught me English and Latin at Greencoat's. I still see him around town occasionally, looking very doddery. He must be well into his seventies now."

"Can I have it back?"

The fact that the poet was still alive, and local, and distantly associated through my father with me, intrigued me and, as a result, caused me to subtly modify my estimation of his poetry; as you might favour your native landscape over a foreign one simply for its proximity, however inferior and nondescript it was by comparison. I looked through the telephone directory. There was just one 'Somerset, A.' listed in our area. His address was given as 6 Asphodel Mead which was on the other side of the town. I wrote to him in a careful copperplate on my mother's Basildon Bond:


'Dear Mr Somerset, I am writing this letter to you because I wanted to say how much I enjoyed reading your book 'An English Poesy' which I have recently acquired. There was one poem I liked in particular although I thought all of them were very good. It is a sonnet and it is dedicated 'To C****'. I thought this was very well written and interesting because I have had similar thoughts about clouds like in the poem. Another reason I thought I'd write to you was because you used to teach my father English and Latin at Greencoat's, the same school that I am currently attending and where English is my favourite subject, although I am not very good at Latin. I hope to be a writer myself one day, although I am not sure that I can write poems, and I also keep tropical fish. I am nearly fifteen years old. Yours sincerely …'

When I read the letter back to myself, I wondered for a moment who could have written it. Somehow the words were not my own. They were like a version of me prepared by an adult in order to win the approval of other adults. It also contained at least one outright falsehood, and one heinous omission: Chloë Singleton.

So what, I thought. He won't reply. He's a poet. He has other things on his mind.

I posted it.

The following evening, the phone rang just as I happened to be passing it. I picked it up.

"Hello?" I said.

"Hello? To whom am I speaking?"

I assumed the call was a wind-up. Surely, no one spoke like that in real life, not these days. But I played along and told him my name.

"*This* …" he announced, grandly, "is *Arthur Somerset*." The 'no less' was implied.

"Oh, hello," I said, and an unbidden nonchalance entered my voice.

"When I received your letter I took the liberty of seeking out your number in the telephone book," he said. "It wasn't difficult since you are blessed with such an unusual surname. It sounds Anglo-Saxon. Where does it come from?"

"My parents."

Some instinct made me prematurely deadpan with him, or perhaps his phoning with such undue haste after receiving my fan-letter had fractionally diminished his status in my mind.

He wasn't deterred. "It sounds like the name of a proud longbowman at Agincourt," he said. "Thank you for your fine letter. You write beautifully for a fifteen-year-old. Letter-writing is an art form in decline, like so many art forms these days. You say I taught your father. I remember him well. Does he have dark hair?"

"Well, he *did* have *some* hair."

"Yes, I remember him perfectly now. A good all-rounder. Wasn't he a sportsman?"

"No," I laughed.

"What House was he in?"

"I don't know."

"Well, what House are *you* in?"

"Ethelred's."

"Ethelred's? A fine House! Your father was almost certainly an Ethelrodian himself. We always endeavoured to promote the hereditary principle at Greencoat's. I'm sure people would take a very dim view of such a practice nowadays; they'd think it far too old-fashioned. Do send your Pater my warmest regards."

"I will."

There was a pause, during which I heard a dog yapping in the background and another, more distant, but shrill, voice of chastisement. I wondered if it was his wife's.

"Would you like to come for tea tomorrow?" he said. Before I had the chance to answer with a polite refusal, he continued, in a voice which was a strange hybrid of entreaty and command, "Come for tea. Directly after school. I should like to meet you. It's so rarely one meets young people these days. They have such a bad reputation but I sense you're going to hearten me and splendidly break the mould. You've got the address. 'Summer's Lease.'"

"'Summer's' ..?"

"'*Lease*.' It's the name of the house. From Shakespeare's Sonnet XVIII." Somehow he contrived to say the number in Roman numerals. "Make sure you knock as well as buzz: sometimes we can't hear the buzzer, if we're in the garden. Knock firmly. I shall expect you at 4 o'clock."

And then he simply put the phone down. He didn't say 'goodbye'. I assumed this must be the old-fashioned way of doing it, when phones were made of Bakelite and stood on teak tables in panelled hallways. I stood there for a while, in a trance, puzzled, and at the same time gratified and discomforted. Then my father came by.

"What *are* you doing?" he said. "You look like you've seen a ghost."


The next day, after school, I went there. Out of some obscure sense of transgression, I told my parents that I was going round to Andy Green's to make an offer on an Angel fish of his that I had long coveted.

Asphodel Mead wasn't what I had been expecting. I had been expecting something hidden, pastoral and idyllic, a place where you could hang out with shepherds and shepherdesses, a dreamlike purlieu of our unremarkable Essex town which had hitherto remained miraculously undiscovered. In reality, Asphodel Mead was a cul-de-sac, a dead-end of oatmeal bungalows, with barren aerials. *Bungalows*. It didn't get much lower than that. But then, I imagined, Arthur Somerset was old and couldn't manage a flight of stairs. In front of each house a patch of baked lawn was circumscribed by mean municipal wire fencing. Parked in front of one 'chalet bungalow', with two fake Georgian windows in its roof, was an orange Datsun *Cherry*. There was a dead sapling fastened to a stick and some distraught flower beds. On the gate of number 6 was a palette-shaped piece of wood bearing the legend 'Summer's Lease' written in a looping cursive, like the lettering at the beginning of an old romantic comedy, or the end.

I hesitated for a moment, unnerved by the abrupt confounding of my expectations, before taking a deep breath and walking down the broken concrete path. First I rang the doorbell, then knocked, in line with my instructions. Immediately, I heard the hysterical yapping of a dog. Through the frosted glass I discerned the shapes of two human forms in what appeared to be an embrace, or fusion, or struggle, I could hardly tell which; like amoeba. Then one of the forms moved to the side, like a cell dividing, and the other came towards the door, still indistinct, and stood there for a moment before sweeping it open.

This, also, was not what I had been expecting. I had imagined Arthur Somerset to be a portly colourful bohemian figure, sporting a fedora and a cravat, redolent of pipe smoke. Instead, I found a thin and wiry man wearing tight pale-grey chinos, hush-puppies, white socks, a salesman's shirt of pale grey stripes, through which was visible a string vest, and a threadbare tank-top the colour of weak tea. He had a Hitler moustache – an apostrophe beneath his nose which accented it into an exclamation mark – and a few wisps of errant coppery hair. He looked like the sort of man who might try to sell you insurance or encyclopedias, then offer you something more dubious.

"You're the school boy?" he said, as if he'd ordered a school boy in the same way that you might order a pizza or a minicab. "You're five minutes late."

I was surprised by his sharp nasal tone which was so different from his ebullient solicitous, even fawning, manner on the phone the day before.

"Hello, Mr Somerset," I said, in my politest school boy manner.

He laughed with a startling high whinny which I knew must be a 'characteristic', something which you might grow to tolerate, or despise.

"*I'm* not Arthur!" he whooped. He looked over his shoulder, down the dim corridor, and shouted, his voice changed suddenly again, as if through some startling feat of ventriloquism, to something ill-tempered and impatient, "Arthur? Your boy's here!"

I heard a distant reply, "Ah! Send him through! Send him through!"

The dog was glowering at me and emitting a deep thrumming sound from its throat, quite alarming in such a small animal. Noticing my nervous glance, the man who wasn't Mr Somerset said, "Oh, don't mind Duchess, she won't hurt you. Come through to the lounge. The old bugger's in there, in a filthy temper, as usual, so I'd mind your 'p's and 'q's."

I entered the hallway and, as I turned to close the door, she – the dog, that is – viciously bit my leg and continued to bite it, despite several powerful back-kicks, as I was led down the corridor with its brown patterned carpet.

When I entered the lounge – and no other word would do for this stiflingly hot brown room – I saw a man struggling to rise from his wingback armchair. This was more like it: he did, indeed, have a cravat, but no fedora. Instead, he had the old school-master uniform of moth-eaten tweed jacket with suede arm pads, a handkerchief sprouting from his top pocket. I shook his hand: he grasped mine with both of his and didn't let go as he hungrily appraised me from beneath a feral tangle of eyebrows. There was something savage in his eyes but something resigned, weary and pleading, something which couldn't understand; and sadness, too. Such sadness. His skin was colourless, like parchment, although there were spidery blotches of red on his nose and cheeks, which I imagined, with a fourteen-year-old's worldliness, were the stigmata of the habitual and heavy drinker. Close up, he exuded a powerful aroma of mothballs, sherry and something unwashed, musky and old-mannish, but complicated with layers of cologne. When he spoke I felt pinpricks of sherry-infused saliva on my face.

"So good of you to come, my dear boy," he said, ardently. Then he held me at arm's length, as if admiring a painting which he might want to bid on. "Let's get a good look at you," he said, and he tilted me from side to side.

"Let him sit down," snapped Adolf (as I now thought of him). "For heaven's sake."

"Yes, of course, of course, how very rude of me," said Mr Somerset, releasing me from his grip at last.

I sat opposite him and began to make plans for an urgent getaway. These men were mad and quite possibly dangerous. If the worst came to the worst I could bolt it through the door into the garden, then be over the hedge and away, away.

"Would you like some tea, young man?" said Adolf, grudgingly.

"No, thank you," I said.

"Sherry, perhaps?" said Mr Somerset, as if that might be more to a fourteen-year-old's taste. I noticed he had a goblet of it on the table beside him and a steamed-up rusting decanter.

"No, thank you," I said.

"Some cordial, then?" said Mr Somerset.

"No, thank you."

"What about some Fanta? We have Fanta for our young callers."

"He doesn't want anything," said Adolf.

"Have some Fanta," insisted Mr Somerset.

"He doesn't want anything," said Adolf again. "Leave the boy alone."

There was a hurt silence, during which I had the opportunity to survey my surroundings in more detail. How was it possible, I wondered, to spend a *lifetime* in a place like this, when I could hardly endure it for more than a few minutes, seconds? The room was dark, crowded and loathsome. There was no television, but instead, where there should have been one, there was a portrait of the Queen and Prince Philip. Behind Mr Somerset, so that it framed my view of him, was a Victorian bookcase gleaming with leather-bound books: Keats, Shelley, Byron, Wordsworth, school-teacher stuff. Above it was an oil painting, in an elaborate gilt frame, of an old man. The legend beneath said: 'Sir Godfrey Somerset, Bart.' Mr Somerset followed my eyes and turned in his armchair.

"That's my great, great, grandfather," he said. "He was, for many years, the Bishop of Rochester. They say he could have been the Archbishop of Canterbury."

"Wow," I said.

"It's by Romney, the greatest portraitist of his day. He only painted the most distinguished of his contemporaries. Worth a small fortune now, I daresay, but, of course, I'd never part with it. Continuity, you see, my dear boy. Continuity."

The rest of the walls, in vivid contrast, were lined with flimsy, apparently temporary, modern shelving, such as you might find in an office. This shelving, I noticed, with puzzlement, was lined with rows and rows of identical grey books.

"What are they, Mr Somerset?" I asked him, pleasantly.

"About nine hundred copies," he said, "of *An English Poesy*."

"Really?" I said.

"Oh yes," he said, now in a tone of reasonable affront. "No one *wanted* them. That would be too much to ask, wouldn't it? that people would want to buy some silly old poems by a silly old fool? How many do you think I sold?"

"I couldn't say," I said.

"Go on," he said. "Guess."

"Two hundred?"

"Fourteen," he said. "I sold fourteen of them. *I* bought seven. I gave a few away, to libraries and bookshops and so on. I daresay that's how you came by yours. The whole debacle all but bankrupted me. You see, my boy, people don't want to read poems any more, at least, not *real* poems. Poems that rhyme, poems that show a bit of craft, of skill, of *tradition*. Poems that have something beautiful and true to say, in the language of our ancestors. They're only interested in … this *modern* stuff. With your wonderful exception, of course. You, young man, are obviously able to appreciate *real* poesy."

"You wait," said Adolf, under his breath. "These dark ages will end and it'll come back. Soon people will come to their senses again. There'll be a second Renaissance!"

"Tell me," said Mr Somerset, leaning in towards me and touching me lightly on the arm, "I'm intrigued. Where did you acquire your particular copy of my bestseller?"

"I won it," I said. "In a raffle."

"What?" He leant forward, cupping an ear. "What did you say?"

"I won it in a raffle."

"A *raffle*?" he said. "You won it in a *raffle*?"

"Yes," I said. "Fourth prize."

At first this seemed to elicit no reaction. Then I watched as Mr

Somerset's face began to crease, and for a moment I thought he was about to burst into tears. But he didn't. Instead, he burst into *laughter*. He heaved and rolled and wheezed, clasping at his belly, eyes squeezed tight. "Fourth prize!" he wheezed. "*Fourth* prize! in a *raffle*! That's … priceless! *priceless*!"

Adolf looked concerned for him. "You'll have one of your funny turns again, Arthur," he sang.

When his laughter had subsided, Mr Somerset topped up his sherry.

"Do you still write poems?" I said, deliberately inciting him: I was already imagining telling someone about this strange meeting in the safety of the future, and I needed a few details.

"You must call me Arthur."

Adolf said, "Tell him. Tell the boy. Tell him what you're working on."

"Oh no, no," said Mr Somerset, waving the idea away, but only as you might an inevitable ovation. It was a lip-service denial, probably often made: I knew I would be told, eventually. And I didn't really want there to be much 'eventually' here.

It was then that I noticed, on the table beside him, next to the decanter, a wad of paper the thickness of a telephone directory. He patted it.

"What's that, Mr Somerset?" I said, against my better judgement, but I felt the innocent enquiry had been expected of me.

"My *magnum opus*," he said. "My *primum mobile*. My … *Historia mundi universalis poetica*."

Adolf said, in a voice of level nasal authority, as if he were stating an accepted fact, "The greatest work of literature in the history of mankind."

"I would hardly say *that*," said Mr Somerset.

"I'd love to read it one day," I said, "but I should go."

"Go?" said Mr Somerset. "But you've only just arrived!"

Adolf was glaring at me. Then he said to Mr Somerset, almost like a command, "Read it. Read your sublime *Historia* now. From the beginning."

"Oh, I could hardly … presume … but perhaps a couple of shortish excerpts? … some of the 'Elysium' passages, you think, which touch on gilded youth? … perhaps our young friend would like that? … but you think the … the whole thing?"

"Of course!" he cried. "You can't read 'excerpts' from the greatest work of literature in the world! Probably the finest Latin poetry since Virgil!"

"It's in … *Latin*?" I said.

"I suppose it does have a certain narrative … *flow*," said Mr Somerset, as if he hadn't heard me, "… and 'we murder to dissect', as Mr Wordsworth so persuasively argued."

"An unstoppable force!" cried Adolf.

"Written in my own distinctive hexameter," said Mr Somerset, "and yet one grounded in the most ancient and revered oral tradition, passed from generation to generation."

"Perhaps another time?" I said. "What about … next Tuesday?"

Mr Somerset laid his sad eyes upon me. "You don't really have to hurry home, do you?" he said, reaching out for his *Historia mundi universalis poetica*. "Surely not on this so special occasion?"

I was deeply conscious that this 'so special occasion' would entail me missing *John Craven's Newsround* and *Blue Peter*. Little did I know that I would also be missing *Nationwide*, *The Goodies*, *Play for Today and The World About Us*. And I would hardly have believed you if you had told me that I would also be missing *Film '76* with the nocturnal hangdog Barry Norman in his office chair, and most of the night-long Test Card too.

As he started to read, I closed my eyes and thought only of my tropical fish, floating in their bright aquarium, the tiny glinting *neon tetra* passing through the lit fronds, while the air bubbles rose and purred towards the surface behind them, finding release in the wider air.

The next morning, just as I was about to leave for school, Mr Somerset phoned. I had been expecting him to call again, but perhaps not quite so soon. Since my visit, I had nursed a growing resentment of him. It had occurred to me that not once had he, or the other man, asked anything about *me*, about my own interests, my ill-formed hopes for the future, my tropical fish, still less my unreciprocated love for Chloë Singleton. I had decided that this lack of curiosity was not an attractive characteristic, even when packaged as the larger-than-life egotism of eccentricity.

My mother, who took the call, said, warily, placing her hand over the receiver, "There's an old man for you. Who is he? Shall I tell him you're out?"

"I'd better speak to him," I said, and took the receiver. "Hello?"

"I know you already have a copy of *An English Poesy*," he said, without introducing himself, "but, since you made such an impression on us, I've *personally* inscribed another copy of it for you, my dear boy. Would you like to come and collect it?"

"When?"

"What about this afternoon? After school. I'll gladly give you some other copies for your more discriminating school fellows."

I told him that I was quite busy at the moment, what with school work and O-levels, and so on, but that I would come and collect it in the next few days. I added, in placation, that I was sure my school friends would love to have copies and that I would collect them when I next came round. I hated him, but I was keen to please him.

"Come this afternoon," he pled, "there's a good boy. We can sit in the garden. I'll make us some traditional rum punch."

"Okay," I said.

I didn't go.

The next day Mr Somerset called to say that he was very upset that I hadn't been true to my word and would I come round that afternoon?

I apologised and told him I would.

I didn't.

The next day Mr Somerset called to say that he was very upset that I had found it necessary to lie to him again and that he would appreciate it if I could collect the book 'as soon as possible' because they had very little space in their house and he had gone to a lot of trouble inscribing it for me.

I told him that I had had no intention of lying to him and that I would come that afternoon.

I didn't.

The next day Mr Somerset called again. He was in tears. He said that he was very unwell and might have to go to the hospital.

I said I would collect the book that afternoon.

I didn't.

The next day Mr Somerset called in tears again and called me a 'deceitful urchin'.

"And I thought you were a gentleman!" he cried. "But now I see you're no different from the rest!"

At that moment, Adolf must have snatched the phone from him: this act of violence set Duchess off in the background.

"Do you see what you're doing to him?" he cried. "To *us*, with your cruelty?"

"Is that … Adolf?" I said.

"Adolf?" he said. "Adolf? Who's Adolf? This is *Cyril*. Cyril Grayling." He announced the name with dignity, as if it meant something, and I did think that I had heard it or seen it before, but couldn't think where. "Oh, and another thing, while we're at it," he went on, rehearsing a list of grievances, "that poem you loved so much in *An English Poesy* – the sonnet? Arthur dedicated that to me – no, I will have my say, Arthur! – to me! For C. *Cyril*. That's my name above the poem, don't you see? He doesn't give two figs for you, 'Colin', indeed! 'Colin'! You weren't even born in 1954, 'Colin'! How could he possibly have dedicated that poem to *you*? It was to me! Cyril! Me!"

I had never suggested that I thought the poem was dedicated to me, since that would have been literally impossible, although he was right about my name. But I didn't bother to contradict him. Instead, I simply put the phone down.

Ten seconds later, it rang again.

I let it.

Mr Somerset phoned every day for the next week. I did not take any of the calls. I had instructed the other members of my family to say that I was unwell and could not come to the phone.

Then, one day, I received a letter from Arthur Somerset. It was twenty-three pages long. I never found the courage to read much of it, although I still have it somewhere. 'My cruel cold belovéd Colin ..' it began.

One day, I asked my parents to tell him, when he called again, that I had left the country, and that I had gone to live abroad, somewhere in the tropics, far, far from England, and that I would never come back again.

The calls stopped after that.

***

In the many years that have passed since then – during which I have lost everything that ever mattered to me – I have never seen another copy of *An English Poesy* and don't expect to.

I believe Arthur Somerset must have died recently – he would have been well into his nineties – because my father showed me the auction catalogue of a local saleroom which had included 'c. 900 copies' of *An English Poesy* in a job lot, 'sold not subject to return'. One of the books, the auctioneer had thoughtfully pointed out, was a presentation copy, inscribed, 'For belovéd Colin, dear new and future friend, paragon of youth. "Thy eternal summer shall not fade." Your loving old fool, always, Arthur Somerset.'

The next lot was catalogued as 'After George Romney. Half-length portrait of Sir Godfrey Somerset, Bart. Modern over-painted print, in faux-antique gesso frame.'

Both lots went unsold.

I have no idea what happened to the original manuscript of *Historia mundi universalis poetica*. It was not mentioned in the catalogue. I suspect the house-clearance people must have chucked it in a skip.

Recently, someone told me that Chloë Singleton had married not long after leaving school and moved to Grays, where she was now merely 'Mrs Whiteley'.

I still think of her, sometimes, when I am staring at my ceiling where memory projects the cloudless sky of that long-vanished summer:

*These clouds are where you are and shine*
*No less in your remoter sky ...*

And I understood, then – as I have come to understand even better now, as my unremarkable life crawls to its close – that there is a terrible fastidiousness in the judgements of the world. It is inescapable and it is never misguided, either in relation to Arthur Somerset's case, or to mine. It seeks out mediocrity like a pig seeks out a truffle, then holds it down, and keeps it there, buried in the earth where no one will see it, or care. We should never begrudge the bright, happy, elected ones who – entirely as a result of merit, of what I can only call 'genius' – dance and play their days away among the stars; then, when night comes, go out in a plume of glory, leaving their long afterglow. We – the remainder, those left behind – grind our penurious days away here on earth, then die in legions, unloved, unsung, unheard of; instantly forgotten.

# Rehab

I used to tell this joke.

"How do you define an alcoholic?"

"I don't know. How do you define an alcoholic?"

"Someone who drinks more than their doctor."

Somehow it doesn't seem so funny anymore.

*

'Benedictine Lodge' is an exclusive private mental health facility set in the leafy rolling country of southern Surrey. Its clinicians and therapists are highly-respected in their various fields and it regularly tops 'customer satisfaction' ratings for similar institutions. While it is best known for its treatment of alcohol and drug addiction – or for what is colloquially known as 'rehab' – it also treats anorexia and bulimia, anxiety, phobias, obsessive compulsive disorders and a condition that I had not encountered before and which was not an affliction which had troubled any of my many ex-wives: sex addiction.

Stella, my sister, had handed me the clinic's shiny brochure in the car and I was impressed. In my other hand was the nearly empty bottle of whisky whose discovery, concealed in the chest of drawers of her guest room where I had been staying while I 'sorted myself out', had been the instigator of our first serious conversation on the subject of my excessive drinking, and, now, the cause of my admission to the facility.

We turned off the main road and passed through some impressive gates. I peered between the trees to get my first tantalising glimpse of the buildings which were to be my home for the next 28 days. Set on a hillside, they were constructed in the prickly 'Gothick' style and painted a uniform creamy white which stood out dramatically against the broccoli of the trees behind. They were far more extensive than the word 'Lodge' had led me to expect. I noted that the buildings included a chapel with elaborate traceried windows, topped by a Quasimodo-style prickly flèche.

As the car came to a gravelly halt, I took what I suspected would be my last swig of whisky for a while (if not for ever) and then, taking this fact on board, felt a dizzying sense of the enormity, and at the same time the absolute necessity, of what I was about to undertake.

In the reception area there was little to disabuse you of the impression that you were entering a luxury hotel. There was an aquarium, a rubber plant and light orchestral music. A man in a smart formal uniform, not unlike a waiter, wheeled a trolley of clunking bottles past, which I assumed to be of the medicinal variety. While my sister tended to some administrative matters on my behalf with a young woman at the front desk, I was taken to a consulting room where I was seen by the Director of the clinic, the amenable Dr Vines. There were no obvious signs that he was a doctor: no white coat, no stethoscope, no distant imperious manner or judgemental frowns. He even shook me warmly by the hand.

Having introduced himself and welcomed me to the clinic, he said that he would need to ask me a few questions as part of the formal admissions procedure. He assured me that I would be given my first medication that afternoon, once the correct treatment, based on his initial assessment, had been prescribed for me.

"Can I ask you, Mr Daniels, when you last had a drink?" he said, fingers poised at his computer.

"About ten minutes ago," I said.

Tap tap tap.

"Excellent. And can you tell me, very approximately, how much you have drunk in the last 24 hours?"

"Very approximately one bottle of whisky."

Tap tap tap tap tap.

"That's great. Would you say that you drank whisky mainly?"

"Yes, I would say that."

Tap Tap.

"Splendid. And for what period of time, would you say, have you been drinking heavily?"

"Since as long as I can't remember."

Tap tap tap tap tap tap tap tap.

"Marvellous, *marvellous*. This is all excellent."

There was something liberating in finding it possible to answer these questions with such unflinching honesty and precision. I had long known that I had a 'drink problem' but had always obfuscated it with word-games, euphemisms, and lies. I was aware that alcoholism was quite possibly the only fatal illness that it was possible to joke about without risk of censure: the notion, for instance, of 'the comic drunk', banging into lampposts with blottoed eyes a pair of crosses, was commonplace, whereas you'd find it difficult to get much audience response to a 'comic cancer sufferer'. And any discussion of alcoholic excess – on Radio 4, for example – was always framed in semi-comic terms, or with a sort of knowing and complicit ribaldry. We're all prone to having one too many sometimes, aren't we? It's what makes us human. So perhaps my cirrhosis of the liver could be understood as a charming character trait?

I had tried to pretend, up until this point – and with some success – that every drink was an exception to my rule and that each was, almost certainly, going to be my last before I packed it in. The truth was that, having drunk a bottle or two of wine, I felt, I suspected, how most people felt all the time; that is, normal. Essentially, by drinking, I had reasoned with myself (and I was always *very* reasonable with myself) I was only catching up with everyone else – all those good people who, in their effortless sobriety, had some unfathomable advantage over me – and was, hence, entirely blameless in the matter. I subscribed to the Homeric view of alcohol (the Homer in this case being Homer Simpson rather than the bearded Greek scribbler of epics) when he declared: "Alcohol! The cause of, and solution to, all of life's problems!" There, in that epigram, is perfectly manifest the whole cruel mechanism of addiction. Now, talking to Dr Vines, I began to feel a new lightness lifting my troubled soul, as if I might at any moment float up from my chair and bob around the ceiling, like a balloon.

After our brief interview, the doctor showed me to the door.

I said, conversationally, and to give him some idea of my cultural credentials, so that he knew precisely the quality of drunk he was dealing with, "I notice you have a chapel here, doctor."

He was impressed.

"Most people don't notice that," he said, "since the whole building looks like a chapel."

"Is it still in use?"

"Oh no. It was de-commissioned years ago. Is that the word I mean?"

"I think you mean 'de-consecrated'."

"So I do. Now we use it for Transcendental Meditation and kick-boxing."

He held the door open but I persisted with my normalising small-talk.

"What was the building originally?" I said. "I presume it wasn't built as a hospital."

"No," he said, glancing at the clock. "It was built, in the early 19th-century, as a Benedictine Monastery. Hence the present name."

"Benedictine?" I said. "As in the famous liqueur?"

He added hurriedly, "And then, for many years, it was a private girls school."

I thought, with his proximity at the door, that I caught a waft of fresh alcohol on his breath; then realised it must have been my own, bouncing off him, coming back to chide me.

Back at reception the formalities were nearing completion. I saw that Stella had established a rapport with the nurse, or receptionist, or whatever she was. They were both laughing heartily at something.

"Did I miss a good joke?" I said, determined to be cheerful.

"I asked Ginny what this place was like," said Stella, "and she said it was a cross between a 5-star Country House Hotel and a high-security remand centre."

Ginny said, rather primly, returning to the gravity of the matter at hand, "Do you mind, Mr Daniels, if I search your bag? Should I have to remove anything that is not permitted I will ask you to sign for it. It will then be returned to you on your departure."

"Go ahead," I said, noticing that the bin on the floor beside her was full of squashed cans of lager and half-empty miniatures of whisky, which had presumably been confiscated from previous inductees. "I have just the one bag," I went on. "You won't find any bottles stashed away unless my sister has planted them on me to get me into trouble. I wouldn't put it past her."

While Stella scowled comically at me, Ginny unzipped the bag and I suffered the indignity of having my boxer shorts rifled. At least they were fragrant from my sister's washing machine. Then she brought out the toiletries bag.

"Do you take any prescribed medication, Mr Daniels?" she said.

"Only whisky," I said.

She frowned. She was probably used to comments like this; new arrivals, I was sure, relieved their nervousness by making silly quips when really everything should have been as serious as hell.

She reached into the bag and took out a bottle of mouthwash.

"I shall have to confiscate this," she said.

"Mouthwash?" I said.

"Yes, Mr Daniels," she said, and held the label towards me. "It contains alcohol. Listerine is particularly bad. 26.9%."

"You seriously think that I am going to drink a bottle of Listerine for the alcohol?"

"It has been known. Some deodorants too, believe it or not. Sign there, please."

"I might be hungover the next morning," I said, signing, "but at least

I'd smell nice."

She'd probably heard that one before too.

I had a difficult night which neither Diazepam or Zopiclone could appease. When, at last, I did fall into a fitful sleep – more a troubled delirium – I dreamt that, at around 4am, an air stewardess wheeled a trolley into my room and asked me, in a whisper, if I wanted anything 'from the bar'. I rubbed my eyes but, sadly, she had gone. I believe these are referred to as 'relapse dreams' and that they are not uncommon during the early stages of rehab.

The next morning, at 9am, I met my assigned clinician for the programme, Dr Van der Beer. He was a youthful but homely-looking man in a knitted cardigan with horn-rimmed spectacles which gave him a look of constant owl-ish surprise. He spoke with a pronounced Dutch accent which lent his voice a lilting solicitous quality, as if he were forever praising a child for its impeccable behaviour. On his desk was a framed picture of his young family: a wife, two kids and a dog, all grinning. They appeared to be sitting outside a country pub. Behind him on the wall was an array of framed diplomas, a display which seemed verging on the ostentatious.

"Welcome to 'Benedictine Lodge', Mr Daniels," he said, busy at his computer, presumably to summon up Dr Vines' notes from the previous day. "How was your first night with us?"

Wanting to continue in the candid mode which had been established with Dr Vines, I said, "Not good."

"It can be difficult for the first few days," he conceded.

"Actually, I've always had problems sleeping," I said, nervously conversational. "And my poor old father suffered from terrible bouts of insomnia all his life. He tried everything: herbal remedies, aromatherapy, meditation. Finally he went to see his doctor who gave him some sound advice."

Without looking up, Dr Van der Beer said, pleasantly, "What was that then?"

"He told him that if he couldn't sleep or if he woke up in the middle of the night, he should have a very large whisky. This was years ago – probably before you were born – when doctors were very old, and hadn't been to college."

Dr Van der Beer was still tapping on the keyboard and this went on, it seemed to me, for far longer than my frankly irrelevant comments seemed to justify. For a couple of minutes I just sat there, puzzled at our silence and seeming impasse. Then I began to discern, faintly emanating from his monitor, the sounds of explosions and the rattle of machine-gun fire, a burst of bellicose music; saw the reflection of a miniaturised tank battle in the his spectacles.

At last he closed the game down. "Now I'm all yours," he said, sitting back, and turning a little in his office chair, first this way, then that. "A little later I shall introduce you to some of your fellow guests. We prefer not to use the terms 'patients', 'inmates' or 'prisoners'."

I offered a paltry laugh. "'Guests' is good," I said. "Disingenuous, but good."

"But before we do that I'd like to take this opportunity to get to know a little bit more about you," he said. "I have read the brief notes taken by Dr Vines yesterday but in the hour or so that we now have together we have an excellent opportunity to fill in a bit more detail. And, Mr Daniels, here at 'Benedictine Lodge', this is always a two-way process so please feel free to ask any questions at any time during our conversation this morning. Oh, I almost forgot."

He reached for a decanter on the shelf behind him, which I hadn't noticed up until then since I had been so intent on his owl-like countenance, and he placed it on his desk between us. It contained a golden liquid. Then he fetched two crystal goblets and placed them beside the decanter.

"Drink?" he said.

Was Dr Van der Beer more guileful than I had been led to believe by his knitted cardigan and winning mannerisms?

"What is it?" I said, eyeing the decanter nervously. He grinned at me, and his face remained set in the same grin, until I cleared my throat and said, "Perhaps … a cup of coffee?"

"Oh, surely something a little stronger?" he said. "*Go on.* I usually have a glass of something at this time in the morning, just to take the edge off. You know what they say: a little of what you fancy does you good! And I understand from Dr Vines that you had a bit of a skinful yesterday, so … hair of the dog, eh? Isn't that the English expression?"

There was complete silence as Dr Van der Beer poured a generous portion of what I could only assume was whisky, or a very good imitation of it, into each goblet. This, surely, was some devious trick, or test, or even an outrageously bold attempt at entrapment. Whatever it was, it was a gambit which seemed to represent at the very least a reckless dereliction of duty on his part; and was also, almost certainly, unethical, if not criminally irresponsible. Or it was a joke. A *bad* joke, but a joke nonetheless. He pushed the drink across the desk towards me, like an opening move in a game of chess. I stared at it and found myself paralysed. It was checkmate, after a single move. Dr Van der Beer picked up his drink.

"Chin chin!" he said, and downed it in one, before emitting the obligatory "ughh".

"Is it *real*?" I asked him.

"The whisky? Of course." He put on a passable attempt at a Scottish accent. "A fine Glenfiddich single malt."

"I think I shall pass on that," I said. "It's … a little … early for me. And …"

"Oh go on," he cajoled me, "*live a little*. Just the one. One can't hurt."

Seeing the drink there before me made me realise just how much I wanted it. Abstainers, just as much as drunks, see alcohol everywhere: it's ubiquitous in our culture, it's constantly being forced down our throats. Every Muslim newsagent has its well-stocked silo of bottles and cans. They serve Prosecco in my sister's hairdressers. I was once even offered a glass of it at the dentist. Alcohol, alcohol, everywhere, yet not a drop to drink.

But now, with this abrupt offer of what I craved, no *correct* way of proceeding made itself immediately apparent to me, although my first instinct was, of course, to neck it down in one before Dr Van der Beer changed his mind. If it was not whisky, but only looked like whisky, and I was to drink it, I would feel that I had failed some test. If it were the genuine article, and I was to drink it, I would, similarly, feel as if I had failed some test, but at least I'd have got a drink out of it. That *had* to be factored into the equation. Drunks were always making this sort of calculation, and arriving, with uncanny regularity, at the answer they'd first thought of. That is: what the hell? One can't hurt.

I swigged it back with the requisite, "ughh."

It was real all right.

"*Good man*," he said.

He re-filled the glasses and then reached into his pocket and took out a pack of Rothmans (I didn't realise they still made them). He proffered me the pack and, emboldened by the shot of whisky which was already making my head swim a little, I took one, which he lit before lighting his own and pushing the ashtray into the centre of the table. It was a mass-grave of stubbed-out butts. Then, in a cloud of ovulating smoke, we talked about my drinking history, my possible 'triggers' and what it was that I wanted to get out of the programme, while he occasionally sipped at his scotch, and I sipped at mine too, but rather less regularly, and we both puffed on our Rothmans, and it seemed to me as if these things weren't going to be an issue after all, or to have any sinister hidden agenda.

Half way through our meeting, I needed the lavatory. Dr Van der Beer gave me directions. I found that I had to pass reception where a new person – not the fragrantly businesslike Ginny of the day before – was holding court with a few white-coated orderlies. A transistor radio was playing disco music. It suddenly became clear to me that I should say something to him about Dr Van der Beer's unconventional approach to therapy, which I assumed was not known about amongst his professional colleagues, and thereby absolve myself from any culpability in case he should smell the whisky on my breath, notice any irregularity in my gait or that I should fail a breathalyser test, but as I approached the desk I saw that he was drinking directly from a can of Carlsberg Special Brew and that – it is quite possible that I imagined this last detail – his eyes were pointing in slightly different directions.

Four weeks later it was all over. I am not going to attempt a detailed description of the programme, and certain confidentiality clauses – which, apparently, I had signed on admission, although I have no memory of doing so – mean that I cannot describe any of my fellow 'guests' in any detail except to say that they were a mixed bunch, the youngest being eighteen, the oldest in her mid-seventies, mostly professionals – you'd have to be to afford the fees of a place like 'Benedictine Lodge' – and our number included a token minor celebrity I'd never heard of: apparently she used to present a weekly Food and Wine programme on the BBC. There were no rock stars, I noticed.

In truth, my memory of the four weeks is hazy and confused. It was a time of unrelieved heavy drinking, of long over-emotional heart-to-hearts – a lot of people told a lot of people that they were their best mate or that they loved them, when it was clear they weren't and that they didn't – and the occasional brawl. The Club 18-30 holidays I had been on in Ayia Napa and Cala Romantica were, in comparison, like vicarage tea-parties. Every 'session' or brawl ended with the group standing in an unsteady circle, arms riotously over shoulders, belting out, in heavily-slurred boorish voices, the supplication: 'Grant me the serenity to accept the things I cannot change, courage to change the things I can, and the wisdom to know the difference.' Then we'd all head for the well-stocked bar only to stagger to bed, unruly and vomiting, at 3am.

At the end of my stay, Stella very kindly came to collect me. As I staggered into the car, banging my head on the door frame, which didn't help my appalling headache, she said, "Good God, Jack, you stink like a *brewery*."

"Sorry about that," I said. "It's a tradition that they give you a good send-off once the 28-days is completed."

"I'm very proud that you saw it through to the end," she said, as we headed down the drive, passing the writhing statue of Bacchus I hadn't noticed on my arrival. "Not everyone has that kind of stamina and determination to succeed."

"Several dropped out," I said.

"They relapsed?"

"Not exactly. They just couldn't stand the pace."

"*Lightweights*," she said.

Soon we were driving through the open country north of Dorking which boasted the most extensive vineyard in England. The sun was shining, the birds were chirruping and all seemed right with the world.

"I tell you what," said my sister, after a few minutes of companionable silence, "why don't we stop here for a moment? It's eleven o'clock, after all."

We pulled up outside a picturesque old inn.

"Are you sure?" I said.

She lavished me a beatific smile and gently touched my arm.

"What the hell?" she said. "I'm gagging for a drink and one can't hurt, surely?"

# The Sonnets

Lovers make myths of first meetings, turning them providential, prophetic or mysterious. Paul and Catherine's myth involved a bar, a paper aeroplane and a sonnet.

\*\*\*

Thirteen years later, Paul said, "Catkin? Do you remember the first time we met?"

"No," she said. She was lying, of course: she knew the tale by heart.

He played along. "When I wrote you that sonnet? Surely you remember, Catkin?"

"Remind me," she said, wanting to hear it again, in his words.

"I wrote you a sonnet and made it into a paper aeroplane and threw it across the bar at 'Be at One'. It landed in your drink."

"I don't remember it actually landing *in* my drink but I do remember thinking you were a pretentious twat."

"You should have *said* something."

"Besides, the lousy poem didn't even rhyme, or scan."

Still, she'd kept that portentous piece of origami with a premonition of its significance: it was one of their union's most important documents, a Declaration of Dependence. But where was it now? Could it have gone missing, just as all their photographs had, on their last move? Her heart shook at the loss.

"It did have fourteen lines," he said, in mitigation.

"Now *that* impressed me. I thought, this pretentious twat must be an English graduate."

"How right you were. Top-up?"

"Okay, if you're having one."

They liked a drink when they were cooking and they only spoke like this, with careful retrospective tenderness, when they were both half-cut.

After a while, she said, "Do you remember the first thing you ever bought me?"

"I do, as a matter of fact. A large glass of Cabernet Sauvignon."

"When?"

"About two minutes after I chucked the aeroplane at you."

"*After* the Cabernet Sauvignon. In fact, it was on our first date."

"First date? Did we actually have one of those? I mean, formally?"

"You took me to Nando's, don't you remember?"

"I really know how to show a girl a good time."

"And it was in Nando's that you presented me with a moth-eaten paperback of Shakespeare's sonnets which you had just picked up in some grotty second-hand bookshop for 10p."

"It wasn't some grotty second-hand bookshop."

"No?"

"No. It was some grotty second-hand *charity* shop. How do you know I only paid 10p for it? That doesn't sound like me at all."

"Because you didn't bother to rub out the price, which was nice, you cheapskate. Thanks for that."

"The book was *meant* to be a joke, a reference to my imperfect aeroplane sonnet. A sort of ironic anti-present."

"Yes, and I was sort of ironic anti-grateful."

Of course he remembered the book. Why were they pretending they couldn't remember these things? Was it because – from their present viewpoint, after so much had happened over thirteen years together – it hardly seemed possible that they had happened and happened between them? Were these just creation myths? But he was loving the easy banter between them. It was a conversation he knew he would remember for its sheer fluidity and ease. Since her recent brief unimportant affair they hadn't been this effortless for weeks. Now, unexpectedly, on a Friday evening in June, it seemed as if they were happy again, and perhaps a bit dopey, in their kitchen. They were happy like people in adverts were happy.

"If you remember," he went on, "I drew an arrow pointing at the 10p and a big circle round it and I wrote something like, 'well spent on my good friend …'" But it couldn't last. It couldn't last because of words. So many problems seemed to be about words, and names. He paused, problematically, before speaking the name that he had written in the book and not the invented one – Catkin – that he'd been using for over a decade. "'Catherine'," he said, and it was strange how difficult and unfamiliar her real name felt in his mouth, as if it came from some dead language whose pronunciation was unclear and whose derivation had long been forgotten. And when he spoke of their *friendship*, it jarred in the same way. Were they still – could they possibly still be – *friends*? after so long, irrespective of her lapse?

"I wonder what happened to that book?" she said, and the half-dreamy way she said it belied the panicky feeling she felt just then, of her world in centrifugal disorder; first the paper aeroplane, then their photographs, now the book, this evidence of her life, flying away from her.

"I haven't seen it for years," said Paul, washing his hands, and feeling his own tone beginning to shift, "but it must be on one of the bookshelves somewhere."

He dried his hands and wandered over to the window. Outside, the last sunlight lay in a rectangle of lime across the lawn and the birds were gathering among the grand lit clouds. A vast rearing platinum-edged *cumulus nimbus*, promising a storm, was shaped like the United Kingdom, but facing in the wrong direction.

"I hope it's not lost," she said, from behind him.

"Why?"

"Why? Because it reminds me of you, obviously."

He felt the rallying of his old resentment. "Do you need to be reminded of me?" he said.

She wasn't ready to rise to it. She was already at a disadvantage. There was this recurrent theme between them, never quite a joke, seemingly intractable, that things had once been better, less complicated; that there had been a golden age before her affair had sullied everything. It only added to his fear that he loved her more than she loved him. He didn't know whether the line in a particular song – 'However I look, it's clear to see, I love you more than you love me' – had given rise to his fear or whether his fear had made him more heedful of the line in the song. Either way, the words had always struck him as an unacknowledged commentary on their relationship. Whenever it came up on the radio or CD player – and it often did, since it was one of *their* songs – he always felt the urgent need to speak over it, to blank it out, and he wondered whether Catherine was conscious of it in the same way, or whether she simply didn't notice. There remained these inviolable secret alcoves between them where words hardly dared to trespass.

"You wrote something beautiful in it for me," Catherine persisted, wanting to pull them back to the safe place they had inhabited for the last few minutes, "which I've forgotten."

She hadn't forgotten those words either: she only wanted him to repeat them. But now she could sense that familiar chill in the air, as when a weather-front or depression approaches and the air changes subtly. Tears were running down her face as she looked up from the chopping board where the onions lay like shards of porcelain, and she stared, unseeing, to that far place where memories get projected. For a moment, they both appeared to be staring at the same thing.

He said, "I wrote something like, 'I wish I could say these things ...'" But he said it with a sort of abstraction, now that he was thinking again of the other thing.

She laughed with a breath of air.

"God, I *loved* you," she said, and realised at once her mistake. She meant, of course, that she had loved him with particular force at a particular moment, but it hadn't come out like that, and, already, it seemed too late to retract, or even qualify.

Cornered differently by her past tense, Paul watched her chopping the onions for a while longer while he processed his complicated resentment. There was always this pivotal moment of choice, when you chose either to speak, or say nothing.

The pasta was boiling. He went to the hob and stirred the frothy saucepan, feeling how the hard pasta broke free and revolved loosely and softened with the water, seeing the pristine etched metal of the pan. The spell was broken and the drink was already going to his head.

"So you did love me once then?" he said, at last, having caught her tense like a virus, now returning it as an accusation. "Really? You think so?"

"Paul," she said, putting down the knife.

"Before you decided to sleep with your boss? Is that what you mean?"

"Paul," she said again.

He put the lid on the saucepan, took his drink into the garden and took out a cigarette. His hands were shaking so much he could barely light it.


Catherine's birthday was in May; Paul's late October. Over the years they had been together they had tried, in zealous but good-natured rivalry, to out-do the other with the extravagance of their birthday 'treats'. This was how they referred to them in their private juvenile language.

In year three he had taken her to The Grand in Brighton where their suite had a balcony and a dazzling view of the sea which roared the whole weekend like a badly-tuned radio, almost drowning out the children's laughter and gull-cries.

For *his*, that year, she had rented a converted lighthouse on the Suffolk coast for a week, secretly arranging with his work for him to have the time off. Everything was fine, except that for the first day they had no electricity or hot water (for which they were given a small refund).

Two years before stood out as the apogee of their extravagance. In May, Paul took her to Paris where they stayed in a five-star boutique hotel on the Boulevard Saint Germain. On their first evening, in a restaurant tucked away on the bow of the Ile Saint Louis, they laughed at the corny sound of an accordion and the Toulouse Lautrec posters, realising they had stumbled unwittingly into a tourist trap. The waiters, who were mostly Croatian, were cold and uninterested, the accordion player disappeared after his second break and several errors on the bill, all to the restaurant's advantage, left the nasty taste of commerce in their mouths.

In October, Catherine, who had just been promoted at work, trumped Paris by flying him out to New York where they stayed on the 27th floor of a Midtown hotel swanky enough to have its own uniformed doorman. It was his first visit to 'The Big Apple' and it was exactly as TV and the movies had led him to expect: fire hydrants, yellow cabs, steam rising from sidewalks, cops with guns and attitudes, the effrontery of the 'WALK/DON'T WALK' signs: these things were props, or effects, surely? He was disappointed not to witness a car chase or a drive-by shooting. The view of Manhattan from their hotel window was indistinguishable from a wide-screen film still. Their second night, calmly post-coital, he had sat at the window, nursing a nightcap bourbon (he was in character) and watching the glittering graph of the city laid out before him in resplendent perspective, the red, white and green traffic on Fifth Avenue gathering at junctions, the lights of planes dipping into JFK. The city hummed and whooped, the trash carts brayed and the orchestra of cars maintained their brassy exchanges all night and yet the whole scene remained resolutely unreal to him.

He turned, to watch her.

Catherine had fallen asleep, naked, on the bed behind him, her body's gradients enhanced in the striped film-noir darkness. He was surprised to find that her familiar shape – her broad back, the kick of her hip, the tapering of her fine powerful legs into the sheet's knotting – was both the shape of his desire and of his resentment.

Year twelve brought bad news for Paul and much worse for Catherine. In February, Paul was made redundant. Then, in May, Catherine's mother had a stroke. It didn't kill her; at least, not immediately. For a week afterwards she lay in her hospital bed, amazed at the polystyrene tiles above her as if they were the ceiling of the Sistine Chapel, moving her lips in a private final negotiation with God.

"What is it, mum?" Catherine kept asking her, gently touching her face with the tender precision of someone reading Braille. "What is it, mum? Mum? Tell me. Please. Tell me. What is it?"

She died without saying and they buried her a few days before Catherine's birthday.

Paul and Catherine stayed with Catherine's father in St Albans for the funeral. Mr Maitland seemed okay to Paul, if a little withdrawn, which was only to be expected, but he'd always been a quiet man seemingly weighed down with private preoccupations, so it was hard to tell exactly what he was feeling. But it was strange, Paul felt, how he secretly, quietly, but firmly, loved Mr Maitland without really *knowing* him. All he knew of him was that he had, before his retirement, been a 'writer on church matters', whatever that meant, and had once considered entering the Priesthood until he had been through some 'crisis of faith'. He never spoke of these things and always changed the subject when Paul brought them up in conversation but, still, this sparse biographical information imbued him, in Paul's eyes, with an air of piety, even holiness.

They were still with her father for Catherine's birthday and so, with mixed feelings, they went to an expensive low-ceilinged restaurant in the old part of town: it was, according to Mr Maitland, 'what she would have wanted'. They toasted her memory. "To Mum," Catherine said, from her unique vantage point, and Paul was forced into adding quietly, "To Mrs Maitland" (he'd never felt right calling her Judy), but Mr Maitland just raised his glass and closed his eyes for a moment.

Paul ended up enjoying an evening he'd secretly been dreading. They drank far too much and, over unbidden complimentary brandy, wept with laughter over some stupid joke about funerals which tipped them, for a transfiguring thirty seconds or so, into a sort of delirium. They thought they had vanquished death and that everything might be all right, after all.

Afterwards, the three of them walked back to Mr Maitland's house with linked arms. When they were home, despite Catherine's protestations, her father insisted on putting a CD into the player. For the next few minutes they endured Handel's *Largo* in a wordless trance, and Paul knew the evening, with this sudden veer of mood, was irrecoverable. Mrs Maitland had, apparently, always loved the piece. Mr Maitland wept quietly and Paul pulled a funny face at Catherine – which, later, she swore her father had seen – and soon after they went to their separate rooms in confusion and fury, and the last thing he said to her that night – only his anger, and the drink, sanctioning the use of her real name – was "*fuck off Catherine.*"

The next morning, on waking, Paul's first devastating thought was that Mr Maitland must have heard his words. He rolled over into his fists, foetal with pain.

Downstairs, everything was normal again but it was a brittle normality as thin as a stage flat. The chink of their cutlery as they ate breakfast seemed abnormally loud and detailed, the sound of a dreadful new expediency which Mrs Maitland would now forever be denied: eating.

Then Mr Maitland stopped eating. He put down his knife and fork and placed his hands on both of their arms. He said, very quietly, and slowly, but staring rigidly at the salt cellar as he did so, "Thank you. Both of you. I couldn't have got through the funeral and these last few days without you. I wanted to say that. I know I'm not very good at saying things. I'm just not. But I wanted to say that."

Paul found, in confusion, that he could only look across at Catherine for help.

She folded her napkin in that quick efficient way she had. "Thanks Dad," she said. "You really don't need to say anything. We understand."

"Yes I *do* need to say anything, Catherine," he said, with surprising force. He didn't usually speak out. "I *do*. There were things I wish I'd said to your mother, or, things I said in the wrong way, when I used the wrong words, and now it's too late to put it right. So I'm going to start *saying* things now, and say them right, if I mean them. If they're true."

"Dad," said Catherine. "Please. Don't. I can't bear it."


Later, Mr Maitland dropped them at the station and, having just missed the express, they had no choice but to catch the stopping train to London. They both knew that this journey would be a sort of purgatory. The train stopped and started through the fields and towns of Hertfordshire, past bare miles of winter wheat, and Paul's ugly angry words of the night before kept repeating themselves against the train's rhythm, as did the unspoken words of the apology he couldn't say. He found he couldn't even utter her *name*, not even Catkin. At every stop, it was only the conductor's voice, cataloguing the names of the remaining settlements to Liverpool Street, like the stations of the cross, which broke their silence.

Then, when they were back in London and walking to the tube station, Catherine suddenly stopped, and he stopped, and, wearily, turned to her.

"What now?" he said.

"Shall we start again?" she said.


As October approached, Paul wondered whether Catherine would arrange something for his birthday that year, after everything that had happened. Since their annual 'treats' had become a barometer of the micro-climate of their relationship, a way of reading their ups-and-downs, her decision would always be telling. Of course, there was no way she would *forget* his birthday, but she might want to celebrate it in a more low-key way than usual, in keeping with the uneasy, but not unendurable, calm which had lately settled on them. Since her mother's death, Catherine had been very subdued and she spent a lot of her time on her own, reading in the kitchen, away from him, smoking in the garden, quietly declining Paul's tentative offers of tea. Most nights she slept in the spare room. She said it was because he snored, but it wasn't that. He said a lot of things like, "Are you okay?" to her, and she'd snap back, "Will you stop *asking* me that?" and then light another petulant cigarette. She'd started smoking again. She sat in the garden, puffing on her Silk Cut, and Paul would pointedly close the window because the smoke was drifting through into the kitchen. Was she angry with him for losing his job? Was she angry with him because her mother had died? Was she angry with him because he had told her to fuck off, in her dead mother's house?

Then, weeks later, she mentioned it. They were watching television.

Very calmly, she said – as if it were part of an ongoing conversation – "and on the whole, I'd prefer it if you didn't tell me to fuck off in my parents' house."

"Okay," said Paul, relieved, as if a long silence had at last come to an end.

"It wasn't the *words*," said Catherine, gravely analytical. "Feel free to tell me to fuck off whenever you want. It was *where* you said them. In my parents' house. I mean, my father's house."

"Okay, Catkin," said Paul.

"After my mother's funeral."

"I know. I was stupid, I was drunk. We were both drunk."

"Are you going to apologise?"

"I've already apologised, repeatedly."

"Not for that."

"Okay, I'm sorry I told you to fuck off in your parents' house."

"My father's," she reminded him.

"You know how … fond I am of your father."

"'Fond'?" she said. He just shook his head. Then she said, matter-of-factly, "You're a bastard, did you know that?"

Paul laughed, filled with a sudden rage.

"Me?" he said. "*I'm* the bastard? That's rich. Coming from the woman who …"

"It was *nothing* with him!" she shouted. "If you truly loved me, you'd see that, and understand!"

She left the room. He sat for a moment, in an agony of indecision, wondering at their sheer volatility, and whether he should have said what he had just said. Her mother's death had given her a sort of immunity. Then he called out, with an imploring cry, "Catkin, *please*!"


A fortnight before his birthday Paul found a letter, addressed to Catherine, lying on the doormat. On the back it was embossed in gold Olde English script, 'The White Harte, Stokeley, Gloucestershire' and beneath, bathetically, its website was spelled out in the same antique lettering, as if Chaucer and Caxton might have been familiar with the internet. He guessed it was a booking confirmation and left it there, turned upside down, so she'd think he'd missed it amid the coloured mess of minicab and pizza flyers.

That evening, Paul idly wondered out loud what they might do for his birthday, as if he had had no expectation that they would do anything. Catherine produced the letter from its hiding place on the bookshelf. Paul pretended to gawp, never happy when he was faking it, thinking his deception must always be obvious.

"What's this?" he said, tearing it open, knowing exactly what it was.

Tucked into the folded computerised confirmation of their booking – 2 Nights, Dinner, Bed and Breakfast@£80 per person per night – was a brochure for the hotel whose front cover showed a long uneven half-timbered inn framed by the majestic foliage of an oak tree. The village of Stokeley, the brochure declared, was so 'unspoilt' that it had often featured as a location for BBC period dramas: in one picture the village square was gravelled over and liberally shovelled with authentic 19th-century horse shit, while a man on a Penny Farthing rode by, tipping his hat at a lady in crinoline.

They drove across England, their silence measured by pylons. Every ten miles or so Catherine, who was wearing shades, lit a cigarette, puffing it anxiously out of the window.

"What are you grinning at?" she said, not taking her eyes off the road. She drove efficiently, changing gear in a series of abrupt mechanical movements.

"You," he said. "You actually look quite cool when you smoke. Especially in those shades. That was a compliment, by the way."

"I can never tell with you."

Against solemn organ chords, a voice, burnished and rich as mahogany, filled the car: "Libera me, Domine, De morte aeterna, In die illa tremenda."

Catherine scowled, and said, "Do we have to listen to this gloomy music?"

"It's not 'gloomy music'. It's the 'Libera Me' from a rather good new recording of Fauré's Requiem."

"Great. A Requiem. Just what we need."

She reached forward, removed his offending CD, chucked it in the glove compartment, and slipped in another. Even the airwaves had become a theatre of war. Her compilation CD was, effectively, the soundtrack to 'The Paul and Catherine Story.' Paul knew every song, and the order of every song. When one song ended, he heard the next in his head before it started, like an echo. 'Getting Away With It' was coming up and he planned his observation long in advance. He had to time it exactly right. The singer – his voice oddly wavering, exposed, vulnerable, like someone earnestly having a go at Karaoke – sang, 'I've been walking in the rain just to get wet on purpose … I've been forcing myself not to forget just to feel worse … I've been getting away with it … all my life … However I look, it's clear to see that I love – '

"It's going to rain," said Paul. "Just look at that sky."

Catherine sang the words over him, over the singer, "'… I love you more than you love me …'"

They left the motorway and for miles the road rose and fell through copper woods. Catherine, buoyed by it, turned the music off at last and even squeezed his hand in a silent pact: she loved him just as much as he loved her, that's what he supposed that squeeze meant.

After twenty minutes, they passed a sign that said 'Stokeley. Please drive carefully through the village'. Catherine slowed down. They both looked eagerly to the left and right, hoping there was more to the village than this.

Suddenly Catherine said, pulling over, "That was it!"

"Where?" said Paul. "I didn't see."

He looked over his shoulder as the car whined complainingly in reverse.

"That *is* it," said Catherine, as they pulled up.

"No way," said Paul.

"Yes it is," said Catherine. "The White Harte with an 'e'. Unless there are two White Hartes with an 'e' in Stokeley."

The effect was disconcerting: clearly this was the same White Harte on the front of the brochure but it was nothing like they had been led to expect. Paul at once understood the guile of the photographer: in portraying the hotel through an artificial frame of foliage he had suggested a rural setting quite contrary to the reality, without necessarily contravening any strict laws of representation. The truth of the matter was that The White Harte was on the main road into the village with a car park in front of it and an orange-canopied petrol station a couple of doors away. The building itself had an air of genteel neglect. In the brochure, it had been portrayed in bright sunshine, with an azure sky behind. Now, as they sat in that dead, compacted silence of a stationary car, they heard the first taut pattering of rain above them. Catherine switched the wipers on: they creaked intermittently, like some dull point being endlessly repeated.

"It should be called The Broken Harte," she said.

"With an 'e'."

"I want to go home."

She never cried, usually. Paul masked his surprise with a conventional gesture, placing an arm over her shoulder.

"Hey, hey, hey," he said, tutting and cooing at her like an attentive dove, caressing her cheek. "I'm sure it'll be fine inside. Come on, Catkin. Don't be like that. It's my birthday and it breaks my heart when you cry like that. Catkin? Come on now."

"I wanted everything to be *perfect*," she sobbed, "and I miss Mum! I *miss* her!"

"Catkin, Catkin. Come on. Come on," said Paul, his heart breaking for her, and he lit two cigarettes, and passed her one, and they sat in the car, smoking in silence for two or three minutes, as the rain drummed steadily above them.


There was no one at reception. Paul rang the bell several times. Catherine made a whistling sound through her teeth which Paul knew wasn't a good omen. There was the smell of eggs and that cloying oppressive heat of low-ceilinged carpeted places.

At last, a receptionist appeared and, after making a few cheery remarks about how it was going to brighten up later, smilingly dealt out the forms to be filled in. They only had one bag so a porter wasn't necessary. As they creaked up the narrow staircase with its fire escape signs and buckets of ash, its pale blue and pink prints, its aromas of tea and disinfectant, he felt suddenly, despite their immediate surroundings, very happy, with that best form of happiness which wasn't quite irrational except in its degree: despite the rain, despite the hotel being on the main road next to a petrol station, despite even the fact that it smelt of eggs, he was happy. They were in a hotel, with a village to explore, with drinks and dinner to look forward to and, later, most probably, that advanced type of pornographic sex they only seemed to indulge in when they were away from home, as if they couldn't do it in front of their own furniture.

The room wasn't like he'd imagined it. It was much smaller, for one thing, and the presence of so much furniture – two mini sofas with purple and gold cushions, a small fat-legged table, a desk with a big black television and 'tea and coffee making facilities' – made it seem very cramped; that, and the flock wallpaper. The window, half way down the wall, was squinting at them. Through it, Paul saw the car park, the side of the petrol station, the steady rainfall.

"I'm going to have a bath," said Catherine, from the bathroom door.

"A *bath*?"

"Yes, a bath. Come and look. It's one of those old-fashioned free-standing ones, on legs."

He went to her, and put his arms around her. "So it is," he said. "Room for two?"

"No," she said, firmly. "Why don't you do something useful and unpack?"

She carefully removed his arms, went into the bathroom and closed the door behind her. She even locked it.

Miserably, he reflected that holidays – particularly birthday holidays – weren't for doing 'something useful'. He put the bag on the bed and unzipped it: it exuded a leathery waft of toothpaste. He hung two sets of clothes on the hangers in the cupboard and put two sets of underwear in the chest of drawers and, at that moment, he was struck by one of those errant thoughts which appear from nowhere but which come to surprise the usualness of things: why do we have to be separate beings, he thought, separate objects, with this terrible distance between us? this distance where everything bad happened, with our words always in the way, failing to get across that space? And his thought expanded into the absurdity of the idea of himself as a mere object, standing in a room of other objects, as if he might be just another sofa or lamp or table. Christ Almighty, he thought, I'm effectively an *object*, and time will treat me no differently, and he felt a shudder of fear go through him.

Then he was distracted by a decanter of sherry on the table and he felt a rallying of his spirits. He could have an untimely birthday drink. Beside the decanter was a hand-written note: 'Please help yourself to a glass of sherry courtesy of The White Harte.'

He called out, "Would you like a glass of sherry 'courtesy of The White Harte' with an 'e'?" There was no answer, and so he said, "Catkin? Have you drowned in there?"

He heard the water running. Then he rapped on the door.

"Catkin?" he said. "Would you like a glass of sherry?"

"No thank you," she said. "Two o'clock's a little early for me."

"Well, I'm going to have one," he said, "since it's my birthday."

Her silence could have been interpreted as a rebuke but he resolved not to take it as one, not today. He poured himself a glass and sat on the bed which was too high and too complicatedly upholstered. Her bag, aborted, was slumped forlornly beside him. It was so familiar, this bag – it went everywhere with them – and yet it remained so exclusively, so resolutely, hers. What was it with women and their bags? Were they womb substitutes, something like that? Then he spotted the corner of a white envelope protruding from a side pocket. With a feeling of trespass, he took it out and saw his name on the front, written in Catherine's familiar looping hand. 'Paul', it said, underlined, with a full-stop. No kiss. No smiley face. Just 'Paul'. It wasn't a birthday card. She'd already given him his birthday card that morning. Besides, envelopes for birthday cards were usually square and brightly-coloured. This envelope was rectangular, and white. Bad news came in envelopes like that. He held it up to the light and saw the faint illegible superimposed traces of words. Was that, in her distinctive looping hand, 'I love you', at the end? But no, this would only be her concluding consolation. She was going to end their relationship with this letter, he thought, and on his *birthday*; she was going to go back to the other man, after all she had said, after all her denials.

He glanced at the bathroom door before reaching further into the bag, curious as to what else he might discover, and brought out a clear plastic bag. Inside it there were some pills in a white box.

Fluoxetine. 20mg. To be taken once daily with water.

He looked at them in complete blankness; then, hearing a commotion of water from the bathroom – a sluicing, the gulping of a plughole – he returned them hurriedly to their hiding place, and stood up; and that's how Catherine discovered him as she emerged from the bathroom in a billow of steam, one towel around her body, the other forming a turban.

"What?" she said.

"You're beautiful."

"Oh shut up. You don't mean it."


It was mid-afternoon and they decided to walk into the village. Although they were both dressed for rain, it had stopped raining. There was even some hopeful watery sunlight which made everything seem fresh and new: it was like the opening bars of 'The Pastoral Symphony'. They came to a sign saying 'To the Village' with a painted hand in a gauntlet, its finger directing them up a narrow cobbled street of irregular honey-coloured cottages with colourful doors and crowded window-boxes, their upper windows frowning under the weight of Cotswold stone. It was an impossibly pretty street – a street that demanded comment – yet they walked it in silence, not holding hands. Catherine took out her phone and, wordlessly, took a couple of pictures. Paul wasn't in them, he noticed.

Half way up the street was a bookshop. It was called 'Stokeley Fine & Rare Books' and, according to the scruffy hand-written note in the window, it was open for another half an hour.

"Shall we take a look, Catkin?" said Paul.

"If you want," said Catherine.

"I thought," he said, with a pretence of lightness, "that the point about birthdays was that you could do whatever you want."

A bell jangled as they crossed the threshold. Within, it looked as if a tornado had recently passed through: books of every description lay in piles on the floor, giving it the appearance of a half-excavated hypocaust, and they were stacked on the shelves, in no discernible order, three or four deep. There were also some antique cabinets filled with more valuable stock.

"Good afternoon," grunted the proprietor.

He was sitting behind a desk in the corner with a mug of tea and a woodbine burning illegally in a saucer in front of him.

"Do you mind if we have a look?" Paul said.

"We close in twenty minutes," said the man, which was an answer of a sort.

"We'll be ten."

The man shrugged, and left them to it. His demeanour made his cheerful door-bell seem almost sarcastic. As they passed between the bookcases, Catherine said, under her breath, "I see his charm-ectomy was a great success."

Paul headed towards Poetry. Catherine sauntered over to a pile of Vogue magazines from the 70s which were heaped on a tatty *chaise longue*. She leafed through a couple but was quickly bored.

"*Paul*," she whispered.

"Hey, Catkin, come and look at this."

"I'm going outside. Don't be long."

He turned, hurt. They'd been in the shop for less than two minutes.

"Okay," he said, now puzzled: wondering why, when it was his birthday, he was the one who seemed to be making all the concessions.

He watched her as she left the shop, crossed the street and stood outside a dowdy designer boutique, marked for closure: its window was an identity parade of undressed manikins, their arms set at inarticulate angles in frozen tai chi. He watched her light a cigarette.

She seemed to be hugging herself, full of her ineffable separateness.

Then something caught his eye in a cabinet. He asked the man, "Can I take a look at a book in the cabinet, please?"

The man was put-out, and glanced at his watch. He stood and limped over to the cabinet, unlocked it, and handed the book to Paul, then stood there, watching him, as if he suspected he might run off with it. Paul held it and moved his fingers across the covers. It was bound in a creamy silken vellum, and the pages were of vellum too, with initials coloured in red, blue and liquid gold. As he turned the pages, he read at random the words that made his decision:

'O! let my books be then the eloquence
And dumb presagers of my speaking breast ...'

"Nice edition of the Shakespeare sonnets," said the proprietor, changed slightly, in the hope of a sale. "One of ten copies on vellum. You won't see another."

"It's beautiful," said Paul, quietly.

"It certainly is," said the man, "but it has a sort of *chaste* beauty."

"Yes. Exactly."

"Printed in Subiaco type, not widely used since the Renaissance."

"I'm eating out of your hand. What are you asking for it, I hardly dare ask?"

Outside, Paul put his arm around Catherine.

"You were in there for a while," she said, stamping out her cigarette. "Did you buy anything?"

"That man was so surly I thought it would only encourage him."

They continued up the street, in the listless way of tourists without an itinerary, until they emerged into a small cobbled square. There was a church behind a lychgate, a market cross, a pub and a lit shop.

"I need some more cigarettes and I might get a postcard," she said. "For Dad. I feel we should have invited him to join us."

"Here?"

"Yes. I worry about him, on his own."

"Give him a call. Invite him." He wasn't *entirely* joking.

"It's too late now."

She went into the shop. He stood outside it, wondering at the village's quietness. And then the bell of the church clanked four times, a discord. Catherine came out of the shop.

"You're looking at the pub," she said.

"Let's have a drink."

"It's a bit early," she said.

"I don't know why you're so … *regulated*," he said. "You never used to be. And, anyway, it's my birthday."

"Is it? I'd completely forgotten! Okay then."

They went into the pub, which was empty, apart from the bearded barman who greeted them warmly in a rich local accent. A log fire was burning in the corner from where a black retriever looked up at their entry and wagged his tail. Paul suddenly felt, in that low ancient half-timbered place full of sweet wood smoke, that things were improving. He had stopped worrying about Catherine's mysterious letter. It no longer seemed to matter.

Catherine bought the drinks – a Cabernet Sauvignon for her, a whisky mac for him (a double, because it was his birthday) – and they took them over to the gnarled table by the gnarled fireplace. The dog ambled over to them, with weary tail-wagging sociability, and Catherine stroked his panting head.

"Good boy," she said.

Paul raised his drink.

"Cheers," he said.

"Cheers," said Catherine, and they clunked glasses. "Happy birthday."

"Is it my birthday? I'd completely forgotten," he said. Clearly, this was going to be a running joke for the weekend.

Catherine took the postcard she'd bought out of her bag, and a pen and a booklet of stamps. It was typical of her, somehow, to have a pen and stamps. For a moment she looked at the picture of Stokeley Church on the front of the card, then turned it over, to the unwritten side, applied a stamp, and frowned. Paul watched her as she started to write, her face marked with some withheld discomfort. She had an almost childlike way of holding a pen but her writing was beautiful and stylish, like a font.

'Dear Dad,' she wrote. 'You'd love it here. It's like something out of a fairy tale. Paul and I are sitting in a pub right beside the church and will visit the church afterwards, I promise.' Then she frowned again and looked up and, although her eyes settled directly on Paul's, they were elsewhere. She turned back to the card and wrote, quickly, 'I love you. Catherine. Xxx'. Then she slid the card across the table to Paul and passed him the pen.

"Just sign it," she said, being used to his subversive postcard comments. He thought for a moment and wrote, 'With love from Paul' and pushed the card back to her. She looked at what he'd written. They'd post it on the way back to the hotel.

"Thank you for writing that," she said.

He shrugged. "As you know, I'm very fond of your father," he said, and he was surprised to see a tear skitter down her cheek. "*Hey*," he said, taking her face in his hands and leaning forward to gently kiss it away. "Come on, Catkin. He's okay. He knows you love him, and he loves you, and that's all that matters isn't it, Catkin? Besides …"

"Besides what?" she said, searching in her bag for a Kleenex. She looked up and was immediately struck by the impish expression on his face, something he could never hide. "What is it? What have you done?"

"I haven't done anything."

"Yes you have."

"No I haven't."

"Then why are you giving me your 'found-out naughty boy' look?"

"I may have done something."

"Oh God. What?"

"In the bookshop."

"What? Something from the bookshop? You got me something from the bookshop, didn't you?"

He reached into his raincoat and felt the soft expensive vellum against his fingers.

"Close your eyes," he said.

# The John Stapleton Incident

I once met Valerie Singleton. She was standing on the southbound platform of White City Underground station holding a cardboard tube. I was on the northbound platform. She kept looking at her watch, I remember, as if impatient to get somewhere. She was quite a lot smaller than I imagined but it was definitely her. Of course it all made sense later: White City is the nearest Underground station to the BBC Television Centre where they film 'Blue Peter'.

On another occasion I met Jan Leeming in Orpington. God knows what she was doing there since I happen to know she lives in Wokingham. She was trying to top up her Gas card in the Post Office.

At the time all this was happening I was renting a flat above a pawnshop in Tubbs Road, Harlesden. I was so keen to work in the television or radio industries – but preferably in television – that I spent every hour of the day and night writing television and radio plays. They were mostly thrillers or whodunits but some of them were deeper 'psychological' dramas. There was one radio producer – Terry Sissons he was called – who was very keen on one of my plays and actually wrote back to me. He said that, although they would not be using it "this time", he had enjoyed reading it and that I "should not give up on my writing" (the letter is in a clip frame on the wall in front of my desk to look at whenever I am feeling discouraged). He forgot to send the play back – it was 400-pages long, all hand-written, and the only copy in existence since it would have cost me a fortune to photocopy – so I had to write back to him asking him if he could kindly return it to me. In fact, I wrote to him on several occasions and even included money for postage. I never heard from him again and nor did I ever see my play again. It wouldn't surprise me if someone stole it and it appeared in the West End with someone else's name attached. The play was called 'The Life and Loves of Valerie Singleton' and it documented Valerie Singleton's passionate affairs with John Noakes and Peter Purves and her great love of Freda, the tortoise, who, you'll remember, had her name painted in white on her shell and whose hibernation rituals we used to follow with such rapt fascination from year to year.

I have often wondered if Terry Sissons was any relation of Peter Sissons, the newsreader. It's not a very common name, after all, Sissons. In one of my letters to him I asked him, but since he never replied, I suppose I shall never know.

Things turned pretty bad for me around the time all this was going on. I realised I would have to get a job, not just for my financial well-being, but for my mental health. Soon I found just the thing. A restaurant called 'Double Entendre' on Park Parade (where all the fancy places in Harlesden are) was advertising for a new waiter or waitress. It was a funny sort of place because, although its name was French, there was a sort of American thing going on. It had car number plates and photos of film stars on the walls – one of which purported to be signed by Larry Hagman – and tried to create a 'Cheers' vibe, which is difficult when you're empty half the time. The walls were of bare red brick. They had a television above the bar showing American sport with the volume turned down. The conveniences were for 'Guys' and 'Dolls'. The food was mostly burgers and spare ribs and hot dogs and pizzas and fajitas: Tex-Mex I suppose you'd call it. They called chips 'French fries'. When I started working there, I was on £4 per hour + tips. This was the mid-1990s and there was a depression.

I'll quickly run through the other waiting staff who worked at 'Double Entendre' because I want to get on to the main subject of this story (as I'm sure you do) which relates to the famous TV presenter John Stapleton.

First there was Penny who had been at drama school and wouldn't let you forget it. She was noisy and brash and she wore flamboyant scarves to cover up her many love bites. She could be quite cutting when she wanted to be. Then there was Jo who was great fun but seemed to have boyfriend problems all the time so she had to keep going off for a 'ciggy' at the back where there was a metal staircase. Ironically, it was a fire escape, where she puffed one fag after another. I always referred to Penny and Jo as 'the girls'.

And then there was Barry. How could I forget 'Barry the barman'? What a character *he* was: if it had been the bar in 'Cheers' he'd have been our Ted Danson. He told me, when we went out for a drink one evening, that he had been a 'bartender' in New York for many years at a place on Broadway and he did have a slight American accent. He had these amazing stories about all the famous people he'd served drinks to, including, on one occasion, Richard Gere, who drank only non-alcoholic cocktails. Then he had to move back to England to look after his mother who was disabled.

The extraordinary event that I am about to relate took place on a damp Tuesday afternoon in November. There wasn't much going on in 'Double Entendre', as you can imagine. In fact, it was empty, although that didn't seem to deter Whitney Houston from letting her heart out over the speakers. I was sitting at the back, gossiping as usual with the girls, when the door opened and a smartly-dressed man walked in.

"He's mine," I said. He looked like a tipper.

I greeted him and showed him to table 6, by the window, which was one of my allotted tables for the lunch shift. It was only when he had sat down and was studying the menu that I had the chance to study *him*. There was absolutely no question about it, no 'might be, might not be': it was definitely 100% John Stapleton, the top TV presenter. I could hardly believe my eyes. He ordered one of our Chilli Dogs ('just the way you like it, but go careful on the chilli!') with a serving of our 'world-famous chunky French fries' and a 'Bud' from the bar. He also ordered a side-dish of garlic bread ('Now you know why you don't see so many vampires around here! It stinks!').

I could barely contain myself. After I had taken the order I went straight up to Lizzie and said, "Look who just walked in."

She glanced over at the table.

"My *God*," she said, her voice reduced to a stage whisper. "Is that who I think it is?"

"John Stapleton!" I confirmed.

"Get me his autograph!" she demanded, tugging at me imploringly. I think she was too star-struck to ask him herself.

"Okay," I said. "I'll ask him when he gets the bill."

I went into the kitchen with his order. The surly chef – I haven't mentioned him until now, and for good reason – was sitting in the corner reading a tabloid (he was always reading a tabloid) and smoking nastily. We'd often thought that could be an issue with Health and Safety, his smoking in the kitchen like that. He was called Terry and he had puffy bags *above* his eyes which made him look like a boxer or streetfighter.

"Guess who just placed this order," I said, nonchalantly. He said nothing. "Go on," I said. "Guess."

"How do I know?"

"John Stapleton," I said.

"John *who*?"

"Stapleton. Off the telly."

"Never 'eard of 'im."

"You've never heard of John Stapleton? He used to present 'Good Morning Britain' and 'Watchdog' with his wife, Lynn Faulds Wood, who, I notice, is conspicuous by her absence. That might be something for the gossip columns!"

He said, "You can gossip all you like 'cos I've never 'eard of any of 'em."

"Come and take a look," I said. "You're bound to recognise him."

Terry, squashing out his cigarette in someone's *Pasta Arrabiata*, came reluctantly to the circular window, like a porthole, in the kitchen door and stuck his moustache against it.

"Where is 'e, then?" he said, "this famous bloke I've never 'eard of?"

"Table 6," I said. "By the window. Dark hair. Wearing a suit."

"Table 6 is empty."

"What?"

"Table 6 is *empty*."

He was right. There was nobody sitting at table 6. I went back into the restaurant thinking that perhaps he'd changed tables. Perhaps he hadn't wanted to be by the window where any passer-by could gawp at him. Celebrities had to be careful of things like that. But the restaurant was deserted: Whitney Houston was Saving all her Love for someone else. When I asked the girls about him, they stated flatly that no one had come in and that the table had been empty all along. I had to sit down at that point. I could have sworn it was him, *sworn* it. And Lizzie, too, *she'd* seen him – she'd even asked me to get his autograph.

For the rest of the afternoon the girls became fed up with my insistence that John Stapleton had come in. Finally, when I had just finished another detailed reconstruction of his entrance and run through the details of his order again, Penny said to me, "Okay, so this famous John Stapleton we've never heard of came into the restaurant, ordered chilli dogs and garlic bread and then walked out or just disappeared into thin air. Fine. We believe you. Now can you please shut up about effing John Stapleton and go and do your job?" Except she didn't say "effing."

Only towards the end of my shift did I realise what had actually happened that day. John Stapleton hadn't come into the restaurant. I had invented the whole thing. What would John Stapleton, a top television presenter, be doing on his own in Harlesden on a wet Tuesday afternoon in November in a place like 'Double Entendre'? It seems ridiculous, thinking back on it now.

But what of 'Lizzie', I hear you ask, the mysterious waitress who had corroborated my sighting and so keenly coveted his autograph? There was no-one called 'Lizzie' working at the restaurant, and never had been. It seems I made her up too.

# The End of the Circle Line

He opened his eyes and lay, breathing. Light crept through the curtains, like gas. From one of the neighbouring gardens a dog was barking its urgent incomprehensible information. A distant train gave a solitary trombone call. All else was still. The telephone waited on the bedside table.

His breathing slowed as the dream dispersed and he concentrated on the ovoid shadow of the lampshade lengthening across the ceiling. Then he heard, among the sounds of the new day, something gathering in the air, like a storm: the first plane coming in. As a child, living near Gatwick, he'd loved that sound for its comforting suggestion of homecoming, of safety. The memory of it filled him with an unexpected calm – as when a swimmer, in some cold sea or pool, moves pleasantly through a current of warm water – and he said to himself, it continues, it goes on; people are still moving across the surface of the world. He thought of the plush night of Europe with its bright diagrams of towns from which this plane had emerged to begin its final descent, over Hammersmith. Then, with an abrupt superstitious impulse, he lifted the corner of the curtain just in time to see the plane's fleeing tail, a single technological wink, before it slid smoothly out of sight towards the peachy continent of dawn, broken over the rooftops. Its sound began to fade, only for another to start from off far to the east: they were piling up in their holding patterns, coming in from New York and Bangkok and Shanghai. He thought of the passengers, disorientated by time zones, gin-and-tonicked, caffeinated, buckling up and gazing down at the passing coal fire of London, its crags orange and steaming, the vast organism of the city spread as if on some petri dish, fed from the dark by cruising veins of light.

He moved towards her.

"Are you awake?" he said.

She didn't answer. She was asleep, or pretending to be. He watched the undulation of her back with that sense of trespass he always felt when looking at her, even when she slept, even after twenty years of marriage. They were not right for each other: he was going to have to speak to her about that at some point in the next twenty years or so. Then, as if in answer to his thoughts, she turned over to face him and said the word, in a clear half-waking voice, "shop". He allowed himself a grudging laugh. *Shop*, he thought: how easy your dreams are, compared to mine. You're dreaming of a shop and I'm in hell. Then came the thought's swift collateral of guilt, and shame: *who do I think I am*? What does my suffering amount to, compared to the world's?

He puzzled over the meaning of her arm-crossed face, a face he'd once held, once loved, once leant in towards – to her astonishment, and his – to kiss, on a train. Now, that face meant something different to him. He'd seen past it to another person he was now unable to love. Why were people meant to look beautiful as they slept? Asleep, you were meant to look as God intended, before the world got to you and had its way: Edenic, prelapsarian, innocent. If anything, he thought, his wife looked uglier asleep than she did awake and that familiar anguish came back to him, that old feeling that he could have done so much better, *so* much better – in fact, could be living a completely different version of his life, somewhere else, with someone else, someone better, or even alone – if only he hadn't met her at a party, if only he hadn't had dinner with her, if only he hadn't had dinner with her again, if only he hadn't kissed her on that train, if only he hadn't taken her hand, if only he hadn't gone to bed with her, if only he hadn't gone to Paris with her, if only he hadn't proposed to her in the garden of the Musée Rodin, if only he hadn't married her, if only he hadn't … his thoughts always ended with this pleading inefficacy, this infinite regression, of 'if only'.

Her features were relaxed into their natural contempt for him: the dry, shapeless mouth, the bladish glint of eyeball, one nostril skewed and provoking, pressed into an oysterish ruck against her fist.

How has this happened? he thought. How am I here? How are we together, sleeping in the same bed? living in the same house?

In the bathroom's fluorescent autopsy he took two Paracetamol washed down with water from the tumbler by the sink. Then he coughed violently, and motes of light circled him, like electrons. There were two full packets of Paracetamol in the cabinet, a bottle of whisky in the kitchen.

He entered the shower. For two minutes the water drummed. He stood beneath it, motionless, head lifted, eyes closed.

Afterwards, as he shaved, the mirror showed the apparition of a stranger. It made him reflect vaguely on the meaning of things, on life, death, the passage of time, everything. Casually, he wondered – as he guided the Bic beneath his nose, staring at someone he supposed to be himself – if there was a God or a heaven or a hell, or if, when you died, was that *it*? Was there nothing after, like before? Then he couldn't find the flannel and so he used the towel to wipe his face and dab it dry. He thought of human flesh, like pastry.

When he returned to the bedroom he had the uncanny sensation that he was absent to himself and that the room was pointing in the wrong direction. Everything was wrong. Surely there was no way he could go in, not on the Underground, not like this.

He half opened the curtains. It was Tuesday out there. He lay on the bed. He still had a few minutes.

His wife opened her eyes.

"What time is it?" she said.

"Six thirty," he said, and remembered his dream. He gasped.

"What?" said his wife.

"Nothing."

"What's wrong?" she said, but that question, so often asked, now always came as an accusation from her, something from which all sympathy had long been jettisoned, leaving only a cruel demand.

"What's wrong *now*?"

"Nothing's wrong," he said.

"You're not still ..?"

"Oh," he said, and drew the word out like a commentary on his whole damned condition. She was going to mention last night, all those stupid things he'd said about himself that had seemed so true at the time – so vitally true and needing to be said – but which now, now … Why could he not remember, when he had drunk too much, never to say anything? Why could he not remember, if he couldn't say it sober, not to say it drunk?

The night before, they had reached a point in their argument when he had stopped speaking altogether, as if he had finally escaped the cycle of anger, accusation and counter-accusation, and he was free of her, and he could leave her. He'd thought she had lost her power over him, her malign spell, on which he blamed his whole disaster. Now he had woken to find it still there, only more potent than before, the whole thing starting all over again.

"All that stuff you were coming out with last night," she said, her voice sleepy and playful with derision, "about concentration camps. What do you know about them?"

"Nothing, nothing."

The dream came back again: the three starved manacled figures, face-down on the ground, burning in the sun, the desert beyond beneath its boiling orange sky, the robed man with his pail of water, pouring water over each in turn, each raising its head, gaping with obscene relief, for air and water. Who were these people? Who was the man trying to help them? Why were they there, in that desert?

He wished he had never gone to that party in the first place, never taken that book from the shelf.

Two months before he had been at a party. He had found himself in the crowded room, standing alone, holding his tepid glass of white wine without even enough social embarrassment to compel him to engage any of the people around him in conversation. They had all been discussing property prices and what had happened in New York, and the effect of what had happened in New York on property prices. He had turned his attention to a bookshelf and, in order to conceal his isolation and boredom, had removed a book at random, but with the pretence of decisiveness, and opened it. There he had found, as if they had been waiting for him, a sequence of three grainy black and white photographs in which he had witnessed the worst of all possibilities, an extremity of suffering which he had visited only in the darkest excursions of his imagination, fed by newsreels and documentaries – being trapped in one of the Twin Towers, being burnt alive in a cage by ISIS, being in a gas chamber, being buried alive – when the instrument of death was worse than death itself – but he could not, he would not turn away. The pictures were of an experiment on a living man at Auschwitz, a word that snagged on his brain like barbed wire. They showed this man, starved and tethered to a metal chair. The chair was in a decompression chamber. In the first picture the man's face was blank, full of the hopeless dejection of capture, as, faintly puzzled, he watched the doctors beyond the glass. In the second you could see his fists straining against the leather bands, eyes tight, mouth gaping. In the third his head was tipped forward and blood had drawn lines down either side of his face.

They'd blown out his eardrums.

In the kitchen, in his dressing gown, he drank a pint of water down in one, then, after a gasp for air, another. There was a tiny but brilliant twist of light oscillating on the tiles by the sink. He could not locate its source. It reminded him of something he'd once seen, refracted on the hull of a boat. Then he saw that the sun had come out in the garden and that the patch of lawn was shining with hoar frost. He imagined someone finding it beautiful.

He looked at the telephone and thought: I could call her now, quickly; I could whisper some assurance to her, some promise.

But he didn't. Instead, he did something unusual which made him wonder if this day was going to be different from other days: he picked up the remote control and turned on the television. SKY News. On the screen a young man and an even younger woman were sitting on a sofa in their overlit studio. They had mugs in front of them, newspapers and magazines scattered about, like you might have at home. Beyond the tilted blinds was London, or at least a simulacrum of it: Big Ben, St Paul's, The London Eye, The Tower, bunched together in impossible proximity. They blazed in light. In their studio, their perpetual summer, there was not a dab of shadow. He wondered, if there was a heaven, it would be something like this: no shadow, no sin, but no hiding place either, just the radiance of the divine bathing the righteous, the saved. The idea made him feel trapped and panicky with nowhere for his cheating soul to run, or even to look away; it made him think there could be nothing he could even want, not even paradise.

On the screen there was footage of the Twin Towers burning, falling into smoke. The voice-over was saying, "… already there is talk of rebuilding them, exactly as they were …"

The kettle thrummed and clicked. The metal pot where they kept the teabags was empty except for its residue of black dust. He thought of his mother's ashes. Then he feared they'd run out of tea bags. He went to the cupboard. There was a new box of PG Tips Pyramids. He took it down. As he pressed open its sharp cardboard teeth, the smell of tea rose into his face and he remembered, with an unexpected immediacy, the cards they used to give away with it, which, as a boy, he would paste into albums. Dinosaurs, space rockets, wildlife, motor cars: he had thought, then, the world was waiting for him, and that it was good.

He boiled the kettle again and poured the smoking water onto the teabag in the mug. The water turned a transparent copper. He stirred it, squashing the teabag, granular and porridgey, against the side. He left it there for ten seconds or so – she didn't like it too strong – then fished out the teabag with the spoon and flicked it into the pedal bin which gave up its waft of last night's cigarettes. He clicked two Canderel in and added a splash of milk. He stirred it. The water turned to mud.

He looked at the television. There was an advertisement for detergent. A man in a white coat, too blandly good-looking to be a real scientist, was grinning at him. He was demonstrating something in a laboratory. He held up a very clean and very white shirt, and smiled. The words came with the finishing jingle.

*Ariel. Concentrated Cleaning Power.*


He took her tea up and placed it on the bedside table.

"Hey," he said. "Tea."

"What time is it?"

"Seven."

She sat up. She picked up the mug and sipped at it.

"I had two really weird dreams," she said.

He went towards the wardrobe.

She said, "Do you want to hear about them?"

"Go on."

"In the first, I was in a shop. But it wasn't like an ordinary shop. It was selling bits of humans."

"Bits of humans?"

"Yes. Arms. Legs. Heads. Stacked on top of each other."

"That is weird, actually. What was the second dream?"

"I dreamt about you."

He noticed the new tone in her voice which may have been signalling a truce, after last night. To say you had dreamt of someone would always be a kind of compliment.

"What happened?" he said. "Did you kill me? In the dream?"

She said, "I came to this evil place – I can't describe it, unlike anywhere I've ever been – and I couldn't find you. It was as if you'd left me there. I walked along this corridor. On either side there were cubicles with red light bulbs, like in a brothel."

"I wouldn't know."

"I remember feeling I had to get out so I left the building and went up this path to a gate where there were three roads leading in different directions. And I knew that you had gone somewhere, to a beach, where you were with other people. I knew you were happy with them, happy without me. But I didn't know which way to go, to find you. I couldn't find you. I'd lost you."

"So what did you do?"

"I woke up … and realised it was true."

"Realised what was true?"

"That I'd lost you."

"Oh well," he said, manufacturing a sort of laugh, "I'm still here, I'm afraid." He threw his next line away, without a moment's hesitation: "I'll be late tonight."

She said nothing. He opened the wardrobe.

"I can't find that red tie you bought me," he said.

After a while, she said, "Why?"

"Why can't I find that red tie you bought me?"

"No. Why will you be late tonight?"

"I told you. There's a meeting."

"When did you tell me?"

"I can't remember. Yesterday?"

"A meeting on a Tuesday evening?"

"Yes. Why shouldn't there be a meeting on a Tuesday evening?"

She didn't reply.

He called over his shoulder, "Why shouldn't there be a meeting on a Tuesday evening?"

His clothes were in a line, hanging. They reminded him of an identity parade for someone, not unlike himself, seen running from the scene of a crime. Under his dressing gown, as if ashamed of his nakedness, he stepped into his boxer shorts. He took off his dressing gown and hung it on the metal hook by the door. Then he put on his striped shirt, his suit, his socks, his shoes, the noose of his tie, conscious the whole time of his wife lying in the bed behind him, watching him as he assembled himself into an executive.

Turning away, she said, "I hope she's pretty."

In the private viewing room of his head people were jumping from the back of a truck, jogging towards a pit where men waited with guns.

Outside, he headed for the station. It was raining. His vision was blurred and kaleidoscopic with it, or with tears, he hardly knew which. For a moment, he thought the air was full of cinders or ash before he realised it was a flurry of snow. His brogues made the crunching sound of sentries on the shrapnel of ice. People who seemed to know exactly where they were going hurried past in a dark huddled swarm. They were all heading in the opposite direction. He was conscious only of their dark undifferentiated mass.

Then something caught his eye: a poster on a billboard by the entrance to the Underground. It consisted of a sequence of three photographs of a man's head. In the first, the man looked despondent; in the second, expectant, vaguely quizzical; in the third, his head was thrown back in a grimace of joy. He stared at the poster for a while, not sure what it was trying to sell him. Happiness, perhaps? Happiness itself? Was that it?

Paralysed by indecision, he stood by the station entrance and smelt burning on its breath. He heard the crash of trains from deep within, like cattle trucks.

Somewhere down there one of them was coming to get him.

In the phone box, he dialled, and, as he waited for her to answer, he read the cards of the prostitutes. He pushed the money in.

The familiar voice said, "Is that you?"

He said, "Listen. Just *listen*, will you, for once in your life? This is the end. It's over. It can't go on like this, do you hear me? It has to stop."

He put the phone down and closed his eyes. Then he pushed open the door and stepped into the street. The rain spat in his face and the sirens jeered at him. In two minutes he would descend the escalator.

# A Holding Pattern

Most evenings during the holidays Robert and I would meet on the village green and head off, under the cover of darkness, for the end of the runway. The darkness was crucial to our operations: it brought to them an illicit clandestine quality.

Robert knew everything there was to know about the airport and aeroplanes. He knew which way they were coming in, how many would be circling over Sussex and Kent, and why the United flight from O'Hare was twenty minutes late. By eavesdropping on the secret radio channels with his home-made transmitter he had gained a sure grasp of the alpha and omega of control tower jargon, of holding patterns, beacons, guidance systems, slots and stacking, the significance of lights, a knowledge that was deeply impressive to an amateur like myself who knew nothing of how the world worked and who felt, with the strength of a moral conviction, that all such knowledge should remain the preserve of adults. For me, one plane was much like any other but Robert knew them all by name and marque, from the ageing twin-props which served the Channel Islands with their alert square-eyed cockpits, to the elephantine Jumbos with their pendulous batteries of tyres which were collected up and tucked away so neatly after take-off. Jumbos were his favourite and aroused his greatest excitement: he could spot them from miles off by the configuration of their landing lights and the deep plain-saw drone of their engines. They were the loudest too. Robert loved the *noise* of planes, that distinctive bisection of sound: the high whistle, the low thunder.

All I knew about airports was that there were planes that needed to get away and there were planes that needed to get home and the art was to let them do both with as few crashes as possible.

It was a twenty minute walk from our village to the end of the runway, a walk which we always made in silence. Robert was never one for small-talk, or talk of any kind. We could go a whole evening and only say a few words to each other. Ours was a pact not of words, but of action, of observation, of surveillance.

From a distance, the airport's proximity was marked by a sporadic roar of engines, a halo of orange in the night sky and a whiff of aviation fuel in the air. As we headed towards it, there were houses and trees and street lights; then there were trees and street lights; then there were street lights. Finally you came to the place where even the street lights stopped. Everything stopped. The world changed here: all the points by which we triangulated our existence vanished, and there was only night. The black sky with its crust of stars – a single frozen shot of all that was – was suddenly more real than the earth we stood on. Gazing up, it was as if we were pitching into the vacuum whose awning threatened to smother you beneath even the *idea* of infinity. In an infinite universe, if something was possible, however remotely – that there was another Robert and David out there, for instance, standing at the end of some alien runway – not only would there be another Robert and David out there, there'd be an infinite number of Roberts and Davids out there. My head span at the thought of it.

"There's an infinity down there too," Robert said, with that dark gurgle in his throat which wasn't quite laughter, and he turned from the vertiginous sky to look at his feet and the planet beneath. It was the first thing he had said in half an hour. "There's no 'up' or 'down', just emptiness for ever and ever, in every direction."

A chill went through me and I wanted to go home, back to my family and to the safety and familiarity which I had to pretend, for Robert's sake, I despised, so that he wouldn't think he was the only who was miserable at home.

Over the surrounding acres, cleared of anything taller than a human being, the wind stalked like some predatory beast, roaring in our ears, cracking in our anoraks. The road ran straight beside the perimeter fence for half a mile or so with bare ploughed fields on the other side, their corrugation brought into relief by the low security lighting.

About half way along, an installation of lights on poles in the shape of a V heralded the end of the runway, or its beginning, and this was where the planes came over, taking off, or coming in, depending on which way the wind was blowing, or on the whims of the controller. Most of our evenings were spent here either standing by the fence or, when a security vehicle drove by in its striped livery, squatting in the drainage ditch which ran beside it. We were committing an offence just by being there and we knew it. Everywhere, wired to the fence, there were signs drawing attention to our transgression: **No Trespassing. No Photography. No Loitering. No Smoking**. Little wonder we gazed with such longing through the screen of hexagonal wire towards that forbidden theatre where shining planes rolled out of immense hangars, gleaming tailfins cruised above a sea of white fuselage, and little excitable buggies rushed around with their lights spinning. Another sign by some metal gates said: **Keep Clear. Emergency Access Required at all Times**. We knew what thrilling eventuality *they* catered for: the inevitable crash. We were certain that we would one day witness it and this expectation – this hope – was probably our real but unspoken reason for being there every night and accounted for that vague sense of disappointment we invariably had when, sometime before midnight, we trudged home together and parted wordlessly on the green to return to our separate custodies. Still, we thought it was only a matter of time before we witnessed some disaster. Every successful take off, every successful landing, we reasoned, made a crash statistically more likely, so there was ever more reason to remain, ever less to go: the law of increasing marginal returns. We knew, with our premature sense of the world's injustice, that the night we *didn't* show up would be the night of the crash. Therefore we went virtually every night, to cut the odds of missing it. Here was the very mechanism of addiction, and while I was partially and unwillingly a slave to its pattern, it was always more evident and more potent a force in Robert. It was the same mechanism, perhaps, that would drive him, eventually, to alcoholism and suicide. Years later, I heard – through a mutual acquaintance – that he had hanged himself in his garage.

My parents had started wondering what I did with my evenings, assuming it was something wasteful or even delinquent, like breaking windows or shoplifting or glue-sniffing. I didn't tell them the truth – about which I was beginning to feel an obscure unease, even a sort of shame – but told them that I went round to Robert's to play Pac-Man and watch TV. Realising that these pretexts weren't particularly convincing, I mentioned that he had a sister, duping a degree of diffidence in this revelation, as if his sister might be the true reason for my visits. Robert did indeed have a sister but I had never met her; besides, she was twelve. My satirical father ignored my subtle implication of a romantic tryst: subtlety was not on his register.

"You seem to spend all your time with him," he said. "There's something not right about the boy. Why don't you see other people for a change?"

The strength of his dislike for Robert had never been fully explained to me but, in truth, his comment echoed reservations I was beginning to have myself. I *was* spending too much time with Robert, even *I* could see that. I needed to be seeing other people, people who weren't so fixated. Who knows? Perhaps even *girls* ... At least I should be opening myself up to the possibility of seeing girls. Members of this strange and dangerous tribe were occasionally to be seen outside the village's pebble-dashed Youth Centre or hanging around the bus stop, chewing gum in time to the solipsistic itch of their Walkmans, or going into Crawley to crawl the Arcade and get chatted up by boys and drink cider and smoke cigarettes with them in the public toilets behind the Job Centre. I naturally wanted a part of this delectable romance: it was just stupid that I was wasting my life watching planes with Robert instead.

Although I would have said at the time that Robert was my best friend in the sense that I saw him more than anyone else, he was my best friend *only* in that sense. And I was beginning to think that there was something not quite right about him. I was beginning to think, in the language of my urbane older brother, that Robert was 'a loser.' I was beginning to think that Robert was going slowly but surely crazy.

Then, one day, I broke the pattern. I didn't go to the green. I just … didn't go. I sat on my bed and looked at my clock. It said it was exactly 9.00pm. This was the time we always met on the green. I did not move. Then my clock said it was 9.01pm and nothing happened. Then it said it was 9.02pm and nothing happened. I continued sitting on my bed. When it was 9.03pm and still nothing had happened, I thought, 'this is easy. I could get to *like* this. I am exercising my willpower by doing precisely nothing.' By 9.30pm I was watching *Kojak*.

The next day I did exactly the same thing. I didn't go, and, in just the same way, nothing happened. The world didn't end. We had simply stopped seeing each other. And Robert did nothing about it, as if tacitly colluding with the 'plan'. He didn't come round to my house, he didn't phone me, he didn't put a note through the door, demanding to know why I had abandoned him. I could surely have invented an excuse; I could have said that my parents forbad me going out since I had to concentrate on my revision. But I was never required to deploy this wholly convincing excuse that was available to me. And, as each day went by, through those long summer school holidays, and I didn't see him again, it became incrementally easier to do the same the following day, and the day after that. Without explanation, Robert and I ceased to be friends. We unravelled, and went our separate ways. The cycle was broken.

With my abrupt freedom, I began pursuing other interests. I realised that if I was to meet girls – and even, who knows? possibly even have some sort of relationship with one – I needed first to find out something about them: where they lived, what they liked doing, and –

perhaps most crucially – what their bodies were like. My brother – who, unlike me and the rest of my family, hadn't inherited the sexual repression gene – had once spotted me eyeing the top shelf in a newsagent where the forbidden magazines were lined up in a riot of colour, mostly pink: backs, buttocks and the beginnings of breasts.

"Well do you want a *Mayfair* or not?" he snapped, in answer to a question I hadn't asked.

I was affronted. "No I do not want a *Mayfair*," I said.

"*Mayfair* or ... *Razzle*?"

"Perhaps *Mayfair*."

I went outside immediately, shaking violently with fear. I couldn't watch. Presently, he came out of the shop and proceeded to wave the dirty mag in my face, singing "Mayfair, Mayfair, Mayfair!" If I had had the temerity to make such a purchase myself, I would at least have diluted it with a *Surrey Advertiser* and some Spangles, even pretended it was a last-minute afterthought. My worldly brother felt no such lack of clarity on this matter. Porn was porn. Hurriedly, I folded the silky magazine into my inside pocket and tried to change the subject, as if what had just taken place was of no special significance.

I would possess that magazine for many years, until it became creased and torn from hurried concealments, folded and folded again, marked with the familiarity of guilt.

At that time, with O-levels imminent and the holidays nearing their end, I dedicated my evenings to study. At least, that was the impression I wanted to give. When my parents, who were quietly satisfied that I had relinquished my inexplicable attachment to Robert, looked in on me, with the regularity of prison guards, they found me huddled over a slippage of text books in a cocoon of light. They must have considered me miraculously transformed. Little did they know that concealed beneath my dog-eared text books was splayed – the whole gorgeous length of her laid out for my unfettered eyes – supine pouting Adèle, finger picking at her lower lip, hipped and breasted, on her satin bed; or big fun-loving Mandy in her bubble bath, just able to squeeze one soapy nipple into her mouth while still peeping at me, a leg cocked against the tap; or Belle, soft-focus on a leaping swing in a woodland glade, caught, à la Fragonard, in a hazy sunbeam; a swing whose ascent allowed, in one scandalous shot, a glimpse of the dark fur between her legs, the suggestion of an opening. Adèle, Mandy and Belle all seemed so nakedly happy and so eager to share their bounty with me that it never for one moment crossed my mind that they might be real people; or that I might, one day, meet and love someone real.

Soon, with summer gone, I returned to school and its smells of disinfectant, spam fritters and wet satchels. The resumed routine made everyone muted and well-behaved. Old enmities were discarded; teachers gentle; we, compliant. There was something almost sanctified about that atmosphere of those first two or three days, before they turned rough again, and edgy, and ugly.

Robert made no attempt to re-establish our liaison. It was as if my presence or otherwise was immaterial to him. I began to see that there was a fundamental difference between Robert and myself but I didn't know whether this was because he had a part missing or an extra part that I didn't have. He was a loner who didn't care about anything but his own very specific interests; I was gregarious, a generalist who courted popularity; he was always exactly the same, in mood and manner, and even dress; I twisted and moulded myself to fit whatever situation I was in, to conform. He was always unhappy; I was ... well, I was unhappy too, but in a different way. My unhappiness was the sort you could write poems or songs about: it was indulgent. I didn't really know what his sort was like but I knew you couldn't write poems or songs about it. Instead, I sensed his unhappiness was like an affliction, and, at the same time, I sensed a peculiarly *adult* quality to it. Adults, I sensed – from observation of my own parents and their friends who occasionally came to somber gatherings at our house in their saloon cars, then left before ten – were unhappy in the same bleak inward unknowable way that Robert was unhappy; they had no choice. Robert had just got it too soon, and too badly. And, in the end, it killed him.

Then, something happened, and everything changed forever.

One evening, I was surprised by a violent knocking at the front door. Usually visitors used the bell. A moment later I heard my mother calling me: "Robert's here!" There was a wariness in her voice, a conditionality, the vaguest hint of a question, which made me think she wasn't too happy that Robert was here. Leaving Belle waiting for me on her swing, I galloped down the stairs. My mother, still standing sentry at the door, threw me a rueful look and an irked puzzled warning expression which I couldn't fathom, but then she left me to it.

Robert was standing on the doorstep where my mother had left him, beyond the half closed door, so that my first sight of him was of a dark shape through the frosted glass. When I fully opened the door, I saw the meaning of my mother's expression: Robert's face was blackened with paint, or mud. For a moment we stared at each other in silence. I resisted the temptation to laugh.

He said, "Come with me now."

"Where?"

"The runway. Now."

"I can't," I said. "I don't want to."

"Why?"

"Because I'm bored of it."

I was surprised to find my heart pounding at my unexpected confession, my assertion: this was uncharted territory.

He looked at me from the white circles of his eyes. There was a strange sour smell emanating from him.

"Come with me now," he said again, with the word-for-word repetition of a savant, or a robot.

"To hide and watch planes?" I said.

"No," he said. "Not hiding. Come with me now."

Something in the voltage of his excitement was catching, or perhaps hypnotizing. We continued staring at each other for a while longer.

Then I said, forming my reckless decision, "Okay."

I grabbed my coat, shouted some excuse to my parents and, before they could find fault with it, closed the door firmly behind me. We ran. I didn't look back in case I saw my mother's anxious face in the window, or my father's angry one.

It was cold out, a sweet woody October evening, and our breath bloomed in it. I noticed that Robert was carrying a bulky flashlight rather than the small torch he'd carried before. I also noticed he was dressed entirely in black and realised, with an irrational movement of jealousy, that, all this time, he must have been visiting the runway without me. *On his own*. And in the interim he'd got himself kitted out.

Once beyond the houses and the dim glow of their curtained windows, Robert ran so fast that I could barely keep up with him: I could only place him in the darkness by the jolting beam of his flashlight. To my surprise, when we reached our usual viewing point, he continued running, and a few seconds later I found him squatting beside the fence, by a gorse bush. It took me a while to get my breath.

"What is it?" I said, heaving, bent double.

He said nothing. Instead, he aimed the flashlight into the bush. Beyond the tangle of gorse I saw the hole in the fence, a hole large enough for a human being to pass through.

It was then that I felt – probably for the first time in my life – that stomach-sinking sensation which accompanies the apprehension of something which is both unspeakable and yet inexorable, the sort of feeling which, I am sure, is common on deathbeds or in doctor's consulting rooms after the delivery of a dire prognosis; or on Death Row, when, along the corridor, you hear the chink of keys and catch the footfall of guards, and their priest, and the clock comes round, finally, to the appointed hour, to the last infinitesimal second. It was the sort of feeling I had coming to me, one unthinkable day, one unthinkable moment: and this was a premonition of it, a rehearsal.

"You can't go through there," I said, reasonably; but, in reality, shaken to my core. "It's against the law, it's dangerous."

He disappeared into the gorse. I shouted after him. Then I went and held the fence, like a caged animal, and saw him on the other side, a dark shape wriggling on his elbows and knees with a peculiar gyrating motion, like some strange new form of life, half-human, half-reptile, burrowing forward.

"Robert!" I shouted, in a hoarse whisper, but I delivered my next words plainly, in my usual speaking voice, as if they were absolute facts. "They will get you. They will arrest you. You will be killed."

He ignored me and continued his frantic wriggling. There was nothing I could do but follow him. I had told myself that I must rescue him. I had told myself that I must stop him, that he was being a danger to himself and to others. Already, my motives were being prepared for the police; already I had rehearsed my tone of whingeing exculpation.

I found that the wire of the fence had been cut. Robert hadn't 'found' anything, I realised: he had made this way through the fence himself, with the aid of wire-cutters. I pushed forward, feeling the coarse vegetation pulling me back, the ends of the wire snagging on my coat, but emerged the other side relatively unscathed. All at once, everything fell silent. There was no wind. I smelt grass, soil, the earth. The airport seemed to be having one of its infrequent intermissions. It was like wandering into someone else's vast empty house. I could just make out the shape of Robert in the distance, and saw, with horror, that he was crawling in the direction of the runway itself.

"Robert!" I shouted. "You're crazy! You'll get us killed! That's far enough! Come back here!"

I was surprised to hear in my voice the yapping impotence of a school teacher or parent. But, still, I followed him and, after a few heartbeats, found myself lying beside him, right at the runway's edge, where the tarmac flaked forlornly into grass, and you realised how thin everything was, just pasted onto the surface of a black sphere. On either side of us, lights shone fiercely and emitted a low humming sound. Otherwise, there was an unreal stillness, and peace.

"We should go back," I said.

He took something out of his pocket: a small bottle with a gold top and a gold label. Wordlessly, he held it towards me.

"What is it?" I said.

He held the label forward. Now I knew what I'd smelt on him earlier, that sour dangerous ugly smell: whisky.

"Where did you get it? Your father?"

"No. I nicked it. Here."

He shook the bottle at me.

"No," I said.

He shrugged, and swigged. Then swigged again.

For a while we lay still. The silence amazed and disconcerted me. Far off, by the airport buildings, we saw the sleek gleaming planes waiting in rows. I expected at any moment a security vehicle to come weltering towards us.

At that moment, the more generalised fear of discovery led to another more pressing one. I realised what I had done. When I had left my bedroom a few minutes earlier – startled at the knock on the door, my mother's voice – I had left my copy of *Mayfair* open on the desk in the plume of lamp light. For all I knew, at that very moment, my parents might be staring into the eyes, and the breasts – and God knows what else – of Belle on her swing ...

"I've got to go back," I said. "Robert, I've *got* to go back."

"You can't go back," he said. "It's too late."

"What do you mean, 'too late'?"

Then I noticed that his gaze had become transfixed at something over my shoulder. With a feeling of mounting dread, I turned to see what he saw. It was coming in from the west, that familiar constellation seeming to hang suspended in the darkness.

"A Jumbo," was all he said.

We both watched in silence as its lights lifted and fell, balancing and re-balancing about a central pivot: it was lining itself up for the runway.

"Robert, I'll stay for that, *then* go," I said, realising how puny and infantile my compromise sounded.

But he couldn't hear me now. The sound had hit us: that distinctive plangent whine, that bottomless roar. And then, as it passed over the fence, the Jumbo seemed suddenly to rear *upwards*, a shining apparition, the whole machine caught in the up-reach of light, the expressionless imperious cockpit, the flaps lifting and falling with nervous readjustments, the markings and lights of the runway reflected in its silver underside, the tyres hanging down, the streams of exhaust forming whorls behind, like angel's wings.

Robert leapt up. I knew instantly what he was going to do. I tried to grab his leg but he pulled free of me and I found myself holding what was left of him: his shoe. I screamed after him but it was too late. He ran – lopsidedly scampering, hopping, in his single shoe – into the centre of the runway, aiming the flashlight towards the oncoming plane. I saw it swoop directly over him and saw him leap up at it and then fall to the ground and a moment later the plane touched down with twin puffs of smoke and we heard its engines go into reverse thrust and for a moment it was like an earthquake had hit us and Robert was jumping up and down and screaming into the air, "I touched it! I touched it!"

Then, something else happened. There was an explosion. The plane exploded. It turned off the runway far too fast, like a toy, and one wing ploughed into the ground and was pulled clean off, sending it lurching sideways while the other leapt skywards. There were more explosions which lit the grass for a moment so that every blade had a tiny shadow and then we saw the plane burning and I knew immediately, with a savage boy's instinct, that no one would survive.

I stood, frozen, hands clasped on either side of my head. I could see Robert's silhouette against the wild gold flames. For a while he stood entirely still, watching the plane, now on its side, burning. The fire crept on its surface like a liquid. There were no people running, or crawling. And for a while, nothing else happened, except the plane burning, and the people inside it burning.

Then we ran like we had never ran before, we ran to the hole in the fence and back to the village. Already some people had come out of their houses having heard the explosion; they had spilled out of the pub onto the green and were standing there with their pints and cigarettes.

By the side of the road, Robert collapsed, and put his head in his hands. I stood beside him. I was still holding his shoe, the sole caked with mud. I let it fall.

"I *touched* it," he said, with a stifled cry.

"You were nowhere near," I said, thinking he would want to be freed of any blame. I put an arm over his shoulder. It was the first time I had ever touched him. "It was nothing to do with you."

He pushed me violently away, and shouted, with joy, "I *touched* it! You saw me! I made it crash! It was me!"

There was something exultant, even demonic, in him: his eyes gleamed in the darkness. Then he lifted his head and looked back in the direction of the airport. I turned my gaze to follow his. Black smoke was creeping towards us through the trees, as if the darkness itself had taken form and was coming to get us. Something beyond boiled and roared. Then I heard the first wail of sirens.

# Getting to Know You

Yes, I remember Gunnersbury. I remember how, one afternoon of heat, we pulled into the station and the doors of our train opened to admit a wall of sheer sound: the homogeneous chirrup of school children. Adult conversation tends to ebb and flow and constantly check itself, like the adult mind; children's talk, in contrast, is constant and happy as birdsong. A modern novelist once described the sound of a school playground as 'safe panic'. The children, prim in their racing-green jackets and toggled caps, were standing on the platform in decorous pairs and I noticed, with a movement of tenderness, that they were, uniformly, holding hands. Although this uniformity suggested compliance to an instruction, still, it touched me terribly. I love the company of children and so felt some disappointment when they didn't board my train but instead were marshalled to the other platform, from which, I supposed, they must have been catching the next District Line train in the opposite direction, off to some tedious museum, no doubt, or exciting zoo, or to marvel at the execution block in the Tower of London with the great axe beside it – which is the only thing I remember about it from my own school visit, so many years ago now.

A young lady, perhaps in her early twenties, boarded my train and sat directly opposite me. I made a note of this because the train was all but empty and she could have sat anywhere she liked. We must be grateful in later life, I suppose, for not being absolutely hideous to our fellow human beings, or even remotely sinister. But it is only a natural instinct – a safety mechanism, perhaps – to position oneself, in a closed container like a train, as far from any other human being as is technically possible: in an empty train, to seat oneself next to another would invite suspicion, even hostility. Think of the most salient example of this spatial discretion: the public lavatory and the mathematical precision with which one – and I refer here to the unfortunate male of the species – selects a urinal, utilising an ever diminishing golden mean to avoid the roving eye, knowing wink or suggestive nudge. I tend, myself, towards the fragrant cubicle where you find, circumscribed in marker pen and often with such chaste precision, the genitalia of either gender, and the telephone numbers where they might, conveniently, and for a modest price, be obtained.

But this young lady, I should say, had, of her own volition, deliberately elected to sit directly opposite me. I felt as if I had been singled out, *chosen* in some way, and I watched her with renewed interest. I am always keen to make new friends; strangers, after all, as the adage goes, are only friends you haven't met. Sometimes I would play this game with my fellow travellers: I would watch them intently until they looked back, and then I would grin broadly, with great creases in my face, revealing my gold front tooth. Now I watched this particular young lady as she crossed her legs – shapely lithe powerful legs, too, in jeans, with a glimpse of brown ankle and the tiniest mark of a tattoo, just there, which looked like an ancient Eastern character – and removed a book from her bag. I always take a keen interest in other people's reading matter and have, on occasions, even seen people reading one of my trifling books of light verse, in the manner of Arthur Somerset, which I have self-published over the years. The temptation is to ask them what they think and then to reveal my identity with a flourish – "there, you see, that's *me* on the back, with the gold tooth, and my little biography!" – but I never do.

You can tell so much about a person by what they are reading; at least, you can tell the important things. But then we must remember that people read books on trains for three reasons: to be immersed *in* them, to publicise their erudition or originality *by* them, and to hide *behind* them. Her book was called *A Short Introduction to Poker Hands* which disappointed me: it seemed an unlikely choice for a young lady. Did she lead a dissolute lifestyle in the gambling rooms? She turned to a page about half way through, the corner of which, I noted, had been folded down to mark her place. On this page I could see, in black and white, illustrations of playing cards laid out in a sample 'hand'. She studied it with a frown of concentration. On the upper half of her body she wore a scruffy black 'bomber jacket' with a complicated assortment of pockets, fasteners and togs. Around her wrist, in addition to a number of colourful bangles, she was wearing a discreetly expensive watch. I could not catch its make but guessed it must be a Chopard, of which I have a sizeable collection at home. Her hair was black and short-cropped, revealing pleasant ears, which she then concealed, even as I watched, behind a pair of improbably large headphones, from which, a moment later, I heard the distracting *tsk-tsk* of her popular music. It always amazes me that the youth of today need to be entertained on so many levels and at the same time.

All along the carriage with its twin rows of orange nooses lay discarded copies of *Metro* in various states of disrepair. I picked one up, buttock-imprinted, from the seat beside me. The headline concerned the apparently random 'brutal' – it's always 'brutal' – murder of a young man the day before in Stratford, East London. There was a picture of him, grinning, on the front cover – clearly oblivious to his destiny – with an arrogant provoking twist to his mouth and an air of shambolic dissolution about him, typical of modern youth, I'd say. Frankly, he looked like a nasty piece of work: you'd think they could have chosen a more sympathetic picture of the murdered man. The story read: 'Ryan Smith (21), from Edmonton, North London, had lived with his girlfriend for two years, and it had been their dream to marry and have children together. Ryan had been successfully attending an NVQ City & Guilds course in plumbing, and had been a hugely popular figure in Edmonton. His parents were both said to be "heartbroken".' I felt I knew him, too well. 'Police are looking for a man seen running from the scene of the crime,' the report went on, in less flowery language, 'described as being white, of average height and build'. Well, it could be *me* then: *I'm* white, of average height and build. How ridiculous. You might as well say, 'police are looking for a man seen running from the scene, with two legs.'

After the brisk beeping the doors slid with a rumble of stage flats and the train, producing an escalating whine – like something out of vintage science fiction – moved off with a dangerous over-acceleration which you felt in the pit of your stomach. I threw my newspaper aside, as if tired of the world's futile and indiscriminate violence. The young lady glanced at me for the first time, and for a moment – which held so much fragile promise, and caused my heart to swoop, as if with a magnetic impulse towards her – our eyes met, and I saw that hers were a seraphic blue, the blue you might see folded into the vestments of the Virgin at the foot of a Renaissance crucifixion. Although her manner was outwardly confident, even, perhaps, a little confrontational – the way, for instance, she had sat herself down directly opposite me, as if daring me to look at her – there was also in her a sort of wariness, a vigilance, which you see so often in people in cities. They cower a little, as if expecting at any moment a terrible finishing blow to the back of the head.

At that moment, the conductor – they call them 'On-Board Supervisors' or some such nonsense – walked past in his bright orange waistcoat, whistling something from Rodgers and Hammerstein ("Getting to know you. Getting to know all about you"). The interruption of his whistle acted as a catalyst to my developing relationship with my young lady and we exchanged a brief smile on the strength of it. It was as if the florid absurdity of the man's whistling, and the inappropriateness of his cheerfulness on this dull commuter's day, had cemented our bond of normality. I realised now the inevitability that something should pass between us. Now that we had, as it were, acknowledged the other's objective reality, this reality became something we could only ignore by an imposition of will, whose absence was itself a sort of presence, as much a passenger on the train as we were.

Finally, she started it. She looked suddenly anxious. "Excuse me," she said, removing her headphones. "Is this the Overground or the Underground?"

It was so rarely that anyone initiated a conversation with me that I had to collect my thoughts and my very strong feelings for a moment. "The Overground," I said.

"Thank you," she said, thinking that was to be the limit of our intercourse, and she started raising her headphones towards her perfect little ears with their pink lobules, like scallops. I imagined, in a sudden transport of sensuality, pressing their fleshy resistance between my fingers.

"The Overground is orange," I told her.

"I'm sorry?" she said, angling her head.

"You needn't apologise," I said. "Orange is the corporate colour of the Overground network. Its other distinction is that it has interconnected carriages, unlike the Underground where, at least in its older rolling stock, the carriages are separated by doors. But the Overground runs on the same rails as the Underground: they share the same gauge." I made this last statement significantly. She looked at me, baffled, the headphones still detained, but she was not, I suspected, entirely un-amused by my surfeit of information; particular this last point relating to the gauge, which I always stressed. At worst, she thought me a harmless crank. "The trains follow the same route," I continued, encouraged by her incipient smile, and a nervous twitch in her left eye, "at least for part of their journey. They part company at Gunnersbury. Whereupon the Underground heads towards Upminster, and the Overground makes its way, eventually, to Stratford. They have different destinations."

I almost used the word 'destinies'.

"Thank you," she said. "And does *this* train go to Kew?"

"Indeed," I said. I had, for a long time, found many alternatives for 'yes' but none for 'no'. "If you mean Kew *Gardens*. Kew *Bridge* station is on the other line and is on the north side of the Thames. Kew Gardens is the next stop."

"Thank you," she said.

"The botanical gardens at Kew were founded in the 18th-century," I began. "They contain the world's largest collection of plant specimens. Comprising 101 hectares of gardens and botanical glasshouses … "

At that moment the train began passing over the Thames with a hollow rattle, and, although I had witnessed the beginnings of fascination in her eyes, I had to bring my discourse to an abrupt conclusion.

Ah, Old Father Thames! How does it go? 'What does he know? What does he care? Nothing for you or me. Old Father Thames keeps rolling along, down to the mighty sea … ' Being a keen observer of human behaviour, I have often noticed, on my regular journeys on this route, how people tend to abandon their reading matter – even if their reading matter is the floor or the posters for West End shows which litter the walls – to gaze out at Old Father Thames in all his different moods and lights: sometimes bright, silver and quivering, like mutating foil; at others, dun, khaki. I have marked a sort of dreaminess pass over their countenances at this time, as if they had undergone some form of transformation and the river had awakened some atavistic memory of being water dwellers, before, being driven by curiosity and ambition, we made the tactical error of crawling out onto dry land, exchanging the buoyancy of water for the crushing weight of gravity. But my young lady had reburied herself in her Poker book, with her headphones back on: she was not remotely interested in the scenery, any more than she was in the history of Kew Gardens, or *me*, and I found myself despising her for it, and I decided there and then that I would no longer attempt to engage her in conversation since she clearly had no intention of revealing anything of any importance to me. In truth, I felt extremely angry, and I made my decision.

Shortly we were passing behind the back gardens of the large villas of Kew. I have always found back gardens infinitely more interesting than front gardens, and trains, uniquely, provide an excellent means for admiring them. Front gardens are, most often, little more than pieces of propaganda or publicity, a 'joyous shot at what things ought to be.' Observe their careful paving and privet, the ornamental wheelbarrow. They tend towards the prim and formal, like a letterhead. They are an introduction; they have all the emptiness – and yet the promise – of a handshake between strangers. You only shake hands with people you hate, a friend once observed. I reflected upon this and found it to be true: you shake hands with politicians, work-colleagues, clergymen after sermons and the Master who has just caned you. Yes, front gardens are very much like handshakes. But back gardens, by contrast – with their paraphernalia of paddling pools, slides, gazebos, garden furniture, vegetable patches, compost heaps, deep trenches – are like bear hugs in comparison. They reveal so much more. Back gardens are *honest.*

We pulled into Kew Gardens. My young lady stood up.

"Goodbye," she said.

I said nothing; instead, I displayed to her, through a salivated and puling grin, my single gold tooth. Then, after waiting a couple of seconds, I followed her out of the train, and the doors, with their dark rumble of thunder, closed behind me.


The next morning, the train was less busy than usual. I normally catch the 9.36 from Richmond to Stratford. This gets me into Stratford at about 10.41. I never travel in rush hour, if I can help it. After rush hour, people seem happier, more knowable, with all the commuters safely locked up in their offices and factories. You'll see little groups of widowed ladies off on some foray or other, perhaps to see an exhibition at the V&A and to lunch afterwards at the latest fashionable bistro on Beauchamp Place; families out for a daytrip, the young ones with their little button noses pressed against the hoary glass; the occasional wary tourist, wishing they'd gone the scenic route, and beginning to suspect they may have got the wrong Stratford.

I picked up that morning's *Metro* and emitted a self-congratulatory

"Hah!" which earned some censorious glances from my fellow passengers.

There she was – a lovely picture of her – and right there! on the front page! I read her details with my customary thirst, and an immense gratitude. Katherine Ashmore (26), 'had been a hugely popular student at Imperial College, where she had been studying for a post-graduate degree in Mathematics, specialising in Probability Theory. A seasoned traveller – who had recently spent a year in Borneo – she had for the last six months shared a flat in Camden with her boyfriend, who was also a student at Imperial, and who was said to be 'heartbroken' at the news. A police spokeswoman said there appeared to have been no witnesses to the brutal murder yesterday, just behind Kew Gardens station, and which appeared to be completely motiveless.' 'Brutal' again: these hacks have such a limited lexicon when describing the infinitely varied act of murder, its unique intimacy. And yet I felt as if I knew my young lady so much better now: her name, her age, her occupation, her hobbies and interests, and so forth. Even her sexual orientation. Now, she was like an old friend to me, and I would never forget her.

But what they didn't tell you was the manner in which Katherine Ashmore (26) had been dispatched, so quickly, so soundlessly, with a single cut from behind and a gentle deposition down the embankment. I am always very respectful of my new friends and ensure that all of their clothing is neatly arranged, as it was in this case, so that it might appear that she was merely sleeping there, on a bank 'where the wild thyme blows.' For Katherine Ashmore (26), I placed coloured leaves about her head with those lovely ears, like a revetment, and uttered a short prayer. There is a dignity in this kind of ceremonial. In the beautiful words of Nahum Tate which close Dido's tragic tale: 'With drooping wings you Cupids come, to scatter roses on her tomb. Soft and gentle as her heart, keep her watch, and never part.' Funnily enough, I *did* keep her watch. And when I got home that evening, I pasted her story into my album, just below that of Ryan Smith's (21), to join the dozens in my safe-keeping. I keep the album in my study, to peruse when I'm feeling lonely. It is bound in purple morocco by Bayntun of Bath and has 'Old Friends' stamped in gilt on its cover.

# The Last Shot

All the way from Victoria the elderly gentleman had shared our compartment, watching the crawl of south London's terraces and chimneypots with a wistful attentiveness which would only have been possible in a foreigner. When the train plunged into the tunnel under the North Downs the abruptly black window presented a snapshot of the three of us in its reflection, like a composition, and for a while I watched the image of him, and wondered where he was from, and where he was going, and why. Then, with daylight switched suddenly back on, we passed over the gridlocked girdle of the M25, symbolically revoking the big city, only for the landscape to resume its tired conversation with commerce, just when you'd hoped for something better. Unlike our companion, whose silence transmitted something ineffably benign, I had long been neutered to the barrenness of the area around Gatwick, as if I could no longer really see it: the lorry parks, the trading estates, the warehouses, the gull-plagued landfill, the profusion of new red houses sprawling over the low hills. This had once been the beginning of the ancient Wealden forest which had filled the home-sick centurion with dread: *Anderida*. Here and there you'd see the remnants of a distant rural past in an ancient hedgerow, an arthritic oak or a half-timbered farmhouse, all cowering under the pylons which strode the land like stretcher bearers.

It wasn't until an hour later, long after our train had diverted from the main line, that there was anything to look at or worthy of a photograph. Arundel. I always made a point of indicating the view to Helen (my wife, who was the third person in the compartment) despite the fact that we'd passed it countless times before. If this view was the property of anyone's, it was hers, not mine, to share. She had been born and grown up not far from here, in a Georgian house which was not quite a farm, yet not quite a Manor, in that architectural hybrid typical of Sussex, a county which, largely, eschewed the grand gesture for the homely and picturesque. Across the meadows, from where the cattle didn't bother looking up from their vegan brunch, the castle was mirrored in the river and, to its left, the prickly apse of the Cathedral reared atop the little hill. It was like a French medieval fortified hill town, but with a Waitrose.

Presented with the notable view, he chose, at last, to speak. "That's some castle," he said. His accent confirmed his nationality which his *Fodor's Guide* and Burberry overcoat had already led me to suspect: we had spent the last hour and a half in the company of an American. He took a camera out of his United Airlines bag, a big old-fashioned Leica, and photographed the view.

"It's fake," I said.

"Excuse me?" he said, cupping his hand behind his ear. "I'm afraid you'll have to speak up, sir: my ears are bad."

It seemed strange to be called 'sir' by a man who was almost certainly twice my age. He had ashen translucent skin, like papyrus, and sad watery colourless eyes; his neck hung in loose folds.

"It's fake," I confirmed, and felt Helen grow cold beside me. "A stage set. A romantic fantasy. The whole thing was built in the 19th-century. The Cathedral. Even most of the castle."

The American didn't seem to see what was wrong with that. "Well," he said, "it's mighty pretty, whatever it is."

Helen, as usual, apologized on my behalf. "I'm sorry about my husband," she said. "He has negativity issues."

The American held up his hand. "Not a problem, mam," he said. "I'm very grateful for the information."

The bubble of our silence was burst and so could no longer be endured. Silence, when framed by sound, soon becomes intolerable. Now we had to do the introductions. He was Hal from Milwaukee, he told us, adding, "Bear Country." We shook hands.

My wife said, "And what brings you to England, Hal? Are you here on vacation?" This first-name thing, and the easy appropriation of an Americanism, were both typical of her: she was, after all, a 'marriage

167

counsellor' (ironically). She was used to finding the right level, the right word, for any eventuality.

"Kinda, I guess," said Hal. Here was an idiomatic American direct from Central Casting: he should have been sitting on a rocking chair, smoking a pipe on some southern veranda while the crickets chattered. He was Grandpa from *The Waltons*; he was that man who drove a lawnmower halfway across America to see his estranged and dying brother. "I guess you could say that I'm here on a ... well, a kinda pilgrimage."

"A pilgrimage?" said my wife, who I knew would be thinking of Chaucer.

My heart sank. A 'pilgrimage'. He was a Bible-belt nutter. I could say goodbye to my *London Review of Books* which lay unread on the seat beside me, still in its plastic sheath.

"I better explain," said Hal, "before you think I'm some kinda crazy person. My wife – Hilda – she was born in Chichester." He pronounced the first syllable to rhyme with 'eye' but I remained resolutely straight-faced. "When she was twenty her family emigrated to Canada. I was working out in British Columbia at the time – I was in the logging business back then – and, well, I guess we fell in love and we got married and had three beautiful children and I was blessed with fifty-three years of a very happy marriage. And then, last year, she got this cancer, and she passed away very quickly – you know, it eats you away, until there's nothing left – and, I don't mind saying to you good folks, it was a great shock to me" – his voice quavered momentarily, buoyant on the helium of grief, but he got it back – "and so in a way it was a relief when she passed, because I couldn't have watched her suffer, I couldn't have done that, Helen."

Helen, transfixed by the use of her name, reached across and touched his leg. "You *poor* thing," she said, and I noticed, with horror, that her eyes, in the sunlight, had filled with tears: the effect produced wasn't unlike a rainbow.

"So, now," continued Hal, squeezing her hand back, "what I'm doing is coming to visit the place she grew up all those years back. We never did make it across the pond when she was alive. That's what you call it, isn't it? 'The pond'? There was always a reason to put it off, you know how it is. And so we put it off and put it off until it was too late, until she was too ill to travel ..." He glanced at his camera. "And on the way, I'm taking some photographs of my journey and when I get home I figured I'd put them into one of those big albums and then one day the grandchildren will get mightily bored looking at them."

We laughed with that exaggerated laughter which comes to relieve solemnity.

"I think that's a beautiful idea," said Helen. "And I'm sure they won't be even slightly bored, Hal."

"Well, I guess it's good to have a record of this thing. I've been taking some photos around London and the hotel I'm in. I guess I figured it would be good for the grandkids to see where their old Grandpop Hal 'hung out' when he was in England, and where their old grandmom was from all those years ago."

"Let me take *your* picture," said Helen.

"My picture?" said Hal. "Why would I want a picture of my ugly old mug?"

She grabbed his camera and, before he could protest, she took him.

"Oh, you're like Hilda, I can see that," he laughed, taking the camera back. "The feisty type, but in a good way. In fact, you even look a little like her, when she was your age."

I didn't particularly want to hear this. "Chichester's interesting," I said, pronouncing it correctly. "Of course the Cathedral is 'worth a detour' but it's not one of the great English Cathedrals."

"Always negative," said Helen, to Hal. "He never has anything good to say about anything."

"I was going to say," I said, "that the spire collapsed in the 19th-century ..."

"See?" said Helen. "'The spire collapsed'."

"... *let me finish* ... and they rebuilt it even taller and more pointy than the first one. Is what I was going to say. There. Is that positive enough for you?"

Helen gave Hal a look of forbearance, as if they already had me in common: their foe.

"Now I'd very much like to take *your* picture," said Hal.

Immediately, my body clenched in revolt. I hated being photographed. And I particularly hated being photographed with my wife. It was as if I didn't want to be seen with her, caught in the camera's propaganda.

"Both of us?" I said.

"Of course both of you!" laughed Hal. He picked up his old camera and pointed it at us. "Smile!" he said.

We moved, awkwardly, together, smiled, and even held hands, for his sake. He captured us.


He was to leave the train at Chichester. We were going on a few more stops to Southbourne, which was the nearest station to where Helen's parents lived. Already, I could feel that unnatural weight that this sort of parting has: our acquaintance too short to be worth prolonging with an arrangement, yet too poignant to be relinquished with a mere 'see you'.

As we pulled into his station, Hal stood. "Well," he said, "I mightily enjoyed meeting you folks. I guess this is my stop. You look after yourselves now."

He opened the door and stepped onto the platform. Then he raised his hand, and I sensed he was about to say something valedictory, even sentimental. I knew what these Americans were like.

"Goodbye Hal," I said, cheerily. "Don't miss the Pallant House Gallery!"

"Take care," said Helen.

While the train waited, and panted, Hal leant back in towards us, and said, almost confidentially, "Love each other. While you have time.

Will you do that for me? will you love each other, for old Hal?"

An old-fashioned whistle sounded, an emblem of departure. Last chances. Hal slammed the door and mouthed his wise words about love again. At last, the train moved off, and we watched him, one arm raised in a salute, slide into our past.

Then I saw what had happened. I pointed at the seat opposite.

"Oh shit," said my wife.

His camera was sitting on the baking seat, its shuttered lens accusing us of something.

There was nothing that we could do, immediately. Certainly the situation didn't merit pulling the emergency cord. We agreed that we would hand the camera into Lost Property at Southbourne. Helen suggested going back to Chichester and trying to find him. I said this was a ridiculous idea. We were already late for lunch and how would we find Hal in a place like Chichester? He could be anywhere.

We sat in silence. I thought to myself: this marriage is over.

At Southbourne the station office was closed. But now Helen was absolutely determined that we should do something. I saw her father sitting in his car, one of those surprisingly ordinary cars that posh people have. When you might expect an old Bentley, they actually have a brand new Nissan, smelling of plastic. Helen sat in the front beside him; I sat, automatically, in the back. In the car's abrupt muffled enclosure, Mr Monckton glanced at me in the mirror. I always thought I detected wariness in his eyes; distrust even.

"Good journey down?" he said, nicely enough.

"Yes thank you," I said, adding the name he insisted I use instead of the more natural 'Mr Monckton': "William."

Helen, breathlessly, told him about Hal, and showed him the camera, and told him of all the photographs he'd taken on his visit. "All his memories are there," she said. "He was going to make an album for his grandchildren. There's no way of getting in touch with him, unless," she implored her father now, by tugging at his arm, "we go back into Chichester and see if we can find him, can we?"

"We *can't* do that," I said. I wanted my gin and tonic.

"Chris is right," said Mr Monckton. Starting the car, he went on, "I've got an idea. You said he took some pictures of his hotel in London? Let's take the film into SupaSnaps in Southbourne and get it developed. They can do it in ten minutes, if you pay a bit more. If we can find out what hotel he's staying in from his pictures, we may be able to contact him that way. Otherwise we have nothing to go on apart from the name Hal and the fact that he's from Milwaukee, and I imagine, I don't know why, that there are quite a few Hals in Milwaukee."

"Brilliant plan, Mr Monckton," I said, and seemed to smell a saving whiff of juniper.

"Do call me William," said Mr Monckton.


After we had had the photos developed, we drove for ten minutes out of the town and into open country. Like a lot of posh people, the Moncktons lived *near* somewhere rather than actually *in* somewhere. The second line of their address, after the name of the house, was 'Near Southbourne' and it was this very imprecision which seemed to imply something nearly territorial, a custodianship of land.

We turned off the lane and passed through the familiar sandstone gates surmounted by two alert heraldic stone eagles. This arrival, which we had made many times before, always seemed to me to have a filmic quality about it, and as the car crunched along the gravel drive, lined with topiary, and the façade of the house came into view, I had my usual grounds for unease. I had grown up in a semi on a housing estate in a modern landscape that consisted entirely of rectangles: lawns, picture-windows, drives, caravans. Coming here always made me feel as if I might be suspected of marrying Helen only for my own advancement, so that I might indulge in the experience of being driven along a gravel driveway just like this.

Mrs Monckton was waiting with the gin and tonics and a hug. I liked Helen's mother much more than I liked her daughter. In the kitchen, with its vast black Aga, there was the smell of roasting chicken. Their black retriever came and wet-nosed me and whipped me with his powerful tail. I began to see the possibility of deliverance.

Helen told her mother about Hal and the photographs.

"Shall we look at them now?" said Mrs Monckton, adding as a caveat to her intrigue, "although it does seem shamefully voyeuristic."

"Yes," I said, and added, as an aside to my wife, encouraged into recklessness by my drink, "I hope there's not lots of pictures of little boys' winkies."

"Why on earth did you say *that*?" said Helen. "What is the point of saying something like that?"

"Come on now, you two," said Mrs Monckton. "Don't start, please. We're going to have a nice peaceful happy lunch and afternoon together, aren't we? Aren't we?"

"Try telling *him* that," said Helen.

Mr Monckton took out the wallet from SupaSnaps. It still had a chemical smell. Inside, there were only four photographs, as the man in the shop had said.

"Not much to go on," I said.

"It must have been a new film," said Mr Monckton, already sensing disappointment.

We gathered around to look. The first picture was a mystery and we observed it in a puzzled silence. It appeared to have been taken on the moon. Was Hal an astronaut? Bursting over the curved horizon was an explosion of light. On closer inspection we saw that the horizon was, in fact, a man's hand, almost certainly Hal's. The explosion of light was a flash in a mirror behind it and you could see the cord for the light.

"He probably took that by accident in his hotel room," said Helen. "He must have started a new film for his Chichester trip, bless him."

The second picture was of a distant Arundel, blurred into a fairy tale.

We looked at it without comment until Mrs Monckton said, "That's Arundel, isn't it?"

"Yes," said Helen. "Christopher insisted on telling him it was all fake."

"It *is* all fake," I said.

"For Christ's sake," said Helen, under her breath.

"*Stop it*," commanded Mrs Monckton.

The third photograph was of Hal, sitting on the train, smiling.

"That's Hal," said Helen.

"He's *exactly* as I imagined him," said Mrs Monckton.

"Hal from Milwaukee," I said, in an exaggerated American accent, "'Bear Country'!"

"He didn't talk anything like that," said Helen. "Why are you being so negative about him? You did nothing but mock him the whole train journey. It was completely embarrassing. I felt ashamed to be English."

"That is absolute rubbish," I said.

"I do wish you two would stop fighting," said Mrs Monckton, wearily.

I sometimes detected in her endless conciliation a degree of maternal anxiety, as if she might take her daughter to one side and say, 'Is everything all right between you and Christopher?'

"Let's look at the last one," she said, and I felt her hand gently pressing on my shoulder, as if she wanted to gently direct me on a new course.

We stood for a long while, staring at it. The room's silence had the air of things falling into place. Wordlessly, with the picture before us, I looked across at Helen and felt a wave of grief go through me which was so intense, so unhinging, that I had to gulp at my drink to assuage it. She returned my look with a blankness which was, I felt, touched with a kind of entreaty; as if she, too, might want to salvage something from our unhappiness. It was, I realised, the first time we had looked into each other's eyes for a long time, perhaps even years.

Then we both turned back to the last photograph on the table, a photograph in which a loving couple – holding hands, sitting happily together in a train one bright ordinary summer's afternoon – smiled at a stranger they would never see again.

## Domestic Bliss

Nothing happens here. Or nearly nothing.

At dawn and midday they bring down the machine with its food tubes, and again at six. At seven, Dr Webb comes with my medication.

Apart from that – nothing.

It was eggs again for dinner today. It's always eggs. Eggs, eggs, eggs. Boiled, fried, scrambled or poached. I asked for them raw but they refused me.

It is dark here. I feel trapped. The walls of my cell contract. I hear only my own blood pumped by my heart's engine, beating the old tattoo: me, me, me.

It is as if I have been here for an eternity. I want to get *out* into the world, to be my own man again.

How long am I to be detained here against my will? They say it could be as long as nine months. I say, in that case, kill me, smother me with a pillow. Smother me with kindness.

Sometimes I hear a man howling in the next cell, like an animal, or chattering like a monkey: the same meaningless word, over and over. They say he lost his wife. And sometimes a hatch opens in the door and an eye appears at it. It swivels from left to right. Then the hatch slams shut. Am I now some circus freak to be gawped at? One day, I shall take that eye out with a fork; then my own.

I would like to know what crime I have committed to warrant this imprisonment. Have I killed anyone? No. Except perhaps myself. Have I wronged anyone? No. The same applies. Have I broken any laws? None that I am aware of, or recognise.

Counsel for the Prosecution, ladies and gentleman of the jury, I humbly submit my plea: my crime is that I love my mother. Seriously. That's it. I love my mother. You'll say, who doesn't? and I would concur. If loving your mother is a crime, I plead guilty! And yet we all love our mothers, so how can we all be guilty of the same crime? I maintain we can't, Your Honour. The Court may adjourn! Case dismissed!

As if.

I shall consider the word mother. Or, mummy. Mummy's better. Mummy's all in the mouth, wholly labial. It is the noise you make at the teat, murmuring for more; it is the sound of nurture and nourishment. Whereas daddy's thin, tinny and tongue-tied, kept for repetition on the palate where it trips and rattles like a faulty part.

You can always count on a mummy's boy for a fancy prose style.

What is 'love'?

In my present solitary confinement I have had a long time to ponder that vexing question I can tell you. My O.E.D. pussy-foots around a definition without ever committing itself. To the word 'love' it allows *eleven* senses (including 'nothing' in tennis) but two will do for mummy and me. In its first sense, I persist, in spite of everything: that is, with that 'warm affection, attachment, liking or fondness'; but in its second, I glory: 'Sexual affection or passion or desire, relation between sweethearts'. I shall always be mummy's little sweetheart.

Don't expect any Freud-egg couch-potato psycho-babble clap-trap from me. Save that for Dr Webb and her eyebrow-raising note-taking ninnies. For I know why I love my mother even if a whole army of men in white coats can't see the remotest joy in her little pink ankles. And I can tell you this: it has *nothing to do with my father* (the italics are mine).

Nothing.

No, the reason I love my mother is quite simple and I shall state it plainly: she's a stunner, a babe, a bit of all right, a ten-out-of-tenner, a real humdinger, a jaw-dropper, a foxy-lady, a bomb-shell, a glamour-puss, a cutie-pie, a femme-fatale, sex-on-legs, drop-dead gorgeous, my very own yummy mummy, a mother I'd like to … and, yes, once she *was* my succubus.

Therein lies our tragedy, hers and mine.

And perhaps my father's too. Perhaps my father's too.


To look at, you'd think she was in her early forties rather than her late sixties. Once, a waiter, wielding an enormous pepper-grinder, mistook her for my girlfriend! Another time, she was wolf-whistled in the street by some builders, and I felt so proud of her on my arm as I marched, cock-sure, beside her, her proud little soldier.

She knows how to use her body and the ornaments of her gender. Her figure has lost none of its full and sculptural shapeliness; still, it buds with the propensity for motherhood. Some mothers, as they grow older, gravitate physically towards the earth and come to resemble large earthenware pots. Not mine. Without recourse to cosmetic or surgical contrivance, she retains her vernal bloom. Her body, with its sweet and secret intersections, its passages of great lyrical beauty, is the Eden from whence I was ejected, and whence I yearn to return.


Just because you love someone doesn't mean you can't be friends. As long as I remember – which is about thirty-four years, if you include that first phase *in utero*, which I can summon as if it were yesterday (the pulse, the deep redness) – I have empathised with my mother and taken her side. There have never been between us any of those unnatural divisions which often pre-figure tragic consequences. Think of that most salient example, 'King Lear', although there it is a father and a daughter who have a falling out – over nothing – and everything falls to pieces. With me, the natural inclinations of childhood and early adolescence – 'pre-puberty' – have never withered to mere kindliness or, worse, to that doting sentimentality with which some sons treat their mothers when they obtain to middle-age. My own early inclinations have flowered and come to fruition, transforming into something worthy of a mother's love. It is precisely these feelings which Dr Webb and her cronies – not to say 'society' – consider a crime. But a crime against what? Can a crime which has no victim really be deemed a crime? If it is a crime at all, it is a crime against 'conformity', nothing more. 'Conformity' indeed: a corrupt system which imposes the same rigid template of acceptable behaviours on all of us from without, so that it is little wonder that each of us, in our innermost being, feels such a closet insurgent or so shameful and worthless an aberration. But at least the word 'conformity' has room for a suggestion of disparagement: one could hardly imagine deploying it with approval ("Oh, he's an excellent fellow – so conformist!") unlike its callow ugly sister 'normal' which approves of and, indeed, *embraces* its dullness.

People have said that my feelings are not 'normal'. What do they mean by that? Surely 'feelings' and 'instincts' have no social context? no legislature? They exist by their own 'norms'. Do they not see that the presiding deity of our viscera pre-dates the flimsy laws we've made for ourselves and yearns to overthrow them? It is the reason we can never find peace.

These same people, these habitual peddlers of 'normal': have they never loved women themselves? women who not only resemble their mothers but *are* their mothers? Have they never, being kissed goodnight at bedtime, experienced an illicit stiffening?

I must now talk briefly, and with reluctance, of my father. I do so only to present to the dis-interested reader a complete picture of my domestic arrangements, against which you must judge my whole conduct. My father was always a cold and distant figure, although one given to public affability. He was far more interested in the small manufacturing firm he managed than in his only issue. You might say, he had an issue with his issue. Sometimes I wonder why he kept me at all. Some only breed, I feel, to chide their offspring later for their own mistakes; their children become batons of guilt in a generational relay-race.

How I despised his petty commercial preoccupations. He considered himself to be at the apex of a tremendous hierarchy, which, at one time, he wanted me to take my 'natural' place in. He used that word. Did I really want to waste my life working for a company that manufactured breast pumps? The truth is that I have no innate respect or genetic pre-disposition for hierarchies; I mean, of course, those man-made ones which scaffold our frail civilisation. It is just not possible for me to reduce myself to deference towards any other human being merely because they sit behind a desk, wear a uniform, have a certain rank, drive a certain car, are of a certain age, or are my father. If he taught me anything – and he tried to teach me everything – it was only through my adroit mis-application of his example. I learnt that, if anything matters, it matters in the realm of the senses alone and not in some dreary Portakabin on a trading estate outside Nuneaton.

I saw his organ of procreation once, his *membrum virile*, his drooping proboscis in its shaggy nest of hair. It seemed to me like a despondent vole, head-hung, sightless and pink.

Who, or what, would I have been if my potential had not occupied a *particular* egg in my mother's precarious hatchery? Nothing? a woodlouse? The Queen of England? I am aware that 'being' is not a privilege granted indiscriminately or on demand, otherwise the universe would consist of nothing more than an infinite compaction of human flesh. We are rare, *chosen*, in some sense. We are elected, and, with each election, billions of others are ruled out, disallowed, consigned to the sheath's gloopy teat, its ribbed polyurethane cul-de-sac.

In this very restricted sense, my conception has been the single greatest achievement of my life, and yet it remains – o paradox of paradoxes! – something I yearn to *cancel out*.

On the whole, I would have preferred parthenogenesis. Why should sexual intercourse be necessary? I wish nothing had come between mummy and me to complicate our simple bifurcation. Her role in the whole unsavoury business of my conception was, I suspect, entirely passive; for her, I am certain, it was a marital duty to be endured. It is the idea of my father's contrasting *eagerness* which disgusts me. I often think of his buttocks clenched and pumping, his jerking spasms and stretchéd sinews. How my mother must have suffered during those interminable nights, staring up at the ceiling as he rocked to-and-fro on top of her suppliant splayed form. Our boudoirs share a wall and I have fashioned a simple but effective listening device from two plastic cups and a tube. Through this device, I am party to his night-time banter, his pigsty grunting, his sweet-nothings which become progressively more filthy and bestial. Once, at his moment of crisis, I swear he called my name, then I heard mother weeping. I wanted, so badly, to go to her but I couldn't, I just *couldn't*, don't you see? And then I think of that single plucky whip-tailed spermatozoa – my dancing partner, disguised as a miniature tadpole (although I prefer to think of it as a quaint little seahorse) – wiggling up and into her lovely velvet interior, straight to a bullseye in her clutch of eggs, puncturing the membrane of my self-contained sphere of albumen with its eager snout. *Getting in there.*

For nine months I hung swaddled in my mother's plush fabric, feasting on her warm egg-white, developing first into a twin-headed zygote, then a realistic little homunculus, wrapped like a prawn about my sucked thumb. On my expulsion, I was a scale model of me, blue-pink, amniotic, tight-fisted and shining, wailing in agoraphobic fear, tugging on the umbilical tether.

And here I am, in prison.

I now view my period of gestation with an almost intolerable nostalgia. Those first nine months were, by far, the best of my life.

After that, things started to go very badly downhill.


It is now time for me to describe my physical appearance. I should hope that, since you have proceeded thus far in my narrative, the details I am about to impart will in no way compromise your estimation of my qualities as a *human being*. So much of our philosophical debate pits the idea of the inner and the outer against each other, as if they were forever, and by their nature, in some irresolvable conflict; soul versus body; mind versus matter; above versus below; son versus father, and so on.

The overwhelming impression I give, to an outsider, is of oafish lop-sidedness. I'm an outsized lolloping thing. It means that, in streets, people tend to give me a wide berth, fearing I might barge into them or veer one way or the other unpredictably, like an out-of-control barrage balloon. My head, swollen and red, and in places split, sutured or fissured, resembles an over-ripe tomato and is far too big for my body (a nickname at school was 'space hopper') and my feet – as if out of some malign symmetrical sympathy – are far too large for my legs ('Big-foot' was another cruel taunt, which was also a reference, perhaps, to my Neanderthal-ish forehead and thick useless blunt fingers which have never played a piano). Still, at my age, I suffer from severe acne over all parts of my body, and, more troublingly, a scaly reptilian crust around the rim of my neck – a sort of ruff – which no doctor has been able to identify, let alone alleviate. I grate it sometimes, like Parmesan. When a sample was sent to a

Cambridge research laboratory – they were not told of its human origin so as not to influence their findings – they claimed that it probably came from a rare, possibly even extinct, Colombian tree lizard.

But enough. You have been very patient as I have extemporised but I trust you will hear me out and bear everything I have said in mind as I conclude by outlining the events which have led to my internment in this terrible place.

I must take you back nine months or so – since time here is unmarked I cannot be certain how much of it has passed since my detention – and to the chalet bungalow in Asphodel Mead which was, supposedly, our 'family home' but which, to me, always felt like a place of exile. My mother, my father and I were taking our usual tea. Thankfully, the television provided the conversation and mitigated the palpable tension that always existed when the three of us were together. Suddenly, my father started berating the poor record of a supplier to his company who, once again, had failed to 'deliver the goods'. In consequence, an order from Mothercare for five hundred breast pumps had been forfeited. As he prattled on with this inconsequential drivel, I happened to look across the table to find myself gazing directly into my mother's eyes, those eyes which were so radiant, so meltingly blue and lovely, not unlike those bottomless pools you read about in love poetry. In that moment, we caught each *other's* eyes and our simple *hypotenuse* (the feminine part of *hupoteino*) coalesced in the fraught space between us, bypassing *him* with its linear intention. It was as if that momentary gaze was a bolt of lightning (the thunder would follow after) and our eyes, the conductors. I knew then, in that instant, that something quite new, profound and irrevocable had come to pass in the relations between us.

My father, interrupting his complaint, and looking up from his Toadin-the-Hole, said, "What are you two grinning at all of a sudden?"

"Nothing," I said.

Mother turned to him with a fake sympathetic smile, so different from the warm inclusive glance she had lavished on me, and adroitly concealed our new secret behind an ostensible interest in my father's affairs.

"It's just *you*," she said. "You and that stupid supplier. How long have they been late with orders? And how long have you been complaining about them?"

I tried at this point to press my foot against her leg, out of solidarity, but found that, frustratingly, I couldn't reach. Although my feet are large, my legs are short; when I am sitting at the table, they do not even touch the floor. I wiggle them sometimes.

"Well," my father said, returning to his gloopy sausage and batter, "I'm sorry that you find my troubles at work a cause of mirth and merriment." Then, looking pointedly at me, he added, "Someone's got to keep this house and home together."

Things happened pretty quickly after that. After the meal, father retired as usual to the lounge, to watch more television, while mother and I did the washing up together. This shared chore was a tradition with us and had always been an opportunity for intimacy, but now it was bathed in the light of a new significance. It was, I suppose, at once the baptism of our love and, on her part, an act of contrition: she was washing *him* off her, for good. As the plates slopped in the sink, our ingenious hands lunged and leapt beneath the foaming opacity like lascivious otters.

After a while, she said, "What are you smiling at, sweetheart?"

"Private thoughts," I confided, implying with my look that they might be private thoughts about *her*. Then I said, "Mother, may I speak to you candidly, on a matter very close to my heart?"

"Of course you may, darling," she said.

"I wonder if, from now on, I might call you 'Joyce'?"

She stopped washing up and looked at me with a puzzled frown.

"Can you call me Joyce?" she said.

"Yes," I said.

"If you'd be happier and more comfortable calling me Joyce, then yes, of course."

"'Mother' makes you sound like some old maid and 'mummy' is just baby-talk. So, if you harbour no objections, I shall call you 'Joyce' from now on. Sometimes I might even abbreviate it to 'Joy'."

"Whatever you're happy with, darling," she said. "It'll take me a little while to get used to it, I imagine, but I'm sure it won't be long before it seems completely natural. And your father?"

"What of him?"

"Presumably you'll want to call him Norman?"

"No," I said. "I think I'll stick with 'father' for the time being, thank you very much."


Two days later, I asked Joyce out. I timed it perfectly. It was Mother's Day. Although I recognise that annual observance for what it is – the cynical contrivance of card manufacturers – I have always held it in a special reverence. It was the middle of the afternoon and father was at his Portakabin. Joyce and I met on the landing. Simultaneously we had emerged from two doors, she from her boudoir, I from the bathroom where I had been working at my crust with an emery-board over the toilet bowl.

"Do be careful, sweetheart," she said to me, "you're getting shavings all over the carpet. And you're *bleeding*."

"Joyce," I said, dabbing myself with a scented tissue. "As you know, today is your 'special day'."

"You're good, aren't you? You never forget."

"And this year, to celebrate, I would very much like to take you out for dinner, if you have no objection?"

"Objection? Why ever should I object? It's a lovely idea. But I don't want you going to any unwarranted expense."

"My benefits have accrued for just such an eventuality. I thought I might take you to the new Greek Restaurant down by the station, 'The Stuffed Vine Leaf.' Everyone speaks very highly of it."

"I love Greek food. You've got a date, darling. We'd love to come!"

There was, of course, a difficult pause then. I said, "I'm sorry, Joyce, but … 'we'?"

"Yes," she said. "Your father and I."

"Joyce," I said, quite sternly. "This is Mother's Day, not Father's Day. Let him take his own mother out."

"Darling, you know very well that Granny passed away five years ago. I do think he would be terribly hurt if you didn't at least ask him. He's been so worried about work recently that it might do him some good to have a nice family evening out."

At that moment, the telephone rang. Joyce answered it. It was *him*, of course, the cuckold, calling from his Portakabin. As he spoke, I pressed my ear to Joyce's downy cheek and heard everything that passed between them. Apparently he had to go to Market Harborough to sort out the problem with his pump supplier once and for all. Furthermore, he would almost certainly have to stay overnight there, at the Premier Inn. This struck me as being the single most serendipitous news of my life.

Then, to my horror, Joyce said into the telephone, "Norman? Your son would like to have a word," and she thrust the receiver into my hands, mouthing, "Ask him."

"Hello father," I said, coldly.

"Hello," he said. He could never bring himself to utter my name, still less call me 'son'.

I said, "I just wanted to let you know – so that you didn't find out later, from a third party – that I have asked Joyce out for dinner this evening and I am delighted to say that she has said yes."

"Who is 'Joyce'?" he said.

"Your wife," I said.

There was a pause before he said, warily, "Go on."

"What more do you want to know?" I said.

Again, he paused, before saying, uncertainly, "I'm not sure."

"I'm taking her to that new Greek restaurant by the railway station," I said, almost conversationally. "It looks very romantic with the candles and private booths and so on. The reviews speak highly of the moussaka and several comment that it's 'ideal for romantic couples'. Obviously, I'd have loved you to be there too but now you'll be in Market Harborough and, in addition, I need hardly point out that you are *not* my biological mother and so, for these reasons, Joyce and I will be going alone … just the two of us … Father? … Are you there? … Father?"

That damp Tuesday evening, Joyce and I were the only patrons of 'The Stuffed Vine Leaf.' We shared a candlelit booth in the window: no longer did we feel it necessary to hide our love from the world. The walls, which were daubed with whorls of white plaster, were crowded with paintings of aquamarine bays, picturesque harbours and ancient ruins, while, in the background, there was the cheerful metallic sound of a *bouzouki*: we might almost have been on Lesbos. Most of the meal was spent in a happy but contemplative silence as we gazed at each other over the table and tried to play footsy under it. I did not think things could get much better than this, until Dimitris, our waiter, came to take our order and said to me, with a nudge, "I wonder if your beautiful *young girlfriend* would care for a complimentary *ouzo* as an aperitif?"

I chose that precious moment – in which I felt that our bond had first been recognised, and, more importantly, affirmed – to reach across and ardently grasp Joyce's hands, having first taken the precaution of laying a serviette over my burgeoning loins. As above, so below; and vice versa.

Greek food was new to me and a little oily to my taste and the half-bottle of Retsina we shared, Dimitris assured us, was meant to taste like that. But we both knew it was not the food or the wine that we were there for: it was the intimate ambience and the opportunity for

Joyce and I to spend some special time together and to get to know each other better, freed from the presence of you-know-who. In our new-found freedom, we spoke, warmly, of our hopes and fears and dreams, and I began to realise just how much Joyce and I had in common, and, at the same time, how much father's constant and overbearing presence had been, up until then, only an obstruction to our intercourse. I began to consider, in that flickering booth, some means of permanently eliminating him from our affairs.

Dimitris was clearly enamoured with us and seemed inconsolable when it was time for us to leave, tempting us to linger with the delights of the sweet trolley or with a nightcap. When, at last, he brought the bill, there were two After Eight mints tucked in with it and he'd even added a smiley face beneath the total where it said 'Service Charge Not Included'. And, if I'm not mistaken, he gave me a knowing wink as he took my money away, as if he knew full well the riches and joys that lay ahead for me in the maternal bed!

Afterwards, Joyce and I walked arm in arm back towards her orange Datsun *Cherry*. She was, touchingly, wearing the fur stole I had presented to her on the occasion of her sixty-fifth birthday which she had clearly been keeping for just such an occasion as this. I had fashioned it from a fox which I had bludgeoned to death with a spade in the back garden and then flattened in my father's trouser press. It had marbles for eyes, now misplaced, which lent it an oddly indisposed hangdog expression.

"That was a lovely meal," said Joyce, squeezing my arm. "Thank you, sweetheart."

"You're more than welcome, Joyce," I said, suavely, feeling very *galante* and sophisticated to be striding along at her side. I couldn't help noticing how people stared as we came by and exchanged breathless words in our wake. Like Dimitris, they must have assumed we were two young lovers out on a first date!

We entered the narrow alleyway which would take us to the car park and it was here that I gently detained her. This, I knew, was the time and the place for my great declaration.

"Joyce," I said. Then, with greater emphasis, "Joy."

"Yes, my darling?"

"I love you," I said. "I *love* you. I've loved you ever since first I nestled within your womb, since you bore me, since I first set eyes upon you, since you held me in your arms, suckled me at the teat …"

"Goodness me, that was an awfully long time ago!"

"Joyce, I love you!"

She said, hesitantly, uncertain of our new language, "And … I love you … very … much … too."

Her reply, anticipated as it was, overwhelmed me. Of course, I had always known that Joyce shared my feelings but now that I had heard her utter those magical words, and in this heightened context, I was unprepared for the urgent passion it wrought in me. It pains me to say that, for a moment, I lost my self-control and, the next thing I knew, I was smothering her face with a hundred burning kisses, weeping and laughing at the same time in a mad ecstasy, crying out her name and then, as she staggered backwards, reeling with delight, I found her warm mouth with mine and attempted, with my tongue –

Joyce, thankfully, acted with greater restraint, showing the wisdom of her years. She already knew that we should not rush into this, however much we both wanted it; she knew we mustn't jeopardise everything by losing our heads at this early stage. With some force she pushed me back against the wall of the alleyway so that my head collided painfully with the brickwork.

"What are you *doing*? What are you *doing*?" she cried, in a transport of desire.

"I'm sorry, I'm sorry," I gasped. "I'm taking things too fast!"

"What are you talking about?" she demanded. "What are you 'taking too fast'?"

Despite the violence and the passion of her reaction – or perhaps because of it – I knew that we were now set on a course from which no one could deflect us.

When we were back at the chalet there was the inevitable anti-climax. At first Joyce and I sat in the lounge in a companionable silence, watching the television, my hand beginning to creep over the ribbed damask of the settee, sideways, like a crab, towards her thigh.

Suddenly, with a swift decisive movement, she turned the television off with the remote control and turned to face me.

"Do you want to tell me what happened earlier this evening?" she said, gravely.

"How can mere words, Joyce, ever hope to grasp the ineffable?"

"I'm not going to tell your father. I think it's best he doesn't know, for now …"

"Yes. He'd only get jealous. I don't want him getting involved, Joyce. He needn't know about anything, just yet. We must choose our moment carefully."

After a pause, she said, "'*Jealous*'?"

"Obviously he'll have to know at some point," I said, feeling all at once very calm, controlled and clear-headed, "but it's not a priority. The priority right now must be *us*. You and me. That's what we must concentrate on now. There may even be the possibility, I have been thinking, of removing him from the equation altogether, if you get my drift." I gently drew a line across my throat. "No questions asked."

She said, "You're talking very … strangely and I'm not sure I altogether like it. It's making me extremely uncomfortable."

"Then let's not talk," I said, and I hushed her by placing my thick thumb on her lips, knowing that she might become over-emotional again.

"But I think we *should* talk," she said, taking my hand firmly away and replacing it on the settee, "so that I can try to … *understand*, to make sense of …"

"There'll be plenty of time for us to talk in the future," I said. "Joyce, I share …"

"'*Future*'?' *What* … 'future'? What do you mean by 'the future'?"

I had to close my eyes for a moment of forbearance, before continuing, "… I share all your feelings, Joyce. We both know we can't go on *hiding* things anymore, we can't go on … *pretending*."

"'Hiding' what?" she said. "'Pretending' what? I don't understand. You're frightening me now."

"I know," I said. "It *is* frightening! It is! It's bound to be, at first."

"But what is? what is it that you're talking about? I feel like you're talking about something I don't understand."

I noticed that she was trembling with excitement, her eyes flaming with desire.

"Neither of us can fully expect to understand it or grasp it right now," I said, calmly. "It's going to take time. We must take things slowly."

"What 'things'? What are you talking about?"

I did not reply. She needed to take this at her own time. There was a much longer silence then and when, finally, I looked across at her I saw that she was lost in thought. What I would have given to read those thoughts at that moment! Then she took a deep breath and, as if coming to a portentous decision, she stood up, and said, with a pretence of coldness, "I'm going to bed. And I think you should too."

My heart shuddered at her proposition. This was all happening even faster than I had anticipated. Our 'vegetable love', to quote the wily Metaphysician, had begun!

She stood and left the room and I heard the familiar whine of the stair-lift. I wondered whether to follow her immediately or whether I should give her time to prepare herself. She might want to take a bath and apply lotions, unguents and perfumes, to get herself 'in the mood'. I too would make my own preparations. I might grate some more of my ruff away, so that, during our proceedings, it wouldn't scratch her delicate skin. I might also apply a little powder and mascara and put on some of the frilly pink lady's underwear I had procured from the launderette.

I lay back on the sofa and closed my eyes, revelling in the delicious suspense, but then – it must have been the Retsina, combined with the evening's heightened emotion – I fell into a deep sleep.

What dreams I had, what emissions!

I ascended the stair-lift to heaven. This took three minutes. Once released from its leather strap, I stood on the landing at her boudoir door, gathering myself. Then, timidly, I knocked.

I heard her voice, distant and dreamy, calling, "Is that you?"

"Yes, Joyce, it's me."

"Come to me," she cried. "Come to mummy!"

Entering her sanctuary and closing the door softly behind me, I was astonished to find the room dancing with the light of a hundred candles which she had placed on every available surface. The sight caused me to gasp and then laugh out loud, with joy, and gratitude.

"I thought I'd make it special," she said, and pulled the covers back to reveal her nakedness, whereupon I fell at once, with a great swoon, into her tightening arms.

That night, Joyce was everything that I had ever wanted, and hoped for, and more. Slowly, gently, with infinite care and delicate sensuality, she instructed me, a novice, in the holy sacrament of love: how far here, how far there, what to do with this bit, what to do with that bit, where this goes, where that goes; how not to *rush*. Perhaps these are things that, finally, only a mother can teach her son. In short, I worshipped her with my body and my soul, and we were, at last, united in one flesh.

But then, after perhaps half an hour of our love-making which had become ever more explorative, something happened. Suddenly, she stiffened beneath me.

"What is it, Joyce, my love?" I said. "Am I hurting you? Am I being too rough?"

"I thought I heard something … downstairs …"

I looked up from her moist socket. "It's nothing," I said.

The next moment we were kissing passionately. Then she froze again.

"What is it?" I said, beguiled more than irritated by her constant distractions.

When she replied, her voice came, throaty with horror. "There is someone in the house," she whispered, and then she repeated it, yet more darkly. "*There is someone in the house*. Coming up the stairs. Don't you hear?"

We both listened again and heard the low clunking whine of the stair-lift. The three minutes of its operation seemed to last an hour. When it stopped, there was a pause, not dissimilar in effect to a drumroll, and I saw two dark shapes, as of cleft hooves, beneath the door. Then the handle slowly began to revolve and the door, with a creak that started low but rose to a high whine, opened. There was a lone male figure standing in the doorway, engulfed in a profoundly dark shadow by the wardrobe. For a moment he seemed shaped like a bat with enormous webbed wings hard and corrugated behind him. I shook my head to dispel the illusion and, at that moment, the figure stepped forward into the candlelight and I saw that it was my father.

"Norman!" Joyce cried, half extricating herself from me. "You're … home!"

Then he did something which I would not have expected a man to do who had just found his wife in bed with another man: he removed his jacket. This seemingly innocuous act was, in its cold self-control, almost as terrifying as if he had been wearing a leather mask and wielding an axe.

And then he spoke.

"What's going on *here*?" he said, and what struck me most was the absence of anger in his voice, the absence of any outrage. There was not even a hint of disapproval; even, perhaps, a degree of curiosity, even of … *interest*.

Joyce brought up the pillow to cover her nakedness. "Norman," she said, "there's a perfectly innocent explanation. It's not like it looks …"

I could not tolerate this retraction. "But it *is* like it looks!" I cried. "He has to know! We can't pretend this isn't happening anymore! The lies have to stop!"

"But, Norman," said Joyce, placing a finger on my lips to quieten me, "I thought you were staying the night in Market Harborough."

Hurriedly loosening his tie, he said, "The meeting was over more quickly than I had anticipated. It was all quite amicable. In the end there didn't seem much point staying the night. I'm sorry, I should have phoned but I thought you might have gone to bed and I didn't want to wake you."

He removed his shirt, kicked off his Hush Puppies and started on his trousers. We heard the jingle of his buckle, the swift zip of his fly, the elasticated snap of his Y-fronts. As he approached, completely naked, his voice came more throatily, and deep, "My wife, my son: at last, my family, together as one, as we were always meant to be! My happy, my perfect family unit!"

"Father!" I cried, dumfounded by his urgent priapism.

"Norman," purred Joyce, with approval.

I turned over to encompass her heaving body and re-inserted, from behind. Then I felt his furred arms about my shoulders and a strangely-familiar blunt poking at my tail. At first, I submitted to the grossness of his carnality merely to placate him; but, as our rhythm built up, and I began to accommodate the sensation, I found myself beginning to enjoy it and encouraging it, and in a few seconds the three of us – mother, father and I – were thickly grunting in unison as the bed shunted repeatedly against the wall.

This is the closing scene of our drama, across which I must now draw the curtain. Is it a comedy, a romance or a tragedy? Can it, possibly, be all three?

Just now I heard Dr Webb approaching, the ringing of the guard's keys, the clatter in the lock, the grating squeal as the heavy door opens and she wheels in the machine with its tubes, its tubes …

She has attended to me. Soon I shall sleep. And, as I drift away, I like to summon that final tableau to my mind's eye, to see the beast with three backs we made that night of Mother's Day. That night, I became a sensual intermediary, an interpreter, a translator of love. Being impotent myself, and free of disease, there was no risk: our only transmission was of energy. I became a condom for my father's rod and my mother's intrauterine device. Each thrust of his I channelled through her and became the sounding-board, for him, of her arched and rising back. And as we moved together, united at last in one rapturous embrace, I was to feel, for the first time, the thunder-raps of an encroaching bliss engulf me. It was a feeling that seemed, like that tender and nostalgic eternity which precedes conception, to have about it something of the quality of Nothingness.

# Asparagus

The escalator which should have conveyed him smoothly up to Arrivals was out of order. After a flight that had already been beset with trivial inconveniences, Patrick now had this further one to contend with and he lugged his bag up the metal steps with that sluggish extra heavy-footedness you experience when ascending a stationary escalator.

Emerging onto the concourse, he was pleased to spot his sister before she saw him. This gave him a feeling of unaccustomed separation from her, as if he was seeing her as she really was and not merely as an extension of himself. He was struck by her immobility amid the hurrying crowd and by the look of troubled introspection on her face: she was worried, that much was clear. His plane had been delayed by two hours and he saw, with a movement of tenderness, how her lips moved with some private incantation; how she glanced twice at her watch even in the short time it took him to reach her. He called her name and they hugged briefly. Then she held him at arm's length, studying him.

"You're unhappy," she said, with her unsettling clairvoyance.

"Oh no, not really," he said, unhappily.

"Did you have a drink?"

Normally, this issue would be raised later in a tactful aside at the villa but, after recent events, the subject of his drinking had become more pressing and now it couldn't wait. His answer took the form of an action. He breathed his unsullied fumes directly into her face, making the hoarse throaty sound of escaping gas.

"That's gross," she said.

"Coffee at the airport, water on the plane. Believe me?"

"I believe you … and I'm proud of you."

He was, for a moment, overwhelmed by these words but he maintained his composure: he was good at that. This had been happening a lot recently, the fear that he might at any moment, and on any pretext, 'lose it'. As a result, he was always ready to deflect any kind word or expression of sympathy before it proved to be his undoing.

As they headed for the *Sortie*, his suitcase made the sharp-edged roar of a fighter-jet on its casters behind him. The terminal, apart from the gaudily-coloured shanty town of shops, cafés and car hire offices which crowded its walls, seemed to be constructed entirely of black marble, like a mausoleum, and it weighed heavily on him. Marseille airport always struck him as run-down and seedy, like that raffish city it served: a cross between Paris and Peckham with its grand gap-toothed boulevards and failed modernist experiments, their once-immaculate white balconies now defiled by laundry and bicycles.

They emerged into the furnace of the afternoon. Nothing could ever prepare Patrick for this assault on his temperate sensibilities: the barrage of sunlight, cars and coaches flashing on flyovers, the stench of aviation fuel and eucalyptus, the complexity of crickets, a plane droning anxiously over them, wings balancing, catching the sun. He was comprehensively bombarded. Above the perimeter fence, beyond the palm trees, tailfins were emblazoned with the cryptic insignia which evoked all the disorientation of international travel: a camel on one, a crescent and a scimitar on another; the flat bureaucratic orange of *Easyjet*.

They walked. The roar of his suitcase was augmented by the click of paving, like a Geiger counter.

"I cannot believe you're wearing a tweed jacket and leather shoes," his sister said. "It's a hundred degrees in the shade."

"I don't do tee-shirts or flip-flops."

"I noticed. 'The Englishman abroad'. I'm surprised you're not wearing a panama."

"I am, in spirit."

Through molten heat, the road stretched ahead to the distant spines of the port, rusting container ships, scarred cliffs, the sea.

In the car park they chose not to take the nightmarish coffin-sized lift but to use the stairs instead. Patrick's long-suffering suitcase slammed on each step as they descended. Two levels down, in the dank morgue of cars, Rachel aimed her device at one of them and it duly winked and chirruped back at them, as if possessed.

Stopping to stare, Patrick said, "Rachel, that's no hire car. That's a hire *bus*."

The bronzed 'people-carrier' had evil peeled-back headlights and a snarling snout of predatory gritted teeth. He put his suitcase in the boot, from where even the tail lights glowered at him. Rachel reached over to let him in. Inside, from the car's elevated position, he felt as if he was sitting on an extra mattress: they'd need ground crew to see them out. Belted up, they sat side by side in muffled silence for a while. His sister didn't press the ignition. Instead, she turned to her brother and gave him one of her grave appraisals.

Patrick said, "You're going to have to clarify what that look means."

Although he was staring straight ahead at a concrete pillar covered with dire warning signs about fire hazards and electrocution – flailing matchstick men stricken by flames and jagged bolts of electricity – he knew the look well.

"You will be okay, won't you?" she said.

There was something like entreaty in her voice: she was *begging* him to be okay. He let the window down to admit a hot vinegary fug of petroleum and diesel.

"Of course I'll be okay," he said. "Please don't keep asking me every five minutes if I'll be okay. I'll be okay. Okay?"

"I'm only concerned about you, that's all. We *all* are … Why did you pull that funny face?"

"Because it somehow makes the situation worse if you're *all* concerned about me. It makes it more real and, as someone once said, we cannot bear much reality. Listen, Rachel. For one week, just the one week of this holiday, I want to pretend that it isn't real, any of it; I want to pretend the whole business at the school isn't happening and I want to pretend that Frances didn't die, okay? Let me have those pitiful delusions for just one week and then I promise I'll go back to being a complete wreck again. Come on now, let's hit the road and get some 'air con' going in here."

"And you'll be civil with Roger?" she said, starting the car.

Roger was Rachel's husband. He was a Senior Sales Negotiator at Foxtons.

"Yes," he said, patiently, "I will be civil with Roger, if he's civil with me. Rachel, I get on fine with him. The idea that there is this great enmity between us is largely a figment of your over-active imagination. Can we go? I'm suffocating."

"Yes," she said, with a malevolent grin, "you certainly are."

"Leave the nimble wordplay to me, okay? I'm the English teacher."

Smiling privately, without indignation, she drove. She didn't really mind him, so much. As they headed up the ramps, even though they were doing under thirty, the tires squealed: it was like Starsky & Hutch. At last, the chilled air began to circulate and Patrick let the window up.

Out of the car park, Rachel negotiated the convolutions of the road system which seemed, like so much in and around Marseille, to be in a perpetual state of reconstruction or repair. There was a clutter of builder's signs, barriers and hoardings. Standing by the roadside, a black gantry, some sort of piling machine, emitted a choking pneumatic clatter. An abandoned building site with barely-begun walls of ill-fitting breeze blocks was desolate, like a modern Pompeii. It crossed Patrick's mind that you rarely saw an abandoned building site in England: here, they seemed to be indigenous to the latitude, like vines and olive trees and wild lavender.

A woman commanded, "In two hundred yards, turn right."

Patrick, having jumped at the voice's sudden intrusion, said, "I hate that wretched 'Satnav'. So … *bossy*. I don't know why we can't just use a good old-fashioned map."

"Well, we can't. Now stop complaining and find some Euros.

There's a barrier up ahead and we have to pay a toll."

Soon they were on the *autoroute.* Cars, dusty but glinting in the brittle air, nudged ahead or fell behind in a gentle vying with each other, inhabiting their own smooth linear dimension. The passengers of these cars, Patrick thought, all seemed to belong to the same subset of people, reduced to near-identical shadowy profiles; just as motorcyclists, leathery, masked and visored, were all the same person, usually a man. This was why the trope of the female motorcyclist worked: you assumed it was a man until she removed her helmet and shook down her long mane of blond hair – it was always blond – while the traffic cops, who had pulled her over for a minor violation, could only stand and stare.

Patrick said, veering suddenly into brightness, sensing afresh the wonderful adventure of simply being abroad, "How *are* you, dear sister?"

"Oh, you know."

"Well, I don't really. The business going all right, is it? back in Blighty?"

"I can't complain. The good people of Richmond and East Sheen seem to have an inexhaustible appetite for beige cushions and scented candles, thankfully." She always belittled the success of her interior design company.

"I think you must be providing a valuable social service there," he said.

"Tell me something. Do you ever hear from Anne?"

Anne had been his partner of eight years. She had left him two years before.

"Hardly ever," he said. "She's shacked-up with some 'Loss Adjuster' in Woking. Why?"

"I don't know. I was just thinking about her the other day. I liked her."

"Well, I did too," he said, carefully colluding with her past tense.

200

"The trouble was she didn't like *me*, so, there we go. Let's not talk about Anne."

"What shall we talk about?"

"How are 'the kids'?" He said 'the kids' in the same way that he had said 'air con' and 'Satnav': ironically, but with feeling.

"They're good, although Ben just sits in a darkened room all day doing whatever he does on his iPad."

"That can't be healthy, surely?"

"Sometimes I think he's on a different planet, or wishes he was."

"He's a smart kid. And my Sylvie?"

"Your Sylvie's utterly bereft. She keeps saying, 'Where's Uncle Patrick? Where's Uncle Patrick? Is Uncle Patrick coming today?'"

"Bless her heart," he said, and caught himself grinning, helplessly, in the wing mirror.

"You haven't asked about Niall."

"I was saving him till last. How is Niall?"

"He *seems* fine. Perhaps a little withdrawn. He doesn't laugh like he used to and I keep catching him staring into the middle distance. Can you believe it was one year ago? One year since Frances …"

He supplied the impossible word that would never fit, however many times they rehearsed it: "'Died'."

She made herself repeat it.

"You did the right thing, inviting him here," he went on, "but it wouldn't have been right any sooner. A year is about right."

"We have to think what to do about his birthday, if we do anything. No one's talking about it and it's the day after tomorrow."

"He may want to forget his birthday this year, after last year."

"Do you think he's still in denial over Frances?"

"'Still'? Rachel, he's never been 'in denial'. If anything he's in the opposite of 'denial', if such a condition exists."

"We're being very gentle with him, even a little distant. We're not fussing around him all the time. So don't *fuss*. Okay? We have to give him the time and space he needs."

Patrick noted how Rachel used the phrase 'the time and space he needs' without the alibi of inverted commas. She said it quite naturally. He would not have been able to use the same words without imposing his ironic quarantine on them. Inverted commas beset him like a swarm of eager tadpoles. His constant preoccupation with language, with its baggage of implication, its involuntary revelations, was one of the many penances of being an English teacher, he supposed.

Although Rachel had many things she wanted to ask her brother, not least of all about the current situation at the school and whether the tribunal had actually taken place, something in his testy defensiveness made her hold back, and for a while they drove in silence. Ahead of them was the steely rear of a tanker with the words 'FLAMMABLE GAS' stamped boldly in red across it. Rachel slowed the car, indicated, overtook. As they did so, the tanker's churning growl fell a tone, in line with Doppler.

Patrick said, "How's it going with you and Roger?"

"What do you mean how's it going with me and Roger?"

"'How's it going with you and Roger?' I don't see how I can express it any more clearly."

"Patrick, we've been married for twenty years. You make it sound like we've just started 'dating' – and yes, I know that's an Americanism."

"I said nothing."

"Come on. What are you getting at?"

"Last time we spoke there seemed to be some 'marital issues'. At least, that's what I picked up on."

Rachel pressed a button on the dashboard and a froth of soapy water masked the windscreen for a moment before the wipers swept it away. The road ahead looked sharper, brighter, even hotter.

Patrick said, "So? Come on. How's it going? And, by the way, I saw what you did just then with the wipers: *classic* 'diversionary tactic'."

"Roger and I are fine, Patrick. Fine."

"'Fine'."

"Yes."

"Do you know what 'fine' means?"

"Well I thought I did but I'm sure you're about to tell me otherwise."

"'Fine' means '*not* fine'. In my experience."

"What 'experience'? Of marriage?"

"In my *linguistic* experience."

"That's a new one. Patrick, I'm sorry to disappoint you but when I say 'fine' I really do mean 'fine'." And then she said something which Patrick hadn't been expecting. She said, "You never give him a chance, do you?"

They drove in ill-tempered silence for a while. Rachel put the radio on. A man urgently informed them what they could hardly comprehend: "Un grand nombre d' incendies de forêt sont signalés dans la region de Luberon ..."

"It's all Frenchified," said Patrick.

"*Shut up* and listen ..."

"... On a conseillé aux gens d' éviter la zone si possible ..."

"Can't we find the World Service? There's bound to be some fascinating documentary about irrigation in Swaziland or something."

"No," said Rachel. "And it's not called Swaziland anymore."

Chastened, he turned to watch France passing: the fast pylons, the slow hills, the stationary sky. He was struck by an intense but intangible longing. What was it *for*, this longing? Art? Architecture? History? Geography? Culture generally? Provence, now so immediate beyond the window, seen from the vantage of his dull set-upon English soul, made him yearn for the riches of the whole world. He longed for an intimacy with every walled town, every crumbling church or monastery; but, as he knew, there was just not enough time for all that. It was eternity he craved: was that too much to ask? He was conscious, even in his early forties, that his time was running out. His past had begun to outweigh his future, funerals to outnumber weddings. In time, he would forfeit the world having barely made its acquaintance. This desperate feeling of waste and impatience, at once of exclusion and transport, hit him with the same force in art galleries when he gazed at some Old Master – not at the main event of yet another martyrdom or crucifixion, which were, besides, of no interest to him – but to the distant bluish landscape which lay beyond, wisped with smoke; when he saw, with an exquisite pain, the painted towers and campaniles of an unknown town where he would never go, whose bells he would never hear.

The man on the radio repeated something with a greater emphasis which only seemed to add to Patrick's incomprehension: "... *On a conseillé aux gens d' éviter la zone si possible* ..."

The villa where they were staying, and where they had stayed for the previous four years, was just outside the village of Goult in the Luberon. It was an hour and a half's drive from the airport. Patrick's swift calculation resulted in a satisfactory answer, but it brought a measure of unease. His flight's fortuitous delay meant they would arrive at the villa at around six o'clock, or 'wine o'clock' as his sister insisted on calling it, and not the scheduled four o'clock he'd been dreading. At six a drink would automatically be offered him, or, if he helped himself to one, no one would think it transgressive; the same would have applied if he had arrived at lunchtime, which fell broadly between noon and half-past-two. If, however, he had arrived at three o'clock (borderline) or four o'clock (categorical, hence his previous misgivings), he would have been offered tea or coffee, or some abomination like peach juice, and no amount of irrefutable reasoning (time differences, special holiday dispensations, oh *come on*!) would have spared him that. Of course no one would stop him drinking at any time; it was just there'd be an 'atmosphere', specifically, the 'Patrick's having a drink' atmosphere, and someone might comment on it (Rachel, usually). On these holidays – when Patrick might reasonably have expected a relaxation of licencing laws – drinks were administered, or not administered, with all the strict observance of a monastic order, as if their consumption had been prescribed in some Book of Hours. But he knew that what had happened at the school could make the next few days particularly difficult in relation to alcohol – more than they usually were – especially since he wasn't sure who knew what, or how much. He knew Rachel knew, because he had told her, and he knew that James, his brother, knew, because he had told him. But he didn't know whether their respective spouses knew, or any of the children – he doubted that – or whether Niall knew. He tried to remember if he had mentioned anything to Niall. He thought he hadn't, at least not in any detail, but he couldn't be sure. He'd have to 'play it by ear' (even his thoughts, when they lapsed into cliché, came shrink-wrapped with inverted commas).

An hour later they turned off the *autoroute* and half an hour after that they turned onto the familiar gateless track which led through vineyards to the villa. On their first visit four years before it had taken them two hours and several phone calls to the agents to locate the track since there was no obvious sign. There *was*, in fact, a sign – a wooden arrow nailed to a post with 'Villa Cèdre du Liban' carved into it – but it was overgrown with vegetation. The agents had confided in them that the track's neglect was a deliberate policy on their part, designed to give no impression of the luxurious villa which lay barely a kilometre at the end of it.

Although the villa was of quite recent construction – a fact that had been deftly side-stepped on the agent's website with the use of the term 'traditionally-styled' – it looked like an old Provencale farmhouse with its pink walls, blue shutters and rose-crowded dormer windows. In front of it was a vast sprawling cedar of Lebanon whose leaves projected the gravel parking area beneath with a dance of light and shade. To one side a decked veranda was choked by vines and a burgeoning clematis that smelt sweet at dusk. On the other side, partly concealed by a box-hedge, was the pool and sun-terrace. Beyond was an outbuilding which contained a games room where you could play snooker or table tennis, and a mini-gym equipped with gleaming black instruments of torture. Only Roger used it. Sometimes you heard him rhythmically grunting and the weights ringing, in time, like anvils. It staggered Patrick that anyone could even *think* of using a gym when the temperature was invariably in the mid-thirties.

The car stopped under the tree with a sedate crunch of gravel.

Rachel said, "Madame Dubois has prepared your usual room."

"'Usual' is good," said Patrick, but he was thinking how much he liked her line and how it seemed to complement the luxurious sound of the gravel, the sound of having arrived, in every sense. 'Madame Dubois has prepared your usual room': it was so *decorous*, like something from an old play.

"I'll leave you to it then," she said. "Sylvie and the others will be by the pool, I expect. Go and say 'hi'."

She went into the villa. Patrick took his suitcase from the boot and went to them.

Roger was swimming with his usual length after length of gasping breaststroke, a glittering surge before him. He was in his skimpy speedos and wearing the goggles that made him look like a deranged Nazi tank commander. James, Patrick's brother, and Valerie, his wife, were on sun loungers, James drinking a dirty mug of tea and smoking a roll-up, being careful to puff it away from her. He had dropped out of medical school to become a tree surgeon and had recently expanded into 'garden design', a service he provided for rich people, mostly, who were drawn to his transformative visions for their cramped Chelsea and Fulham backyards. Valerie was reading Houellebecq's latest *succès de scandale* in its original language: hers. She was, like Patrick, a teacher, although, unlike Patrick, she taught at a fashionable sixth-form college in an affluent suburb; they rarely compared notes on their shared vocation since their experiences were so different. Her subject was 'languages', but French, principally. The most important fact about Valerie was that she was French and she only liked things that shared this characteristic with her, so it was always surprising to Patrick that she'd let her standards slip and married his very English brother. The annual holidays in France were partly intended to placate her for her exile in England and, more heinously yet, for her exile in that part of it known as West Norwood, which, according to Valerie, had no counterpart in France. She had once said, "Only the English, and an island race, could conceive of such ugliness," which had caused James to raise a mildly-outraged eyebrow. Perhaps it was true? They sent their preternaturally tall son Louis to the *Lycée Français Charles de Gaulle* in South Kensington so that he would grow up to be a fine young Frenchman. He was nowhere to be seen but that was usual since he was at that age when the presence of parents was one long nuisance and every conversation an interrogation. Ben, Rachel's son, was also conspicuous by his absence but Patrick guessed that he would be sitting in a darkened room doing something on his iPad, in line with Rachel's character study. Niall, the only non-family member present – the London Finance Director of a supposedly ethical petrochemical conglomerate based in Taiwan – was stretched out on his back on the grass with his head under a towel like a discreetly-veiled casualty in a war zone, but he was apparently only asleep; and Sylvie, his sister's youngest at eight-and-a-half, was at once, on seeing him, bounding, leaping over the Lilo, running towards him, and, before Patrick could utter a word, jumping up onto him and putting her arms about him so that, when he span her around, she stuck to him like a limpet. She was weightless and her hair was wet and she smelt pinkly of sweets.

"Uncle Patrick! Uncle Patrick! Uncle Patrick!" she cried.

"Sylvie," he said, in his steady avuncular voice, although he felt like weeping with joy. "Look how *brown* you are!"

She let herself be disconnected from him, with the tugging resistance of Velcro. Returned to the ground, she gazed up at him, her face twisted in the sunlight, her tousled hair forming a golden halo around it, a fist pressed at her cheek.

"I got burnt," she complained, suddenly grumpy in one of her seamless changes of tone, and she twisted round to show off the patch of peeling tomato skin on her shoulder.

"Ouch," said Patrick. "You should put some ointment on that."

"Mummy did," she said.

"Don't you use suntan lotion?"

"Mummy does but I still get burnt. Will you come in the pool now?"

He laughed. When you were eight-and-a-half, everything was now, or never.

"Perhaps later," he said. "Go into the shade, sweetheart, otherwise you'll get burnt some more."

She danced across the grass, happy as a daffodil, singing to herself, "Uncle Patrick's here … Uncle Patrick's here … Uncle Patrick's here …"

Everyone allowed Patrick these important moments with Sylvie. Now they were done with, they called out to him, orderly as a school register: "Hello Patrick!" "Hello Patrick!" Niall pulled the towel from his face. "Hello Patrick," he said, half sitting up, squinting, shaking himself into consciousness. "Better late than never, you daft old bugger. School let you out?"

Only Roger, still swimming, was unaware of his brother-in-law's arrival, since he had his earplugs in and his goggled eyes closed against the surge of water.

"Good afternoon," Patrick announced, raising his arm in a mock salute, full of anxious fake pomposity. "Or good *evening*. It's six o'clock, by Jove. No drinks?" He felt it was good to get that out of the way. When no one responded, he said, "Just going to unpack. I shall be making a statement to the press later."

He went into the villa, cursing himself for saying 'by Jove', and found his usual room ready. Madame Dubois had, indeed, prepared it. Rose petals and chocolates were scattered on the bed. The shutters were closed. A tall white fan whirred in the corner and, very slowly, shook its head at him, in disappointment.

Unpacked, showered, ready for a drink, Patrick emerged onto the veranda to find it deserted, apart, surprisingly, from Louis who was sitting, angle-poised, at the far end of the table, writing glumly but obsessively in a notebook. He was, approximately, sixteen, or he might have been fifteen, or seventeen. Patrick wasn't sure. He always forgot birthdays. This imprecision seemed a by-product of his own childlessness and lack of commitment to the whole biological project, now probably too late to be put right, even if he had wanted to.

"Louis!" he cried, with that exaggerated enthusiasm he reserved for him and which was, considering Louis's private subdued nature, always a little ridiculous and compensatory.

"Oh hi," Louis said, with the characteristic lugubrious fall in his voice which had once earnt him the nickname 'Droopy'. He closed the notebook but kept his hand resting on it.

"How are we?"

"Okay."

"Writing your memoirs?"

"No."

He didn't say what he was writing. Patrick sat at the other end of the table and scanned it. He pretended, comically, to peer underneath it. Then he looked at his watch.

"This is all very … peculiar," he said.

"What is?"

"Well, it's half past six and no one's down here hosing Prosecco down their faces. Where is everyone?"

"Getting ready."

"Getting ready for what?"

"Well, dinner. We're going into the village."

This is what they did every evening and so Patrick couldn't see why it took any special preparation now. Then he wondered if the reason everyone, apart from Louis, was absent was because they thought their presence and their pre-dinner drinking might encourage *him* to drink. Was this going to be a theme of the holiday, after what had happened? a conspiracy to control him? He told himself that it was only their concern, but still, it made him uneasy. He hated the idea that his presence might inhibit them or make *them* feel uneasy and he thought: what a complicated unsatisfactory mess this life is.

He looked at his watch again and wondered whether Louis noticed how fidgety he was.

"I suppose I'll just have to get my own drink then," he said, standing. "I really had expected to be waited on hand-and-foot. Do you want anything? Water? A beer or something?"

Was Louis too young for beer?

"Non, merci," he said.

Patrick – wondering whether Louis had implied some disapproval by his clipped answer – went into the kitchen and opened the fridge door which jangled with its heavy freight of bottles. He took out an already-opened bottle of white wine and poured himself a glass that was so full he had to sip it before risking transporting it. Then he took it outside to find that Louis had vanished.

"Well," he said, sitting down. "That's nice."

"What's nice?"

It was Valerie. She came out of the kitchen and sat opposite him, smoothing a map out on the table before her. She surveyed the creased spread of her homeland in all its miniscule culture-packed detail: the green leaf of France with the red filaments of its *autoroutes*.

"I was beginning to feel I had been abandoned by everybody," said Patrick.

"We're a bit behind today. James will be down shortly."

"You're not having a drink?"

"Later."

"How's college?"

"Oh, you know. The same as ever. We've just had 'LGBTQ' week."

"They wouldn't even know what that was at my place."

210

She looked up from the map with a troubled expression, as if about to say something difficult, and it struck Patrick then that she knew about his problems at work and was, as a consequence, reluctant to ask, in return, about *his* work. Instead, she voiced her habitual concern.

"Have you seen Louis?"

"He was out here a moment ago but he ran away at the first possible opportunity."

"I suppose it's his age: it can't be much fun being sixteen these days."

*Got it*, thought Patrick. Make a mental note, even write it down somewhere: *Louis is sixteen*. Behind him, he heard organisational voices, laughter and a cork popping: he heard deliverance.

"I *loved* being sixteen," he said, and then instantly regretted saying it. It might have sounded as if he were accusing Louis of some deficiency or, worse, his parents of forming some obstruction to his happiness. He said, quickly, "Planning a trip?"

"Yes," she said. "Tomorrow I thought we'd go to the Abbaye Notre-Dame de Sénanque."

There was something both impressive and disconcerting about the way his sister-in-law's voice switched from the dry Anglo-Saxon machinery to the voluptuous sophistication of her mother tongue, as if two different people were speaking.

"Wa-hey!" he jeered, an English lout, a foil to his fogey self, that other pose. He chided himself: I must aim for a greater consistency. And then the thought ran on: I must be as inexplicable to Valerie as English mustard.

She said, "Would you be interested in going, Patrick?"

"Absolutely," he said.

But his enthusiasm belied what he really thought, that an Abbey seemed an unlikely choice for an excursion. Did she intend for the children, the youngsters – whatever the correct collective noun was – to join them? Such things bored them on the whole. Teenagers didn't like old stuff and had no interest in God. They would prefer a beach or a water park, or, better still, to be left to their own devices: specifically, their laptops, phones and iPads. Then he remembered that Valerie was Catholic, and strictly so; James was, in the default English manner, godless, and even, with his connection with trees, a little pagan. It had always struck Patrick that this difference between Valerie and James might be another impediment to the viability of their marriage, a reason for it not to work as well as it seemed to; at least, from the outside.

"Here's James," said Valerie. "And Rachel. Oh, everyone's here all at once ... except Louis, of course. Except Louis."

Patrick turned to see his sister, his brother, Roger, Ben and Sylvie emerge onto the veranda, all wet-haired and freshly laundered, except for James who always contrived to look a little grubby, even after a shower. He was further delighted to observe, unobtrusively, that the adults were holding glasses of Prosecco, except for Roger who always had a beer, and he was even more delighted – although he hid it behind an expression of dutiful forbearance – when Rachel said, with reassuring flippancy, "Have you got a drink there, my dipso brother?"

It was a pleasant twenty minute amble from the villa to the village through the vineyards. The peachy sun was nudging the hills and the air was turning cooler. The night-time cicadas, although still marking time, seemed to take things more easily than those on the day shift. All the way, Sylvie held Patrick's hand and skipped along beside him, not saying a word. She was content simply to *be*. Louis had been, as usual, press-ganged into joining them but he had to show a token resistance. Tall and unhappy, he followed, limping along at the rear with all the enthusiasm of a Tommy heading for the Western Front. Ben idled wordlessly beside him, intent on some hand-held device.

The village of Goult consisted of little more than a single street – the grandly-titled 'Rue de la République' – which meandered prettily up a slight incline, lined with a jumble of irregular houses. At its head, many of the houses appeared to have been carved directly out of the rock so that they had a massive fortified appearance, and yet the windows had frilly lace curtains and flower-boxes. Halfway along the street it opened into a square, of sorts, used chiefly as a car park. At its centre was a modest war memorial with a statue of a head-hung soldier, his rifle laid despondently aside. Beside it, a fountain leaked rather than fountained. Around the square, on almost every available surface, there were flyers for an upcoming local election, some pasted over each other, with the genial frowning faces of politicians, familiar to locals, lauded or lambasted, but as unplaceable to Patrick as the faces on foreign banknotes or stamps; as unfamiliar as their grinning prime-time television presenters. The square grandly proclaimed itself the 'Place de la Libération'. French place-names tended to celebrate some founding ideology, or they swaggered and strutted, recalling martial or revolutionary glories or the dates on which they had occurred; or else they recalled philosophers, or novelists, or artists; in England, place-names, particularly those in the suburbs, were more likely to remember a remote bucolic past of woods or wildlife or meadows … before the town had come along and ruined it all.

The most significant building in the village, in terms of size, was the church, a massive boxy Romanesque structure dedicated to Saint Sebastian whose doors were two draped rectangles through which could be glimpsed isolated shimmers of gold. As they passed by, its bell clanked the half hour, like someone hitting a saucepan with a spoon, and Patrick thought of foreign bells, so deadpan and street-level, and the way they made the church seem as much a part of the daily life of the village as the neighbouring *boulangerie*: you'd pop in to cross yourself at the altar just as you'd pop in next door for a baguette. English bells, in contrast, bloomed remotely in the sky like an aural hallucination, reserved for occasions, either festive or solemn: announcing, or summoning, or warning.

As was their habit, they stopped in a bar for pastis and fizzy drinks. Then they went to one of the restaurants which lined the 'Rue de

République'. These restaurants catered chiefly to the tourist trade and yet the town was otherwise remarkably un-commercialised. There was a shop selling stuff you might actually need: insect repellent, dusty tomatoes the size of tennis balls, huge blue tubs of water which bulged with their own magnification.

Patrick was pleased to sit next to Niall at the restaurant. Apart from their initial greeting, they had hardly spoken since he had arrived. Niall fixed him with a mischievous questioning look.

"So, tell me, what's happening with you and the 'troubled inner-city comprehensive'?" he said, after they had clunked glasses. He always referred to Patrick's school in this way since it was the same form of words Patrick himself had chosen to describe it when he had first got his job there. Its full, and unlikely, name was 'The Academy of Saint Francis of Assisi' which Patrick avoided since it made a notorious South London sink-school sound like a product of the High Renaissance.

"How much have I told you?" he said.

"Virtually nothing. Which makes me only the more curious. You said that there was going to be some sort of 'enquiry' – was that the word you used? What have you been up to, Patrick?"

"I have no secrets from you, Niall, but the whole thing is a bit sensitive and also, frankly, embarrassing."

"Now I'm even more intrigued."

"A couple of months ago I was going through a particularly low patch …" He was going to mention Frances then but instead he gave Niall a significant look which he at once registered and understood, indicating, with a brisk nod, that he should continue, "… and – well, there's no easy way of saying this so I'll just come out with it: one morning I went into school pissed."

"Pissed … as in … pissed off?"

"No. Pissed as in pissed."

Niall snorted. "I'm sorry," he said. "It's not funny, but I thought that's what students did, not teachers. Anyway, you've surprised me,

214

a little."

"Why? What did you think I'd done?"

"Oh, I don't know. I suppose I'd imagined you'd committed a minor indiscretion with some obliging sixth-former."

"You know that's not my style."

"So were you drinking in the morning or were you still drunk from the night before?"

"Both. I wasn't falling-about drunk but it was noticed. My words were slurred a little, and, of course, it was smelt on my breath. That's usually the downfall of the problem drinker: they either smell of booze or of mouthwash and booze. You can't obfuscate the stench of sin."

"Bloody 'ell. A few 'Hail Marys' and you'll be right again."

"With me it's more likely to be a few Bloody Marys. And 'the long and the short of it' was – *is* – that I was reported and, like a naughty schoolboy, was sent home, and now there's going to be an 'investigation' … a 'tribunal' … call it what you will, although they can't seem to make their mind up when exactly. The suspense is killing me. I could lose my job over it."

"Shit," said Niall. "So it's serious."

"Well *yes*. I mean, it's not *quite* the same derogation of responsibility as if you were, say, a sozzled airline pilot or brain surgeon, where you'd be directly putting lives at risk, but, still – call them old-fashioned – the Parent Teacher Association take a pretty dim view of a teacher being half-cut on the job. Even an English teacher."

The waiter took their orders.

Later, they meandered back to the villa in a loose group. Patrick continued what had been a worthwhile conversation with Niall, chiefly for its normality. They hadn't mentioned the tribunal again, or Frances. Instead, they had talked, unusually, of politics, of Brexit, Boris, Trump. Niall had observed that 'Spitting Image', recently revived, was now redundant since reality had become its own parody, politicians their own puppets, the whole reactionary right-wing agenda reduced to single word ciphers. Afterwards, they had smoked over brandies, apologetically deflecting their fumes away from the others. Patrick was that curious thing called a 'social smoker', meaning an 'anti-social smoker'. For him, smoking was only elevated into something more than a disgusting habit when seen as an incremental form of suicide and therefore touched with tragedy, even a sort of hubris. With each happy puff, each willing inhalation of death, he was *teasing* mortality, saying 'come and get me then, if you think you're hard enough, and if you're going to anyway.' Niall had taken it up again soon after Frances's death, having given up years before for her sake (Frances had hated smoking). Now, he had no one left not to smoke for.

When they were on the track the sky beamed with a huge pale moon. It reminded Patrick of those old American films, usually Westerns, in which a filter was used to turn day into a counterfeit night: it was the vivid shadows which gave the game away.

Suddenly Sylvie called out to everyone. She had found a firefly. The scene they formed then, which Patrick observed from a slight remove – the figures in the darkness gathered around a single point of light, like an altar lamp – reminded him of a painting he'd once seen but he couldn't think of which, or the artist's name, or where he'd seen it, or when. It seemed utterly lost to him. He felt a moment of panic at this gap in his head, this occlusion. He felt the world, and its detail, slipping through his fingers, like ash, before he pulled himself together, and took Sylvie's hand in his, and they skipped along together, and he taught her the words to 'We're off to see the Wizard!' "Because! Because! Because! Because! Because!"

***

Patrick came down for breakfast to find everyone already started. No one seemed to notice his arrival, except Sylvie, who watched him as he stood for a moment in the blank refreshed heat of another Provencale morning, a prelude to the same day-long pageant of sunshine and cicadas they'd had the day before, and would have the day after, and the day after that.

"I thought we said ten o'clock," he said.

"Nine-thirty!" they chorused.

His failings were always made public; criticism of him took the form of oratory.

"Nine-thirty? That seems terribly early," he said.

"*I* think it should be ten o'clock too," said Sylvie.

Patrick, smiling at her collusion, took the remaining place between Ben and Louis. Despite the fact that the seating arrangements were random and changed from one sitting to another, he always felt as if he had been somehow put with the youngsters; that he had, in some way, been demoted. He felt the same in the staff room at school where, although he was one of the older teachers, he always felt its most junior.

Roger was seated opposite him, ravenously consuming his breakfast 'special' of bacon and eggs. He was peculiar about foreign breakfasts, always insisting on making his own 'full-cooked English' with the shrink-wrapped bacon he smuggled into France concealed in an inner pocket of his suitcase, like contraband. Patrick couldn't help watching his big hands moving with their over-large other-person's fingernails and the errant image came to him of them moving in the same ravenous way over his sister's body, before he shook it away.

"Could someone pass the croissants?" he said. "And the butter. And the jam. And the coffee. And the milk."

While this was being done, Roger said, without looking up, "How's the head this morning?"

"I can't think what you mean," said Patrick, with a pretence of lightness; but, when everyone laughed, he felt a furious stab of injustice.

The night before, Roger had been just as pissed as he had been; Niall and James more so. He had noticed how his brother seemed to be drinking more than he used to. Did no one remember how, on this very veranda just a few hours before, James had stumbled when he'd gone to fetch another bottle, although Valerie had suggested he shouldn't, and very nearly dropped the two empty ones he was carrying?

But, for now, and for the sake of sociability, he would just have to nurse his dejection and mask it with affability. He was good at that. In truth, communal breakfasts were one of his pet-hates, his least favourite aspect of these holidays, to be endured, the endurance made worse because you had to pretend to enjoy them. He resented the water-treading conversation, the forced hangover-fuelled attempts at hilarity; greasy croissants, unfamiliar butter, sour coffee made sickly with foreign milk; flies. The list of his complaints was a long one.

Valerie said, brightly, "So who is coming to the Abbey this morning?"

There was silence until Patrick said, "I'll come to the Abbey."

"I'd like to," said Rachel.

"Me too," said James, "but only if there's room."

"Count me in," said Niall.

"Kiddies?" said Valerie.

"N'utilise pas ça mot, Maman," said Louis.

Louis was effortlessly bilingual. On those rare occasions when he actually said anything, he would sometimes start speaking in French before realising his error and reverting to English. Sometimes one of his sentences would begin in French and end in English, or the other way round.

Valerie asked him, "Do you want to come, Louis?"

"Non, merci."

"No," said Valerie. "What would be the point of visiting a monastery when you've already taken a vow of silence?"

Sylvie said, to everyone's relief, "What's an Abbey?"

"It's a religious building," said Niall, "where monks do unspeakable things to each other. While Gregorian chanting."

"*Niall*," said Rachel, in mock outrage, but she was pleased to hear some of his old banter again. They'd missed that.

"So that's … how many?" said Valerie, going round the table and counting on her fingers. "Assuming none of the youngsters are coming, that's five of us."

"You don't want to come to the Abbey, Roger?" said Patrick.

He had decided, at last, to be passive aggressive. Roger sawed his bacon.

"Not really my thing," he said, through a mouthful of it.

"Anyway, who's going to look after 'the youngsters'?" said Rachel.

"Good point," said Roger. "You'll need me to stay and baby-sit."

"Bloody hell," said Ben, and Rachel gave him a warning look. "I do *not* need 'looking after' or 'baby-sitting'. Sylvie might, but I don't. I'm fifteen, if you hadn't noticed."

"And I'm sixteen," said Louis.

Patrick thought: how can I remember all this priceless information? Ben: fifteen. And Louis has confirmed he's sixteen. If only he had a pad to write it all down.

Sylvie, tugging at her mother's arm, said, "Can I come too? Can I? Can I?"

Patrick felt, with the helpless vanity of love, that she only wanted to go to the Abbey because *he* was going there.

"Are you sure you want to, sweetheart?" said Rachel. "It might be boring for you."

"I won't know until I've been there, will I?"

"Of course you can come, little one. We can fit six in the car, can't we?"

"I'm only small, after all," stated Sylvie, reasonably, and then stroppily crossed her arms and looked very cross at the fact.

The voice said, politely but firmly, "In two hundred yards, turn left."

219

"If you say anything rude about 'Satnav', Patrick," said Rachel, "I'm driving this car straight into a tree."

Patrick winced at her unfortunate choice of words but managed to say, levelly, "In that case, I shall remain silent on the matter."

In the people-carrier the six of them made a good sub-group, Patrick felt; there were no obvious tensions or 'hidden agendas' among them; they had an easy-going 'dynamic'. Without Roger's sometimes boorish assertiveness and Louis's and Ben's surliness they seemed a light-hearted crew, renewed, as if this excursion was a holiday within a holiday.

"Mummy," said Sylvie, "I need a wee."

"You should have gone before we left."

"I know, but I need one now."

"We'll soon be there, sweetheart."

Valerie said, "Saint Benoît demande à ce que le monastère détienne toutes les choses nécessaires: eau, moulin, jardin, boulangerie et les divers métiers en sorte que les moines n'aient aucune nécessité de courir au-dehors, ce qui n'est aucunement avantageux à leurs âmes."

When she stopped speaking there was silence. Patrick and Niall, who were sitting in the second row, exchanged puzzled looks. Sylvie was sitting between them.

"Was that in *French*?" she said.

"It was," said Rachel. "Valerie, did you *know* you were speaking in French?"

Rachel was driving; Valerie was sitting beside her in the front.

"Bien sûr."

"There you go again! Would you care to translate? I'm afraid I only have some rusty schoolgirl French. In a school exercise, I once translated 'canne à pêche' – fishing rod – as 'a can of peaches'."

"It's about the Abbey," said Valerie. "From the guidebook."

"You memorised the whole guidebook?" said James, who was languishing in the third row, dramatically nursing his hangover.

"No, *mon cher*," Valerie called to him, acidly, "I'm reading it from

Google on my phone, *idiot*."

"What does it mean?" said Sylvie.

"You're good, aren't you, Sylvie?" said Valerie, and she reached back between the seats to locate and squeeze her hand. "At least *you're* interested in Saint Benoît's views on the monastic life. I'll translate it for the rest of you, *étrangers ignorants*. 'Saint Benoît – or Saint Benedict, I suppose you'd call him – demanded, or asked, that monasteries should hold, or have, everything necessary for life; that is, water, windmills, gardens, boulangerie, or bakeries, and so on, so that the monks would not need to go outside … meaning, they would never need to leave the monastery, to go into the world … because that would not be good for their … souls'."

"Blimey," said Patrick. "I hope they had good Wi-Fi."

"Was there a bar?" said Rachel.

Niall, pointing out of the window, said, in an urgent raised voice, "What's happened here, people?"

The car slowed to a walking pace and they peered out. The forest had gone. Instead there was a blackened plain punctuated with the stubs of charred trunks. A pall of sulphurous smoke hung, waist-high, in the air. Just then, three fire engines, their lights glittering but sirens oddly silent, raced in the opposite direction, as if fleeing something.

"I wonder if they know something we don't?" said Patrick.

For a while no one said anything. Sylvie gazed anxiously over her shoulder to the road behind, after the fire engines, one finger detained in dismay at her mouth; then she looked at Patrick.

"What don't we know?" she said. "Uncle Patrick? What don't we know?"


As the guide book, courtesy of Valerie's phone, informed them, and they could now see for themselves, the Abbey was 'magnifiquement situé' in a narrow wooded valley. They parked the car and walked along a rough chalky track towards the ancient stone building with its tower, apse and buttresses. Its setting was enhanced by the bank of trees behind and, in front, a field of lavender whose scent filled the air. The track led them to what appeared to be a modern extension, although one made from the same rough stone. Very un-monastic automatic glass doors admitted them into a surprisingly secular, even corporate, air-conditioned vestibule complete with designer chairs, potted plants and a drinks dispenser. There were two doors for the 'public conveniences'. The door for the gents had a picture of a monk on it and, for the ladies, a nun. For a moment, they stood around, bemused more than disappointed.

"Well," said Niall. "Monasteries have certainly changed since *I* was a novice."

The shop was a large brightly-lit chamber with piped Gregorian chant. Its walls were lined with chunky wooden shelving stacked with bottles of wine and liqueurs. In the middle of the room were a number of cabinets. These contained lavender-related goods – soaps, perfumes, skin creams – although there was one section of a rather more cerebral nature containing books about the Abbey in particular and the Cistercian Order in general. There were also, Patrick noticed, some Asterix, Tintin and Babar comics to distract bored children. With Sylvie at his side, he leafed through 'Asterix le Gaulois' for a while. He'd had an English edition as a child but he remembered all the pictures with an unhinging swoon of nostalgia. Sylvie stared at them with complete seriousness. Then, ruffling her hair, and leaving her there with the comic books, Patrick wandered over to his sister who had chosen a bottle of lavender perfume. She had sprayed a sample onto the back of her hand which she offered for him to smell.

"A present for Valerie," she explained as they joined the queue for the till.

"Funny sort of place, this, isn't it?" said Patrick. "It's essentially a shop with a rather nice monastery attached. Apparently. Somewhere."

"What's that you're holding?"

"'Asterix the Gaul'. In French."

"You're buying it?"

"Yes."

"Who for?"

"Sylvie. Well, me actually."

When it was their turn, the woman at the till looked up, smiled, and sang, "Bonjour!"

This was always a difficult moment. Rachel and Patrick's fumbled attempts at French tended to be counterproductive and to cause either irritation or amusement. But it was necessary to establish that no assumptions were being made; no cultural protocols overlooked.

"Parlez-vous anglais, madame?" said Rachel, apologetically.

"Of course."

She did not seem unduly outraged.

"I'd like to take this, please," said Rachel. Then, brimming with self-confidence, she added, "Merci beaucoup," although she insisted on comically undermining her efforts by pronouncing the 'p' at the end.

The woman, smiling with forbearance, rang the perfume up on the old-fashioned till. It was the first bell they'd heard since arriving at the Abbey, Patrick noted: no irony was ever wasted on him.

"We were just wondering …" Rachel began.

"Yes?"

"Well, we were just wondering … where is it?" She shrugged, fetchingly, looking from left to right. "Où est il?"

"Où est il?" said the woman, still offering her official smile although now it came with a frown of puzzlement.

Patrick said, "Rachel, I think 'où est il?' means 'where is *he*?' As in, where is … *God*? Which is a perfectly reasonable question." He added quietly, "Here."

"Of course," said Rachel. Realising she had no idea how to say 'where is it?', she gave up on French, and stated, simply, "Where is the Abbey?"

"The entrance is up the stairs," said the woman, pointing to the vestibule.

Sure enough, there was a flight of stairs on the other side which they had missed on their arrival, so taken had they been by the attractions of the shop.

"That will be twenty-five euros," she said.

Rachel paid with her card.

Then she said, "Where is Sylvie?"

They turned and saw the others, one by one, stationed around them: James and Niall in the book section, talking seriously; Valerie sitting drinking from a plastic cup by the water-cooler; and no Sylvie. No Sylvie at all.

There was a flash of panic in Rachel's eyes.

"Where is she?" she said.

"She was here just a moment ago," said Patrick.

He put 'Asterix' to one side: it could wait. They searched the shop, calling her name calmly but firmly. Then they went to James and Niall.

"Have you seen Sylvie?" Rachel said.

They both shook their heads.

"Last time I saw her," said James, "she was looking at the comic books with Patrick."

"When?"

"Five minutes ago. If that."

They went to Valerie.

"Have you seen Sylvie?"

"No," she said. "She was over there, with Patrick."

"Oh Christ," said Rachel. "Oh Christ, where is she?"

"Rachel, calm down," said Patrick, feeling the first shudder of panic and guilt. He should have kept hold of her, he should not have let her out of his sight.

"Everyone look for her," Rachel commanded.

There was something steely in her voice.

They searched the shop, asked everyone.

Valerie said, to one group after another, "Avez-vous vu une petite fille? Avez-vous vu une petite fille?"

Everyone shrugged or shook their heads.

Patrick went quickly to the vestibule but by the time he was crossing it he was jogging. She wasn't there. The others had followed him and now they were all calling her name. The panic was catching, spreading like fire.

He saw Rachel put her face in her hands.

He stood, paralysed with fear.

James said, "I'll look upstairs. She might have gone upstairs."

He ran towards the stairs.

Niall thumped on the door of the lavatory with the picture of the nun on it, shouting, "Sylvie? Sylvie? Are you in there? Sylvie?"

Patrick said to the few people who were standing around, not caring that he spoke in English, "Have you seen a little girl?"

They looked perplexed; they shrugged. Someone said something in French. A man pointed outside and said, "J'ai vu une jeune fille dehors. Elle est partie avec un homme."

"Can you speak in English?"

The man said, "There was a … a little girl … outside. She was … with a man."

Patrick ran to the doors which parted to admit him to a world where unimaginable things happened. As he ran, calling her name over and over again, the track passed beneath him as unreal and vertiginous as a landscape seen from an aeroplane. His heart was pounding. He thought he might be sick. He couldn't lose someone again, not now, not so soon, and not Sylvie, not Sylvie. In those few sickening seconds he had already imagined her taken, abused, tortured, raped, murdered. He *must save her*. In the car park a car was backing out of its space. It contained two people. He could not see them clearly, just the indistinct profiles of two child murderers. The car turned and started towards the exit. He ran beside it and beat his fist on its side, shouting for them to stop; then, when the car showed no signs of stopping and even accelerated away from him, he ran ahead and leapt in its path. The car lurched to a halt. Its horn sounded a single angry blare. A man got out, slammed the door and came towards him.

"Qu'est-ce que tu fous?" he demanded, ready for a fight.

Patrick felt a sharp pain in his chest. A constellation of pin-prick lights swarmed before his vision, like amoeba, or galaxies.

He leant forward, clutching his chest and gasped, "I'm looking for an eight-year-old girl … light hair, blue eyes … wearing a red top and green shoes … green shoes …"

He was amazed at his forensic power of recall.

"You'll get killed jumping in front of cars," the man said, in perfect English, but already his tone had changed. "Are you okay?"

"She's missing. There's a girl gone missing."

"We haven't seen a girl. Call the police. Are you okay?"

Patrick nodded – he was okay, he would call the police – but as he staggered past the car he pressed his head directly against the back window and peered in to where he expected to see Sylvie bound and gagged. There were two seats, an armrest, a rucksack, a bag.

The car drove off.

Despite the gripping pain in his chest he ran back to the Abbey. When he reached the vestibule the doors opened for him and he saw Sylvie talking to her mother, the others gathered about her, laughing.

Rachel looked up at him.

"It's okay, it's okay," she said, with a wild gasp. "She was in the lavatory. Niall found her. She's safe. Sylvie, now listen. You must always tell us if you're going somewhere! Always!"

"I was only in the lavatory," she said, looking up at them all, her face beginning to crease, her voice straining against tears.

"No one's angry with you," said Rachel. "We were worried, sweetheart, that's all."

Patrick fell to his knees and wept.


"Well, that went well," said Niall, when they were back in the car.

Valerie was driving with James in the front beside her. Rachel was sitting in the second row next to Sylvie, holding her hand. She was still trying not to cry. Patrick and Niall were sitting at the back. Patrick was shaking but now he was beginning to feel, as the shock and fear began to subside, the inevitable shame and humiliation. He had wept in public. Someone he'd never met had brought him a cup of water. Even after he had calmed down, strangers had stared warily after him, and passed comment.

They had decided to leave the Abbey immediately. As they had walked the seemingly interminable track back to the car a silence settled on them as each pondered the meaning of what had just taken place: Sylvie's disappearance; Patrick's reaction to it.

Patrick thought: they must think I'm losing it. They must think that the pressure of this business at the school, of Frances's death, its anniversary, that these things are finally getting to me. They must think I am on the edge of a breakdown.

As they drove – not sure where, since it was only eleven o'clock, and it seemed too early to return to the villa, because they had said they would be home in time for a late lunch – the conversation resumed, but it had a wary polite feel to it.

Rachel said, her voice oddly matter-of-fact after what had just happened, "You had to take the guided tour. They didn't let you just wander around the place on your own, unsupervised. We'd missed the ten-thirty tour and the next wasn't until two, so, unless we wanted to hang around for three and a half hours …"

"No, you were right," said James.

"And the admission price was fifteen euros each which I thought was a bit steep. I thought monks were meant to take a vow of poverty or something."

They decided, by a majority decision, to go back to the villa.

"Too much excitement for one day," said Rachel.

Patrick noticed that her shoulders were shaking. He glimpsed her stricken face in the mirror even as she carried on talking completely normally.

At the villa, Roger and Ben were setting the table for lunch.

"You're back early," said Roger.

"I'm afraid we've been ex-communicated," said Niall.

James said, "There was … an incident. Rachel will tell you."

"So you didn't get the Abbey habit?" said Roger, and they groaned.

Roger seemed in very high spirits. The bad joke and the premature laying of the table for lunch were evidence of a shift in his disposition since breakfast.

Rachel at once marched Patrick to a shady corner behind the villa, its rougher, usually unseen, aspect which overlooked the field. Here there were some rusting and cobwebbed gardening implements, an abandoned tractor and the sound, and smell, of the goats which wandered freely among the vines. Patrick let himself be taken. He knew what was coming. Clumsily he lit a cigarette.

"I'm not going to ask you if you're okay …" she said.

"Oh go on."

"… but that was quite a performance."

"Rachel, I was terrified. It was *relief.*"

"Do you think *I* wasn't terrified, and relieved? She's my daughter."

"If any harm had come to her …"

"I know, I can't bear to even think about it. But she knows now not to go off without telling anyone. But you went crazy. I mean, really … *crazy.*"

"If it's any consolation I feel like a complete idiot."

She fixed him with her exact eyes; blue, like her daughter's.

"Are you going to drink at lunchtime?"

"Oh I see. That's what this is all about."

"Are you?"

"No. Or, at least, nothing stronger than that disgusting peach juice."

She held him gently against her and they stood together in silence for a while. He let his arms hang at his side as if he were passively accepting some sort of blessing. The beating of her heart belied her outward calm: he felt it pounding, oddly syncopated, against his own.

Then they heard muffled explosions of water and laughter coming from the pool and the ordinary world was back again and, in the light of it, their charged embrace seemed suddenly ridiculous.

Lunch always looked and smelt like a deli, crowded and colourfully laid out on the table in the leafy sunshine. Rachel and Valerie, as part of their maternal pact, shared a bottle of 'mummies' rosé', having already imbibed their customary Mojitos; James and Niall shared a bottle of white; Roger had a couple of beers. *French* beers, but only because the local shop didn't stock 'London Pride'. Sylvie, Ben, Louis and Patrick ('an honorary youngster' as he disingenuously termed himself) had to make do with water or peach juice. Patrick assumed that peach juice was an acquired taste which he had yet to acquire, but he persisted with it. He had reasoned that, since he liked peaches he must like peach juice, but he was now beginning to think that in its reduction from spongey solid to glutinous pulp some Platonic essential quality of 'peach-ness' was lost. Rachel presented Valerie with the lavender perfume, beautifully and inexplicably wrapped – had she brought wrapping paper and Sellotape with her on holiday? – but which now seemed tainted by what had happened shortly after she had bought it, just as lavender, Asterix and Gregorian chant would forever be tainted for Patrick.

Afterwards – apart from Louis who retreated to his room and Ben to his darkened lair – they returned to the pool. Patrick took his Aldous Huxley to the only sun lounger that was in the shade. For a reason that he couldn't quite fathom he was re-reading 'Eyeless in Gaza'. He didn't usually re-read books but he was intrigued to see how it compared to his memories of it from when he had read it thirty years before as an undergraduate. It was the same dog-eared Penguin which he'd bought for 50p in a second-hand bookshop in Oxford, the flyleaf still bearing the price in pencil at the foot of a series of crossed-out climb-downs which had started at an optimistic £2.50.

Roger was snoozing while slowly roasting on the next lounger.

Without opening his eyes, he took a swig from the can of beer beside him. Patrick envied him his recreational style of drinking. Roger drank like he played his soccer: in teams of men, mainly at weekends.

Patrick started reading but after just a couple of lines he found his mind wandering, and, besides, a fly kept tap-dancing on his knee.

"How's the book?" asked Roger, eyes still closed.

"Not bad," said Patrick, laying it aside and stretching. "I read it before."

Whenever Patrick said something that wasn't immediately explicable, or perhaps even, on the face of it, irrational, Roger always allowed a little buffer of silence to register the fact, which, if it were represented in a comic, would be a thought-bubble containing a question mark *and* an exclamation mark.

"So ... why, exactly, are you reading it again?" he said.

"Nostalgia?"

The answer had been intended as a joke, but, when Patrick considered it, he found it to be at least partially true: since Frances had died, he had been thinking over his college days and, more specifically, of his first meeting with her, that near-disaster of her ruined jumper outside the gates of Keble. 'Eyeless in Gaza' was just another aspect of this attempt at retrieval from a period of his life that seemed increasingly lost to him; it was as if those far-distant events were not just isolated and remote in time but had happened to someone else.

He noticed that Roger was reading The Guardian.

"I didn't have you down as a Guardian man," he said.

"No," said Roger. "I'm not really. No tits."

Patrick snorted. Often he felt he didn't give Roger enough credit: it was dawning on him that what he mistook for boorishness in his brother-in-law might actually be a healthy habit of self-mockery.

"Do they sell English papers in the village?" he said.

"No," said Roger. "I found it in the kitchen in an old drawer."

Patrick pondered this puzzling statement for a while. Then he sat up, grabbed the paper and examined the front page.

"Roger," he said, "this paper is two years old."

Roger grabbed it back. "So what?" he said. "It was so good first time round, I'm reading it again. Like you and your," he squinted at Patrick's book, "'Eyeless in Gaza'."

He pronounced 'Gaza' like the footballer.

During the ensuing silence, Patrick wondered whether he should ask Roger how he and Rachel were 'getting on'. He could broach the matter of their supposed marital difficulties lightly: was he still enjoying being married to his bossy sister? It would leave the candour or otherwise of his reply entirely up to Roger. But, when Patrick opened his mouth to address this issue, he found himself saying, "So, tell me, how's the exciting world of London Real Estate?"

Ten minutes later, Patrick's mobile rang. It was Phil Probert from the school. He was the Assistant Vice-Principal.

"Hello, Patrick," he said. "Are you abroad? Your call tone's different."

"Yes. I'm in France." Patrick judiciously said 'France' and not 'The south of France' or 'Provence' to suggest that he might have been languishing in Le Havre or Dieppe. In a caravan. "Phil, can you hold on one moment?"

He stood and started walking across the lawn so that he would be out of earshot of the others and, at the same time, clear of any pool-related noises. For the same reason he hadn't wanted Phil to know that he was in the south of France he didn't want him to know that he had been sitting by a swimming pool. As he walked, even at this significant, possibly even decisive, moment in his life, he registered the broad-leaved, shiny and unnaturally dark-green foreign grass. It reminded him of the artificial grass in butchers' shop windows. He found the shade of an olive tree.

"Okay, I can talk now," he said. "Fire away … Phil?"

"Patrick? Are you still there? It's a very bad line."

"I can hear *you* perfectly."

"Okay. We had a meeting this morning and I just wanted to let you know that the general feeling is that you should be reinstated."

"'The general feeling'?"

"Yes. But there are two schools of thought. One is that you're a bloody good teacher who just made a stupid mistake …"

"It's the other school of thought I'm worried about."

"The other is … well, you can guess the other one. That what you did was highly irresponsible and that it damaged the school's reputation."

"'Reputation'? What 'reputation'? I don't think anything I could do or say could damage the school's 'reputation' any further than it has been already."

Choosing to ignore this remark, Phil said, "There was no vote but I think if there had been one – no names – you'd have won five to two."

"Hardly a landslide."

"No, but better than I had been expecting, in the circumstances."

Phil Probert had always been on Patrick's side – they were borderline friends – but in school matters he had to maintain a pose of impartiality.

"Well, thanks for letting me know," said Patrick. "What happens next? Phil?"

"Sorry, you're breaking up again. What did you say?"

"What happens next?"

"We'll have the tribunal, at some point."

"'At some point'? Why 'at some point'? Why can't they just set a date and then get the damn thing over with? Why these endless deferrals? Phil, really, the tension, the *not knowing*, is killing me, it's affecting my whole life. Earlier today I lost it in a monastery."

"I completely understand, Patrick. Reading between the lines, it seems to me that they're just prevaricating and that they don't really know what to do."

"I just want someone to make a *decision*. Any *decision*."

"Hang in there, Patrick."

"Yes, but for how long? How long? ... Phil? ... Are you there? ... Phil?"

There was no reply. The connection was lost.

Roger came slapping wet-footed across the terrace from the pool. Having swam, he brought with him a whiff of beer and chlorine and a micro-climate ten degrees cooler than the surrounding air. He sat on the sun lounger, removed his goggles and earplugs and pummelled his hair with a towel.

Patrick had put his book aside. He couldn't read. After the call and its lack of resolution he found it impossible to concentrate. He noticed that Roger was watching his wife and daughter in the pool. Patrick followed his gaze. Sylvie loved the water but she couldn't swim to save her life. She had armbands on and was doing a frantic version of the doggy-paddle, her head held up to the sky, her eyes tightly closed as she threshed the water in front of her. Her mother was gently supporting her with one arm and guiding her towards the deep end and the diving board.

Roger said, "Do you ever wish you'd had kids?"

Patrick didn't reply at once. This was partly because he didn't know what would constitute a genuine answer and partly because he was surprised that Roger, of all people, had asked the question. Roger's conversation didn't usually trespass on the personal.

"You mean with Anne?" he said. "Anne didn't want children. At least, not with me. I think she considered me genetically defective."

Roger shrugged.

"With anyone," he said.

"I don't know. Seeing your Sylvie, I might wish I had; but then ... well, I don't know if I could bear so much ..." He had to pause before he could articulate the word he *meant*, without inverted commas: "Love," he said.

Roger picked up his beer and swigged the last of it.

"You get used to it," he said.

"Besides, I'm too old for children now."

"Rubbish. Mick Jagger had one in his seventies."

"I think you'll find that was Mrs Jagger. No, I'm past it. The other day I was cruising on Wandsworth Common – Roger, I wasn't cruising, that was a joke – and there were these two virile young merchant banker types kicking a football around. One of them accidentally kicked it in my direction and so I ran at it and kicked it back with reasonable force and accuracy and he shouted at me, as if he were paying me the greatest possible compliment, 'You still got it, mate!' Imagine that. 'You still got it, mate.' He might as well have called me 'Grandad' or 'Old Timer'. That was … instructive."

Roger stood. He didn't seem particularly interested in Patrick's anecdote, despite it involving a football.

"I need a piss," he said, "and I'm going to get another beer. Do you want one?"

"I'm not allowed drinks before six, by order of the management."

Roger knew what he meant.

"I have a beer at eleven every morning and she never complains," he said. "By the way, Rachel told me what happened at the Abbey this morning."

"Oh yes," said Patrick, as if it was something that might have escaped his mind or occupied only a remote corner of it, whereas, in reality, he had thought of little else after the event, until the phone call. "That was a scary moment in our day."

Roger was watching him. He seemed to want to say something.

"What?" said Patrick.

"I'll tell you – and I never thought I'd say this – but you're a good bloke, Patrick. You're a good bloke."

Patrick could only stare after him as Roger went for his piss and to get another beer from the fridge.

Later, restless, unable to lie any longer in the sun, unable to read, unable to do anything, Patrick went to the veranda and sat in the shade, wondering if this slight relocation might make him feel less unsettled. Helplessly he thought of Satan in 'Paradise Lost' and dully rehearsed the lines 'The Hell within him, for within him Hell/He brings and round about him, nor from Hell/One step no more than from himself can fly/By change of place ...' as if preparing to answer an exam question with the lower sixth. 'Is it possible to defend the view that Satan is the true hero of 'Paradise Lost'?'

He smoked a cigarette and then wished he hadn't. He would have liked a drink. Then he noticed that Louis's notebook had been left on the table in the place that he had been writing in it the day before. Without allowing himself the time for the complications of conscience or second thoughts, he walked over to it, glanced around, and opened it. He flicked through several pages. Some were covered densely, in column after column, with the name 'Celestine'. In one place a column had been violently scored through over and over again, so violently that the paper had torn. The latter parts of the notebook seemed to be filled with a diary and here Patrick's conscience finally drew a line at his snooping. Besides, it was written in French. He closed the notebook, being careful to replace it exactly where he had found it, and returned to his place at the other end of the table. 'Celestine', he thought: what a beautiful name: almost Miltonic, or Shakespearian – like Cymbeline.

Shortly afterwards, his brother came by.

"I'm making tea," he said. "Do you want some?"

"No thanks. I'll stick with water."

James hesitated.

"Could I have a word?" he said.

There was often this formality with his brother. Sometimes he addressed Patrick as if he were addressing a distant acquaintance, or a work colleague.

"Of course."

James sat and expertly prepared a roll-up. With his gnarled hands and worn-down fingernails there was something of the frontier about him. His old-fashioned lighter, with a tang of paraffin, clicked a blue flame. Puffing smoke sideways, he said, "We have to decide about tomorrow evening. About Niall's birthday. Do we celebrate it or not, in the circumstances? Do we even mention it?"

"Niall should decide, obviously."

"Will you talk to him?"

"Do I have to?"

"Yes. I know it's difficult but you're closest to him. He'll be honest with you."

"Okay."

James stood, and stubbed his cigarette out.

"Are you sure you wouldn't like some tea?"

"Sure. Thanks. Is it too early for wine, do you think?"

"Yes. I do. And it is."


Here's what happened.

Frances had died one year before, on Niall's fortieth birthday. The two events were connected but no one knew how. This was the mystery surrounding the circumstances of her death which only compounded Niall's grief with a terrible *not knowing* and which had formed a chasm between him and Frances that sometimes seemed greater, and more terrible to him, than the chasm of her death itself. But, for Niall, the mystery served another obscurer purpose which he would never have admitted to himself: it kept her, in its constant irresolution, still real and present to him; kept her, almost, alive.

Frances had planned a surprise party for Niall's birthday. It was, after all, a big one, forty: half way, if you were lucky. She had secretly arranged that one of his work colleagues would take him out after work and keep him away from their flat until 8pm. This was to give the guests time to arrive an hour earlier, put up a 'Happy

Fortieth' banner, blow up balloons and engender a generally festive atmosphere. Frances had to prepare the food. She had recently abandoned her career in finance, which her heart had never been in, and started training as a chef. Thirty people had been invited and thirty seven had accepted and they would all be requiring her exquisite *hors d'oeuvres*.

But when the conspiratorial guests dutifully arrived at the flat at seven they found it empty. They knocked, calling Frances's name. They knocked again, and, finding the door unlocked – itself a worrying factor – tentatively stepped in. The lights were on but no one was home. Kiss FM was playing on the radio. They called her mobile. It went straight to voicemail every time.

At half past seven, they called Niall: they realised that the 'surprise' element was no longer important compared to his partner's inexplicable absence. He had been in a pub one tube stop away and was with them in a matter of minutes. They looked everywhere for a note. Nothing. There was some food in an early state of preparation and a half-drunk glass of Prosecco. At first they acted as if there must be an obvious explanation which they just weren't getting and they were all still able to laugh and chat nervously while Niall constantly consulted his watch and went to the window and called her mobile again and again. They had some drinks. She'd obviously just popped out for something. That was it. She'd be back. Perhaps she was picking up a surprise guest from the tube station. But after another half an hour had gone by, and they had passed the official starting time for the party, and still they had heard nothing, they all began to get a bad feeling and they settled into an uneasy silence. Someone turned the radio off. People sat or wandered around outside on the pavement, smoking, speaking to neighbours or passers-by who knew nothing. Niall continued to call her every two minutes. "Hi, you've reached Frances. Please leave a message." "Hi, you've reached Frances. Please leave a message." After the tenth call, he stopped leaving messages and just called again, and again, thinking, it would be the next call, the next one that she answered, and she'd be laughing, and wondering what all the fuss had been about.

About half an hour later, just when he was about to call the police, they called him. Frances had been involved in an accident. She had been driving. Her car had hit a tree and she was in intensive care at the Royal Free Hospital. Niall and Patrick went straight there and spent the night at her bedside. What the police had not told them was that she was in a coma. The heart monitor showed her frail continuity, each tick of her life. Watching it was unendurable. "Why was she driving?" Niall kept repeating, his head planted in his splayed fingers. "Where was she going?" Patrick shook his head.

Frances never woke up. She died the next day.

Eye-witnesses claimed that she had swerved the car in order to avoid hitting a child who had run into the road. The man who had presided over her funeral (no one knew who he was) went further than this and suggested that she had intentionally forfeited her own life in order to save that of the child; and then he had reeled off that platitude 'she who saves one life, saves the whole world'. What did that actually *mean*? The fact of death was usually shrouded in euphemism, self-delusion and magical thinking: the dead had 'passed away', they were 'at rest' or 'asleep' or had 'only slipped away into the next room', implying that their absence was a temporary, reversible condition. Niall wasn't having any of it. He refused to believe that Frances's death had been an act of sacrifice any more than that it had been a mere accident. He began to speculate agonisingly and fruitlessly as to why she might have taken the car out just an hour and a half before the party had been due to begin, none of which seemed convincing as an explanation. But there remained one dreadful possibility which he could never quite rid himself of: that she had, indeed, driven the car intentionally into the tree but not for the selfless reason which the man at the funeral had ascribed to her, but to commit suicide. No one else gave this dark possibility the time of day; they dismissed it out of hand. But Niall could not get the monstrous idea out of his head. As a result he thought back in minute detail over their relationship, in futile dissection, to see if he could find anything which might have led to such an act, but he couldn't, unless she had kept some terrible dark secret from him. But she didn't keep a terrible dark secret from him. He knew she didn't because ... he just *knew*. She'd been happy. *They'd* been happy. True, they'd had the occasional argument, but who didn't? They always made up in the end. And, surely, he reasoned, if she had been going to take her life, she wouldn't have chosen that evening, of all evenings; and, surely, she'd have left a note, wouldn't she? Surely she would have left a note. Wouldn't she?

It was one of the traditions of their annual French holidays that each evening they went to a different restaurant in the village. Goult had enough places to satisfy this whim. That evening they went to the café in the square opposite the church which also combined as a bar, tobacconist and post office. James had an egalitarian soft spot for it and called it 'The Caff'. It was different from the other more up-market places in the village both in its clientele, who tended to be earthy local types who turned up in battered 2CV vans, and the cuisine: it served burgers and pizzas and chicken wings, the stuff *real* French people ate who were no more likely to eat Coq au Vin than they were to adore Piat d'Or. The mismatched assortment of metal tables, each with a metal ashtray at its centre, and painted metal chairs, uniformly chipped and rusting, were still hot to the touch after their day spent baking in the sun. But the chilled wine from the local vineyards was perfectly good and less expensive than elsewhere.

As they arrived at their table, Patrick deliberately placed himself next to Louis. Ever since illicitly reading his notebook that afternoon he had felt a mixture of guilt and concern for the young man's welfare, even his mental wellbeing.

"Do you mind if I sit next to you?" he asked.

Louis didn't look particularly put-out but, then, neither did he look particularly put-in.

"Pas du tout," he said.

"Now let me stop you right there, buster. You can have the pleasure of my company on one condition: you speak in English. I have schoolboy French so if you need to ask the teacher to pass the ruler – *règle* – or rubber – *gomme* – then I'm your man. If, however, you need directions to Marseille railway station … I'm actually fucked."

After they'd ordered and the drinks had arrived, Patrick said, "Louis, can I tell you a story?"

"A *story*? Last time someone told me a story I was about ten. What kind of story?"

"Something that happened to me thirty years ago."

"It's about Frances, isn't it?"


Patrick had known Frances long before either he or she knew Niall. They had been at Oxford together. He had been at Brasenose, she on the other side of Radcliffe Square, at Hertford. He was studying English; she, History.

Their first meeting had been inauspicious but Patrick, when he was to analyse it later, felt that it had something of the goofy romantic comedy about it and was therefore, in its way, encouraging. She'd be Meg Ryan and he'd be … well, himself, of course, his bumbling ineffectual self. It was the third week of his first term. He had been cycling along Parks Road beside that gloomy ecclesiastical pile of bricks called Keble when he noticed a young woman cycling a short distance ahead of him. He felt, even from his distant view, that she would be beautiful: it was something about the fall of dark glossy hair across her back, the elegant but powerful pressure of her legs on the pedals. He wondered, automatically, assuming her to be a student, which college she was at. Then her bike went over a speed bump and a jumper fell out of the rear basket and landed on the road. She didn't notice and carried on. Patrick called out to her in words that would, in retrospect, make him cringe: "Excuse me! Madam! Madam!" But what else could he call her? She turned, and stopped, and *was –* obviously – beautiful. The jumper was lying in the road between them. Patrick sped towards it, swept it up with a flourish that aspired towards gallantry and then started cycling with it, holding it out towards her, like a trophy. He felt the whole thing had a sort of courtly vibe. But when he was only a matter of yards from her, he felt the jumper violently tug from his grasp. It had become snagged in the front wheel of his bicycle whereupon it managed two revolutions before it seized up the whole mechanism and he came to a juddering halt and very nearly toppled over, which would have completed his humiliation. The woman, unable to conceal her annoyance, turned her bike and cycled towards him as he, kneeling in supplication, attempted to extricate it from the spokes. It wasn't torn – at least, not obviously – but it was twisted into a knot and smeared with oil. Muttering an apology, and wincing, he handed its sorry remains to her. It was, in a way, quite funny – how his well-meaning act of chivalry had so badly misfired – but she didn't seem to find it the least bit amusing. Instead she said, "Bloody hell, it's *cashmere*." Patrick didn't know what this fact portended, nor that these words would later be significant as the first thing she ever said to him. "But thank you, anyway," she added, grudgingly; then, shaking her head, cycled off into his history (as he thought then) and into his extensive back-catalogue of near-misses and almost-had-beens.

Then, just a fortnight later, Patrick found himself standing next to her at a party in New College. Oxford was a small place, especially if you were an undergraduate. Recently, he had often tried to recall the occasion for the party and who had invited him but all these precious details were lost and gone forever, the memory of them now eternally out of reach, beyond the horizon of recall. He wished now that he had asked Frances if she remembered anything about that party. What was it for? Who had invited her? and him? Who had they had, at that early stage, in common? It seemed important to him that he should retrieve this kind of circumstantial information, as if it might be used in evidence against him, to incriminate his former self for the crime of not knowing how happy he had been.

"I'm the person who destroyed your cashmere jumper," he said, by way of introduction. "Can I get you a drink to make up for it?"

She didn't say 'no'.

They spent the rest of the evening together, making constant references to her ruined jumper and his complete and utter hopelessness: it became a useful running joke between them, although one that he would always be the butt of. He offered to pay for it to be professionally cleaned or even to buy her a new one, a proposal with which she concurred with alacrity, and Patrick was very pleased for this, since he knew it would provide an opportunity to meet her again. But, as it turned out, he didn't need such an opportunity. As the party had begun to deteriorate, Patrick had taken her to the college's cloisters – to his amazement, she confessed she had never seen them, but he let her off because it was her first term, and this wasn't her College – and he remembered, more intensely than anything that night, dancing with her there, wheeling her around and around on the grass under the spreading branches of the great holm oak which at one point he even attempted to climb. It was a strange thing to have done but he only realised that the next morning. They ended up going back to her cramped and surprisingly untidy room in Hertford, and, inevitably, they had sex, in a fumbling friendly sleepy way. Although he didn't stay the whole night, he didn't get back to Brasenose – admitting himself stealthily with his college night key (or 'shag-key' as some referred to it) – until four o'clock in the morning.

They began a relationship, although they never strictly defined it. There was, he was sure, an assumption between them of fidelity and exclusivity but they never signed anything. Frances was properly feminist about it: she had no intention of being defined by any relationship. The trouble was that she didn't tell Patrick this. He was more than happy to be defined by it. She was quite a 'catch', after all. Then one day, in the middle of the next term, Patrick found her with another man – a third-year engineer from St Peter's, which only made matters worse – and it was over.

They did not see each other for the rest of the term but the following term they bumped into each other on Brasenose Lane, a meeting which was inevitable sooner or later. Patrick was surprised at his own lack of rancour and by how absolutely he had forgiven her for her betrayal; she was impressed by the same things. Their relationship began again, this time as a friendship uncomplicated with matters of the heart, or flesh. It grew to become the central and most important friendship of Patrick's, and Frances's, life.

After graduating, Patrick and Frances had moved to London, Patrick to Wandsworth and Frances to Belsize Park. He had started his teacher training and she began working in the City. Patrick didn't disguise his contempt for her choice of career which he thought was a waste of a history degree and, worse, capitalistic and immoral and venal; her excuse was that it would be a stop-gap to earn a few pennies before she did something completely different and unexpected which would also be a waste of a history degree, like becoming a chef and owning her own restaurant.

Frances met Niall on a boozy bankers' night out in Soho and the rapidity with which their relationship established itself took them both by surprise. Suddenly, overnight, they were 'an item'.

When Patrick was introduced to Niall a few days later – Frances had coyly described him as 'her new friend' – he was astonished to find them holding hands and, a few days later, this astonishment was compounded when he found out that he was moving in with her. He thought: how did all *this* happen, and with such undue haste? He didn't, at first, trust Niall, partly because he was a banker and partly because he had a residual possessiveness over Frances. He thought him over-bearing; he thought he had a 'superiority complex'. Niall didn't trust *him* because he seemed to have an unclassifiable relationship with Frances about which, he suspected, he wasn't being told the full story. After this initial resistance, they grew first to tolerate each other – for Frances's sake, who seemed to need them both – and then, over the years, to like each other, until they began thinking of each other as friends independently of Frances, and would sometimes even forget that, if it hadn't been for her, they would never have met in the first place.

By the time Patrick had finished telling the story, concluding with the terrible events of the year before, the complimentary house cognac was being served. Even Louis had one.

Patrick said, as they clunked the glasses together, "I don't know if that tale has a moral. Perhaps – if there is one – it's a hackneyed one: that we should try to grasp the world while we can, even if it results in failure, or humiliation, because you never know what might be around the corner."

He watched Louis carefully for his reaction. There was no obvious one. And then he thought two terrible things at once, so that they became the same thought: Louis is wiser than I am, and knows more than I do; and he knows I read his notebook. He knows I read about his Celestine.

"What do you reckon?" he said.

Louis said, with a shrug, "J'ai déjà entendu des histoires commes ça."

***

The next morning after breakfast Patrick said, "I see you are consulting the dreaded map."

Valerie looked up from it and said, "Qu'est-ce que ça veut dire?"

"You're looking at the map again. You know what happened last time you looked at that map. That's right. It ended up with weeping, on my knees, in a monastery. Do you want that all over again? Do you?"

He was pleased for the opportunity to make light of it. The event still troubled him. He felt he must do this with everyone: assert his *normality*, the fact that he operated under the same guidelines as everyone else, the fact that he could maintain his composure along with the rest of them. She smiled, a little, and he sat opposite her. The breakfast things had been cleared away but there were some gritty breadcrumbs on the table which he picked up, one by one, and put in his mouth.

Over breakfast he had announced that they would be celebrating Niall's birthday that evening, having consulted Niall privately about it, and that they would be doing it in style, going to what was reputed to be Goult's finest restaurant that evening. It had a Michelin star. He had booked it online that morning himself, having first checked with Rachel and James that they were prepared to countenance the extra expense. Everyone was relieved that the matter was resolved.

Valerie said, "I am planning a trip this afternoon to Ménerbes."

"You're keen on your excursions."

"Otherwise we just lie in the sun all day drinking Prosecco."

"Thank you for saving us from that particular Circle of Hell. What's in Ménerbes?"

"Peter Mayle."

"Oh God. 'Peter Mayle' as in 'A Year in Provence'?"

"Yes, and, you're right, he has a lot to answer for. It was that ridiculous book which made the English fall in love with Provence and come here each summer in their hordes. And then when the book was made into a TV series … well, that was 'the last straw'. The English invasion was complete."

"Voilà!" said Patrick.


Later, he went into the kitchen to put the coffee on and found a stocky woman stooped over the sink, vigorously scrubbing at it with a Brillo Pad. It was Madame Dubois, the laconic housekeeper who came in for a couple of hours each morning to tidy up after them. This chiefly entailed putting their many empties noisily into refuse sacks.

That percussive ringing sound seemed to express her disapproval of their excesses, their whole 'lifestyle'. Seeing her there, Patrick felt that slight affront of someone who had expected, and hoped, to be alone in the kitchen; he felt he deserved it after another drawn-out communal breakfast. But he always felt uncomfortable in her presence, as if he was complicit with the system which condemned her to this shameful drudgery, and so he over-compensated with an exaggerated cheeriness.

"Bonjour!" he sang.

Without making eye-contact she nodded briskly and then, to render any attempt at a further verbal exchange between them out of the question, ran the tap at full power and stood there, looking at the floor, waiting, as the water thrummed in the sink.

He thought: she *despises* us.


It was lunchtime. Patrick was in the field with Sylvie and Ben. The tall grass, golden in the midday sun, was jumpy with insects and bristling with thistles, while the crickets flexed and ratcheted around them like fishing reels. Rachel had sent them on a vital mission to find some wild mint to put in whatever it was that she and Valerie were preparing for lunch, or possibly into their Mojitos.

"It is absolutely imperative we locate mint," said Patrick.

"This is so bloody boring," said Ben. "Mum's always sending us off to forage for exotic ingredients."

"I'd hardly call mint 'exotic'," said Patrick.

"What does it look like anyway?"

"Mint?" said Patrick. "Minty."

"Thanks for that, Uncle P. That's really helpful."

Sylvie said, "Is this mint?" and shoved something green in his direction.

"No, Sylvie. That's a weed."

"They won't know."

"They will know, sweetheart, because it's not *minty*. It might even be poisonous. Don't forget, we're not in England now. Abroad, dangers and threats lurk around every corner. Johnny Foreigner cannot be trusted. You can't be too careful. Take it from me. That's why we did Brexit."

Ben produced a concessionary snort.

"I saw a snake here once," said Sylvie, and promptly yawned.

"Sylvie," said Patrick. "I *was* joking you know. About Johnny Foreigner."

"I *know*."

"Or, at least, it was an attempt at irony. Do you know what irony is?"

"Is it like ironing?"

"Yeah, that's right," said Ben. "Ironing."

Patrick scowled at him.

"Ben, in his rather rude way, has actually just demonstrated it perfectly," he said. "Irony is when you deliberately say the opposite of what you think is true."

Sylvie thought seriously about this for a moment.

Then she said, "You mean, like grown-ups do?"

"Yes," said Patrick. "Just like grown-ups do."

Ben sat on the low wall.

"This is so bloody boring," he stated again, flatly, kicking his heels against the stone. "I can't believe that we're in a field, in France, and it's, like, two hundred degrees in the shade and we're trying to define irony."

Patrick said, "You should have brought your iPad out."

"It's too bright in the sun to see the screen."

"I was being ironic."

"By the way, Uncle P.," said Ben, "are you sure you're warm enough in that jacket? Wouldn't want you catching a chill."

"When abroad, Benjamin, it's important to set a good example for the natives."

"Is *this* mint, Uncle Patrick?" said Sylvie.

Ben said, "No, Sylvie, you idiot. It's a *weed* just like the last one was."

"Ben," said Patrick, warningly.

Under his breath, Ben said, "She's just so bloody ... *annoying*."

"Let's have a look, Sylvie," said Patrick. "No, sweetheart, Ben's right, but it's much more like mint than the last one. I think this must be some sort of clover. Can you find one with four leaves?"

She scoured the ground, keen to find him anything. Then she picked something up and handed it to him.

"What's this?" he said, holding it up between his thumb and index finger as if it were a priceless jewel. "An acorn! A *French* acorn! Thank you Sylvie. I didn't know they had acorns in France."

"*Durr*," said Ben. "Where d'you think French trees come from?"

"Irony, Ben," said Patrick. "Irony."

He revolved the smooth green shape in his palm until some superstitious impulse made him drop it, discreetly, into his jacket pocket.

After lunch, which did not include mint, a group of them set off on the twenty-five minute drive to Ménerbes. Present were Valerie, Rachel, Patrick, Niall and *Louis*. Louis's willing inclusion – he'd actually *volunteered* – had surprised them all and quietly pleased Patrick, who felt that the previous day's symposium on love might have been instrumental in encouraging his sociability. Perhaps Louis's exile was coming to an end and he would make friends with them all and bare his heart. Sylvie had declined to join them, saying, with the world-weariness of her eight-and-a-half years, that she was "just too tired". Patrick suspected that her experience at the Abbey had put her off excursions.

After they had parked and were walking into the town, the phrase 'tourist trap' inevitably came into Patrick's mind. All of the signs were there: shops selling knick-knacks, scented candles, expensive women's clothing, execrable artworks and ornaments: unnecessary things, most of which were painted white, or beige. Their doorways wafted the air-conditioned scent of potpourri and joss-sticks into your face. You couldn't buy a loaf of bread for love or money. The church was locked and the museum closed for the afternoon. An 'art gallery' sold idealised paintings of the town before it had been ruined. It only had time for visitors now, visitors who wore a faint look of pique that they didn't have the place entirely to themselves but were forced to share it with so many lousy tourists; the very same tourists who had ruined the place by making it so commercialised and, well, *touristy*.

They stopped outside a typical shop in the main square. It was called, all in lower case, 'espaces'.

"My God," said Patrick, surveying the tasteful spot-lit window display, "look at the overpriced tat. Eighty euros for a rusty watering can."

"I like overpriced tat," said Rachel, and went in.

Patrick had to remind himself that overpriced tat – her own judgement, not his – was her bread and butter. There was a particular series of Harry Enfield sketches, set in a terminally-pretentious 'boutique' in Notting Hill, which she loved, despite the fact that it ruthlessly satirised her business.

He watched his sister talking to the elegant woman within. She wore a Hermès scarf swept around her long neck. They exchanged business cards.

Afterwards, they explored the town for half an hour and then went to a café which had an extensive view south from its elevated position on the ramparts. Vineyards undulated, in a misty heat, to the velvet hills. There was a leaning funnel of smoke rising from some distant forest fire. The Mediterranean was just visible on the horizon, a plain of gaseous quicksilver with a solitary tanker set atop it: it looked like a target. Patrick watched all this with an old yearning: the sea was that one earthly province which human vandalism couldn't desecrate, but then he thought of the tonnage of plastic waste and raw sewage, the massacre of dolphins and whales for the sake of tinned tuna. He looked at his watch. It was twenty past three. Would it be permissible to have a glass of wine? He decided against contravening the rules of the Book of Hours, feeling that even the circumstances of Niall's birthday would not overrule them. If it had been twenty past four he might have risked one but a drink at twenty past three seemed transgressive, even on holiday. Was he turning into one of those sad people whose days were a gritted-teeth countdown to the first viable drink?

Having ordered his smoothie, he was miffed, and not-to-say a little impressed, when Louis had the temerity to say to the waiter, casually, without feeling it necessary to ask anyone's permission, "Une bière, s'il vous plait, monsieur." And then, when the waiter asked him what *size* of beer he wanted, he replied, without hesitation, "*Grosse*", and demonstrated the size with his hands. Then Niall ordered a bloody *glass of champagne*, because it was his birthday, only for Rachel and Valerie to order Mojitos. Patrick had no choice but to endure the martyrdom of his smoothie in silence. He consoled himself that he would at least have gained some brownie points from his sister.

He turned to the view. As he did so, he noticed that his arm was resting on a boulder which jutted out over a ravine which fell in a series of dark crags into a deeper darker chasm. Further along, the cliff-face had been secured by wire mesh to stop rock falls onto the road beneath. Then he noticed that the boulder he had been resting his weight on had a metal bar secured over its hot flank which had been calibrated with centimetres. This was presumably to measure any movement and to give warning when it might become insecure, and fall. It seemed as if the whole cliff and the town itself were on the verge of collapse. Perhaps at some point in the geological future, or much sooner, they would pitch into the valley on a tectonic slide into that terrible fissure. Gently, so as not to trigger the catastrophe, he removed his arm. As he did so, a siren began to wail, first low in its register but gradually rising in pitch and volume until they were all clasping their hands to their ears. Because it filled the air so completely it was impossible to locate its source; it seemed to have no *direction*. It was as if the whole universe was consumed in a howl of cosmic distress and terror, like the sound that might warn of a nuclear attack, the end of the world, of everything.

At last, the noise began to subside, and, finally, stopped altogether. Beyond the leafy fencing of the café, the town resumed its life as if nothing had happened. A church bell, unconcerned, sounded the half hour. A moped buzzed past laden with water melons, ridden by an un-helmeted man with bare feet. The warning had been a warning of nothing.

Patrick removed his hands from his ears and threw a relieved smile at the others but he was shaking violently, his whole body prickling with perspiration.

"What the hell was *that*?" he said.

The waiter said, "A drill."

Patrick laughed, even.

"A *drill*? For what?"

He cowered instinctively as a jagged fighter jet tore the sky above them with an impossible loudness; then two more, just as loud, trailing whorling ribbons of smoke.

That evening they went to the restaurant which Patrick had booked for eight o'clock. It had several features which distinguished it from the others in the village. For a start, it was tucked away down a side street off the 'Rue de la République' and was therefore a place you had to know by repute rather than stumble upon by chance. Management were very strict about bookings: even a ten-minute delay, as the website made clear in its strangulated but proper English, might result in the loss of your table. He was pleased, then, that, as they took their seats, he heard the church bell ringing eight. Their table was on a terrace which projected from the rear of the restaurant giving views of the jumbled terracotta rooftops of a lower part of Goult they hadn't even known existed. The waiter was stone-faced and starchy: he made a creaking sound as he handed out the menus. Rachel, giggly and high-spirited, saw him immediately as a challenge. She announced that she would make him laugh at least once by the end of the evening. She and Valerie even shook on it. The menus were unlike the laminated sheets of the lesser establishments: they came in padded purple bindings with silk tassels which wouldn't have looked out of place on a pulpit. This was to ensure their *à la carte* prices were not an anti-climax. A silence settled on the party as they leafed through its stiff pages, until Roger voiced their general concern by stating, flatly, "*Jesus H. Christ* on a bike."

"Agreed," said Niall. "I wonder if they do mortgages?"

"I'm definitely having one of the veggie options," said Rachel.

"My apologies, everybody," said Patrick. "It's a little more expensive than I had anticipated. The website is a bit cagey about prices and now I see why. Shall we skip starters?"

"It might make more financial sense to skip the mains instead," said James, "*and* the starters. Perhaps just stick to bread and tap water."

"I'm paying my bit," said Niall.

"No you are not," said Patrick, who was sitting next to him. They'd been through this on the way there. "I'm paying for you. It's your birthday present. You're not getting anything else."

"The prices are written out as words," said James. "'Vingt-huit', for example. No mention of Euros, just 'Vingt-huit'. That should always set the alarm bells ringing. For God's sake, will someone order the wine to soften the blow of these prices?"

"Le vin le moins cher est de trente-cinq euros," said Louis.

"Clarify?" said Rachel.

"Sorry. The cheapest wine is thirty-five euros."

"I think I preferred it in French."

They ordered the cheapest wine.

Niall said, quietly, "Patrick, there really is no need for you to pay for me. It's going to bankrupt you."

"Don't be ridiculous."

"You're a school teacher."

"What's that got to do with the price of fish?"

"Quite a lot, actually. The 'Loup de Mer' is forty-eight euros. I imagine a teacher's pay, even at your exalted level, is pretty modest."

"Well, it's more than the unemployment benefit which I will probably be claiming in a month's time so take advantage of me while you can."

Niall thought about this reasonable proposition.

Then he said, brightly, "Okay!"

At last the wine arrived. Rachel took this as an opportunity to make the waiter 'corpse'. She offered to taste it and then performed a very creditable impression of an oenophile, sniffing at it, holding it up to the light, swilling it around her mouth as if in a washing machine, finally pretending to spit it out. The waiter remained unmoved. He was familiar with the routine.

She gave up.

"That's fine," she said.

When the waiter had gone, Valerie said, to Rachel, "You're going to have to do a lot better than that to win him over."

Patrick rapped on the table to get everyone's attention.

"I think," he said, raising his glass, "that there's an obvious toast demanding to be made. May I have the honour of proposing it? Here's to Niall. To Niall on his birthday!"

They raised their glasses and chorused, "Happy birthday!"

If it had been any other restaurant they would probably have sung it.

Now Niall wanted to say something. He pinged his glass with his fork.

"Listen, you lot," he began. He half stood, then seemed to decide against it, and sat again. "The booze has gone to my head a little, I'm afraid, and … I'm not usually given to making speeches … but I wanted to say a few words … a few *serious* words, actually." Everyone subtly adjusted their faces, giving him permission to be as serious as he liked. "I wanted to say how much this time spent with you all … my stand-in family, can I call you that? … how much it has meant to me over the last week and a half. As you know, one year ago a terrible and inexplicable event took place … inexplicable on many levels … and … well, there's never an easy way of saying it … a better form of words … or a euphemism even … we just have to get used to it, the bare fact … Frances … died."

It had been said, at last. The matter was at hand and incontrovertible: Death. It stalked them even at the table of a Michelin-starred restaurant in Provence.

Niall looked around the table, acknowledging each person in turn, waiting to make eye contact, wanting everyone to know how much they counted to him.

Then he said, "And so, if I may, I'd like to propose another, far, far more important, toast, to someone now ageless." He raised his glass. "To Frances."

They said together, solemnly, "To Frances."

"To Frances," said Niall again, and then added, more distantly, "wherever she may be."

When, inevitably subdued, the conversation resumed around them, Patrick said to his friend, "Well done."

Then they had to apply themselves to the evening's chore which now, when viewed through the prism of mortality, seemed even more an irrelevance: ordering. This was made more difficult by the fact that the menu was only in French. Valerie and Louis helped out as best they could.

"Pity they don't have pictures," said Roger, "like in McDonald's."

Niall said, "What in the name of all that is holy is – and forgive my pronunciation, Valerie, and Louis – 'Filet de Maigré Parfumé au Ras-el-Hanout, Fenouil et Riz Rouge de Camargue' when it's at home?"

"And what are 'asperges'?" said Rachel. "I'm probably saying that all wrong. 'Asperges'."

"Sounds like a syndrome," said James.

"'Asperges' is asparagus," said Valerie.

"It's actually the cheapest starter, or the least expensive," said Rachel. Then she posed herself an important question: "But do I *like* asparagus?"

"It makes your piss smell funny," said Roger, "or is that something else? Artichokes?"

"Thanks for that, dearest," said Rachel. "Asparagus, asparagus, asparagus. I can't remember if I like asparagus. I like asparagus *soup* so I must like asparagus, mustn't I?"

"It's fairly bland," said James, "so you might not have very strong feelings about it either way. It's like lettuce. No one hates lettuce but no one loves it either." He added, melancholically, "I'm a bit like lettuce."

"Ne sois pas idiot," growled Valerie, kicking him under the table.

"Asparagus, asparagus, asparagus," said Rachel, half to herself, as if meditating on the subject. "Asparagus, asparagus, asparagus."

Patrick said, calmly, "Rachel, will you stop saying 'asparagus'?"

"Why?"

"Please. Just stop saying it will you?"

"There's no law against saying 'asparagus', is there? In fact, we have an inalienable right to say 'asparagus' as much as we please. Asparagus, asparagus, asparagus …"

Patrick had reason to notice his sister's more-than-usually high spirits. Everyone joined in with the joke, everyone started chanting, "Asparagus, asparagus, asparagus …"

Except Patrick.

He sat for a while, barely tolerating it, until their voices began to grow louder, echoing off the surrounding walls, which themselves seemed to be closing in on him, and then he shouted, "Would everyone … *shut the fuck up*? Please? Just *shut the fuck up*?"

Some people on the next table looked over. The waiter glanced from behind his beaded door.

Everyone shut up and stared at him.

Rachel looked mischievous.

"Asparagus?" she said, in a meek squeaky apologetic voice.

Patrick leapt up and pulled away from the table, knocking his glass of wine over. He stepped down from the terrace and walked, half jogged, along the side street in the direction of the village square. He had an odd sensation then of the unreality of the old flagstones passing beneath him, and this sensation of out-of-bodyness, this sense of viewing things from a great height, which often afflicted him at moments of heightened anxiety, seeded a further thought which seemed to him quite new and even radical, strange for it never having occurred to him before: how was it possible that his arms and legs moved? how was it possible that he made them move? There seemed to be no special effort involved on his part; no hiatus, or even causal effect, between intention and result, not even a corresponding thought or intention. No, your arms and your legs just moved when you wanted them to. It was as simple as that. And inexplicable.

These thoughts, these baffling diversions, began to disperse when he reached the square and he dismissed them with the resolution that he must appropriate and assert his 'normality', must rid it, once and for all, of its inverted commas. It wasn't helping him, this pointless questioning, analysing, of everything. He must aspire to the condition of mere animalhood, of being, of being what he *was*, beyond the futile self-interrogation of his consciousness. He could move his arms and legs. So what? He should live with it. It was just how it *was*, like everything.

Sitting by the fountain, he fumbled for a cigarette, looking around to see if anyone had followed him, half expecting to see Rachel or James or perhaps Niall hurrying towards him, but there was just the busy crowd outside the post office restaurant. Their opulent clamour filled the night. It was easy to imagine his sister, just after he had stormed off, saying to everyone, in her placatory way, "Leave him. Leave him."

He finished his cigarette and immediately lit another, but then, when he was half way through it, in furious indecision, he stamped it out and stood. He wondered what he should do. Should he go back and apologise? He couldn't, not yet. He was still shaking, still unreal, or real in a new way. He went, without thinking, into the church.

Inside, the only light came from a cluster of candles near the altar. In the cool semi-darkness he could make out that the church was made from the same rough stone as the houses at the other end of the village: it seemed more hollowed-out than built. At first sight, the interior appeared to be free of any decoration, certainly not crammed with the usual gilded bric-a-brac he associated with Catholic churches in southern latitudes. He passed, through a ghostly caress of incense, towards the altar. There was a painting hanging there in an immense baroque retable, lit from beneath by a single artificial light. Even in the dimness he could see the poor quality of it and the crudity of its composition. It was divided, exactly, in two, across the middle. In the top half, the Virgin and Child and another, time-travelling, Jesus were sticking out inarticulately from the bluish-pink pillows of heaven, like finger puppets, while fat-cheeked *putti* blew trumpets at them from their flaky golden sky. These happy levitating beings gazed down with apparent equanimity on two darker earthbound figures in the murkier lower half who peered upwards and, tearfully, with light-pricked eyes, wrung their hands, longing for this other, happier, state of being. Patrick did not know who these sublunary figures represented; presumably they were saints or martyrs in waiting since they had that doomed look. You could see they had it coming: the rack, the wheel, the fire. For all of its absurdity, the painting at least portrayed a vision of the world which offered the possibility of redemption. With a shiver, he turned to the candles again – nightlights in their little tin bowls – and lit one from another, placing it in its holder. In this manner, hope was passed on. Then he went back towards the door, turned once more to look at the altar and to pick out his own candle in the group, but when he turned back to leave the building he saw Niall striding across the square towards the church, smoking. Despite his stride, he looked more preoccupied than purposeful. Quickly, Patrick backed away, out of sight behind the door, and then, feeling dizzy, he sat in the last row of seats and placed his head in his hands.

A moment later he heard clipped footsteps and echoes of clipped footsteps. Niall had entered the church. Patrick raised his head from his hands and watched as his friend walked down the aisle towards the altar. He watched him take a candle and light it, serendipitously, from the very candle he had lit himself. Then, it appeared, to Patrick, that Niall *crossed* himself, or had the church's flickering ambience made him imagine it? Patrick and Niall rarely talked about religion but Patrick remembered one conversation not long after Frances's death. Patrick, safely abstract with Rioja, had wondered out loud whether or not there was a deity – his code for 'an afterlife' – and Niall had said how he could 'never go back to *all that*.' Patrick wished now that he'd asked him what he'd meant by 'going back' and 'all that', by that dismissiveness. What was he dismissing?

Niall turned and started towards the door. When he was just a few steps from it, he stopped, and peered into the gloom.

"Patrick?" he said, in his normal speaking voice, conceding nothing to the unspoken rule of silence. "Is that you?"

"Yes, I'm afraid so," said Patrick, in a whisper.

Niall got the whispering thing.

"What are you doing in here?" he whispered. "Are you *praying*?"

"It can't do any harm," Patrick whispered, standing and walking towards him. "Can it?"

"Pascal didn't seem to think so."

They both turned, as if on the same impulse, to look at the altarpiece.

"It's a seriously shitty painting," whispered Patrick. "Look at the way the figures stick out of that cloud at such weird angles. Perhaps there's no perspective in heaven. And Jesus looks like Noel Edmonds."

"'The First Noel'."

They watched the painting in silence for a while, half expecting Noel o wink at them.

Niall whispered, "Can I ask you a theological question?"

"Yes, but you may not get a theological answer."

"Do you think there's an afterlife?"

"No," whispered Patrick, adding hurriedly, as he thought of Frances, 'although we can't know that for sure, of course."

"If there was one, how would you imagine it?"

"Oh, pretty corny, really. Not unlike the upper half of that painting, I suppose. Clouds, sunshine, attractive countryside, a complete embargo on suffering, no work of any sort, a general air of goodness permeating the ether, a tangible sense of relief, even a certain amount of smugness and self-satisfaction ... we made it! ... and, it goes without saying, all this lasting for ever and ever without end, Amen."

"Wouldn't you get bored?"

"Oh probably. But give me boredom over fear any time."

"Once I may have believed all that. But no longer. When earlier, in my toast to Frances, I added that small but significant codicil – 'wherever she may be' – I was under no illusions. The illusions have long been discarded. I know she's nowhere; not here, not 'up there' and not 'down there' either. She's nowhere. She's not even in the canister of ashes the crematorium gave me as a souvenir."

"You can't know that for sure," whispered Patrick, conscious that his lip-service agnosticism was beginning to wear thin with repetition.

Then Niall said, back in his normal speaking voice, "For God's sake, let's get out of this place. I can't take any more of this sycophantic whispering."

They left the church and stepped into the square. It bloomed with the sounds of a civilisation at peace with itself, dining, drinking, talking: *la douceur de vivre*. Standing by the leaking fountain and the forlorn soldier, they lit cigarettes and absorbed the pageant for a moment

Patrick said, "Do you think I've lost my marbles?"

"Not at all," said Niall. "I never thought you had any marbles in the first place. I'm joking. Patrick, we understand that you're under a lot of stress with everything that's going on at the school right now, and, of course, with Frances, and all that stuff. We all have different ways of dealing with 'stuff'. Or not dealing with it. We all have our crosses to bear."

Patrick was struck afresh by his friend's generosity. Of all of them, Niall had the greatest cross to bear.

He said, "I hope the others are as philosophical and understanding as you are about it."

"Of course they will be. They love you. They're your family. I don't have one of those. At least, not like you do."

"You never talk about your family."

"You're very fortunate to have all that."

"There you go again: not talking about your family."

"My family don't exist in the same way that yours do. I was an afterthought, a mistake, and I don't want to talk about it. Come on. Let's go back. Everything's fine. No one's going to say anything. It'll be as if nothing happened."

"Is that healthy? Pretending nothing happened?"

"In this case, yes. And I promise no one will mention asparagus ever again. What was going on there, with that whole asparagus thing?"

"Nothing," said Patrick. "I over-reacted."

They set off.

"You seem to be fizzing with a dark energy," said Niall.

"Niall, I need to talk to you. I need to talk to you about something very important."

"Can it wait until the restaurant? They'll be thinking we've absconded."

"I need to talk to you in private."

"Okay, but later then, back at the villa."


When they returned to the table no one said anything or even seemed to notice them. As Patrick and Niall took their places, eyes were not diverted, conversations were not curtailed. Only Sylvie gazed at them, unaware that her gaze was something, itself, that might be observed. They re-entered the flow of things, and, with perfect timing, the starters arrived. The conversation resumed, and it was as if nothing had happened earlier. But then, a little later, when Patrick was talking intensely to Louis, there was one moment – a moment that he would remember for the rest of his life – when he casually let his eyes roam to his sister's to find that she was gazing directly back at him, and, for a while, in their shared silence, they held each other's eyes expressionlessly, until Rachel's features softened into an absolving smile which Patrick acknowledged with a quick nod, before turning back to Louis who was telling him, at last, of his love for the beautiful, remote and mysterious Celestine. Celestine was in the year above him at the *Lycée*. He was also, as it turned out, a man.

Back at the villa they played 'Charades'. Although it was nearly eleven, Sylvie was allowed, as a special dispensation, to play one round. It took a little while for them to get 'The Little Mermaid'. Then, as she left to go to bed, everyone called out, as usual, "Goodnight Sylvie!" and she ran off. She would be fast asleep in five minutes, dreaming of mermaids.

Patrick was anxious for the games to end. He hated organised fun but he had other reasons to be impatient as one round of 'Charades' stretched into another, and then, as midnight was passed, it seemed as if they might start a game of cards – worldly Roger wanted to have a go at Poker – until Rachel decided it was time to call it a day, and when Rachel, who was at the centre of things, left, everyone else would soon follow.

At the end, only Louis remained, apart from Patrick and Niall. He stayed and sat with them for a further ten minutes. Patrick felt divided: he wanted, of course, to encourage Louis's new-found sociability and his desperate need for solace and advice regarding Celestine, of whom he had spoken to no one else in the world, but at the same time he felt the urgency of his need to get the talking with

Niall over and done with and that could only be done when they were alone. At last, at one o'clock, Louis bad them good night, and left.

Patrick and Niall sat for a while in silence. The bulb suspended above them, visited by moths and other more pendulous night-insects, created an alcove of ferny light, like a miniature self-contained world. As the candles began to gutter on the table, their waxy smell hung in the air along with the drowsy scent of the clematis.

"Poor Louis's in love," said Patrick, at last.

Niall gave a grudging laugh but made no comment.

Patrick stood, went into the kitchen and poured two brandies. He came back out and placed them on the table between them. Then he lit two cigarettes and passed Niall one. He said, "So, I need to talk to you."

"I sort of got that idea," said Niall. "I'm hanging on your every word. In fact, I'll go further than that. You're actually making me nervous with all this … *build-up*. What is it that you want – no, *need* – to tell me?"

"It's about Frances."

"I thought as much. So? Speak, for God's sake."

"It's about that evening, one year ago."

"Go on."

"It's something I should have told you a long time ago, something I should have told you on the night itself."

"For God's sake, get on with it then."

Patrick noticed that Niall's hands were trembling.

"That evening of the party," he said, "I was in a great rush. There'd been a meeting at school which had overrun and so I was very late and I had been given firm instructions, by Frances, that I should be at your place by seven at the very latest, to help with the setting up of the party and so forth. And I was not in the habit of being late for Frances."

"No. None of us were late for Frances."

"So I was desperately getting myself ready … when my phone rang and it was her. Frances."

"What time was this? What time did she phone you?"

Niall always hungered for any details about that evening, however seemingly inconsequential: anything that might help him understand.

"I know exactly what time it was," said Patrick, "because I checked the clock. It was twenty past six."

Niall made a calculation. Then he said, "And why did she phone you?"

"She phoned me to ask if, on the way to the party, I could get some asparagus."

Niall snorted.

"Why do you laugh?" said Patrick.

"Well, *asparagus*. The idea of it. Who cares? Why are you telling me this? It doesn't matter."

"It does matter, Niall. I assure you, it does matter a great deal."

"Okay. I'll take your word for it. So – did you get the asparagus or not?"

"I refused to. I said, no, I won't get your wretched asparagus, I'm late as it is, you want me to be there at seven so I'm going to be there at seven. And she'd done this before, with other exotic ingredients that she always managed to forget until the last moment. It was never a pint of milk. I told her that if I had to get some asparagus it would mean that I'd have to go to Waitrose, which was out of my way, and bound to be packed at that time on a Friday evening, and I'd be stuck in a queue at the tills … and so on, and so on, making lousy fucking excuses not to get some stupid asparagus."

He paused. It was time to reveal his black-hearted soul.

"Actually," he went on, "the truth was that I just couldn't be bothered. I wanted to get some drinks down me, I wanted to get into the party spirit, I didn't want to be stuck in some interminable teetotal queue at Waitrose."

"So, can I take it that you *didn't* get the asparagus then?"

"I didn't."

"So, why is this …?"

"Relevant? I'll tell you why it's relevant, Niall. It's relevant because then, after I had been going on and on about why it was absolutely impossible for me to get the asparagus from Waitrose, she interrupted me, and said, not angrily, but firmly, 'Okay, fine, forget it, I'll go and get it myself … in the car.'"

Niall stubbed out his cigarette and immediately lit one of his own. He drank some brandy and would not look Patrick in the eye. Instead, he moved his finger back and forth across an ebony-stained knotted fissure in the table.

Patrick said, "So, that's why she was driving at six-thirty that evening. She was going to get some asparagus which I couldn't be arsed to get. Because I didn't want to stand for five minutes in a queue. Because I wanted to get some drink down me."

Niall said nothing. He continued to smoke. There was a glazed look in his eyes.

"Are you going to say anything?" said Patrick.

Niall shook his head.

"What is there to say?" he said. "Frances was driving to get some asparagus. There you have it. Now I know."

They sat in silence for two minutes.

Then, just as Patrick was about to speak at last, Niall said, "Patrick, I know what you want. I know why you've told me what you just told me. You want forgiveness. But I can't give you forgiveness."

Feeling suddenly nauseous, tether-less, sinking, Patrick said, his voice raised a tone, croaky and breaking with fear, "Why?"

"Because it's not in my power to. Only Frances could forgive you. But she can't. Because she's dead."

He stood. He stubbed out his cigarette. He downed his drink and took the glass into the kitchen. Patrick heard a tap running. He guessed Niall must be pouring himself a glass of water. He waited for him to return. Perhaps he would bring the remainder of the brandy out. He waited. Then he turned to the bright window of the kitchen and called, "Niall?" There was no answer. He stood. He went into the kitchen. It was empty. No one was there. He heard the fridge give a shaky tremble, like a sigh or death rattle, then stop. Then he saw Niall's glass, washed, upside down, on the draining board.

\*\*\*

Breakfast. Nine thirty on the dot.

Patrick, taking his seat, said, lightly, "Niall not down yet?"

"Nope," said Rachel. She passed him the coffee and a look.

"Thank you. And could I have a croissant and the butter please? Where is he?"

"I imagine," said Rachel, "that he's still fast asleep. How long did you two stay up last night, carousing?"

"We didn't stay up 'carousing'. We went to bed shortly after you."

"Yeah, right. So who drank all the brandy?"

"We didn't drink 'all the brandy'. There were a couple of inches in the bottle, if that. I'll replace it, if you're so bothered. It's not like Niall to be late. He's usually *early*. Sylvie. You know which is Niall's room, don't you?"

"Yes. It's next to my one."

"Will you go upstairs and check on him? Just knock on his door and see if he's coming down for breakfast."

"Okay."

She stood and, with a patter of bare feet, ran into the villa.

Rachel sang, "You're *fussing* again. I thought we'd agreed there wasn't going to be any fussing around Niall."

"By 'we'd agreed'," said Patrick, "what you really mean is that you gave me a five-minute lecture in the car."

"Now, now," said James. "Could I possibly trouble you for some salami, Ben?"

Patrick couldn't eat. Instead, he drank some black coffee. He turned towards the kitchen, yearning for Niall to appear, wakeful, smiling …

fine. At last, Sylvie skipped through the kitchen and came over to him.

"He's not there," she said.

"Did you knock?"

"Yes. His door opened and I looked in and he wasn't there."

"Did you call for him? He might have been in the shower? Or …"

"I did call for him. His bed hadn't been slept in. It had chocolates on it."

Patrick said to Rachel, "Madame Dubois hasn't been in already this morning, has she?"

"No," said Rachel. "She comes in at ten."

Sylvie confessed, "I ate one of the chocolates."

Patrick and Rachel exchanged a look.

Sylvie said, "*Niall* won't mind. He always lets me have his chocolates."

"Of course he won't mind, sweetheart," said Rachel, distractedly. Then she said to Patrick, "What on earth did you two get up to last night?"

"Nothing. We talked."

"About?"

"Stuff. Stuff you talk about."

"Did you talk about Frances?"

"Yes, a bit."

"You see, this is what happens if you *fuss*. Was he okay?"

"He was fine. Fine-ish. He went to bed. I *thought* he went to bed. But obviously not."

"Perhaps he felt like sleeping in a field," said Louis.

"Christ," said Patrick. "Where did he go?"

"There he is," said Valerie, pointing.

Niall was walking across the gravel towards them carrying a shopping bag. He waved with his free hand. The shadows of the cypress tree made him flicker as he approached. Patrick noticed that he was wearing the same clothes he'd been wearing from the night before. He came to the table and put the bag on it.

"Everyone's gone very quiet," he said.

"What did you get?" said Rachel, brightly.

"Some bread and fruit and wine and olive oil and stuff," he said. "It's market day in the village."

In silence, he took his place among them at the centre of the table.

After a while, which was filled with the wordless chink of cutlery, he said, "Can someone pass the bread? Bread please. And shall we have some wine?"

No one said anything. Patrick exchanged a look with Rachel. James raised his eyebrows hopefully. Sylvie just looked puzzled.

"Wine?" she said. "It's breakfast and even mummy doesn't have wine for breakfast."

Roger snorted.

Niall said, "I was joking."


Later, when Louis, Ben and Sylvie had been 'volunteered' into tidying away the breakfast things, Rachel said, "All this talk of wine and brandy reminds me that reserves are getting dangerously low. I'm afraid another supermarket run is due."

Niall said, "I'll go."

"You don't have to."

"I don't have to but I'd like to. I think the drive would do me good."

Rachel wasn't sure what he meant. She was worried about him.

Roger, who was lying back in his chair with his eyes closed, sunning his exposed furry chest, said, "You're not insured for the hire car, mate."

"So?" said Niall. "I'm a careful driver. It's only a few miles. Kilometres. And I'd like to go, it would be good for me, to have time … and space."

"You're not insured," Roger simply repeated.

Rachel was looking at Niall intently, trying to read him.

Then she said, uncertainly, but keen to make any dispensation for him, "It'll be okay."

Roger made a whistling sound.

"On your own head be it," he said, "but I'm telling you, it's … irresponsible."

"You can't go on your own anyway, Niall," said Rachel. "You'll be buying half the European wine lake so you'll need at least another pair of hands."

"I'll go with Niall," said Patrick.

"You're not insured either," said Roger, but then rolled into the sun and seemed to give up.

"Can I go too?" said Sylvie who had finished putting things away and was now comprehensively bored.

"No, you stay here, sweetheart," said Rachel. "Let the boys go on their own. You're going to have a swimming lesson with daddy this morning, remember? Without the armbands?"

While Niall fed the location of the supermarket into Satnav, Rachel handed Patrick, who was sitting in the passenger seat, the list she had compiled.

"Jesus Christ," said Patrick, unravelling it. "What's this? 'War and Peace'?"

"Stuff we need."

"Hang on, hang on. We *need* almonds? No one *needs* almonds."

"Have I put coffee pods on there?"

"Yes."

"They must be Nespresso-compatible."

"Okay. They must be Nespresso-compatible. I have *no* idea what that means."

"Niall?" said Rachel, bypassing him, even as he let the window start to rise. "You heard that, didn't you?"

"They must be Nespresso-compatible," he said.

The gravel applauded as they started moving.

"And don't forget the rosé!" Rachel called after them. "We've got barely enough to last the afternoon! The situation is critical!"

Patrick noted how his sister was quite capable of making light of alcohol dependency one moment while sternly admonishing him for it the next. He watched her receding in the wing mirror. She was standing with one arm detained in the air as if struck into immobility by some fearful misgiving or dread. And she was still standing there, watching them, when they turned onto the track.

Niall wasn't speaking. Patrick turned to look at him.

"That was funny with Roger earlier," he said.

"What was?"

"Him getting all 'uppity' about you driving without insurance but not once offering to drive himself … You know I *had* to tell you what I told you last night."

Niall said nothing.

Patrick said, "Can we talk about it?"

"I'd prefer it, on the whole, if we didn't."

Patrick toyed with the idea of not talking about it but he couldn't not talk about it.

He said, "I completely understand that you are angry with me."

"I'm not angry with you."

"You have a right to be."

Niall said nothing; just minutely shook his head.

"You have a right to be," said Patrick again.

"I'm angry at the world, not at you. The fact that you couldn't be arsed to get some asparagus is neither here nor there in the big scheme of things. You can't impose meaning on things retrospectively. You have to judge them by the conditions that existed at the time."

"What do you mean? What do you mean 'judge'?"

"You couldn't be arsed to get some asparagus. *Fine*. You meant nothing by it, at the time: it was an act which, in any other circumstances, would be trivial and forgotten about. Venial. Subject closed. End of story."

He let his window down, fumbled for a cigarette, lit it.

They drove in silence. Patrick wondered if Niall had been offering up at least the possibility of forgiveness by conceding that he had 'meant nothing by it', and did not 'venial' mean just that? that the act was forgivable? Something kept nagging at him: the need to clarify, to have the forgiveness made explicit.

The woman said, "In two hundred yards, turn right."

When they came to the junction with the main road, and were waiting to enter the stream of traffic, Niall tossed his still-lit cigarette out of the window.

"You can't do that," said Patrick.

"Why not?"

"It's a fire risk. Haven't you seen all the posters warning about forest fires?"

"Oh, for God's sake, Patrick, I threw it onto the *road* … What are you *doing*? *Patrick*?"

Patrick jumped from the car. He walked around to Niall's side. As he stamped the discarded butt out, repeatedly, until there was nothing left of it but a black stain, a car drew up behind them. Beyond the sun-bleached windscreen, the shadowy driver, troubling as a photofit, thrummed his fingers on the wheel and then, when Patrick looked in his direction, gave an imploring shrug of Gallic exasperation. Patrick mouthed his apology, jogged back to the passenger door and slammed it shut after him.

"Happy now?" said Niall.

"Yes. Although the man in the Peugeot isn't."

They sat waiting for a gap in the traffic while the car behind revved and revved its engine.

"No good doing that, my impatient French friend," said Niall, eyeing him in the mirror.

Patrick said, in as casual a voice as he could muster, "Where were you last night?"

"What do you mean where was I last night?"

"Your bed hadn't been slept in this morning."

"You went into my room?"

"No. Sylvie did. She was after your chocolates."

Niall pulled out into the road. Patrick noticed that he had turned left, not right as they had been instructed to. He chose not to mention it. He was already in trouble for fussing over the cigarette.

Instead he said, "So where were you?"

"I went for a walk."

"At one-thirty in the morning?"

"Yes, at one-thirty in the morning. Can you please just let me drive?"

"Where did you go? ... Niall, where did you go?"

The woman said, "When possible, make a U-turn."

"Does it matter where I went?"

"It does to me, yes."

"I walked for a while."

"And then ... ?"

"And then I went into the village."

"You went into *Goult*? Was anywhere open at that time of night?"

"Only the church."

"So what did you do?"

The woman said, "When possible, make a U-turn."

"I went into it."

"The church? And then ... ?"

"I slept there."

"You slept in the church? The whole night? Weren't you spooked?"

"No. In fact, I felt at home. Safe. And that painting isn't as bad as you make out, you know."

Patrick tried to imagine Niall lying on the marble floor by the votive candles, flat on his back, like an effigy, staring up into the dark ceiling. Perhaps he had found some faith there, on that cold floor; or re-found some. Or, if he had not found faith, at least some peace. *Requiescat in pace.*

The woman said, "When possible, make a U-turn."

The supermarket, or 'Super-U' as it was called, occupied a long low smoked-glass building not unlike an airport terminal. After the contingent mess of the dual-carriageway, lined for its whole length with car showrooms, factories and warehouses, the supermarket's clean-lined modernity came as a relief. The walls demarcating the car park consisted of waist-high wire cages densely packed with sculptural blocks of pale granite. They secured two trolleys and entered the building. The air inside, after the black heat of the tarmacked car park, was bracingly chilly and smelt, refreshingly, of cheese and washing powder. Cheerful tinkling piped music, barely audible, was a subliminal incentive to consumerism: it made every happy shopper feel part of a bigger plan.

Niall decided that they should divide the job in two and then go their separate ways. He tore the shopping list in half and gave Patrick the lower section which consisted mainly of afterthoughts, Patrick thought, fiddly stuff which would take some hunting down, like almonds and fresh mint. The upper half contained the important stuff, the stuff they needed. Then he saw that Rachel had added at the bottom of his part 'LOTS OF ASPARAGUS', but had, thoughtfully, drawn attention to her harmless joke with a smiley face. Still, he was grateful that Niall hadn't seen it.

As he wheeled his trolley to start at the other end of the building so that they wouldn't keep running into each other, he realised why Niall had introduced this 'division of labour' scheme: it was more than mere expediency. Back at the villa, he had said he needed 'time and space' – and hadn't Rachel said something similar of him, in the car? – and that was tantamount to saying he wanted to be on his own. Cruising across the faux-marble floor – the trolley with a juddering tic in one wheel which was transmitted through his arm like an extra heartbeat and pulled him constantly off course – he felt, suddenly and unexpectedly, on familiar territory. The interior of the supermarket was almost indistinguishable from his local supermarket in

Wandsworth with its bright aisles with multi-coloured products stretched to vanishing points beneath a dark tubular ceiling. He noticed how there was a dearth of specifically French produce in favour of international or generic brands which were, perhaps, more common to a particular demographic irrespective of nationality; here, stacked high for the ordinary man and woman in the street were Kellogg's Cornflakes, Coco Pops, Nutella, Robertson's jam, Heinz tomato ketchup, Heinz baked beans – did the French really eat baked beans, like *normal* people? – Vimto, Nescafé Gold Blend, Lipton's tea bags, Persil, Listerine, Brillo pads; there was on display in one corner, where a saleswoman sat behind a desk, a suite of flouncy garden furniture which wouldn't have looked out of place on the patio of a semi in West Norwood. Then you looked outside and saw the walls of granite, the cruel sun on the tarmac and the dusty coniferous shoulder of hill, all rendered silent and sepia by the smoked glass, and you realised you were at a quite different latitude from West Norwood, after all.

It took a while to load everything into the back of the car. They had to put the third row of seats down and even then it was tight. Patrick counted twenty-five bottles of wine. They worked in silence, a silence that cried out for words between them. When it was done, Niall went to the driver's seat and Patrick to the front passenger's.

As they drove through the car park, with the sound of bottles clanking worryingly from behind, he made the decision to put the radio on and to do so without soliciting Niall's assent. Other people, he had noticed, weren't always asking for permission to do everything – Louis's under-age beer in Ménerbes, for instance, he kept thinking of that – so why should he? Did he have some set of properties, or restrictions, which marked him out from all other adults? Making a resolution to change the habit of a lifetime, he pressed the button. A song came on which he immediately recognised. It was by Keane.

"Turn it off," said Niall.

Patrick did as he was told, immediately. The silence, highlighted by its brief interruption, yearned for an explanation. And then, with a sinking feeling, he remembered that Frances had been a big Keane fan. She'd seen them in concert, twice. 'Love is the End' had probably been *their* – Frances and Niall's – song. What were the chances of that? of all the songs in all the world? and here in France, on French radio too? What were the chances? So much for his freedom; so much for his exercise of free will. He thought: there is some malevolent force at work in the cosmos, some demonic director, or puppeteer, who delights in organising the world along these lines in order to thwart even our goodly, but earth-bound, intentions. What was the point of trying to be in control of things when you were up against that? He decided to do nothing from then on, in the face of such an adversary, except comply, and submit, and endure. And what was it, after all, that he had to 'endure'? what terrible privation, what suffering? A car journey, made in silence. In the grand scheme of endurances, it didn't even register. He could endure twenty minutes in a car, in France, in the South of France, going back to a luxury villa with a boot-full of booze … and almonds. He was in paradise.

At the junction their silence was calibrated by the tick of the indicator.

Patrick forced himself into saying, "You're not using 'Satnav'?"

"I know the way back," said Niall. "*Jesus*. Why won't any of these wretched French people let me in?"

He pulled, impetuously, into the road, forcing an oncoming car to brake violently, sound its horn and flash its lights. Patrick watched this performance in the wing mirror.

"If they drove on the right side of the road it might help," he said. "By the 'right' side of the road, I mean, of course, the 'left' side."

Leave it at that, he thought: my futile joke, my pose of fogeyness and xenophobia, even my tweed jacket with the elbow pads: all dishonest, unmeant. That's enough, be silent for the rest of the journey, don't enrage him further.

Niall was staring rigidly ahead.

Patrick watched the car behind them receding in the mirror, then saw another take its place, and another, and two more. The cars seemed to be retreating more quickly than before, piling up behind them. One flashed its headlights as they overtook. Ahead, he saw that the hyphenated white lines of the road were rushing at them like tracer bullets: they were picking up speed. The car's engine was snarling and straining, transposed up a semi-tone. Surreptitiously, he checked the clasp on his seatbelt and gripped the armrest. It occurred to him that they were not insured. The speedometer said 120. With relief, he realised it would be in kilometres per hour, not miles. After a few more thumps of his heart he saw that had increased to 140. He pushed back into the seat; felt himself *being* pushed.

"Niall," he said.

When they were doing 160 Niall started weaving between cars in order to overtake. This lane-changing seemed more reckless than their mere speed since it had an air of swagger about it. It would certainly attract the attention of the police. When Niall found himself blocked behind a peculiarly intransigent driver ahead he began sounding the horn and flashing the lights until the car pulled out of his way.

"Niall," said Patrick. "Niall."

He looked over to him and saw that he remained impassive and stone-faced, the tension only visible in his white-knuckled grip of the steering wheel, his eyes set on the veering race track ahead.

"Niall," he said.

A cliff of rock reared and raced beside them. Patrick, in passing, noted that it was sedimentary with slanting layers of grey and white rock. He thought: beneath everything – the lawns, the flower beds, the trees – there was always this final impediment of stone: we were space-bound on a bare rock, after all. Then he remembered Sylvie's acorn. He reached into his pocket and grasped it tightly, like a prayer bead, closing his eyes as he did so, waiting for the impact, for annihilation.

Which didn't happen. He wasn't annihilated, *yet*. Life was only ever a deferral. But when he opened his eyes the cliff was at a safer distance and they were slowing and re-joining the flow: a car even slid past them, although its occupants stared at them. He was surprised to feel a kind of deflation as normality – a brittle normality – reasserted itself, with its vista to the afternoon, and the next day, and the one after that, stacked up in a silent unknowable countdown to the last one of all. Niall even bothered to indicate when he took the left turning. Soon they would be back at the villa and Patrick would have a large brandy – a very large brandy – even though it was eleven in the morning – he owed himself that, after this – and they would talk over what had happened, everything would come out, at last. And when everything was said and when everything was understood, everything could, at last, be forgiven. *Tout comprendre, c'est tout pardonner.*

With a burst of relief and this saving image of brandy and cigarettes and redemption, he gasped, "Jesus, Niall …"

They arrived at the track. Niall turned into it and, at once, pressed his foot down on the accelerator, as far as it would go. There was a churning of grit, a nasty engine snarl. Patrick, sitting bolt upright, clasped onto the side of the seat and glanced at the mirror. He saw a cloud of dust rising in it. It wasn't over, yet. Then it would be over. In a matter of seconds the engine was making that desperate straining sound again. The whole car vibrated. Patrick closed his eyes, counting away his remaining seconds. The time, the place, the *type* of his death was entirely in the hands of an external agent. He was completely powerless. Niall had total sovereignty over whether he should live or die. And he was completely powerless, too, when Niall drove the car straight into the Cedar of Lebanon.

The woman said, "You have arrived at your destination."

Patrick stirred. He knew he had been unconscious but he had no idea for how long. It might have been seconds, or hours. He had been woken by the voice and the blare of the car horn, a held unresolved chord that had an almost physical presence in the air.

Something was pressing into his chest. He thought for a moment that he had been folded in half by the impact, his back and his legs broken. But it was the airbag. The airbag had saved him.

He sat up and looked around himself, dazed. Everything was dancing in the dappled sunlight from the tree, even the smoke that was tumbling from the bonnet. They were half in the tree and half under it, and it was leaning and moving above them, in the Mistral.

The woman said, "You have arrived at your destination. You have arrived at your destination." And kept saying it.

He turned to look at Niall who was slumped into his own airbag. His had saved him too. "Niall," he said, and reached out to press his arm, tug it. "*Niall.*"

Niall grunted as he returned unwillingly to consciousness. There was a bruise above his left eye and a rivulet of blood ran from his nose to the corner of his mouth, but, apart from that, he seemed unharmed. Slowly, he turned to Patrick and offered him a helpless broken smile. He even managed a chuckle as he spoke.

"Sorry about that," he said.

"About what?"

"Well, driving into the tree. You must have noticed."

This was his old banter.

"Yes. I did think it was a bit strange, but I guessed you must have had some perfectly good reason for it. The bonnet's on fire, by the way. I just thought I'd point that out."

"I sort of ... forgot to stop."

"It's an easy enough mistake to make."

It took a sort of bravado, Patrick thought – and perhaps mild concussion – to be sitting in a burning car (which, presumably, could explode at any moment) and to be having such a conversation.

Niall said, with his old drollness, "My instructor never told me that I shouldn't drive into a tree."

"However were you meant to *know*?" said Patrick. "Oh well. The car's a write-off – and uninsured, of course – but we appear to have survived reasonably intact. That's the main thing. The fire's a bit of a worry, of course. It seems to be getting worse. We should think about getting out soon, assuming the doors aren't jammed. Can you move everything?"

At first, Niall didn't understand Patrick's question. Then, realising what he meant, he experimented with his arms and legs, as if discovering himself and his possibilities all over again. He could *move*, he could interact with the world.

"Everything appears to be in working order," he said. "We seem, despite my best efforts, to be … *alive*."

"Yes," said Patrick. "I'd noticed that."

"What shall we do about it, do you reckon?" he said.

"Live, I suppose. There's nothing else. Then get out of the car. That's something we should consider, quite urgently."

"You know, Patrick, I think I know what happened that night, a year ago. I think I understand."

"About the asparagus?"

"No. Not about the asparagus. About something important. About Frances. I think she drove the car into the tree to spare that child's life."

"Yes," said Patrick. "So do I. I think that too."

At the sound of voices he turned to look over the horizon of his strange new planet. Through the smoke, now flecked with flames, he saw his sister, his brother, Roger, Valerie, Louis, Ben and his beloved Sylvie: the living, running across the gravel to save them.

Printed in Great Britain
by Amazon